Praise for Virna DePaul

"If you're looking for a hot, sexy, emotional read, Virna DePaul delivers!"
—*New York Times* and *USA Today* bestselling author J. KENNER

"Virna DePaul creates yummy alpha heroes."
—*New York Times* bestselling author TINA FOLSOM

Praise for *Awakened*

"Barrett and Nick's electrifying chemistry, coupled with a clever and intricate plot, makes this one amazing read."
—*RT Book Reviews*

"A nifty romantic suspense to sink your teeth into."
—*Fresh Fiction*

"Virna DePaul did an amazing job."
—*Smitten with Reading*

"I am more than satisfied. Between the great character and good plot, a paranormal romance fan couldn't do any better."
—*The Jeep Diva*

Praise for *Turned*

"A captivating start to a fascinating new series with a hero that's to die for."
—Bestselling author RHYANNON BYRD

"With *Turned*, Virna DePaul delivers a sexy and exciting new take on the vampire novel, one that comes complete with a kick-ass heroine and a to-die-for hero. I can't wait for the sequel!"
—TRACY WOLFF, bestselling author of *Ruined*

"*Turned* is intense, intricate, and insomnia-inducing (plan to stay up way too late!). Virna DePaul puts the awesome in the awesomesauce of paranormal romance."
—JOYCE LAMB, curator,
USA Today's *Happy Ever After*

"Plenty of action, an intriguing plot, a crisp narrative and stellar pacing pulls the reader into the story and keeps the pages turning."
—*RT Book Reviews*

"DePaul's first Belladonna Agency paranormal will appeal to readers who like their vampires sexy [and] their heroines spunky."
—*Publishers Weekly*

"The chemistry between the two was great and made for some very sexy scenes."
—*Fresh Fiction*

"*Turned*, first book in the Belladonna Agency series by Virna DePaul, is a page turner and grabbed me from the beginning and had me reading until the wee hours of the morning."
—*The Jeep Diva*

"This is an author whose work continues to delight."
—*Just Talking Books*

Praise for the Novels of Virna DePaul

"Seducer and protector—this vampire has it all."
—*Fresh Fiction*, on *A Vampire's Salvation*

"Virna DePaul is amazing!"
—*New York Times* bestselling author LORI FOSTER

"Incredibly well written, different, and hot."
—*New York Times* bestselling author LARISSA IONE

"A gripping tale! DePaul creates the perfect blend of danger, intrigue, and romance. You won't be able to put this book down!"
—*New York Times*
bestselling author BRENDA NOVAK

"If you have not yet started this [Para-Ops] series . . . you are really missing out."
—*The Book Reading Gals*

BY VIRNA DEPAUL

The Belladonna Agency Series
Turned
Awakened

Filthy Rich
A Vampire's Salvation (e-Original Novella)
Arrested by Love (e-Original Novella)

Filthy Rich

A Novel

Virna DePaul

BANTAM BOOKS
New York

A Bantam Books Mass Market Original

Copyright © 2015 by Virna DePaul
Excerpt from *Turned* by Virna DePaul copyright © 2014 by Virna DePaul

All rights reserved.

Published in the United States by Bantam Books, an imprint of Random House, a division of Penguin Random House LLC, New York.

BANTAM BOOKS and the HOUSE colophon are registered trademarks of Penguin Random House LLC.

ISBN 978-0-345-54249-6
eBook ISBN 978-0-345-54250-2

Cover photograph: Innervision/Shutterstock

Printed in the United States of America

randomhousebooks.com

9 8 7 6 5 4 3 2 1

Bantam Books mass market edition: November 2015

This book is dedicated
to my family and friends
who've supported me
throughout this wild writing journey.

Thank you to Sue G., Gina W.,
and the entire RH team
for making me feel so welcome
at Random House.

Special thanks to all my readers for your support.

Finally, love to Craig, Josh, Ethan, and Zach.
For always and forever.

Filthy
Rich

Chapter One

"Go. Just go. At a party like this, you could meet the love of your life."

Cara Michal didn't bother rolling her eyes, mostly because her friend Iris was giving out unwanted advice over the phone and couldn't see her do it.

"I work on Wall Street, Iris. The guys I work with, the ones attending this company event, aren't interested in love. Even if they were, I'm not."

"Well, apparently you're not interested in fun or sex, either. Jesus, Cara, just how long *has* it been since you've been on a date?"

This time Cara did roll her eyes, but smiled. Usually Iris wouldn't have to ask the question—knowing someone since high school made it so questions like this were usually irrelevant—but their monthly mani-pedi meet-up had been forfeited for the last six weeks due to Cara's intense work schedule, and Cara had barely managed to respond to Iris's multiple texts with a simple thumbs-up or "ugh" face. She'd barely had time to eat and sleep, let alone check in with her friend. She missed Iris. Thankfully, the huge project she'd been working on was over and she'd be getting back to a seventy-five-hour work week instead of what had been closer to a hundred. And maybe get back to dating, too, although she doubted it. The last few dates she'd accepted had been more trouble than they were worth, and she wasn't eager for a repeat.

"It's been awhile," Cara admitted. "But I knew when I started the four-year analyst program at Dubois & Mellan, that's what I was signing up for. That's why they pay me the big bucks," she added dryly. Earning a six-figure salary three years after graduating college wasn't anything to scoff at, but the reality was that it didn't go very far, either. Not for a single woman living in Manhattan with the kind of responsibilities Cara had, anyway.

"By this time next year, that'll all change. You'll get your bonus for completing the program, dole it out to your family, and finally listen to me when I say you need to seriously rethink your chosen profession and do something you love," Iris said, confidence in her tone.

Another thing about knowing someone since high school was the freedom they felt in handing out unwanted advice. Cara bit her lip and counted to five before answering. "I love analyzing numbers," she pointed out.

It was mostly a true statement, but there were other things she loved more. Things she might have tried out as a career if her life had turned out differently, like teaching high school math, or computer engineering. Only Iris knew the true reason Cara had become a Wall Street analyst: after her father had died, she'd needed to make good money and make it fast, and if she had to sacrifice her personal life to do it, so be it. But that conversation was one Cara would rather avoid. Iris was trying to help, but sometimes her brand of help simply made Cara feel a restlessness she couldn't afford. "You know it's not as easy as that," Cara said quietly. "If the firm offers me a permanent position, I'll have to take it."

"Even though the work is killing you?" Iris said.

"Overly dramatic, much?" Cara responded dryly.

Iris sighed. "Dead horse. Moving on. You still haven't answered my question. Have you gone on any dates in the last few weeks that I'm unaware of?"

"Um, I went out with a colleague a couple of times, though we also talked shop so I could justify it." Greg Johnson was like many of the junior stockbrokers that Cara knew. Tall and attractive. Young. A bit cocky. Rock-hard abs and biceps threatening to bust the seams of his designer clothing. A dazzling smile made more dazzling by teeth whitening. Summa cum laude at Yale. And yet over the course of a couple of dates, he'd proven to be uninspiring. Besides, dating coworkers wasn't high on her list—too many chances for things to go wrong, and when they did, the inevitable awkward silences and gawky avoidance moves in the hallway would ensue.

"You're talking about that guy Greg from your office, right? You had dinner and drinks a couple of times. You said you were bored. Hardly a date, in my book."

"You mean because we didn't end up between the sheets?" They'd started off at one of the French restaurants near their office—where Greg had attempted to illustrate his knowledge of fine dining and wine. But while his overly loud and cocksure attitude had attracted the fawning attention of a couple of sleek young women at the bar, it had flattened her libido. Once the check came and he'd tried to convince her to go with him to a nightclub, she'd pointedly suggested making it an early night.

"Not exactly, but I detect a noticeable lack of enthusiasm about this guy," Iris said. "And no wonder. He sounds safe. Just like every other guy you've dated the past few years. Would you like me to fix you up with someone?"

"No thanks," Cara said quickly. "I can manage. Besides, you and I seem to go after men that are complete opposites."

"Yeah, but that hasn't always been the case. Remember Tony Spokane?"

Cara's mouth tipped up. Did she ever. Tony Spokane had been the high school cigarette-smoking bad boy, complete with leather jacket, motorcycle boots, and long hair. He'd also been the one thing that had ever threatened to come between her and Iris. When Cara had realized that, she'd given Iris the all clear. And if she'd continued to periodically daydream about Tony and that dangerous self-assured glint in his eye, long after he and Iris had stopped dating, well, she'd kept that to herself. Just like she kept to herself the fact she still occasionally daydreamed about bedding a bad boy. Someone sexy and powerful and as far from the high-finance men she dated as one could get.

"Old Tony turned out to be more your speed than mine," Cara said. "And now that I think about it, most of the guys you date bear a strong resemblance to old Tony."

Iris snorted. "True. And that's not necessarily a good thing. At least you meet employed guys."

"There is that." Cara leaned back in her chair. Iris had been an artist, actress, gossip blogger, and stand-up comic. At the moment, she was waiting tables in Brooklyn at a dive that served nachos and two-dollar cans of beer to poets and artists. The borrowing type. Another reason Cara had passed on her friend's offer—yeah, sure, Iris's boyfriends were sexy as hell, but so totally unreliable.

"So this guy Greg doesn't make the cut? Not even for a good old-fashioned roll in the hay? Didn't you say he's sexy?"

"Sexy body . . . not too sexy of a brain. And his self-serving attitude isn't all that sexy, either."

"Is he going to be at the party tonight?"

"He wants to go together, but I haven't committed." Cara sat up straight again and fiddled with a pen, tapping it on her desktop. "Some important client of ours is throwing it. Attendance is strongly encouraged, which translates as show up and suck up. But I get so little time off as it is; hanging out with my coworkers is not how I relish spending it."

"What's the occasion?"

"Something big with D&M is going to be announced, I think. Maybe a new contract. Or someone's retiring." More likely checking in for an extended stay at a mental-health rehab facility. It happened in her line of work. A lot. Between the intensity of the work weeks—surgery residents had nothing on stock market traders—and the pervasive alcohol and drug use that came with trying to stay on top of the game, people crashed right and left. Not her, though. She stayed on the straight and narrow. Did her job and only her job.

Maybe that's why lately she'd been feeling so . . . uneasy. Discombobulated. Like her world had shifted off center and she was standing at a tilt. If her high school crush on Tony had taught her anything, it was that there was a wild side to her. Granted, a small one, but one that needed to break free every once in a while. Nowadays all she did was work. And work. And work. Except for those rare times she went by herself to dance in nightclubs, and that obviously wasn't cutting it anymore. But what would? Finding her own modern-day Tony Spokane to pine after?

As if.

She rubbed her temple, trying to dull the slight headache she felt coming on.

"Whatever it is, you should probably hear the news firsthand," Iris said, interrupting Cara's thoughts. "And the thing is, you really *don't* get out much."

That was true enough. "I suppose I'll go."

"As if there was any real doubt," Iris snorted. "You live and breathe that job, Cara."

"Yeah. Unfortunately." Exhaustion hit, settling into her bones, causing her to drop her pen and lean back in her chair. How much longer could she push this hard? A memory of her childhood, her family on the shore during summer, swam into her mind. How gentle and relaxed and warm that day had been . . . her and her brother, Glenn, chasing waves up and down the beach, their mother reading a book under the sun umbrella, their father combing the beach for seashells . . . Just as quickly, the mental image slipped away, leaving her with the sting of nostalgia and the strong desire to be back there, on the beach with her family and her once-idyllic childhood. Impossible, yes . . . "But . . ."

"But what?"

She started. She hadn't realized she'd said the word out loud. "I do have three weeks of vacation that I've never used," she said. "Maybe I'll actually take a few days to escape." She tried to imagine it. Warm sand and water. A frothy drink in her hand. Nothing to do but read a good book and flirt with a hot cabana boy or two. Not quite like her childhood experience at the Jersey shore, but something similar . . . something relaxed. Maybe the Bahamas or even South Carolina. Someplace where she could hear the roar of the surf at night and feel the heat of the sun during the day.

Yeah, right, like she'd ever take the time off work and go somewhere.

More realistically, she'd probably stay close and spend most of the time with her mother or Glenn. Visiting her brother in his residential treatment home, Windorne Care Home, wasn't the most relaxing of events. She normally tried to see him once a week, but those visits were often stressful and rushed. She counted her blessings that her mind was healthy—she couldn't imagine how difficult life was for her brother, who had had treatment-resistant schizophrenia since his late teen years.

"You seriously should. But never mind the three weeks. Tonight would be, what? Three hours of your precious time?"

"Maybe four. I have to get there and back. The party's being held at some private house along Long Island Sound."

"Ritzy. Classy. That means you also need to spend some time finding something appropriate to wear in that black hole of a closet of yours. Seriously, you're in dire need of some retail therapy. All you have in there are suits, suits, suits. Navy, black, gray. Blouses, blouses, blouses. Cream, ivory, white. You know, Cara, there's nothing wrong with dressing up a *little*, is there? God, with your long blond hair, skin an angel would pay to have, and body made for . . . well, you know. You never play up those amazing assets of yours, and you should."

Iris was exaggerating about the plethora of work clothes in Cara's closet, only slightly. Over the last year, she'd found herself wearing a slinky dress, her blond hair loose and over her shoulders, and her face heavily made up—complete with smoky eyeshadow and mattered lips—while inside a nightclub, grinding to the heavy beat, losing herself in the thick crowd. She hadn't told Iris what she was doing, although she felt guilty about keeping a secret from her friend. It was as if she'd found a small way to break free of the burdens working at D&M placed on her.

"I'll do my best not to embarrass you, Iris."

"You don't embarrass me. You make me damn proud, honey," Iris said, a rare show of emotion in her voice. "You do so much for your family, I just wish you'd take some time to live *your* life for a change. I hate seeing you give so much of yourself and take nothing in return."

Cara closed her eyes and took a deep breath, then forced herself to smile. Iris couldn't see it, but maybe she'd hear it in her voice. "It's not forever, Iris. I'm lucky. I'll have my time eventually."

"When?"

When I win the lottery, she thought. But although not having to worry about money would certainly make her life easier, it wouldn't solve all her problems. This desire to break free being one of them. And the lack of datable material would be another. She cleared her throat. "I'll start by trying to have a little fun tonight. Promise."

"Call that guy," Iris said quickly. "Greg. He might be egotistical, but maybe being around a hot dude might get you in the mood."

Maybe. Probably not. But Iris's suggestion was worth considering. After disconnecting with Iris, Cara called Greg. As the phone rang, she hesitated.

She didn't want to go, she realized. Still, her hesitation confused her. Did she not want to go to the party, or did she not want to go with Greg? This was a work-related function. Whether or not she would be bored by either Greg or conversations with her coworkers shouldn't matter. Yes, work-related functions were boring, and rightly so. It was far better to maintain the status quo than let loose and get crazy. And some of her work friends would be there, too. Gail from three doors down. Tammie, another analyst. It would be nice to chat with them. But God, she wanted more. Wanted to no longer be swimming in monotony. Wanted to no longer feel like she was twisting around in her own skin, held down . . . held back.

But where were all these thoughts coming from? This restlessness, this desire for more, wasn't her. She was exactly where she wanted to be. Working hard. Making a decent living but still cognizant of the fact that everything she was working for could be taken away from her at any moment, the way it had been taken away from her family—from her dad. She could never let her guard down. Never get too comfortable. People took advantage of those who had weak walls. Who trusted too much. And when people swooped in for the kill, they left only devastation.

It was probably just Iris's talk of love that was throwing her off. As streetwise as her friend was, Iris was a closet romantic at heart.

Thankfully, she'd flushed that out of her system a long time ago. Romance was for those who had time and money to waste. Not her.

When Greg answered, she caught her breath, then found herself saying, "Greg, it's Cara. I, uh, decided to go. Did you still want to attend tonight's party together?"

This. This is why dating coworkers is a bad idea, Cara thought later that evening as she watched Greg enjoying himself without her. *Because now that I've confirmed I never want to see him again, I won't be able to avoid him.*

As soon as the thought formed, Greg caught her gaze from across the room and smiled before turning back to joke with his posse, something he'd been doing for the past twenty minutes. Cara quietly snorted, and drained what was left of her drink before setting her glass down on a marble table with a *clunk*. Greg's ability to be pleasant had disappeared about five minutes after they'd arrived—apparently he turned obnoxious in social settings when surrounded by his friends. Loud laughter. Male-snarky comments about the females in the company. Scanning women's bodies up and down the minute they entered the room, letting his gaze linger on their breasts. And ignoring her, almost to the point of being rude.

Actually, Greg *was* being rude. Earlier, he'd tugged her into a corner and attempted to kiss her. When she'd tried to gently push him away, he'd felt her up. Fortunately for her—or for Greg, she wasn't sure, since she'd just about kneed him in the balls—her friend Gail had come up and initiated a conversation with her, leaving Greg to gape at the other women at the party.

By the time Gail had taken off, Greg had found his group of likeminded friends and was studiously avoiding her. Cara had ended up refreshing her own drink twice, and he'd still not moved from his coterie.

So obnoxious. In fact, obnoxious to the point where Cara had decided wandering the party by herself was infinitely preferable to spending any more time than necessary in Greg's company. But a drawn-out conversation about equities with Jackson Riley, one of the young traders who sat in the bullpen on her floor, had her swallowing a plethora of yawns. She'd been right in wanting to avoid this party—boring would be a kind word. At this point, she greatly regretted the fact she'd come to the party at all and wanted nothing more than to run home, change into her pj's, and dig into a container of ice cream while watching one of her favorite movies on Netflix. Gail had already taken off, claiming a headache, and Tammie never had shown, leaving Cara on her own. Her boss, Max Dubois, had awkwardly chatted with her for a short while before noticing one of their big clients and abandoning her at the drinks station. The host of the event, apparently a major client who owned the house, hadn't even made an appearance.

The uncomfortable feeling that she didn't belong here was beginning to get to her.

Turning abruptly, she headed to the grand foyer that adjoined the living room. She looked around at all the fancily dressed people drinking their fancy drinks in the fanciest house she'd ever been in that no doubt belonged to some blowhard who was probably as boring—both in bed and out—as Greg. Not that she knew for sure Greg was no great shakes in bed, but it was a pretty safe bet given the few clumsy kisses he'd planted on her after their previous meet-ups, and his roving hands from earlier in the evening—hands that made a mammogram seem sexy.

In the foyer, more well-dressed guests milled about, drinks in hand, polished shoes traversing gleaming marble as their owners inspected and clearly coveted this painting or that vase as music boomed from discreet but powerful speakers. Her head throbbed in time to the beat. Here, close to the bar, the crowd was mostly young and predominantly male. Larry Gills, one of the more senior traders, was the eldest, even more so standing next to Rafe Sampson, the young and overly eager trader who followed Larry around like a puppy dog. John Turner, another old-timer, looked out of place with his salt-and-pepper hair and slight paunch as he stood next to the young men whose rock-hard bodies indicated any leisure time was spent at the gym or rock climbing. It was as if a trading office building on Wall Street had emptied out and arrived en masse to drink hard and talk business and brag, before the last train or hired drivers got them back to Manhattan.

Which, of course, was the case. The majority of D&M was here, at the party, along with a few people she recognized as clients.

The gathering seemed sedate on the surface—no one laughing hysterically and no dancing on tabletops. But Cara knew that the legendary orgies of yesteryear weren't quite consigned to the past. Crazed parties with strippers and whatnot, staged for big clients who expected no less, still happened behind closed doors, far from the ears and eyes of lawyers specializing in sexual harassment cases with potential multimillion-dollar payoffs. The movie *The Wolf of Wall Street* hadn't been too far off the mark.

Getting blasted was still considered okay. But it wasn't just booze that fueled the pulsing energy beneath the relatively polished manners of the guests. Some of the traders snacked all day on the same uppers they'd been prescribed since first grade, boosting the effect with the newer Modafinil. Whatever it took to make them feel smart and perform at peak was cool, as long as they literally kept their noses clean. The older guys in the office still reminisced wistfully about white powder and nosebleed binges, but plain old cocaine was passé. These were games she didn't play and avoided at all costs. Too bad her date seemed to be in the thick of it all.

Cara was pretty sure that Greg's unexpected obnoxiousness was being ramped up by something synthetic, another strike against him, now that she was keeping track. She could barely tolerate boredom, but never drugs. She refused to touch any of it, preferring to rely on self-generated energy and natural drive. She oversaw the direction her life took, every single step, from personal to financial to professional. That necessitated maintaining control, and Cara didn't associate with anyone who might endanger that.

Right now she was feeling slightly less than composed. She needed a breather. Plus whoever was deejaying had amped up the volume on a dance mix that on nights when she was alone in a club would have her moving, but now only made her want to leave. Or find earplugs.

Automatically, she began moving toward the front door, which was framed with high arched windows revealing a glimpse of shimmering black water beyond the vast lawn. Built on a spit of land that jutted out into the water of Long Island Sound, the mansion was extraordinary, with wraparound views.

The glamorous North Shore setting was in every way the opposite of Ashtogue, Long Island, the blue-collar town where she'd spent most of her childhood, growing up in a white clapboard house built on the usual concrete slab. The other houses on her block looked much the same, except for the ones with added second floors or gabled rooms built on when more kids came along. The small lawns were carefully maintained or patchy with dandelions, depending on how much time the owners had to fix up their small piece of suburbia.

She'd loved her home. It had been humble, yes, but she'd known only love. Respect. Admiration. Her father had made her a swing out of an old tire and would push her so high she'd swear her tiptoes touched the sun. Glenn had dragged home a few pieces of plywood from a construction site up the block and together, she and her brother had built a tree fort in the old alder in the backyard, where she'd sit on hot summer days, reading her favorite books and dripping Popsicle all over her legs.

But that was before everything came crashing down.

Later, after she'd grown up, Cara had never wanted to revisit her childhood home. She preferred to remember the town the way it was. Before her family had gone under. Way before she'd moved to the outskirts of New York City with her brother and widowed mother. Long before her father had died.

She pushed through the crowd, but no one among the noisy guests paid the slightest attention to her, which was perfect. She needed some moments of peace and quiet to regroup. It would be nice to breathe in air that didn't smell of five-hundred-dollar-a-bottle perfume and expensive liquor and costly ambition. When the front door opened, only one power couple stepped inside, but Cara could see more cars coming up the circular drive.

Two Bentleys. A Maybach. Bringing up the rear, a couple of shiny new Mercedes Benz sedans, the poor relations. The nouveau riche were always followed by the strivers. She hated to think of herself as being in the last category, but it was difficult to deny. She was always striving to leave her past behind and move toward a kinder, gentler future. It wasn't massive wealth she craved, but what she did want—respectability, comfort, and stability—necessitated accumulating a healthy supply of cash without going overboard and without advertising it, either. Take her outfit—a simple cream skirt and blouse that Iris would hate but would grudgingly approve of on her. Add the fashionable shoes—designer, sure, but sturdy. Nothing outrageously expensive. Subdued enough not to stand out. Stylish enough to project class.

The old adage was true—it took money to make money. It also took money and quite a lot of thought and planning to project an image that you were not to be messed with—but also not *worth* messing with. Stay in the know and swim with the sharks, but at the same time stay off everyone's radar.

The experiences her father had gone through had taught her well. She'd watched in silence as his world—and the world of her family—had been ripped apart. As a child, there was nothing she could do but observe. Take notes. Assess what worked and what didn't. In one fell swoop, she'd gone from the laughing kid with the skinned knee and perpetual book in hand to the silent observer, solemn and determined.

For the most part, projecting a confident and quiet exterior was what Cara excelled at. But not now. Not tonight. Somehow having Greg ditch her for his Adderall-sniffing friends and not having Gail or Tammie at her side, she felt amazingly alone. And off her axis. Like the facade she'd worked hard to put up had slipped and she'd been exposed somehow. Now she felt like she was swimming in a fish bowl, vulnerable and alone.

Abruptly, she changed direction and headed up the mahogany staircase that rose in a classic curve. No way could she take one more inane conversation about work—she was done. As she reached the landing, the throbbing music and incoherent chatter behind her died down, as if someone important had just arrived. Whom it might have been didn't matter—she just needed to get the hell out of there. She didn't pause, didn't look back, and instead moved even faster, practically running, until she finally turned a corner and made it to the next floor, which was dimly lit, quiet, and most important, unoccupied.

Most of the doors in the long hallway were closed, but not that of the nearest room. She peered inside to see an impersonal but serene space dominated by a long, angular black leather sofa outlined with bronze studs. A low glass table stood in front of the sofa. A white cashmere throw, tossed over one well-padded arm with meticulous casualness, seemed to have been left there for anyone.

Cautiously, she stepped inside. The thick charcoal-colored rug beneath the minimal furniture muffled her footsteps. She decisively closed the door behind her. Then, leaning back against it, she closed her eyes. With a twist of her mouth, she acknowledged that if someone was watching her, she'd likely resemble some airheaded actress in a horror movie, fleeing for her life before finding temporary sanctuary. Briefly, she imagined Greg wearing a hockey mask and wielding a chainsaw. She laughed out loud, then swiftly cupped a hand over her mouth to stifle the sound.

It wasn't like anyone could hear her. She opened her

eyes and looked around again. In a gigantic house full of guests, she was completely and utterly alone. As if Iris were nagging her from afar, Cara wondered how it was she could end up solo at a party with so many available—and good-looking—men. Not her fault—it was just that none of them were the right kind of man. That was nothing new.

Was Iris's implication—that she hadn't been laid for way too long—the thing that had her churning from the inside, or was it something else?

Or maybe she was just frustrated that all her hard work, all the years spent pounding the books in first her high school then her college library, was all for nothing.

She glanced around the room, knowing there was no way she'd ever get so rich as to afford a place like this. Or even know anyone this wealthy. She pushed away from the door and wandered around the room, realizing it was far more spacious than she'd thought at first glance. She studied the stark beauty of the understated decor more closely. Everything looked new, though nothing was ostentatious. Their host was likely someone who'd made it big on the Street, and relatively recently at that. Presumably a financier or hedge-fund king who could afford the best had added the property to his real-estate portfolio. She didn't have the feeling that anyone actually *lived* here.

Cara ran a hand over a wall covered in something that wasn't wallpaper, but something luxurious, with an unusual texture. Natural. Shagreen? Was that the right word? No—that was shark skin. Shantung. That was it. A heavy silk. She closed her eyes once more. Opened them. Immediately wanted to close them again. She hadn't eaten before their arrival and she'd waved away the catering-company waiters circulating with trays of canapés. Clearly, an empty stomach, combined with her late nights at the office and the drinks she'd just downed, was making her drowsy.

She rubbed her temples. Thought about going back downstairs. Bit her lip. One more conversation about numbers crunching or equities or fair trade values with someone like the young trader Jackson or her boss, Max, and she'd scream. No, she'd much rather stay here. And if Greg wondered for half a second if she'd retrieved the rented car from the valet outside and abandoned him to find his own way home, even better.

She paced the room. After only a brief hesitation, she kicked off her high heels, sat on the sofa, then swung her legs up to lie down. Yeah, no way she was going back down there. The party might be in full swing, but it was definitely over for her now. She could call a cab to come get her, but not just yet.

The cool leather of the sofa invited her touch. No doubt about it, whoever owned the mansion had taste. Of course, that was easy enough to buy.

The enveloping silence of the room enfolded her, easing her into something like sleep. An elusive sense of contentment and safety washed over her. She surrendered herself to it.

Until what felt like only moments later, an odd sensation brought her out of it.

A hand caressed her cheek. Her slowly returning consciousness registered it as masculine, strongly so. Startled, Cara opened her eyes and struggled to sit up even as she clutched the cashmere throw that now covered her. It was soft. And it smelled good. Clean. Spicy. Even before she sensed movement, she knew a man was there—and that it was *his* scent she was enjoying.

Almost frightened, she looked up into the intent dark gaze of the man standing over her.

He was well over six feet, with broad shoulders and a lean, athletic build, wearing a suit that even her drowsy mind registered as expensive and definitely custom made. His eyes were brown, his hair even darker, maybe black. It was hard to tell in the shadowy room. But it looked messed up, not styled, in contrast to the rest of his appearance.

A strong jaw had a tense set, but she could guess what he looked like when and if he smiled. There were faint lines on either side of a mouth that had a sensual fullness. His lips tightened for a fraction of a second as he looked back at her, his expression somehow radiating sensuality and displeasure all at once.

Of course he was displeased. She'd rudely intruded into his private space. An automatic apology hovered on her lips, but for some reason she couldn't get it out. All she could do was stare at him, transfixed, and sternly tell herself that no, she couldn't stand, grab his face, and pull him down for a kiss to see if he tasted as good as he smelled.

The fact she wanted to was a bit of a shock.

Her stomach quivered and she swallowed against a dry mouth. A racing heartbeat had her parting her lips to breathe. Wow. She wanted this man, and bad.

Chapter Two

Cara considered herself plenty experienced. There had been times in her life she'd enjoyed the company of men. When she'd had boyfriends. Sex. But her desire for men and their bodies had always seemed, while probably quite normal, nonetheless slightly unremarkable. Her girlfriends in high school—including Iris—had burbled on and on about boys and how wet they got when the boys walked by, but her? Yeah, she'd thought Tony Spokane was hot, and had felt a little flutter in her belly when she kissed her first boyfriend—had even climaxed the very first time she'd had sex, losing her virginity to her college boyfriend Alec—but somehow the fantastic glittery experience her friends talked about had bypassed her.

Until now.

As seconds stretched together, the man standing over her focused on her mouth, her eyes, as if caressing her face with his gaze. The intensity of her instant attraction to this stranger was anything but unremarkable.

It was his eyes that really did it to her. The heat in their depths was startling. The quivering in her belly radiated out, lower, and she felt herself getting wet . . .

wetter than she'd ever been. Wet enough that if she weren't careful, it would show on her cream skirt. She fought against the wild notion that he wanted to take what he saw: her. Right now. Right here. Any way she wanted to be taken.

She fought even harder against the notion that that was exactly what she wanted. And that she yearned for him to show her ways to be taken she'd barely even heard of. Ways Iris probably knew about.

But he stayed where he was. His hands were in his pockets. He'd put them there *after* he'd touched her. Unless she'd just dreamed that tender caress, of course.

"You weren't enjoying the party?" His deep voice reverberated in the room.

Conversation, she reminded herself. First step in meeting someone new was to converse, not strip naked and jump their bones. She hesitated, then said, "Everything was beautiful. First class." *I'm just more an economy class kind of girl*, she thought, then mentally slapped herself upside the head. Why even think that when a gorgeous man was staring at her? When he'd obviously covered her up while she slept? *Watched* her while she slept?

He smiled slightly. "You weren't enjoying it," he said decisively. His calm self-assurance was very different from the young guys she worked with, although he didn't look much older than they did. He was probably thirty. Just. But he had a tough, ruthless look about him, as if he'd literally fought his way to the top of the world.

Oh, God, she suddenly realized, this had to be his house. Everything about him lent credence to that fact. She'd stumbled into his private sanctuary. But instead of seeking confirmation, she asked, "What time is it?" Slowly, she moved the cashmere throw down her body, touching the buttons of her cream blouse first to make sure she wasn't carelessly revealing herself. Every button

was in place. It was her imagination working overtime
that made it feel like they'd jumped loose and given him
a glimpse of her lacy bra before she'd opened her eyes.

"After midnight."

She rose from the sofa, straightening her rumpled
clothes. "I have to go." Somewhat awkwardly, she
slipped a foot into one high heel, then the other, and
stood tall. He was still a whole lot taller.

"You can stay in here for a bit if you like," he said
indifferently. "The party's winding down."

"I guess this must be your house."

He inclined his dark head in a nod.

"Spectacular. Really nice." Cara told herself not to
babble. "I'm sorry, we weren't told who owned the
place."

"I'm Branden Duke."

A nice name. A regal name. But this was no Prince
Charming. Too haunted. Too harsh. But gorgeous,
nonetheless. "Nice to meet you, and thanks for the offer
to stay, but . . ." She glanced beyond him and swallowed. The door was behind him. Closed.

He'd opened it, seen her sleeping, and come in, closing
it behind him. Why?

As if he had picked up on the nervous question that
buzzed in her mind, he turned and strode to the door,
opening it again. But he came back.

Two things registered. First, she wasn't being dis-
missed. Second, he wasn't blocking her way, and that
appeared to be deliberate on his part. He'd known she
felt threatened and had immediately reassured her. With
actions, not words. In her world, that immediately set
him apart from most.

She stepped toward him, fully intending to make a
swift exit—and made the mistake of looking up. His
dark, burning gaze hypnotized her for a moment longer.

He raised a hand and ran his fingertips over her sleep-flushed cheek as if he couldn't help himself.

Again.

Cara was mesmerized. The unexpected contact was tender and also erotic. Familiar.

Tempting.

This man in no way resembled Tony Spokane. He wasn't a boy playing at being bad. He was simply bad through and through. In all the best ways possible.

"Don't." She was barely able to breathe out the single word. She wasn't angry or afraid—just wildly confused by his daring and her own crazy reaction. He dropped his hand.

"Are you here alone? Do you work for—"

Frightened by the intensity of her attraction to him, she blurted out, "I came with Greg Johnson. He must be wondering where I am."

Right. As if Greg looking for her would be some kind of protection from this man. If Branden Duke wanted something, wanted *her*, a little competition would hardly put him off.

Besides, she didn't *want* Greg to come looking for her.

At the top of the list of the Reasons Why Not, which were coming back to her, was the inevitable watercooler talk between the guys, discussing the party and instant replays of their conquests. She didn't want to become Topic Number One during that bull session. But getting caught up here with this man, who had some mysterious connection to her company, wouldn't do, either.

Branden's gaze flickered. "Greg Johnson. The stock-broker from Dubois & Mellan? He's gone."

Great. That meant Greg had taken her ride back to Manhattan with him. *Bastard*, she thought, but without much heat. After all, she'd contemplated doing that very thing to him. "You know him?"

"We were introduced tonight."

"Great. Well, I really should be going—"

Cara stepped back, nearly falling when her leg connected with the low glass table. Branden reached out and held her arms, the strength in his large hands flowing into her somehow. She swallowed hard, reluctant to shrug him off.

The spell he'd cast didn't break. Seconds passed. A minute. He didn't release her. Instead, his soft grip slowly turned into caresses, with his hands smoothing over her arms and then up her neck until his hands lightly framed her jaw.

She still didn't pull away. All she wanted to do was give in and see what happened.

"I'm thinking Greg Johnson doesn't deserve you."

"And you do?" The statement just popped out of her.

He smiled ever so slightly. Cocked a challenging brow. Stared at her with eyes filled with a taunting dare.

So what if we're strangers, it said. *You want to kiss me. So why not kiss me?*

She could think of many reasons why not. But she didn't want to think. The lingering dreaminess of being caught unawares and the intimate solitude of their chance encounter dissolved her resistance. In a heart beat.

She rose on her tiptoes to give him her mouth, loving the ebony fire that blazed in his eyes just before she made contact. The kiss was a brush of the lips at first, then a searching, urgent opening of her mouth as his tongue met hers. Branden Duke kissed with expert sensuality. The strong body underneath the fine suit conveyed a rising heat as she relaxed against it, not surrendering just yet, but savoring the pleasure of a scorching kiss from a real man.

In its own compelling way, it was another first kiss. But absolutely not innocent, though his sensual skill made her feel like a beginner. Never, never had she so much as dreamed a kiss could be so powerfully erotic.

The desire he awakened could easily turn into obsession.

She didn't know how much time passed. The kiss continued. His hands glided over her curves—front and rear, but mostly rear—but he didn't try to get underneath her skirt or blouse. She liked that. She thrilled to his touch, enjoying the subtle slide of material over her hips as he pulled her closer and made her move for him. He knew exactly what he was doing, bringing forth visions of platform beds and silky sheets and ropes tied around her wrists—

She immediately flinched at the erotic vision of her bound and helpless to this man's hands and mouth. Whether it was at her movement or because he'd guessed at her thoughts, his kiss became rougher. His touch more possessive, pressing her against him with an unmistakable air of dominance.

She couldn't help but respond. Cara raised her arms and draped them over his shoulders, breaking off the kiss to nuzzle his neck and press her nose into his heated skin, warmed by that delicious spicy scent. His chin rested lightly on her head and he groaned as she rubbed her blouse- and bra-covered breasts against his front, shamelessly enjoying the feel of her nipples tightening against the fabric.

He drew in a sharp breath, and then abruptly set her away from him, leaving her disoriented and cold. His grasp on her arms was hard, frantic yet conflicted, as if he wanted to keep her at a distance but was unwilling to let her walk away completely.

She gasped and let her head loll back, eroticism making her spine grow weak.

Then he landed his blow. "Maybe I was wrong. Maybe

Greg was just your way of getting in here. Are you look-ing to trade up? Is that it?"

Instead of flinching this time, she actually recoiled. How could he have thought that? *Why* would he have thought that? Just because he'd aroused her with his kiss? Her spine snapped up, rigid, and she shot him a glare.

He frowned, his grip loosening enough that she could rip herself away. She backed up several steps and simply stared at him. She couldn't help it. He'd shocked her and she knew by the expression of regret that instantly flashed across his face that she probably looked like he'd slapped her.

He held up a hand. "But I could be wrong."

His voice snapped her out of her paralysis. "You think?" she asked nastily. She immediately turned and strode toward the open door. She gasped when his hands gently grasped her arms from behind, stopping her in her tracks. She stiffened, but when he didn't roughly pull her against him, she forced herself to relax. *Let the bastard grovel,* she thought. She'd enjoy it. Then she'd mentally knee him in the nuts and get the hell out of here.

"I'm sorry," he said quietly. "You . . . that kiss . . . it took me by surprise."

You think? This time she asked the sarcastic question silently. His tone seemed genuinely perplexed and she relaxed even more at his willingness to admit he *could* be taken by surprise. It was a concession of vulnerability he probably didn't make a habit of giving.

Deliberately, she took three testing steps forward. As she'd expected, he didn't try to stop her, instead letting her go completely. And he didn't try to force her to turn around when she just continued to stand there, trying to get her bearings.

Cara felt dizzy. She didn't want to feel that out of control. But she didn't want to leave. No, she wanted this man, in every way she could have him. But a wanton kiss that had just sort of happened was one thing. Sex with a stranger, and she'd admittedly seemed headed down that unexpected path, was quite another. For him to imply she'd been lying in wait for him had been insulting . . . but understandable given where he'd found her and how she'd initiated that mind-blowing kiss.

With a sigh, she turned to face him. "I understand why you thought what you did. But you're wrong. I was just looking for a place to be alone. I wasn't expecting . . ."

At her trailing words, he sighed. Ran his hands through his hair. "Neither was I. But I liked it. I don't suppose you'll forget what I said, though."

The expression on his face—playful hopefulness— actually had her stifling a laugh.

"I think it's best I go." She slid her hands over her skirt and checked those blouse buttons. Still in place, every damn one of them. She hadn't known it was possible to get that turned on fully dressed.

"Do you really?" The playfulness was gone. His tone seductive. The look in his eyes posing another question altogether: *How about we have sex instead? All night long?*

God, the guy could switch it on and off. It was probably second nature to him. He was obviously used to getting his way.

"Yes," she said, shifting her attention off him and onto the door. She needed to get out of here . . . before she did something to embarrass herself. "The party is over . . ."

"That's right. The only people left are the ones who have something I want."

At the emotionally charged tone in his voice, she

turned her attention back to him. His gaze seemed to include her in the category he spoke of.

"Another woman? Or two?" she asked for some foolish reason.

Branden smiled. Big and wide. He was gorgeous, period, but when he smiled . . . she felt like someone who'd seen the sun for the very first time.

"More like a baker's dozen," he replied.

Okay. That raised some unpleasant questions and answered a couple of others. She hadn't been his Sleeping Beauty, just a girl who conveniently conked out in an upstairs room. And it was clear he was no Prince Charming, even if he did own this cool waterfront castle and kiss like a sex dream come true.

"Oh. I see." Cara gave him a thinly stretched smile and sauntered to the door. If the party had degenerated into some sort of upscale orgy, she wanted no part of it. She needed to get a taxi.

"My driver can take you home. He's in the porte cochere. Tell him I sent you."

His voice caught her as she stepped out into the hall, and she immediately halted. Her initial instinct was to politely decline. She didn't. She needed an escape hatch and he'd just given it to her. She wasn't about to turn him down. Without even saying thank you, she walked quickly to the mahogany staircase, going down the stairs with silent speed.

From below, Max Dubois, her boss, noticed her as she glided down the staircase. Loudly, he called out to her. "Cara, I didn't realize you were still here! I—"

"I'm sorry, Max, but I have to run," she called. True to her word, she practically ran to the foyer to grab her coat, which had her wallet in the pocket, from the front closet. Only once she was at the front door did she allow herself to look back and up.

Branden Duke was watching her, his strong hands

resting on the banister of the upper landing where he had remained. Even at this distance, the intensity of his dark gaze was unsettling. He didn't seem happy that she had escaped.

Tough luck. Cara told herself she should have known better than to fall asleep in a lion's den. At least she'd never given him her name.

If she was lucky—and smart—she'd never see him again.

Despite the cold night air, Branden kept the car windows rolled down, craving the bracing rush of wind. He needed to clear his head, and a solo drive in his latest luxury sports car did the trick. It had taken an eternity for the remaining guests—the junior brokers and their managers, plus the execs who were in on the takeover—to be ushered out. The wives and girlfriends in attendance had clustered together, chatting. A few of the officially unattached females, easy to spot by their microscopic skirts and staggeringly high heels, had been bold enough to come up the stairs and thank him for the party.

That had pissed him off, but only because he hadn't liked seeing them on the second floor. Where *she'd* been. Where they'd been together. He didn't want anyone intruding on those memories, no matter how innocuous or swift the intrusion.

He knew her name now.

Cara Michal.

Based on their conversation upstairs, he'd assumed she was Greg Johnson's date, not an employee of Dubois & Mellan. And because he'd known the other man had abandoned her, Branden hadn't had any qualms about acting on the potent attraction he'd felt from the moment he'd seen her sleeping on his sofa.

He'd known he should wake her and get her the hell

out of his house. Instead, he'd given in to the temptation to look at her, then to touch her. He'd wanted to rouse her, see those thickly lashed lids flutter open to reveal the color of her eyes.

When they had, he'd sucked in his breath at how spectacular her blue eyes were. They reminded him of a cross between aquamarines and sapphires. He'd wanted to kiss her then and there. He'd waited to see if she'd kiss him. Not simply because he enjoyed a challenge but because she was a stranger. Even when his cock ached to bury itself inside a woman—even when it ached in a way it never had before to bury itself in *her*—he knew better than to give in to temptation and jeopardize all that he'd worked for.

She'd snuck into his private domain. If she kissed him first, no matter how things progressed from there on out, she'd have a very hard time crying foul, especially because he'd have the security footage to back it up.

Thank God she actually had made the first move. He'd quickly taken over, shocked at how fast he'd surrendered to his need to touch her. To have her. When she'd rubbed against him, he'd barely stopped himself from shoving up her short skirt and bending her over the sofa so he could plunge inside her. His out-of-the-blue comment about her looking to "trade up" had to be the stupidest, most egotistical, idiotically impulsive thing he'd ever said. Granted, she'd stepped back and he'd gained a few seconds of breathing room. But by the fire in her eyes, he knew he'd gone too far.

Why in God's name hadn't he been able to control himself?

He slammed the steering wheel with an open hand. The car veered and he corrected it with a furious yank in the opposite direction. Too bad he hadn't been able to do the same for himself when she was there, her luminous eyes never leaving his as she tried to straighten her messed-up clothes, not sure whether she should stay or go.

She was different from the women he was used to. Like no other, in fact. Despite the fact that she was obviously capable of taking care of herself, she brought out his protective instincts.

His desire to protect her—if only from himself, he thought with renewed anger—had continued even after she'd left. He'd had every intention of seeing her again. And soon.

But then he'd heard Max Dubois call out to her. And when he'd gone downstairs to see to his remaining guests and spoken to Max, he realized he'd been wrong.

He learned her name. And he learned she *did* work for Dubois & Mellan.

As such, she was now his employee.

He'd just bought the company.

The big announcement was supposed to have been made at the party.

Only that hadn't happened.

He'd missed his chance when he, like Cara, had gone upstairs for a moment's peace. He'd found her instead.

Any hope of peace had been shot to hell.

Even now, hours later, even after learning that she was his new employee and that it would be wholly inappropriate for him to jump into bed with her, Cara Michal stayed on his mind. He couldn't get her out no matter how fast he drove.

He flicked the gearshift and allowed the car to leap forward. That had been one hell of a kiss from a once-in-a-lifetime lady. He couldn't help but imagine doing more with her. In a variety of thrilling ways, starting on the couch she'd been reclining on. He'd spread her out, with one of her legs thrown over the back of the couch, and the other hanging off the edge while he buried his face between her thighs, lapping her up.

Thinking about the soft, silky goddess he'd been privileged to hold and wanted to hold again, Branden sped up even more. Damn. It was as if she'd slipped through his fingers, never to be recaptured. Even worse, he would see her again, but not the way he wanted to. He drove faster, angry with himself for letting her leave without getting another taste of her.

He slowed down a little, trying to snap himself out of his irritable mood. Stone bridges, ideal hiding places for an officer in a black-and-white, spanned the long curves of the roads on Long Island's North Shore. Zoom through and they'd get you on the other side. Especially if driving a Maserati.

He glanced in the rearview, almost expecting a blast of red whirling light and wailing siren. There wasn't even another car. At four in the morning, he had the road to himself.

Plenty of room and plenty of time to keep right on thinking about Cara. But he'd be better off turning this roaring beast of a car around and doing that at home. No sense risking another speeding ticket.

He slowed even more, then pulled over to the side of the road, and in the dark, clicked on his Bluetooth. A few minutes later, he'd sent out various texts, some business, and one to his youngest sister, Jeannette, reminding her to turn in her application for college on time. He hadn't finished college himself, but he'd made sure his half sister and stepsiblings had received an excellent education. All but Bethany had done just that. Bethany was currently pursuing her dream of being an actress on Broadway, and Branden was damn proud of her, just as he was proud of all his sisters. Jeannette was in her final year of high school, and he'd be damned if she didn't go to an excellent university.

And it would be up to him to make that happen. Their mother was an absolute failure when it came to finances ... or deadlines ... or taste in men. And Jean-nette's father—all of Branden's stepfathers, to be truthful—was an asswipe of the highest extreme. No way would the man ever be able to put his amazing and beautiful daughter through college.

A beep told him a text had come in. He flicked a glance at the screen on his car and read a message from Jeannette. *Big bad bully. Don't you know what "gap year" means?*

Yeah, right. There was no way he'd let her get away with flitting all over Europe, taking a "gap year."

Don't you know what self-sufficiency means? he texted back.

She responded with an emoji with a tongue sticking out, then added on a selfie of her holding a blue martini in one hand, the other hand flashing him a peace sign.

He chuckled. Spunky and cute. But this was a school night, and she'd better be drinking a virgin mocktail, not a real martini. He thumbed in, *Get back to Mom's house, now, or you'll have to scrub my toilets if you want your allowance.*

Jeannette responded with another selfie, this time with her pulling a despondent face and car keys in hand.

In a half hour, he pulled into his long driveway, click-ing the remote to operate the security gate. The staff would have gone home—most of them were locals. He paid them well to not live in. Branden preferred to have his house to himself when not entertaining, though he didn't spend much time at the place.

After entering the house, he mounted the stairs and looked into his sanctuary. Immediately, he thought of Cara. What instinct had brought her there and who had left the door unlocked? The memory of Cara on the black leather sofa, her gorgeous curves all too evident under the white cashmere throw, dogged him. That golden hair, flowing like spilled honey as she moved restlessly in her light sleep. Her blue eyes when she'd awoken, disoriented and just a little frightened to see him.

He'd stood there like a fool, drinking her in. He'd been amused by the wary look in her searching gaze. Intrigued by the way she'd seemed flustered, checking her blouse to make sure it hadn't come undone when other women would have leaned closer and tried to lure him in. He suspected she could take his face off with a single swipe of her pretty claws if he had dared to try anything. So he'd dared her instead. With just a look. But she'd gotten his message.

And she'd taken his dare and raised the stakes on him.

Branden sat down on the couch and stretched out, catching a faint and tantalizing whiff of her perfume on the throw.

Fuck it. He couldn't have her. Not if she worked for him. Not given the true reason he'd purchased Dubois & Mellan, one that had nothing to do with business. If he made money on his new acquisition, fine. But he had plenty of that.

Still, even if he couldn't have her, he could fantasize about doing her. He let his hand slide down and opened his fly. He gave in to the impulse, encircling his achingly stiff rod with a steel grip. Yeah. The same fingers that had stroked her sweet cheek and investigated all that luscious womanliness, curve by curve, tightened as he got himself off in pulsing jets. Intense, solitary satisfaction. Job done.

Yet his cock didn't feel like quitting. It wanted her. *He* wanted her. Naked. Vulnerable. Begging for pleasure beyond her wildest dreams. Tender and erotic to begin. Kisses that started at her mouth and moved down, down, down. Then he could really open her up. See what made her cry out. How deep she wanted it and where. Rough and raw if she liked it like that. Then sensual and slow. The mix had to be magic. He wanted to make it unforgettable.

Because the fantasy of her was going to have to last him.

Tomorrow morning, it would have to be all business between them.

But Branden knew keeping things strictly professional with Cara Michal would be impossible.

Chapter Three

When Cara woke up, her corporate studio apartment was still dark. She flung off the covers and padded barefoot into the bathroom, dreading what she would see in the mirror after less than five hours of sleep.

She switched on the light and peered at her reflection. As postparty reflections went, it wasn't too bad. There was no major puffiness or wild-kingdom streaks, since she'd removed her makeup before tumbling into bed. After dropping her nightgown on the bathroom floor, she cranked up the shower spray and stood under it.

An unforgettable man was very much on her mind, and he hadn't left it since that kiss. As she lathered the bath puff she recalled the ride back to the city in Branden's limo, which had revved up the fantasy. If he'd been in the backseat with her, she would have succumbed to his powerful allure before the skyline of Manhattan had appeared. She'd made a few comments to the driver, attempting to strike up a conversation, hoping for some clue as to who Branden Duke really was, but the driver had remained stoic. Silent. He'd pulled up smoothly to the front of her condo building, exited the vehicle, and come around to her side to let her out, then had ignored the tip she'd tried to hand him.

Well trained.

Even as she'd been driven down Long Island in silence, the sound of Branden's low voice echoed in her mind. Her body seemed unable to forget the sensation of his hands gripping her. Stroking her. The taste of his mouth. His scent. She almost felt like she'd slept with him. Her ragingly sensual desire had surfaced again in her dreams, stimulating a wildly improbable fantasy starring Branden Duke. He'd been nameless, a dark lord of lust. As she rinsed the shampoo from her hair she thought about how she'd reacted in her dream—letting him taste her, then demanding to taste him. But he'd always gotten the better of her. God, the thought made her quiver.

She hadn't known she could actually dream triple-X scenarios of such intensity. They hadn't made much sense, but it didn't matter. She closed her eyes and felt his dream hands moving all over her, liquidly sensual, hotter than the water beating down on her bare skin.

Her own hand slipped between her thighs, but Cara denied herself the satisfaction. In a way, that would be surrendering to Branden Duke's allure, and even in the privacy of her own place, she could not let that happen. She needed to wipe him from her mind and get to work.

Once out of the shower, she wrapped herself in a thick towel and closed her eyes to dry her straight hair, feeling more in control now. Flicking a brush through the length, she combed it into her usual shoulder-length bob, a style that made the most of her natural honey-gold color. Cara dabbed a healthy glow from a small bottle onto her cheeks and outlined her blue eyes with a soft black pencil. Two swipes of tinted lip gloss and she was done. Glancing at the clock on the wall, she realized she needed to hurry.

Heading back into her bedroom, she didn't bother to switch on any other lights, preferring to raise the blinds for a peek at the skyline, drenched in the deep blue of predawn, without being seen herself. Windows in nearby tall buildings were starting to light up. Some were residential but most were offices. The Street got up early.

So did Cara, as a rule. On weekdays anyway, unless she'd stayed up too late working or watching nature documentaries. On weekends, when she was actually able to go out, she gave herself more leeway, especially if she'd had a late night dancing holes in her shoes.

After choosing a tailored but feminine suit in a dark shade, she dressed quickly in her walk-in closet, a routine that hadn't changed in the three years she'd been working for Dubois & Mellan.

The mirrored closet was a touch of luxury she appreciated. The rest of the apartment was nice enough. But it wasn't her own and never would be. One of these days she was going to buy her own place. It wouldn't be in Manhattan and it wouldn't be like this. It would be something simpler. Homier. But not being allowed to hang pictures or have a dog or pick a paint color other than white or beige was the price she paid for corporate living quarters with free Wi-Fi and cable and a location that couldn't be beat.

Her apartment was somewhere to sleep and watch TV, that was all. She'd never entertained there. The most she did for herself was occasionally nuke some leftovers for a late-night snack. The fridge was teeny and so was the microwave.

Dubois & Mellan had financed the construction of the building and owned several floors outright. The biggest apartments were reserved for visiting executives, but one of a handful of coveted studios had been offered to her on a temporary basis as part of the signing package. She was lucky to have it. She did pay rent, but at below market rate. Housing costs were a near impossibility in New York otherwise for a newly minted economics grad without a trust fund or rich parents who could cosign an astronomical lease.

She gave one last look around as she put on her parka and wrapped a warm scarf around her neck. The apartment was nearly as spare as the long hallway she went out into. After flicking her multiple locks closed, she entered the elevator, which was empty when she got on.

Something about the claustrophobic space made her think of Branden Duke again. If she ever got trapped between floors, she would want it to be with a man who triggered all her erotic layers . . . a man like Branden Duke.

Her stomach clenched and her mouth went dry. God, the night before, after he'd woken her up, all she'd wanted to do in his upstairs hideaway was rip off that fine suit and expose the magnificent man beneath.

Cara let her head loll back against the paneled wall. Just how he had unleashed so much sexually charged emotion in so little time wasn't something she understood.

Damn and double damn. She must be lonelier than she thought. Iris had to be right—she needed to go out. Date. Hell, she needed to get laid. But easy sex just wasn't her. That's why she danced; to experience her erotic side without adding the complicated factor of men. The discreet club not far away from her apartment, where 90 percent of the men were gay and 10 percent undecided, was where she could dance with anyone, have a fabulous time, and not get asked for her phone number. All that and great nachos.

The elevator reached the first floor. The soft stop that bumped her brought her back to reality.

She murmured a good morning to the doorman, who opened the lobby door for her, and went out into the chilly early morning air, shivering a little but feeling refreshed by the nip.

She pulled her sunglasses from her bag and shielded her eyes from the sun's first rays that barely penetrated the narrow streets of New York's Financial District, a closed-in space lined with old stone buildings jostled by towering glass skyscrapers. Young professionals, heads down, eyes on their smartphones and earbuds plugged in to get a jump on the overseas markets, crowded the sidewalks. One bumped her, hard, and didn't bother to apologize. Not that she expected him to—she'd long ago learned that the small-town values she'd been brought up with didn't translate to New York streets.

A gleaming SUV passed her, a little too close, and before she could edge back away from the street, a black town car whipped past, an older, well-dressed and coiffed woman in the back, a smartphone glued to her ear.

"Maybe get off the phone and tell your chauffeur to avoid using pedestrians as bowling pins," Cara muttered under her breath as she came to a stop at a light, waiting with the edgy crowd of pedestrians for it to change.

Glancing around at the cars surrounding her, she noted the small, glowing squares of light in half-seen hands behind every tinted window. London had been up and running for six hours. Tokyo, twice that long. Every second counted in the twenty-four-hour business of making megamoney.

Just in case, Cara took her phone out and checked a news feed. She didn't want to get caught in the elevator looking clueless in case the global markets had burped somewhere and caused a sudden sell-off. A quick scroll showed nothing of interest. Then she glanced at her messages. Greg hadn't called, which meant she didn't owe him much of an explanation, if any.

The crowd surged around her, almost knocking the phone out of her hands. The light had changed. There was no hesitation on Wall Street. She quickly stepped forward, joining in the current of business suits, and shoved her phone back into her coat pocket.

A few minutes later she ducked out of the flow of businessmen and -women and stopped at a quilted-steel pushcart.

"Morning, sunshine. The usual?" the man behind the glass panel asked. In the three years she'd been coming to his pushcart, the older man with the cracked glasses had never asked her name, but he knew she liked a small coffee with two sugars and a dash of cream. And that she sometimes indulged in a donut.

"Thank you," she responded. Back home she would have known this man's name, if he was married, how many kids he had, and their grades. But here, in the heart of money, that kind of intimacy was avoided.

He snapped on a lid, sliding the cup through the window with a wink and a cheerful good-bye, taking her dollar before the next customer stepped up.

Holding the hot cup with care, she went through the bronze doors of Dubois & Mellan. The offices were located in an old-fashioned temple of finance with soaring columns on either side of the entrance and two half-hidden statues, female nudes with downcast eyes, supposedly representing Virtue and Prudence.

Like either would get you anywhere on the Street.

There were a few of her coworkers in the spacious lobby. Some always beat her in, no matter how early she got up. Even in the lobby of D&M, it was the same deal as the crowds of pedestrians moving through the vehicles on the narrow streets of the Financial District. Eyes glued to phones. Ears plugged with buds. She nodded and smiled to the few who caught her eye, but they didn't get off their phones to say hi as her heels clicked over the terrazzo floor.

The hustle and bustle made it easy to be invisible and indulge in a little people watching before she had to be imprisoned behind a desk and stare at columns of numbers. She had decided long ago that Excel software was user-friendly as Microsoft products went, but it sure as hell wasn't her friend.

And speaking of friends . . . or rather, *not* friends . . .

She took a sip of coffee and headed to the security setup at the far end of the lobby, wondering what she should say to Greg when she saw him. She knew she should be more pissed he'd left her stranded. It would be perfectly within her rights to verbally lash out at him. And yet, she'd rather just be done with him altogether, she realized as she stepped behind Rafe Sampson, one of her coworkers, in the security line. Rafe swept his gaze over her and raised his brow, and she had to wonder if Greg had said anything to Rafe about her at the party last night.

Greg had ultimately done her a favor by leaving her to the mercy of a host she hadn't been introduced to, not knowing that she'd eventually catch a ride with Branden's limo driver. Now she had the perfect excuse to not see him again outside the office.

But the memory of Branden's dark gaze came back to her with unsettling intensity. She could still imagine the brush of his hand against her cheek, even though it hadn't happened. She had to have dreamed that. Not the kiss, though. Or the heavy petting.

The memory aroused her. But something deeper lay just below her arousal: a purely emotional desire for his touch. A sharp pang of longing coursed through her for several seconds before she could shake it off. Or rather, she tried her best to shake it off as she entered the security setup and swiped her magnetic ID through a computerized turnstile, waiting for the buzz to sound.

What was it about Branden Duke that had her so fully in a tizzy? Why was her body reacting in such an intense and new way? Was it that he was sex on a stick and the men she'd dated before had been bland? It couldn't be the fact that he was filthy rich—money was something she needed, but she wasn't starving for it. And she'd never compromise her values simply to hook up with a rich dude. As different as she and Iris were when it came to types of men, they had one thing in common: neither felt compelled to go after a man because of his money.

Maybe it was simply that he didn't seem cookie-cutter: all the men she'd dated in the last few years had seemed to have been popped out of the same mold.

Branden Duke hadn't come from a mold. He'd have broken the mold. Made a new one. And broken that one behind him.

That had to be it—she was simply attracted to his differences. His uniqueness. That hint of bad boy that made her finally, *finally*, coax a man onto a dance floor with her so she could tease him with the brush of her body and the promise of more to come.

It took another swipe of her card before she was validated. After the machine beeped, she stepped through, continuing toward the much more modern part of the lobby that led to the new structure built above the old one. Dubois & Mellan commanded the uppermost floors. Clients were supposed to be impressed by the spectacular view. A few, the megarich, didn't even seem to notice the skyscrapers or the bridges or the expanse of harbor, as if they owned it all and couldn't be bothered. There was such a thing as too much money.

The view still impressed her. There were days when she didn't quite believe she worked in a place like this. Cara, along with five other D&M employees, ID badges around their necks, entered the elevator. Inside, she leaned back against the mahogany paneling, steadying herself for the whoosh upward and worked to ignore the loud laughs of Rafe Sampson and his perpetual side-kick, Larry Gills. Both men irritated her—too loud, too obnoxious, and sharing too many details about the party the night before.

A few minutes later, the doors opened and she straightened, following the men, and walking out onto thick carpet that softened her footsteps and all other sounds. Well-heeled clients and visitors experienced a respectful hush as they entered the brokerage and private invest-ment firm of Dubois & Mellan, a workplace hush that, like others, had long since supplanted the hectic scream-ing and rushing around on trading floors.

Which was still how a lot of people imagined stock exchanges. The reality couldn't be more different.

Behind the scenes, the office tended to be noisier than the halls that led to it, even though most trades were executed in split seconds through high-speed computers on the other side of the Hudson River in New Jersey, sometimes in anonymous buildings she could see from her office.

Walking through a maze of right-angled turns, headed to her office, she heard the soft call of her name. She stopped at the office a few doors down from hers and leaned against the doorframe, smiling at Gail.

"Sorry I bailed so early," Gail said, her voice strained. "How was the remainder of the party? Did you meet the host?"

At the mention of Branden, Cara found herself sud-denly inhaling, then worked to calm her idiotic body's even more idiotic response. She liked Gail, and had shared a few personal details with her over lattes and the occasional shopping foray, but letting the woman know even a hint of what had gone down between her and Branden the night before would not work. Instead, Cara nodded at Gail—slightly older but a replica of who Cara would be someday: conservatively put together, a neat and tidy hairstyle that lacked any verve, and muted makeup. A body that had edged its way to No Return and was one croissant away from tipping over the edge.

"I'm afraid I ducked upstairs and avoided most of the activity—had a headache," she said. At Gail's understanding smile, she added, "I did meet the host, though. He's intense. But in a good way."

The buzz of Gail's phone grabbed the older woman's attention, and she waved a hand at Cara, indicating they'd pick up the conversation later.

Cara heaved a deep breath of relief and headed on. Her office was another huge perk, considering that she had just turned twenty-three when she'd joined the company. It even had a window with a thin slice of the spectacular view. Thick translucent glass panels set into the interior walls afforded an illusion of privacy from the general commotion. Never having to deal with the distractions of a cubicle where anyone could look over her shoulder meant she got a lot more work done—and meant she could hide out and stay late. Her office felt more like home in some ways than her apartment.

She was grateful for a lot of reasons to have a door she could close, and that had been true from the get-go. Cara kept a safe distance from most people in the firm, unwilling to risk the emotional connection. She had Iris for that. Yes, she'd occasionally gone out shopping or to lunch with Gail and Tammie, but they'd kept conversations superficial. The few times she'd gone out with Greg amounted to the only occasions she'd broken her rule against office dating. She knew why she'd finally accepted his dinner invitation—she'd been overworked and lonely, and he was nothing she couldn't handle.

Not like the mysterious Mr. Branden Duke.

At the door of an office on the other side of the department, a group of people stood in a huddle. Many more than usual for this hour of the morning. Something was going on, but Cara was in no mood to engage in office gossip, or to find out whatever sports event was big news. She was grateful to reach the door of her office without being seen.

But why was her door closed? The office cleaners usually left it open. She turned the handle and stood frozen on the threshold, a sense of cold easing over her. Greg.

"Hiya."

She closed the door behind her with a sharp click, frowning at Greg and not answering his cheery greeting.

There was a wad of filthy chewing gum stuck on the sole of one of his wingtips. Maybe he didn't know that. But he still looked way too comfortable, reclining with his feet up, uninvited and unwelcome.

"Why are you in my chair?" she demanded. "And why are your feet on my desk?"

"Gee whiz, Goldilocks." He swung his legs off her desk and got up. "At least I'm not sleeping in your bed. Mind if I ask where you ended up last night?"

She set the take-out coffee cup on a low bookcase and hung up her coat, even more annoyed. "Mind if I ask why you left me without a ride?"

He frowned. "Look, you're the one who ditched me—"

She sighed and interrupted him. "You're right. Because we both know we were bored out of our minds with one another. Thanks but no thanks, Greg. Let's do what we should have done three dates ago and get back to being colleagues. Now, if you don't mind, I have work to do. I know you must, too."

Greg shook his head. Cara realized that he was looking over her shoulder. She followed his gaze.

The translucent panel revealed the shadow of a tall

man who had just stopped in the corridor when someone else's hand tapped him on the shoulder.

"Who's that?" Cara murmured.

A female voice that she vaguely recognized—Ashley? Emma? She didn't remember the staffer's name—bubbled a welcoming hello.

"I think that's our new boss," Greg said quietly.

Cara just stared at him. "What are you talking about?"

"He's been making the rounds. Him and his entourage. Although I think most of his posse is still on the lower floors. But he's on our floor now. I'm surprised you didn't bump into him already."

"Why didn't I know the company had been sold?"

Greg shrugged. "He just bought D&M. Boom, like that. Paid cash. Not a lot of fanfare. Makes sense—he seems like the quiet type. But you don't have to make noise when you can swing a hundred-million-dollar deal overnight."

That wasn't monster money on Wall Street, but it was a lot more than Cara would have thought the company was worth. But she hadn't heard a word about plans for the company to be sold. Unless Greg was pulling her leg.

"D&M was bought? Are you kidding me?"

"Nope."

Cara felt her stomach tighten. Drinking her coffee would only make that worse. She didn't even bother to remove the lid, and instead tossed the cup into the refuse bin. Wow. They'd been sold. It happened.

So much for her reasonably good mood. She had never taken this job for granted considering it was a four-year program with the option to hire her on permanently, but she'd had the security of those four years. Something told her that was no longer the case. Acquire and fire, that was how it went, especially in this business. Handshakes all around, and then the heads began to roll. She told herself not to panic. The cardboard boxes came before the pink slips. No trace of either. She hadn't heard muffled sobs from the cubicles or the screech of packing-tape dispensers sealing up everyone's hopes and dreams and knickknacks.

But she could probably kiss her three weeks of accumulated vacation good-bye.

Something struck her. "Wait—you said he seemed like the silent type. Did you meet him already?"

Greg shrugged. "I didn't know he was our new boss at the time, but I met him last night. Guess you didn't."

No. She'd been upstairs napping and then making out with the homeowner. Branden Duke. Maybe she should have stayed downstairs and been a good girl, as usual. She would have met the new boss then. Would have learned about the sale of D&M. No wonder her boss, Max, had tried to talk to her as she'd come down the stairs from Branden's office—he'd wanted to tell her the news.

A slight commotion in the hallway drew her attention back to the silhouetted man.

"Looks like he'll be stopping by your office soon. I'll leave you to meet him on your own," Greg said.

"Right." After he left, Cara's gaze fixed on the translucent panel. She needed a minute or two to compose herself. The shadow stayed away. She heard nothing other than the subdued voices outside.

She smoothed her suit, which wasn't wrinkled, and shoved miscellaneous paperwork into the nearest drawer. There wasn't much clutter. No framed mottos, no kitty cat art, no personal photos. A single orchid sat on the corner of her desk, its elegant magenta blooms adding a little color.

Cara made a beeline for her chair and got busy pulling up files on the screen, opening her top desk drawer for her hair clip and her reading glasses, which she shoved onto her face. She didn't really need the glasses to work on the computer, but they made her look capable and serious. A good hard pull on the hair clip and she looked almost stern.

She was typing gibberish, sitting superstraight and focused on the monitor, wishing she'd asked Greg the man's name. It would have been nice to be prepared—to know the new owner's name, at the very least.

"Hello."

Oh no. Cara swallowed hard. The masculine greeting startled her beyond belief—not because the man had snuck up on her, but because the sensual timbre of his voice and the way it reverberated in a quiet room were unforgettable.

She swiveled in her chair to face Branden Duke.

"Um. Hello," she said, forcing herself to not stammer. There were several words for the way she felt. Bewildered. Flabbergasted. Blindsided.

He wore an expression of professional neutrality, but his gaze still seemed to pierce her. With her seated and him standing, he appeared taller than he had last night. But still sensual. Still different. Still unique and sexy and breathtaking.

Oh, God. She'd initiated a sexual encounter with her new boss. And clothed or not, it had been hot. Was it possible he'd planned it? Had he known . . . he could have known . . . hell and damn. Had he set her up? And as his employee, did she dare ask?

What was she supposed to think?

Cara took in the details. He was even better looking in the clear, cold light of day. His thick hair, the get-your-hands-in-it kind she preferred and exactly what she'd done while kissing him with unabashed lust, wasn't quite as dark as she remembered—more brown than black. There was the strong jaw she'd caressed and there were the faint creases around his mouth that suggested a smile even when he wasn't smiling.

Which he wasn't. And unlike last night, there was no hint of amusement or warmth in his gaze.

Wait—he didn't think she'd come on to him as a way of working her way up the corporate ladder, did he? Nerves sent her stomach churning.

She cleared her throat, wishing he would start the small talk. Where was the HR representative when you needed her? Peggy Noyes normally showed the new hires around and she was great at small talk, Cara thought desperately. Oh hell. She couldn't just sit here. She half rose.

"Please, don't get up," he said cordially. "Mind if I sit down?"

"No, of course not." She whipped off her reading glasses and set them down, indicating a teak chair, one of two. Hoping her hands weren't shaking. "I just—wasn't expecting this. I mean, you. I wasn't expecting you."

He moved the chair closer to her desk and settled his long frame into it, resting his hands on the polished wood armrests. The subdued elegance of his suit emphasized his remarkable physicality and self-assurance. By dark of night or in broad daylight, Branden Duke radiated ultramale confidence. And he was unbelievably sexy.

Her mouth went dry. Thank God he wasn't mentioning, not even hinting at, what they had done last night. Yet. He had amazing self-control. Unless he was trying to drive her crazy all over again. God, what was she supposed to say here?

"I was sort of saving meeting you for last," he said.

What did that mean? "Oh. Great. I mean, thank you for the ride last night. I got home safely." She winced and whispered, "Obviously."

He nodded. "It was my pleasure."

That wasn't a reference to their full-on make-out session, right? It couldn't be. He simply was being polite. right? The silence stretched, long and uncomfortable. She'd have to do it. Talk about what happened the night before. Clear the air. But was she ready? Nope, not yet. "So . . ." she said. "You're my new boss . . ." *And I kissed you. And you thought I'd been lying in wait for you. Literally.*

"That's right. I've had my eye on Dubois & Mellan for some time. Your company seemed like a very attractive acquisition."

"It's not my company. I consider myself lucky to work here." Her words had come out strong, confident, but inside she was a mess, thinking things like, *I'd like to keep working here. Please don't fire me. And please don't be the type of asshole who'd make my job dependent on sleeping with you. Because as much as I'd love to do exactly that and dreamed of it last night and even fantasized about you in the shower this morning, that's so not going to happen. Even if it means losing my job . . .*

For a moment, his expression softened. "You're far too modest, Cara. But I find that particular trait, along with everything else about you, quite . . . enchanting."

She sucked in a breath. How gallant. And a little old-fashioned.

Before either one of them could say anything more, a booming voice came from the hallway outside her office. "Branden, where are ya?"

The voice belonged to Max Dubois, the company founder—and her boss. The boss she shouldn't have blown off last night when he'd tried to inform her of the company's purchase.

For a long moment, Branden didn't take his eyes off

her, nor did he reply. Then he called out softly, "I'm in with Cara, Max."

The other man appeared in the doorway. "Ah, right. Hi, Cara." Max beamed at her, then turned to Branden. "I woulda introduced you two if you'd waited for me. Quit walking so fast."

It was more a question of leg length, Cara thought. Max was barely five feet tall and paunchy, with curly gray hair and shrewd blue eyes.

"She's one of our rising stars," Max informed Branden. "The one I was telling you about last night."

What was up with Max? He'd never singled her out for such extravagant praise. Maybe he wanted Branden Duke to know what a fabulous deal he'd made.

"Oh, I'm just a worker bee," she said lightly. Her self-deprecating comment seemed lost on Branden, who inclined his head in a nod, casting an appraising look at Cara that made her nervous—and snapped her back to something like reality.

Max turned to Cara. "I tried to tell you at the party, but you took off before I could introduce you to the host—and D&M's new owner. The announcement was supposed to be made at the party but Branden here got tied up."

Cara felt herself blushing and Branden's mouth quirked.

"Anyway," Max continued, "deal done. We signed on the dotted line at dawn. Now I can retire. Get in some golf, chase divorcées. Boca Raton, here I come."

Definitely too much information, although Cara figured that Max's jokes and chatter were for Branden's benefit, not hers. Generally speaking, Max barely noticed her, even though Dubois & Mellan was considered a small firm by Wall Street standards. But Cara smiled politely.

"Congratulations on the purchase," Cara said to Branden, but didn't quite meet his eyes.

"Hope you like your new boss," Max went on. "Of course, you might not see that much of him after today. He's bringing in a few folks to work the day-to-day aspect of the business. The Duke likes to operate behind the scenes. Bet you never heard of him."

The Duke? What an odd nickname. But it fit the man. Whom until last night, she'd never even heard of. "I hadn't," she said reluctantly.

Branden didn't seem to mind her truthfulness. The creases framing his sensual mouth deepened for a second but he still didn't quite smile. "Then I've been successful."

"Never mind his bullshit," Max said bluntly. "Believe me, he's a mover and shaker on the Street. A real big, swinging—never mind. How many companies do you own now, Duke?"

"Five."

Max guffawed. "Used to be fifty. And all of them were worth twice what he paid for them upon divestiture. Just don't unload this one too soon, Duke. I'm kinda sentimental about it."

Cara had nothing to add.

Branden had bought the company and could sell it if he wanted to, but she hadn't been fired yet. If she was . . .

If she was, she'd be out on the street. So would her mother and her brother. She wasn't worried about herself. She could crash with Iris. If needed, her mother could stay with a distant relative. But her brother . . .

Her big brother, Glenn, had always been her biggest supporter. He'd always stuck up for her. Taken her for rides on his bike. Let her hang out with his friends. But then, after he turned seventeen, over the course of a year, he'd changed . . . become withdrawn. Apathetic.

Flat, like he had no emotion. Until he started seeing things. Believing things. Hearing things.

Things that were not there.

Schizophrenia, they'd learned. And even after the difficulty of coming up with a diagnosis, came the even more significant difficulty of finding treatment. Glenn's mood disorder was severe, and didn't respond well to conventional treatment. Meds helped, but only to a degree. He'd found a balance in his life by living in an assisted-living facility, but it was private and cost a small fortune.

A fortune she paid for.

Panic rose in her throat but she valiantly pushed it down, reminding herself that if she lost her job, it wouldn't be too long before she found another. Dubois's recommendation would get her in anywhere on the Street. It could even be time to move on if it turned out that she didn't like her handsome new boss.

The old boss slapped him on the back. "And I like this girl, too. Watch your step with her. The watercooler talk says she doesn't fool around."

Cara hadn't ever seen Max Dubois hanging around the giant blue plastic bottle. But there was a touch of protectiveness in his remark that was nice—and unexpected. She was suddenly sorry the funny little man was departing the firm he'd founded before she got a chance to know him better.

"Noted," Branden replied, his gaze steady on hers.

Max moved around restlessly, as if he wanted to get going. "Listen, Cara, you gotta stay in touch. I mean that."

"Thanks, Max. I can't believe you're going so soon, though."

"Ah, this guy knows what he's doing." Max gave Branden a conspiratorial grin. "I never woulda sold him the company if I thought he didn't."

The younger man returned a cool smile. "I promise not to run it into the ground. Neither will the staff I'm bringing in."

Cara wondered where Branden knew Max from. They seemed to be more than business acquaintances. There could be a family connection, however remote. Besides the considerable age gap, the two men were nothing alike and had to have radically different management styles. Didn't matter, she reminded herself. She had to keep her nose to the grindstone, do her job to the best of her abilities the way she always did, and she'd stay safe.

Oh, and avoid any more steamy encounters with Branden Duke.

"Okay. I'm holding you to that." Max offered a breezy wave of farewell as he exited, calling loudly to another colleague down the hall.

Branden lifted his ankle to his knee, looking even more comfortable. The combination of easygoing authority, sensual good looks, and fine body plus seriously long legs could be her undoing. She almost couldn't believe she'd been close enough to feel everything he had without actually putting her hands on certain parts. Why hadn't she taken advantage of the moment?

Arousal shot through her. Once again, Cara met Branden Duke's dark gaze straight on. He seemed to be sizing her up in exactly the same way but with much more confidence, as if he knew exactly what he wanted from her.

But what was that? What did he want? She'd be happy to share her financial expertise, such as it was. Although his success was reason enough to guess that he probably didn't require her knowledge.

Her best bet would be to lie low and figure out what the hell Branden Duke was all about.

"So," he began. "You'll meet some of the personnel I'm bringing in later. The IT team, a new office manager, and a few other specialists. Right now I'm trying to get a scope on who does what, and how well they do it. Tell me what is it you do for the company that's unique."

Cara hadn't expected him to put her on the spot. If only she hadn't been touted as a rising star when she really was just a worker bee, a team-playing, dedicated, loyal, hardworking, humble bumblebee silently buzzing with annoyance as she looked at him. "Ah—what exactly do you mean?"

"Your analytical methods, innovative approaches you've come up with, that sort of thing. Let's start with the most difficult problem you ever faced here."

That would be you, Mr. Duke.

"Well. Let me think."

"Is it really that difficult a question to answer?" he asked.

Or rather, to Cara's mind, taunted.

She lifted her chin.

Game on.

Chapter Four

Cara stood, and on weak knees made her way to the file cabinet at the corner of her office. She hauled out hard-copy files and printed reports, slapping them down on the desk and turning them around so Branden could read the highlights as she pointed them out. In the last six months alone, Cara had analyzed several multimillion-dollar deals in development that no one but she thought would ever turn a profit. In the end, management had followed her advice and D&M had raked in a fortune. A tiny fraction of which would hopefully plump up her year-end bonus.

But as she explained the spreadsheets, throwing out facts and figures and pointing out profit margins, it took all her effort not to focus on how closely he paid attention . . . how his gaze flicked from the papers on her desk to her face, then back again, eyes smoldering in intensity . . . how the corner of his mouth crooked up when she got excited over explaining a formula she'd come up with . . . how he would occasionally stroke his gaze over her, as if sizing her up.

How his scent wafted over her and how she could feel

his body heat as she stood leaning over her desk, their heads almost touching.

And yet she managed to keep her composure. Succeeded in explaining her work. Kept the conversation focused on her work and didn't so much as hint about the night before. And didn't let herself get overpowered by this dark and enigmatic and amazingly sexy man.

"So that's what I do and how I solve problems," she finished up with barely controlled heat. "Is that what you were looking for?"

"Yes." He rotated the papers back around. He'd barely looked at them. However, she had a disconcerting feeling that he'd taken in the most relevant information at a glance. That, and Max had probably already informed him of her work and the results.

"I have copies," she added. "You can take all that with you." *And leave my office,* she thought. *Before either of us brings up last night.* She couldn't do it—couldn't discuss what had transpired between them, which had her insides twisted up in a multitude of knots.

The frosty hint went right by him. It was possible that he was somewhat impressed by her diligence and acumen. Or maybe he was thinking of how her ass felt under his hands the night before. She couldn't tell.

"That's not necessary," he said affably. "But thanks." He remained sitting in his chair. The side chair that Max Dubois had let her pick out for her office along with the desk was now, of course, Branden's chair. He didn't even have to leave if that's what he wanted. God, she wished he would so she could think. So strange this guy pressed her on button so easily.

Tapping his long fingers on the sleek wooden frame, Branden looked idly around her office, skimming his gaze around the space, over her low bookcase, and across her near-barren desk. He frowned.

Did he have a problem with it being neat and clean?

She thought a little uneasily that maybe it was *too* neat and clean. She didn't want to give the impression that she had run out of work to do after helping to put the company's balance sheet squarely into the black for the next quarter and beyond. But she also had no desire to show off her personal life through photos and tchotchkes.

Oh yeah, that's right . . . she had no personal life.

At least the orchid was pretty.

His gaze stopped at her monitor and then moved to her face.

"One of the first things we plan to do is revamp the computer system," he said at last.

"Great," she said with no noticeable enthusiasm. Then she brightened. A really ingenious IT team might manage to screw things up for weeks and they'd all get an in-house vacation. "But don't tell Max. I think he chose the software himself."

Branden only shrugged. "It's out of date. We need to get up to speed." He gestured to the papers, then spoke again in a normal tone even as he stood and rounded the desk toward her. "Great job on the reports."

He stopped next to her and leaned close, not quite whispering in her ear, but close enough. "About last night . . ."

Her knees shook. There it was . . . mention of the night before. She should have taken the initiative and brought it up first. Admitted to her mistake. But he'd beat her to the punch, and now she needed to respond. And *not* by jumping him. "It didn't happen," she muttered.

"Yes it did," he said in a low intimate voice. "I'd like for it to happen again. If I'm not mistaken, so would you. Last night I thought you were dating one of my new employees . . . But now that I know you actually work here . . . it can't."

He fell silent, his gaze seemingly filled with regret.

"Of course not," she whispered. She quickly glanced at her open office door. What the hell was he doing, starting this discussion here? Now? While he was standing so close? It wasn't smart. It was madness. And ironically, even as he was telling her nothing could happen between them, the fact he so clearly wanted something to happen was turning her on like crazy.

She sucked in a gasp, inadvertently catching his attention. The corner of his mouth went up in a wry grin. Oh yeah, he knew she wanted him. Damn.

"Last night I was tired," she said, keeping her voice low. "My behavior was out of line and won't be repeated."

"I don't doubt it," he said, not exactly looking pleased.

Cara sat back down and put on her reading glasses, then stacked the papers in no particular order, taking the glasses off again and putting them on top of the papers. The hair clip chose that moment to slide off. She twisted around to grab it before it hit the floor, then jammed it back into the desk drawer and pushed her hair in back of her shoulders. Cara knew her cheeks were flushed. Short of pulling out the rice powder she used to eliminate shine and getting the emotionally revealing color down to geisha white, there was nothing she could do about it.

"Now that's how I remember you," he said in that low, now-even-more-intimate tone. "It's no wonder I—"

A trilling voice announced the imminent arrival of its plump owner. "Oh, Mr. Duke?"

Branden didn't flinch. Didn't move back even a centimeter. "We'll have to continue this conversation later, Cara."

"Why? It's over," she murmured.

"It should be. Yet I'm finding it more difficult to accept than I should."

"Mr. Duke, are you in there?" The voice of Peggy

Noyes came again. She still hadn't appeared when Branden stepped back and returned to the other side of her desk.

"Yes, I am."

"And you, Cara?" Peggy Noyes tended to talk in questions. Her face appeared, but not the rest of her. "Oh goody. You've met Mr. Duke, but there's someone else you have to meet. And here she is."

Everything but the trumpet flourish, Cara thought. It wasn't even nine yet and she'd had enough surprises for a week. Heart still beating wildly, she refiled the papers and reports with trembling hands.

The sound of soft footfalls made her look up. The woman who entered Cara's office was stunning—young, with a controlled waterfall of glossy black hair and delicately outlined doe eyes. Gold earrings and a couture corporate outfit completed the look.

"Deena Raj, this is Cara Michal," Branden said.

"How do you do." The smoothly cultured voice had a slight but noticeable edge. Had the woman overheard them talking? Maybe. Her gaze barely took Cara in before she walked over to Branden and rested a possessive hand on his shoulder.

Cara expected Branden to flush or shift guiltily. He didn't. His gaze stayed firmly on Cara. She, on the other hand, did her best to dismiss him and focus instead on the woman beside him.

Who wore a diamond solitaire nestled next to a wedding band on her slender left hand.

Branden did not strike Cara as the married type. Not even the divorced type. Chances were Deena Raj didn't own him despite the way she'd so clearly staked her claim.

She had to be whom Branden had meant when he kept saying *we*. Cara was instantly on guard, knowing that she would have to be that way all the time if this was her other new boss. The woman was nothing short of perfect.

"Hello." Cara rose, smiling automatically. Deena's flawless lips curved as Branden stood up to retrieve the other side chair, setting it next to his. They both sat.

Two against one. Inherently not fair. Cara was grateful for a desk. She needed a defense against all that good breeding and fine tailoring. Not to mention the calm stares they were giving her.

"Sorry to spring so much on you at once, Cara," Branden said. He could switch from warm to cool in an instant. Yet another reason to be wary of him. She acknowledged the insincere apology with a fractional nod as he continued.

"Deena's heading up the IT team and she'll be in charge of revamping the system, as well as the new installation. Not that she does it personally," Branden added.

Of course not. That's what minions were for. The lovely and faintly imperious Deena seemed born to give orders to hapless minions.

"She designed the system and wrote the code," he added.

"Really. That's great."

Branden and Deena made no comment. Cara sensed a slight chill in the air. She struggled for something appropriate to say and settled for, "Will the name of the firm change?"

"Not right away. There's a lot to do first," Branden said. "Deena and I have worked together on takeovers and purchases before, of course. It's almost a routine with us. But every company is different."

Cara had a sneaking suspicion that these two did way more than work together. The subtle personal warmth in the discreet looks they exchanged, the way they stood just an inch or so closer than mere colleagues ever would, the occasional light touch of Deena's lovely hand on Branden's suit sleeve—yeah. Big fat clues, each and every one.

It was entirely possible that Deena spent a fair amount of time in Branden's great big bed with her long legs wrapped around his bare back, revamping his system for him.

Cara chided herself for her uncharitable thoughts, which she would keep to herself. But she would still think them.

"Well, just let me know what you need me to do," she said.

"Everyone will receive a detailed memo," Deena said. "Plus individual attention. You'll meet Mike Gaunt, our office manager, soon. I understand that your analyses show some insight." That was not exactly praise. Good ol' Max had just thrown her to these two wolves so he could go bang golf balls into outer space.

"Mr. Duke and I were just going over six months' worth of reports," Cara told her. "I can prepare a complete file for you if you'd like hard copies of anything—"

"That won't be necessary," Deena purred. The interruption was soft but definite. "Your entire hard drive has been downloaded into our new server for our own analysis."

The beautiful lips curved again. Cara couldn't call that expression a smile. But the informal meeting seemed to be at an end, for which she was grateful.

"I see. Let me know if there's anything else I can do to help."

"We will. Branden, shall we move on?"

We again. The possessive little word grated on Cara's ears. She avoided Branden's gaze as the two of them got up to leave.

"Yes, I think so," he said. "Cara, thanks so much. I

appreciate you taking the time to chat and I do apologize for interrupting you this morning."

"It's your prerogative," she said. "Stop by whenever you like."

"I will." His voice was a dark promise, one that made her shiver.

They went out, Branden holding the door open for Deena, even though it was obvious that it would have stayed open on its own.

Cara waited until they were well away before she got up and closed the door with a quiet click. Down the hall, by the watercooler, she could hear the excited chatter of her colleagues. The purchase of D&M was big news—and understandably, people wanted to discuss the changes. But not her. Not now. Too much closeness at the workplace made her nervous.

Making out with the sexy boss made her ultra nervous.

She went back to her desk and tried to get to work for real. It took longer than she would have liked for her to calm her racing heart.

She began breaking down data input for a new report, a process she found calming. Numbers did what was expected of them, unlike people. She concentrated on the latest predictions for obscure commodities that might be worth much more by the end of the day.

It couldn't come soon enough for her.

At lunch, both Gail and Tammie stopped by. "Sushi?" Gail asked brightly. "We can talk about the sale and make bets on who gets fired first."

"*And* bet on who will get into the new boss's bed first," Tammie added, a naughty smile on her face. Younger than Cara by two years, the girl had asked Cara to go clubbing with her several times, but Cara had always passed. Tammie was too aggressive, too intent on finding a man to marry. She probably had every intention of being the girl who got into Branden Duke's bed first.

Cara had to wonder if she'd done things differently the night before, maybe she would have ended up winning Tammie's bet. She also had to wonder why the thought of Tammie pursuing Branden and being the one to warm his bed instead made her want to scratch her friend's eyes out. It wasn't a feeling she liked. Not in the slightest.

"Sorry, I need to get going on this new project," she said. "And let's hope none of us get fired—I need this job."

The women excused themselves, and later a delivery boy brought up a sandwich and soda she'd ordered earlier, which Cara ate at her desk.

By the time the office emptied of employees, she was barely aware of the diminishing light outside her window.

Cara wrapped up her self-imposed assignment and left. Bundled in her scarf and parka, she went down a crooked old street that led to the waterfront park at the very end of Manhattan. This time of day, without the pressing need to get in early to work, she liked taking the alternate route home.

Even from where she was, she could see waves smashing against unseen pilings in the near distance, throwing sparkling spray up in the air under park lamps that had just come on. The wind was coming straight off the ocean, chopping the gray-green water of New York's harbor into a million whitecaps.

Elsewhere in the city, you could forget Manhattan was an island. Not down here.

She walked along the waterfront, headed home, loving the smell of the ocean and the cries of the wheeling seagulls, slashes of white against the darkening sky. At the corner, a block away from the office, she noticed a low-slung car crawling through traffic—an Italian model, she figured. Probably worth a cool hundred grand. The color, a deep navy with thin rally stripes highlighting its aerodynamic lines, was relatively subdued, but the overall effect was intentionally flashy. Both she and the car came to a stop at one of the streetlights. When the window rolled down and the man in the driver's seat gave her a nod, she caught her breath in the back of her throat.

Branden Duke.

"Don't worry—I'm not stalking you or anything," he said, giving her that crooked grin she was growing familiar with. "Seems we left work at the same time. Need a lift?" The question was casual, like he was in an ordinary car in some little town.

She swallowed, working to gain her composure. "No thanks. I live two blocks away."

"You sure?"

She nodded. "I can walk faster than you can drive around here."

"We could meet down here sometime, you know. Outside the office."

"Why would we do that?" she asked, trying to look innocent.

He smiled at her, a real smile. "Because we have that conversation to finish. Among other things."

She should have corrected him. Told him they'd never be finishing that conversation. But then she remembered the gleam in Tammie's eyes when she'd suggested making a bet about which woman was going to bed Branden first. And for some reason, instead of blowing Branden off, she said, "Um . . . maybe. I guess."

His smile broadened, but his attention was jerked away by a change in the streetlight. "Until then, take care, Cara."

With that, he drove off, negotiating slowly over potholes and around construction barriers. The car was built for speed but down here, five miles an hour was about as fast as anyone could go.

For the second time that day, despite reassuring her nothing personal could happen between them, he'd made it patently clear that he *was* interested in her.

He stopped at a red light up ahead. His flashing right blinker hypnotized her for a few seconds.

Cara seriously hoped he wasn't watching her in his rearview mirror, staring after him like an idiot. She snapped out of it and looked into a shop window instead, but the reflection showed the car well enough.

She knew the street he was about to turn into had no outlet. It ended at a new residential tower, the kind that had separate elevators for luxury cars so residents could actually park right on their very own floor.

Unless he was visiting or picking up a friend to go somewhere else, it was possible that he lived in the tower. If he did, in addition to the mansion on Long Island Sound, he most likely ruled his world from one of the penthouses, complete with wraparound terrace and sweeping views. Too close for comfort.

The light where he was waiting went to green. Despite herself, Cara looked away from the window at the fabulous car, which gleamed midnight blue as it made the turn. It was gone in a moment.

Branden Duke had all the toys. Fantasy wheels. Awesome real estate. Limitless money to roll around in. He was a man anyone would envy, incredibly good-looking and exceptionally intelligent.

And now, out of nowhere, he was her boss, give or take a few layers of managers, and he owned the company.

He seemed to be trying to do the right thing—telling her that things would remain professional between them. But even so, he wasn't denying that he *wanted* her in his bed.

He was off-limits.

But tempting. So very tempting.

She'd never felt the way she had when they'd kissed. When he'd run his hands over her body, his touch had been both sensually tender and dominating. She wanted to experience it again and could only imagine how intense the feelings would grow if they were naked. If he was inside her . . .

A seismic shift seemed to grab her, right there on the sidewalk.

He wanted her. Bosses slept with their employees all the time.

There could have been a lit-up billboard above her head, flashing the words *why not?*

What if you never find another man that makes you feel that way again?

That would probably be a good thing, she told herself. She wanted safety and stability—Branden Duke made her feel the opposite.

Oh, God. The feelings he evoked in her had to be quashed down or the fiery restlessness that had bothered her even before that damned kiss would only grow worse.

Of course, the only way to fight fire was with fire. Branden Duke was her employer and thus had access to her personnel file. It was only fair if she found out a little bit more about him.

It was time to find out about the mysterious Branden Duke.

"You seem to be in a hurry, Miss Michal."

"Hi, Joe." Cara gave the stout, brass-buttoned door-man of her apartment complex a frazzled smile and pushed her flyaway hair out of her face. "Yes I am. I, um, have a financial report to finish."

He tsked. "You shouldn't work so hard. Don't forget to have fun once in a while."

Fun. That's what Iris had said she needed, too. Fun. And sex. "Oh, that's part of the plan." She frowned when she looked across the street. "Where'd all that construction equipment come from?"

The building across the street was surrounded by wooden barriers and warning signs. A scaffold had been erected during the hours she'd been away, rising no higher than the second floor.

"They set it up this morning."

"Oh no. I hope the building isn't going to be knocked down. The noise is going to be awful."

"Don't let it get in the way," Joe said.

"Of what?"

"The fun," he said, laughing, before he went out to whistle up a taxi for a waiting resident, not someone Cara knew. She headed for the elevators.

A half hour later, she had everything she needed at the ready. Laptop. Pen and paper. Novelty pajamas from Victoria's Secret for comfort. A pint of Ben & Jerry's Americone Dream to keep her from getting depressed if she found too many photos of Branden with different women.

She jabbed a spoon in the caramel swirl and left it there.

Let the Googling begin.

The swirl had turned to soup by the time she was interrupted by a text from Iris: _Party hard last night? Or hardly party? TXT BK._

She responded: _Party OK but boring as hell and Greg a D*CK. Never dating a coworker again. Did NOT get laid, so don't ask ;-)_

She studiously avoided the mention of groping her

new boss, then returned to her research. She put the pages she'd pulled at random into categories with taps on the touch pad.

Education. She had never heard of the small Connecticut college he'd attended. He had put in two years and left, then started as a trainee at a boiler room operation, according to various bios she'd come across.

Career. Branden Duke was a self-made man, like so many Wall Street moguls. Insider comments on business blogs tagged him as a street fighter and someone who'd been ruthless throughout his meteoric career.

It all fit.

He got respect, according to what little she could dig up on him. Cara would agree that he'd earned it. She knew how difficult it was to climb high on Wall Street. The media liked to make it seem easy for a chosen few. It never was, not for anyone.

His rise to power had taken place before she even got her start. It could happen that fast, if you were tough and smart and unprincipled. From the boiler room, he'd gone on to routine deals for a tiny trading firm to founding his own investment company only a few years later. He had done it all, starting with municipal-bond funds that penny-pinching grandmas trusted and moving on to billion-dollar deals with shady Russian oligarchs.

A ping from her phone told her Iris had texted back. *I want DEETS!*

She thumbed a quick response, *None to tell—except for how wide I yawned*—and drank some of the melted ice cream, coughing from the syrupy sweetness as she set it aside.

Her own highly respectable credentials—she'd gone to the University of Pennsylvania on scholarship for her econ degree and graduated from their Wharton School of Business, then had been hired by D&M right after that—were somewhat suspect in the inner circles of real money men, but only because few women had done what she'd accomplished. Sexism was alive and well, especially among the old guard.

There were still only a handful of women making big money. For a while, Cara had wanted to rise quickly to the executive ranks herself. Then the reality had set in. Great pay didn't make up for gratingly awful colleagues, mostly male. There were a few exceptions. Cheerful, loudmouthed Max Dubois was one. She knew now that he would have helped her if she'd decided on a different career after her first four grueling years.

And now Max was gone.

Another ping. *Did you at least dress sexy?*

Iris wasn't going to leave this alone, was she?

Cara responded. *Sexier than what I wear to the office. Not so sexy I'd be mistaken for a prostitute. Not that THAT would ever happen.* Then she set the laptop aside, still sitting propped up by pillows, and flexed her calves and wiggled her toes. Nothing like pajama-clad research to make you forget you had legs. She'd been at it for over an hour.

The one category she'd spent the most time on had been pretty much a wash: early life. She hadn't found much info on who Branden Duke had been before he'd earned himself the nickname the Duke.

She switched to images for a visual search, scrolling on and on, hunting for a much younger, geekier Branden Duke somewhere in the past. He couldn't always have been so perfect, physically speaking. There had to have been a time when his nose was bigger than his chin and his dark hair hung halfway over his eyes. Adolescence wasn't fair to anyone but a chosen few.

So many Brandens and none of them Dukes. Wait. *Wait.* She scrolled back. Bingo. That had to be him at around seventeen or eighteen.

She rested her hands on the laptop briefly before visiting the page, staying in the image's black box to study Branden's senior yearbook picture, wondering who'd posted it on the obscure site. Him? He hadn't been as good-looking then. Too thin and kinda gawky. But with a killer smile. The big caption over the photo said it all: his classmates had voted him Most Likely to Exceed the Speed Limits of Life.

She squinted at the fine print under the picture, puzzled for a second. "Holy shit," she whispered. Cara sat bolt upright, dragging the laptop onto a pillow to bring it closer. She enlarged the image just to make sure she'd read it right. She had. It said Davies, not Duke.

The name Davies sent a shiver up her spine, and a memory of her father, shoulders hunched and defeat drawn all over his face, slid unwanted into her mind. She brushed the past away, focusing on the future. On Branden.

Why had Branden changed his name? This was the first page that mentioned a different name for Branden Duke, unlike the others she'd read, which were much more recent.

Granted, Davies was a common name. But she'd love to know why Branden had changed it. She'd changed her name from Finch to Michal, her mother's maiden name, before leaving for college. As much as she'd loved her father and hated what had so unfairly happened to him, she'd also needed to separate herself from the scandal that had followed his death as much as possible, if only for professional reasons. Perhaps, like her, Branden was running from something scandalous.

She leaned back suddenly, a thought hitting her hard. Branden couldn't have anything to do with *that* Davies, now, could he? The man who'd turned her world upside down?

She stared and stared at the photo, trying to find a physical resemblance between Branden and the other

Davies, who should rot in hell. No, Branden looked nothing like the man she remembered. Still, it was possible there was a connection, especially with both Branden and Davies being linked to the financial world.

Cara had to find out, even if it meant pulling an all-nighter. She was going to look half dead when she got to work tomorrow, but it would be Friday and she could rest up over the weekend.

But wait. Even though Iris hadn't responded to Cara's last text, she should still be up. Cara grabbed her smartphone and skipped texting, going straight to punching the phone icon.

When Iris answered, she immediately asked, "You awake? I need you to help me do research."

"No." Iris yawned convincingly. "Numbers don't love me and I don't love them."

"Not for work. This is personal."

"Really?"

"Yes. Two laptops are better than one."

Iris laughed. "You seem to be assuming that mine is charged. And is working. Hang on while I go plug it in." A pause. "Yes. You're in luck. And now?"

"I want you to look up someone named Branden Duke." Cara waited. Several minutes went by.

"Wow," Iris said, sounding a lot more awake. "Do you actually know this guy?"

Memories of his scent washed over her. Cara bit her lip, breathing through her nose until her heart rate slowed its sudden increase. "Met him last night at the party, and in the office this morning. He's my brilliant new boss."

"Ha-ha. Sure he is. Looks to me like he doesn't do anything but let models and actresses hang all over him."

"That's, like, twenty photos in five or six years, all told."

"You counted," Iris said dryly. "Does that red carpet follow him everywhere he goes? Do the girls?"

Something stabbed at her gut, and it took a moment for her to realize the emotion was jealousy. Odd. She'd never been jealous about a guy before. "I don't know. The photos are fairly tame, though. But the articles were all about how ruthless he can be, and, um, dangerous—in the financial world, that is. Kinda made me wonder."

"Maybe he pays Reputation.com to make the really bad stuff disappear." Another pause. "Oh. Here's a hard-news site," Iris said. "Huh. He did just buy your company. For a zillion smackeroos. And let me guess. That boring party you didn't want to go to was for him."

"Yes. But I didn't know who he was at first. He never introduced himself to me until this morning."

"Aha. Something happened and you didn't even know his name," Iris said gleefully. "I can hear the shame in your voice."

Oh, God. She hoped not. "Like hell you can."

"Was it wonderful? Are you going to tell me all about it?"

Iris had a highly developed instinct for bad behavior, a talent that had fueled her brief stint as a gossip blogger. But she'd been downgraded to a mere supplier of bits when her page rankings fell and had quit in a huff.

"That's not why I called you," Cara said. She took another swig of melted ice cream. "I found out that he changed his last name. It used to be Davies."

"So?"

"Iris—" She sucked in a quick breath. "Okay, back when we met in high school, I swore you to secrecy about my sordid past."

Cara was being flip, but the memories of those terrible days had never gone away.

"Yes you did. Loyal friend that I am, with my amazing

Swiss-cheese brain and all, I forgot practically everything you said."

"Nice try. I know you didn't. But here's the thing.
Davies was the last name of the creep who ruined my
dad."

Iris didn't respond right away. And in fact, she didn't
know everything. But she knew a lot.

Years ago, when Cara and her mother had to move
out of their little Long Island house to Brooklyn, she'd
told no one except her new friend Iris about the financial scandal that had disgraced her dad, Hank Finch,
and plunged the family into poverty when he couldn't
find work, unfairly accused of fraud he hadn't committed.

He'd been hoodwinked by the comptroller of the
township's pension fund, who'd looted the money and
given it to another enterprising son of a bitch on Wall
Street who in turn had made a fortune and then some
before the Securities and Exchange Commission had
caught up with him. Her father had died of a premature
heart attack before that and her mother had barely survived a nervous breakdown. Even worse, her brother,
Glenn, had suffered his first psychotic break. The doc-
tors who'd finally diagnosed him indicated that the
shock could have triggered an earlier onset of his illness.

Carl Davies was the high-flying trader who'd parlayed
the township's stolen money into a fortune. She blamed
him for what had happened to her dad, her mother, and
even her brother. Hank Finch had taken the fall, not the
comptroller, although the comptroller had later died in
a car accident. And Davies had plea-bargained his case
down to a few years in a golf-course prison. But Cara
held on to her dream of someday clearing her father's
name once and for all.

"Oh," Iris said in a flat voice. "Yeah, I remember him.
You don't think—"

"They're in the same business." Cara copied the URL for the yearbook photo into an email to Iris. "I'm sending you the link to a photo of Branden when his last name was still Davies."

"Branden, huh?"

Iris's dry statement wasn't lost on Cara. Yes, she would have referred to him as Mr. Duke if she hadn't been so attracted to the man. Fortunately, Iris didn't push it.

Several seconds. "Got it. Scrawny but sexy. Interesting how people turn out."

"Iris, I don't know if I'm seeing things by this point or what. Can you look up Carl Davies and compare the two?"

"Uh, yeah. Give me a few minutes. And do something constructive while you're waiting." Cara could hear the keyboard clacking from Iris's side of the call.

"I've been drinking—"

"Not a good idea," Iris warned her.

Cara stifled a laugh. "Melted ice cream."

"Gross," Iris said. "Okay, I got a few shots of Carl Davies from back in the day. Do you want to see them?"

"No." Cara didn't want to explain to Iris that flashbacks to that time still made her feel physically sick.

"No problem. I can compare Branden Davies and Jerk-off Davies for you. Yuck. He looks like those reptiles that live in dark caves. Everything but the forked tongue. Definitely from the 1980s with those big-frame glasses." Iris slowed down and stopped typing. "Okay," she said after a while. "Got the younger photos of Davies and Branden side by side. I would definitely say there's no resemblance whatsoever. But hold the phone. I'll see what I can find on Davies's personal life."

Cara settled back into the pillows, keeping the phone propped on her shoulder. She pushed her laptop away from her for the time being.

"Nothing much," Iris reported. "Carl Davies never had kids. Hey, here's an interview quote from the great man himself. Also from the eighties."

Cara steeled herself. That was before he'd gone to jail.

" 'I love dames and I love dough. I just hate kids. No offense. But we all know the little bastards get in the way of everything fun.' Not much else on him." Iris cleared her throat.

"Carl Davies is a convicted felon who's wanted for fraud in five countries. I don't think you're going to find him on LinkedIn."

"You never know," Iris said cheerfully.

Almost without knowing it, Cara yawned, not stifling it quickly enough.

"I second that yawn. Let's quit for now," Iris said. "My feeling is that the same-name thing is a coincidence."

"But why did Branden Duke change his?"

"How should I know? Maybe his mom remarried and he took on his stepdad's name. Ask him."

"Of course. Why didn't I think of that? *Hey, Branden, are you related to the reptile who destroyed my dad? Just thought I'd inquire.*"

"It's a start. Call me tomorrow. Maybe I'll dig up something else."

"Thanks, Iris. You're a true friend."

"I'm a tired friend. But good night. Try to sleep."

Cara couldn't.

The coincidence of the names still bugged her.

A lot.

She had more hunting to do. There were too many ifs at the moment.

Friday dawned with the rumble of garbage trucks far below. Cara jolted straight up in bed and shot a quick glance at her ringing alarm clock. She'd slept through that insistent ring for an *hour*? She threw the covers off but got tangled up in a sheet and almost face-planted on the decorative rug next to her bed. Not the way to start the day.

After a quick shower, she grabbed the nearest outfit out of her closet—a black suit—and didn't realize until she exited her building that the tights she'd pulled up her legs were dark blue, not black. No time to turn around and go back to her apartment—Branden Duke and her job waited.

A now-familiar warmth spun through her core as the thought of Branden entered her mind. She needed to stop this visceral reaction her body had at each thought of him. A man like Branden Duke would confuse her life, and that she didn't need. She needed her job and security—for her brother, Glenn, if not for herself. As she ran down the street, keeping on her toes so as to not break a heel, she ran a comb through her hair and hoped it would appear dry by the time she entered the lobby of D&M.

Nope, she wasn't so lucky. At the security setup, Rafe Sampson was leaving, probably headed to a morning meeting with a client, and grinned unkindly at her. "Save your wild escapades for Friday and Saturday," he told her, and when she frowned, he laughed.

What a pain in the ass. Like she hadn't ever seen him slip in late before, bags under his eyes and a large coffee in his hand.

As she skulked down the hall, Gail poked her head out of her own office and caught a glimpse of Cara.

"Wow," was all she said, but the word spoke volumes.

Cara groaned. "That bad?"

Gail hesitated, tipping her head to the side and sweeping her gaze up and down Cara's body. "You don't look like you're making the Walk of Shame, but it's pretty close. Need black stockings? I have extra."

"No time." Cara glanced over her shoulder, down the hall. "I'm trying to get to my office before—"

"Don't worry, the new boss isn't in yet."

Cara heaved a sigh of relief. "In that case, I'll take the black stockings. I'll owe you."

Five minutes later, appropriately color coordinated and with her hair partially blow-dried under the hand dryer in the women's restroom, Cara entered her office and sat down heavily in the chair behind her desk. What a way to start the day. Not.

Although a few new faces showed up—some man named Alex, who held a position Cara couldn't quite figure out and whom she had yet to meet, a young Hispanic woman named Graciella, who'd ducked into an empty office and sat with her nose to a computer monitor, and an older man named Frank, who settled down into an empty seat in the bullpen, phone glued to his ear—Branden never showed. Neither did his snooty sidekick, Deena. Cara didn't miss either of them. Plus, when work wasn't distracting her, Branden was ever-present in her rollicking sexual fantasies. She'd known the guy less than forty-eight hours, yet she knew so much about him. A lot she'd discovered during last night's research, but she also knew how he smelled. How he tasted. How strong and gentle his touch could be. How his voice sounded.

And she knew she wanted to learn so much more.

How he looked naked. How he felt naked. How he felt while inside her.

Since none of that could ever happen, she told herself it was all right to fantasize. Besides, the reality of Branden Duke couldn't possibly live up to the sex god status he'd attained in her dreams.

Could it?

God, why had a man suddenly invaded her every thought? Why had she acted all schoolgirlish during the day, checking the hallway and watercooler to see if he'd arrived? Keeping an ear out for the sound of his voice? Checking her emails on a near-constant basis to see if he'd sent one to her?

The man wouldn't leave her mind . . . and she wasn't sure how she felt about that.

Chapter Five

The weekend had not gotten off to a great start, not after another sleepless night fighting off erotic dreams about Branden Duke and more nightmares of her past and the fact that Cara had found herself back at D&M early Saturday morning, ostensibly to work. Finally, after she realized she'd been looking for the silhouette of a tall, intense man, she called Iris and asked her to go to her favorite spa in Chelsea with her. No sense in simply sitting in her office, pretending to work while really lying in wait for a man she barely knew.

She'd had enough of acting like a love-struck teenager.

The private room at the spa held two massage tables. Cara was draped in heated towels, her head swathed in a terry-cloth turban. She looked over at Iris, who was more swaddled than draped, and twirling a lock of hair between her fingers.

Their schedules rarely synchronized, but they really were solid friends as survivors of the same tough high school. Not academically tough. *Tough* tough. They'd shared battered textbooks and sat at graffiti-scarred desks and graduated with sighs of relief.

Iris had instantly befriended Cara, a transfer student

from Long Island, when she and her mother had moved to Brooklyn after her father's death. It had been a long time before Cara told Iris, who not only took everything in stride but told Cara to get over it and just live her damn life.

Good advice. She'd tried to follow it.

She and Iris had taken very different paths: Cara into the financial world and Iris into the arty nexus of Brooklyn. But they stayed in touch and had grown even closer as the years went by.

Iris stretched forward and pulled at the curtain separating the private room from the main interior area of the spa. "What's taking so long?"

"Half-price days are always busy."

Iris dropped the curtain and wriggled back onto the table. "So Greg was a douche, huh?" She caught Cara's wry look. "Definitely not someone you'd ever hit the sheets with?"

"Nope."

"You don't have to be in a long-term relationship to get some action, you know. You could just have fun. Go to the clubs. Meet someone online. All for a little adult fun."

Thinking of adult fun made Cara instantly think of Branden Duke. Butterflies shot through her stomach.

"No way," she said, hoping her voice didn't give away her sudden tension. "Too many weirdos in clubs and online. Way too many."

"Aw, they can't all be weird."

Cara shot her a look. "Oh yes they can, and you of all people should know that."

Iris shrugged her bare shoulders, loosening the towel that swaddled her torso. She pulled at it. "Treat yourself to an obsession. Unless you already have one that starts with B and ends with O-S-S."

Cara said nothing.

Not surprisingly, Iris interpreted her silence as speaking volumes.

"Thought so," Iris said cheerfully. "Time for true confessions."

Cara hesitated, wondering how Iris always managed to hone in on Cara's deepest, darkest secrets. She'd obviously picked up on the fact that Cara's interest in Branden Duke went beyond any possible connection to Carl Davies, the man who'd ruined her life. She'd stayed silent on the subject of how much she wanted Branden, but the desire flaring up inside her seemed like it wouldn't go away anytime soon. Maybe she should divulge a little. Share with Iris her big quandary . . . to go after Branden, or run full-out in the opposite direction.

"Okay, you're on to something," Cara began. "You already know he's handsome and rich. He's incredibly sexy. And . . . I kissed him. At the party. And he's made it clear he wants me. I guess I should have told you that from the get-go."

"You're forgiven. Because I'm also guessing you want him. I've never known you to Google a guy. That's something new for you."

Cara spoke very softly. "I more than want him. My body is hungering for him. For some reason, I want to tease him until his head explodes. Make him beg for what he thinks he's never going to get. And then . . . then I want to give it to him. In the most mind-blowing way possible."

"Huh. That sounds interesting. Could you be more specific?"

"About the fantasy part, no."

"Too bad." Iris sighed. "But why does it have to stay fantasy? Why not treat yourself to some of that?"

"Because I work for him. So do about a thousand other people in different companies. And believe it or not, I think the guy actually has morals. He's trying to keep things professional. *Trying* being the operative word."

"Meaning?"

"Meaning his resolve seems . . . shaky."

"In other words, he gets close to you and forgets things like office rumors and harassment suits. All he can think of is doing you."

"It seems that way," Cara confessed. "But he's right. We can't act on our attraction. Besides, although I do think you're right about his original last name and Carl Davies's last name being a coincidence, there were some gaps in Branden's timeline."

"You're paranoid."

"Maybe."

"You're also pissed that he woke up your inner sex goddess. Or is it more than that? Is Mr. Davies/Duke someone you could see yourself falling for?"

Cara glowered at her. "Based on a brief introduction, him listening as I explained my job, and some admittedly hot chemistry? No. I'm not interested in anything permanent with anybody. I said I want to toy with him, not win his heart."

"No?" Iris murmured.

Their eyes met, but before Cara could reply, the peach velvet curtain parted. Two women in white stood outside. "Ladies? Are you ready?"

"Yes, thanks," Cara said quickly. She looked at her friend again, who smiled. A silent truce was declared.

Blissed out, Cara and Iris just lay there side by side, relaxed to the point of being boneless as warm oil was poured over their backs and the skilled masseuses got to work.

They sighed and moaned occasionally, but that was about it for intelligent conversation for the better part of an hour.

Cara might as well have been alone. Given Iris's teasing, she tried to think of anything and anyone but Branden Duke, but her mind kept going there, drifting to an irresistible fantasy that began with doing to Branden what was being done to her.

It was so easy to imagine him on a table, mostly naked, and herself . . . well, not wearing a white coat, but mostly naked, too. Cara told herself to save the fantasy for later, when she really was alone. Or better yet, don't go there at all.

She surrendered to the healing hands and completely lost track of time, until steamed towels were laid on and brisk rubdowns began. Then their backs were patted dry.

Small, smooth rocks that had been heating somewhere in the room were gently set in place on energy meridians by what seemed to be invisible hands. Voices drifted into the room, and Cara and Iris were left alone.

The voices in the waiting room intensified, but Cara was too blissed out to care until she heard Iris's table creak as she shifted.

"What's going on out there?" Cara asked, staying flat with her eyes closed.

"Dunno. But some client sounds pretty stressed."

There was a clatter as Iris lifted herself up on her elbows, inching forward on her belly. Cara opened her eyes to look at her.

"You're losing your pebbles."

"Story of my life." Iris reached out and moved the curtain of the booth, peeking out. "Wow. She looks famous."

"Who?"

"The woman who just came in."

"Actress?"

Iris pondered that for a moment. "Maybe. Or a television personality."

Cara lifted her head and craned her neck until it hurt.

When she saw who was making a commotion, sudden bile ate at the back of her throat. "Neither. Oh shit."

The woman at reception pushed her glossy black hair back over the shoulder of an impeccably fitted jacket. Her slender hand reached inside a costly Bottega Veneta tote and extracted a wallet to pay for her spa treatment.

Cara ducked back down. "That's Deena Raj."

"You know her?"

"Just met her this week. She's a financial software expert. Branden Duke put her in charge of IT."

"Oh." Iris looked again through a gap that was a little too wide.

"She can see you!"

"I don't think so." But Iris dropped the edge of the curtain, still listening to what was going on beyond the peach velvet.

Cara's head was buzzing. The spa was a short taxi ride from the Wall Street area and popular with the handful of women at Dubois & Mellan. She and Gail had come several times before, as had Tammie. Someone might have recommended it to Deena Raj.

"I hope she didn't see me." Cara swore. "I don't want her telling Duke I skipped out of the office."

"It's Saturday."

"I know that. I came in late on Friday and should put in weekend hours. It's an unwritten law."

Iris gave her a sympathetic look. "At least they pay you well for not having a life." She gathered a towel around herself and slid off the massage table, padding over to grab a pair of courtesy slippers.

"And don't worry," Iris added. "I overheard the reception lady signing up Deena Raj for a stress-dissolving soak in an isolation tank. You can tiptoe out if you have to get back to the office."

"No way," Cara muttered. "I did my time for today. I

just don't like thinking that she and Branden know exactly when I log in and log out."

Iris exchanged the towel for a cushy bathrobe and tied the knot tightly. "Are they, like, a couple?"

The question made Cara cringe inwardly. But she'd made such a point of being nonchalant about Branden Duke she had no one to blame but herself.

"Maybe," she replied. "Except that she has a wedding ring snuggled up to a big fat engagement diamond on the same finger. How'd you miss that?"

"I don't know." Iris made a move toward the curtain as if to check.

Cara scowled. "Stop. You don't have to peek. And by the way, I don't think he gave the rings to her."

Iris's eyes gleamed again. "You're talking scandal."

"These days, there's no such thing. And if my new boss and his second-in-command are maintaining an inappropriate personal relationship, it's none of my business."

"I'm not so sure. Because maybe that shaky resolve you were talking about is really just a front and he's just waiting to get 'inappropriate' with you. Crazy, madly, deeply inappropriate."

Cara threw the rolled face towel at her and missed. "Get out of here."

Giggling, Iris swooped through the opening in the peach curtains and left Cara by herself.

Chapter Six

Monday morning, Cara got in a little late. Again. Like five minutes, not a big deal, but for Cara that was uncharacteristic and unprofessional. Unfortunately, it was also becoming a bit of a habit, one she'd be all too happy to blame on the as-of-yet-not-to-be-seen-again Branden Duke. Unfortunately, she couldn't. Sure, dreaming of him had made for restless sleep all weekend, but he hadn't been the one to call her that morning just as she was heading out for work.

Greg came up to her as soon as she got off the elevator and stepped onto their floor. "Buzz, buzz. All the worker bees are in their cells. Why aren't you?"

"Blow off, Greg, it's five minutes—besides, I had an important call. Not that it's any of your business."

The tart comment didn't seem to ruffle him. "Didn't you get the text about coming in bright and early?"

"No." She paused for a few seconds to survey the main office area. It was a lot quieter than usual, and there were no traders hanging around talking shop or commenting on an online poker game in progress on someone else's monitor. Greg seemed to be right about that. "Who sent it? What's going on?"

A thickset man with a close, bristling haircut came out of a trader's office, smoothing a tie that was simultaneously too wide and too short. Like him.

Greg looked pointedly in the man's direction, then back at Cara.

"Who's he?" she asked in a whisper.

"Mike Gaunt. The new office manager. He's going around and he's taking notes."

At least he wasn't looking at her. She sized him up in a glance. Ice blue eyes. No visible lips. Expressionless face. Over forty, not yet fifty. Never had any fun because he couldn't possibly have a sense of humor.

Great. What a day for her to be the Five-Minutes-Late Girl. It was no use telling Mr. Gaunt, if he should ask, that she'd been set to arrive an hour early. She'd been headed out of her apartment right as Windorne Care Home, her brother's care facility, had called, informing her that he was having an episode. As the sound of her voice, even on the phone, was often able to calm him down . . .

Well, she'd spent almost an hour talking with Glenn on the phone. Most of that time he'd been talking rapidly about a governmental conspiracy and how his phone was tapped. She'd managed to talk him into taking his fast-acting antipsychotic, and the meds had finally kicked in—the last ten minutes of the call had been blessedly calm.

Unfortunately, the phone call and the fact she was late to work hadn't exactly left *her* in a calm state.

Gaunt stopped at a cluster of financial-news terminals and took a seat next to Chip, the intern, who'd been parked there to keep him out of trouble. Chip smiled nervously at the unsmiling man beside him and pointed to one of the monitors.

"Poor kid," Greg said. "But at least you can get into your office without Gaunt seeing you."

"Thanks for the heads-up." She strode away and turned the corner. Most likely Branden Duke had cleared out and left the actual running of his new acquisition to this guy.

She went into her office and was confronted by the soles of a different pair of masculine shoes. Bigger than Greg's. Much bigger. Which was because they belonged to Branden Duke.

Her heart skipped a beat and her mouth went dry. She let her gaze drift upward, mentally caressing him even as she tried not to. The object of her scorching fantasies grinned at her as if he could read her mind. Cara stiffened her spine.

"Is there an invisible sign on my door that says Put Your Feet Up on My Desk?" she asked, not lightheartedly.

"No. Sorry about that." He swung his legs down and stood up. "My back was acting up. Too much tennis this weekend. I play a hard game. Guess it caught up with me."

Cara didn't know how to respond to that revelation of human weakness, so she simply said nothing.

"Anyway, let's start over. Good morning. Nice to see you."

She was rattled by his presence, seriously so. Most likely because it *was* nice to see him. "Sorry I'm late."

"No problem at all. It happens," he said affably.

"That's nice of you, and as the owner you probably can say that and mean it, but the new office manager . . . I don't want to give him the wrong impression," she said. She didn't want to sit in her chair, not when he was standing.

"Don't worry. Mike's not as tough as he looks. Did you meet him?"

"Not yet." She stepped around Branden, catching a faint whiff of fresh citrusy aftershave. His skin was as sleek as his smile. "Is there something I can help you with?"

"Yes. I wanted to take you up on your offer to copy those files."

Cara tried to remember the parts of her sex fantasies in which *she* controlled *him*, but somehow imagining him naked didn't help calm her nerves. "Sure. Just give me an hour."

"Not a problem. I'm keeping Max's assistant. She knows the company inside and out. You can bring the files to her."

Jean had been at Dubois & Mellan longer than anyone else. Cara liked and trusted her, although they didn't hang out at lunchtime or anything. But it was nice to know that there was a friend in front of what was now Branden Duke's office. She was going to miss Max more than she thought.

"I'll do that," Cara stated.

"I'd appreciate it."

She could feel his gaze on her when she glanced down at the morning mail, not quite turning her back to him. Some animal instinct made her not want to do that. His eyes met hers with the same dark intensity, not that she was likely to get used to it, when she looked up. He grinned again and went out through the open door without saying good-bye.

Cara blew out a breath and sat down at last, scrolling through emails and answering the important ones before burying herself in paperwork.

She lost track of time until the phone rang. Cara peered at the little screen. Outside number, one she knew.

"Hello."

"Hi, sweetie. It's your mom."

Cara could tell by the sound of her mother's voice that there was a problem. "What's the matter?"

"Oh nothing. Well, my property taxes. I just found the form under a lot of junk. It's more than I can pay right now," her mother said shakily. "You know how it is, end of the month."

Which was when her mother was most likely to call. Janine Michal Finch had never gotten her life together after her husband's death. It's as if her broken heart had broken her spirit, too. She tried to make ends meet, but her health was bad and she'd inevitably miss too many days at work and would get fired. Money management was a foreign concept for her—Cara's dad had been the breadwinner and the one in charge of the budget and finances before he'd died. Her mother had accepted her financial dependency then, and now, too.

How different her mom was from the vibrant, cheerful woman Cara remembered from her youth. A woman who'd put on disco music and dance in the kitchen with her kids. A woman who once convinced her husband to drive them in an old Chevy across the country just to see the sunrise over the Grand Canyon. A woman who could make cannolis like nobody's business.

Cara couldn't remember the last time her mother had made cannolis. But it had to be before her father had died.

Cara bit her lip and blinked back the sudden rush of moisture in her eyes. Life was what it was now. Her mom was who she was. They were alive. They had each other. That had to be enough. "I'll take care of it, Mom."

"I'm sorry I let it slide. I can pay you back."

"No. Just get caught up. I can cover it."

There was no use in offering financial advice or suggesting a course in money management. Cara had supplemented her mom's fixed income as soon as she'd started making real money.

"How soon can you make the payment?" Her mother's pleading voice sounded faded and weary.

"I have to overnight a check. You know the tax office doesn't take credit cards."

"Okay then." There was a brief pause. "Have you—have you talked to Glenn lately?"

"I just talked to him this morning."

"And how's my sweet boy?"

Cara closed her eyes. Glenn *was* her mother's sweet boy. He was Cara's sweet brother. But that sweetness was often trapped now in the body and mind of a man plagued by intermittent psychotic events, something their mother had a very hard time dealing with. Which is why Cara handled all matters concerning Glenn's care, including the cost of the expensive live-in facility with the staff that was the best they'd found. Windorne Care Home was good to Glenn, and she willingly paid through the nose for excellent treatment of her brother.

"He's good, Mom," she said, deciding not to tell her about the incident earlier that morning. "I'm sorry I'm so busy. I'll call you tonight, okay? We haven't had time to talk."

"That would be nice," her mother said. "You could come out to Brooklyn, you know."

A sense of longing swept over her—longing to see her mother, not necessarily a longing to go to Brooklyn. Visiting the small row house she'd spent her teenage years in was depressing—the furniture was the same, only even more shabby, and the interior and exterior walls needed painting. Her former bedroom was now used to store a jumble of miscellaneous items in crushed cardboard boxes. Somewhere underneath them was her old mattress and box spring and maybe even the desk she'd built out of a door and plastic crates. The neighborhood was sunk between two elevated freeways on the distant frontier of Brooklyn and would probably never be hip. Or gentrified, either, which meant the mortgage wasn't a monster.

Cara tried to help her mother with the house, but it was all she could do to keep up with the missed mortgage payments and property tax payments.

What would her father say if he saw how her mother lived now? Cara could still remember how he'd come home from work each evening and go straight to her mom, kissing her full on the mouth and hugging her, telling her he loved her.

No wonder her mother's heart had broken.

"I miss you, Mom," she said, her throat suddenly constricting. "And I love you. More than you know."

After hearing her mother's soft and loving response back, she ended the call and returned her focus to work. The pale slanting light coming in through her office window was her first hint that the long workday was drawing to a close. Mike Gaunt hadn't made it as far as her office. Cara put him out of her mind and squelched her resentment at the idea of having to justify her job a second time.

The phone rang again. Another Brooklyn number, familiar, but not her mother. She picked up, cradling the receiver on her shoulder while her fingers moved over the keyboard.

"Hey, Iris."

"Hello there. Did you look at Gawker today?"

Cara had no interest in gossip sites. Iris was a devotee. "Nope. Don't read it."

"You should."

"I wouldn't want it to appear in my browser history," Cara said.

"Use your smartphone," Iris singsonged.

She stopped typing. "Why?"

"I'll stay on the line," Iris said.

Cara took out her smartphone and pulled it up. She glanced at the headlines as she scrolled through them until one stopped her cold:

"Hot Mystery Babe Flees
Decadent Slumber Party at Money Mogul's Mansion!"

There was a photo of her outside the grand front doors of Branden Duke's Long Island mansion. She looked disheveled. Wantonly so. The blurb was even worse.

This pouty blonde with honey-dipped hair was spotted in the wee hours trying to escape the pleasure palace of money mogul Branden Duke. Don't ask us who she is. Just tell us if you know. Bonus question: why has Duke muscled in on the exclusive brokerage firm of Dubois & Mellan? Their richest clients want to know if their investments are safe. So do we. Lock up your stocks and bonds and your daughters, New York. The man is too sexy and too smart.

"Holy hell," she breathed. "What is this? Who took that picture?"

"You tell me," Iris said. "Although you look great."

"I look like a hot mess," Cara countered. "All I was doing was waiting for the . . . car."

"Car?"

"Branden Duke's limo. He . . . uhm . . . arranged for his driver to take me home after Greg bailed on me."

"Really? Funny how you keep leaving so many little details out. Exactly what did you do to earn that favor?" Iris asked. "Your lips look . . . hmm. Crushed by passion? And who tousled up your hair like that? You said it was just a kiss. This doesn't look like a girl who got a mere kiss."

Cara stared at the photo.

"This was days ago. How come it got posted now?"

"Gossip sites don't put everything out there instantly. They have to bank a few juicy scoops for when there's nothing going on. What, do you wish they hadn't waited?"

"No, but—"

"I'm telling you that's how it works," Iris said, just full of information that made Cara's head hurt worse. "Otherwise it would all be firemen rescuing teeny kittens, although that works if the kitten is cute and the fireman is sexy and as we all know, a lot of them are. I have the calendar to prove it."

"Shut up," Cara said, a hint of laughter in her tone but still stressed. "Just shut the f—" She swiveled in her chair at a firm rap on the open door. Mike Gaunt stood in her doorway. "Frog up. I'll call you back."

"You frogging well better," she heard Iris say cheerfully.

She whisked her smartphone off the desk and into a drawer before pasting on a wide, fake smile. "Oh, hello. You must be Mr. Gaunt. Please come in."

The stout man entered and chose a chair, sitting down without leaning back. Cara took a deep breath. "Sorry. That was a friend of mine. I usually never take personal calls in the office."

A semblance of a smile appeared on his face, as if Mike Gaunt wasn't too accustomed to making them. "I know. The phone records confirm it."

Not just a manager, she thought with dismay. A micro micromanager with control-freak eyes. Which were boring into her.

"You have a completely clean record, in fact. There are employees here who abuse their perks and privileges. But not you," he said. "You could be our poster person for work-appropriate conduct." That awful pseudo-smile appeared again.

Cara guessed that Mike Gaunt didn't read Gawker. And she thanked her lucky stars for that.

Chapter Seven

"Hmm. It's a little out of focus." Branden had pulled up the photo on his monitor at Cara's request. "Let's get rid of the glare so I can get a better look."

He pushed a button. New blinds with ultrathin metallic slats began to lower automatically, concealing the tall windows inch by inch. The heavy silk drapes in old gold—the color of serious money, Max Dubois used to say cheerfully—had been removed from Max's former office. The old making way for the new.

She nodded.

How could Branden be so nonchalant? Cara could guess. The view had to be different when you lived on top of a mountain of money. A hint dropped on a gossip blog that he was up to no good, financially and otherwise, proved exactly nothing, and he had lawyers and PR flacks at his beck and call to take care of bad press. To say nothing of outside tech specialists who could make oh-so-embarrassing online mentions sink down in the rankings. She didn't.

He touched a few keys. "There. Saved. For future reference."

Should she ask why? On the other hand, she'd saved it, too. Just not on her work computer.

Given the pictures she'd seen of him with different women during her Google searches, and the noticeable absence of any mention of a wife or family, Branden was definitely not a married man, and she was certifiably single, which didn't matter, since a photo like that would definitely give the wrong impression to future employers, if she had to move on. And she very well might. Somebody at Dubois & Mellan could have already seen the innuendo-laced post with her picture. It only took one person to get the whispering started.

Cara Michal. Sleeping her way to the top.

Really not something she wanted on her invisible résumé, meaning the one that headhunters put together when doing an Internet search on new clients. She'd get instantly booted down the ladder, from the top rung to the bottom, and starting over as a cubicle rat at some two-bit brokerage was not part of her career plan or her life plan. She didn't just have her mouth to feed, but her mother's. And most important, Glenn's.

She'd studied the photo after Mike Gaunt had left her office and gotten so worked up that she'd barged in here, wanting to speak to Branden before anyone else did, grateful that Max's former assistant was on break.

"I don't know who took it," Cara said. "Or why anyone would post it."

She looked around, wondering what had become of Max's furniture. The oak desk and matching chairs, relics of the company's early days, had been replaced by new pieces in sleek chrome and leather—including a couch that looked just like the one she'd napped on at Branden's mansion. Just as long, just as black. But much less inviting, with no white cashmere afghan to soften its hard lines.

"The answer is obvious," he said matter-of-factly.

"Because you look sensational. That just-got-kissed mouth and the messed-up hair are made for a tabloid cover."

His reply pulled her attention back to him. "Great. Super great. Is that where I'm going to end up?"

Cara realized instantly that she shouldn't have challenged him. Branden's grin left no doubt as to what was on his mind, besides his awareness that she'd been studying the revamped office. It was his lair now. All the way. The towering bookshelves were gone, too, along with a jumble of aging printouts and thick binders. The walls showed no scars from the removal because expensive hardwood paneling had been installed, covering everything. There was no art. Nothing personal anywhere. The new desk had no drawers and no work in progress atop its highly polished surface.

Contained. That was the word for the new look. If he had anything to hide, it was in the desktop computer, a slim widescreen framed in aluminum. Her sultry photo was tucked away in the hard drive, much to her chagrin. Maybe she shouldn't have brought it to his attention. Somehow she'd just assumed that he'd been told about it, or pinged on it.

Everything around here had changed so fast. She supposed an office could be redecorated practically overnight if it was necessary. But why had he done it? Max had made a point of hinting that Dubois & Mellan was just another acquisition for the great and powerful Branden Duke. She wondered why he'd go to the trouble.

The couch in particular stood out. Wall Street offices weren't designed for lounging around in. And she'd made the mistake of looking at it and then at him.

His dark eyes glittered as he leaned back in his chair and supported his handsome head on his crossed arms, eyeing her with lazy sensuality. "As to where you'll end up, I have no idea. But I can give you a few suggestions. Unless I'm misinterpreting the question."

"Oh please . . ." She couldn't really blame him for the double entendre, considering that she'd taken the initiative from the start. The usual boundaries between boss and subordinate didn't seem to apply somehow. Especially when she was alone with him. For one thing, she couldn't keep her mouth shut. "I didn't mean the couch. I meant a supermarket checkout rack stuffed with stupid tabloids. If that photo hits any covers, I'm going to get rung up with a quart of milk and a dozen eggs."

"I wouldn't worry if I were you."

"How can you be so sure?"

"You're not a celebrity." Branden turned the monitor toward her. In high res, in the darkened office, she really saw every detail. He was right about the effects of the kiss they'd shared. Blurry mouth and embarrassingly dreamy eyes. Cara cringed inwardly.

"If I'd known there were reporters and photographers roaming around your place, I never would have—"

"What? Tried to seduce me?" He was almost laughing.

"Now hold on," she snapped.

"I was kidding. Calm down. And don't worry. I'm not a celebrity, either."

"And yet apparently, despite the fact I'd never heard of you, you're a celebrity on the Street."

"Obviously you have better things to do than read tabloids. I find myself wondering if that's anything besides work."

"Isn't work enough?" she said, evading. From the way he stared at her, he seemed to know exactly what she'd done. "And do you think people will come to the conclusion that Gawker got all excited over nothing?"

He gave a shrug that made it clear he really didn't give

a damn what anyone thought. "I have no idea. Their sphere of influence is New York."

Cara glared at him and pulled her pencil skirt down over her knees. Not that he was looking anywhere below her neck. But damn. The eye contact was still incendiary. "Exactly. Which is where I work and live, and so do you."

"I can take care of myself," he said breezily. "But I appreciate your concern."

"Guess what. It's not all about you." She muttered the words but he heard them just fine. "People outside New York read Gawker."

"I suppose so."

"A hot item can go viral. Reputations get shredded."

He sat up straight, extending his long legs under the contemporary desk as he rested his elbows on the top of it, studying her. "I just don't think yours will. You're not doing anything in that photo except standing there looking gorgeous. Since when is that a crime?"

She felt herself blush. Fortunately, the darkened room hid it. "Sooner or later I'll be identified."

"Maybe that would be to your advantage."

Cara stared at him incredulously. It was possible he was teasing her. "Are you *again* implying that I went upstairs for any other reason than to get away from that noisy party? Or that I set up that kiss?"

"No. It just happened. And it won't happen again."

He didn't seem to really believe that. Not with that lusty gleam in his eyes.

"By the way, you said you went to the party with Greg Johnson," Branden said casually. "Do I need to worry about a brokenhearted boyfriend who's going to see that photo?"

"No. I mean, he's not my boyfriend. Then or now."

"Maybe that's the problem. You don't think he might have taken it?"

Cara shook her head, but not with certainty. "He'd left by then. You said so yourself."

"Perhaps I was wrong. Something to think about, though."

Something for her to think about, he meant. He didn't seem to care either way. But then Greg was a junior employee and scarcely worth the attention of a CEO. "Whoever took the photo had to have known it could cause problems. For you and for me."

"Why? It's not like Gawker knows I kissed you. Just that you were at a not very exclusive party with about a hundred other people. The rest is spin."

"Is it?" She waited for a reply, which he didn't offer. "I assume you didn't miss the bit about you muscling in."

"No." He seemed almost bored. "Most takeovers could be described that way. But even a hostile takeover isn't illegal. Insider trading, market manipulation, now those would be bad. I've never been accused of either."

She noticed the dodge. Which wasn't to say that he hadn't done that and worse. He just hadn't been under suspicion or gotten caught.

Cara felt Branden's gaze return to her. He hadn't spoken, but knowing he was looking at her snapped her instantly out of her momentary reverie. "Well, if you're not concerned, I guess I shouldn't be."

"I'm really not. If you want me to have a word with Mike Gaunt—"

"That's all right. I'd rather you didn't." Cara didn't want that laser-beam focus turned on her, even though she had absolutely nothing to hide. "I just wanted to talk to you before anyone else did," she added.

"I appreciate that." His tone was smooth. "But rest assured, it's not something that bothers me."

"If you want, I could respond to the post. You know, defend you." Cara made one last attempt to crack his composure. "That headline doesn't make you look good."

"It's all bullshit. They really don't have a story."

"Looks like Gawker's trying to crowdsource this one. You read the whole thing, right?" She pointed to the monitor. "Plus that part, where they ask for my name?"

"Noted. And I don't see a single response."

"That could change."

"Websites like that update content several times a day. It'll be gone by quitting time. My advice to you would be to forget about it."

"Do I have your permission to monitor the site during work hours?"

"If you feel the need to, go right ahead. I have better things to do than breathe down your neck."

"Perhaps there's someone who won't be so blasé about the post. Someone who won't want me—never mind." She had been about to mention Deena Raj. The new head of IT had probably started snooping through everyone's hard drive by now.

The look in Branden's eyes conveyed his thoughts on the subject, although he smiled pleasantly. *Don't go there, little girl.*

Cara didn't. She was more sure of the clandestine connection between those two by the minute. "I'll update you if Gawker keeps going with it."

He snorted. "It won't—not without fresh information, and they won't find any. I keep a low profile."

She'd picked up on that during her hours of research on him. This couldn't have been the first time something like this had happened. There had to be a flunky or more likely a team of them somewhere, scrubbing suggestive photos from the Net and erasing scandalous stories. Unless Branden didn't generate any. Which seemed hard to believe. Exactly how he accomplished that was something he didn't seem inclined to share.

Branden leaned back in his chair. "Even if they do, it will have absolutely no impact on your job, if that's what you're worrying about."

"No?" She gestured toward her image on the monitor. "The pit bull you hired to manage us is going to be so disappointed in little me if he sees that."

The disparaging reference to Mike Gaunt just slipped out. Cara was about to take it back when Branden chuckled. "Good description. And accurate. Mike has high standards."

"So I gathered. Did he ever work for the FBI?"

"Go ahead and ask him." The answer was noncommittal, but a ghost of a smile appeared on Branden's leanly handsome face.

"No way. If you don't care, I guess he won't give me a hard time about it. Well, good. So this won't affect our working relationship. We're just boss and employee."

"As far as Mike is concerned, yes. Between you and me, I think you know better than that."

She sucked in a breath. "You said it yourself. We need to forget that ever happened."

"I said we had to keep things professional. Maybe that means we should forget what happened, but I'm having a difficult time doing that."

"Really? Because it's been . . . what? Over three days since we've seen each other? Seems like you haven't had too much trouble putting me out of your mind."

His expression instantly turned serious. "If you truly think that's the case, then you're misinformed. I've stayed away in part because I thought I was respecting your wishes. But maybe you don't know what you really want, after all."

She swallowed hard. Cursed herself for challenging him. What had that been about anyway? She'd actually sounded like she'd felt he was neglecting her.

"I'm sorry," she said. "I don't know why—"

"Don't you, Cara? Because I certainly do."

She shook her head. "We can't—"

"We'll discuss that all later. I don't want you to feel uncomfortable at your place of business."

But he'd be fine making her uncomfortable out of the office?

She raised her chin. "I really don't see the purpose of looking for trouble twice."

"Generally, I'd agree with that," he said softly. "But I find that with you, things are different."

"But—"

Branden got up and walked around the desk, stopping just short of touching her. "I said we'll talk about it later, Cara. But if you continue to push things, I'll be glad to set you straight about my level of interest in you. Is that what you want?"

She was sucking in breaths like a locomotive now.

She immediately turned and walked out. She took the long way back to her office through the maze of right angles and fantasized about doing him on Long Leather Couch number two, really aggressively. Scratching. Biting. Kissing him hard. Riding him harder, straddling him, on top. Making him pay for the intensity with which she wanted him.

She closed the door to her office once she was inside. Anyone who needed to talk to her could take a hint and save it for later. She paced for several minutes, trying to quash the instinct to return to Branden's office and beg him to touch her. She didn't care where as long as she finally felt his hands on her again.

Lord, what was wrong with her?

When her heartbeat stopped thundering and she'd finally calmed herself down, she plopped down in her swivel chair and glanced at the phone. No red light, no voicemails. She tapped a key and looked at the monitor.

No new emails, either. She turned and gazed at the slice of river view without seeing it.

Her mind was whirling and she suddenly remembered Branden asking her whether she thought Greg could have taken the picture.

Greg was just a guy she'd dated a couple of times and who'd brought her to the company party. And ditched her, she reminded herself, only minutes before she'd decided to ditch him. Had he hung around and done more drinking, then given in to a boozy impulse to snap her waiting outside looking slutty? He could have a pal at Gawker or know someone who did. Still, she got the impression Greg's idea of pranking ran more to frat-house hijinks, not malicious hits on someone's reputation.

She stared at the phone, half expecting it to ring off the hook and force her to field what-were-you-thinking questions from colleagues and curious friends.

Hours passed. Nothing happened.

Despite her mind periodically replaying her earlier encounter with Branden, she got a lot of work done. At one point, however, a sinking feeling slammed her in the gut. What if there were other photos? That erotically charged kiss had been sex with clothes on, nothing less. The door to Branden Duke's upstairs lair had been open. They'd been so wrapped up in each other they never would have noticed.

If there was more to come, she wouldn't be able to ignore it. And neither would Branden. Dreading what she might see, Cara checked the website. As he'd predicted, the post was gone.

She felt only marginally relieved.

Hours after Cara came to see him, Branden heard a rap on his office door, then his stepsister's voice.

"It's Deena."

"Come on in," he said without looking up from the newspaper. Good, he could use Deena's thoughts just about now. Not long after Deena had become an investigator with the agency, the SEC had approached him about working with her to uncover shady business practices for them. Most of the time, that didn't involve buying companies, but in this case he'd already had his eye on D&M, so the purchase had served two purposes. He was here to turn a profit on his purchase, as well as help the SEC uncover any underhanded trading at D&M, but both those purposes had slid from his mind.

And he knew why.

The Wall Street Journal lay in peaks and valleys on the couch beside him. He was halfway through *Barron's* weekly issue. Unfortunately, he could barely remember anything he'd read all day.

His mind was filled with Cara Michal. How beautiful she was. How delicious she'd tasted. How it was best to stay away from her, but every time he saw her, he found himself wanting to do the exact opposite. The picture in Gawker hadn't helped. It had brought to the forefront of his mind every small detail that he'd tried to forget about that night and the wild kiss they'd shared.

She'd looked like she'd just been thoroughly fucked rather than just kissed.

And all he could think about was making her look like that again.

And again.

He'd stayed away from her the past few days, trying to do the right thing, and she'd had the gall to accuse him of not being interested. God, he'd wanted to make her eat those words. Show her in every possible way how much he wanted to be inside her and—

"Are you busy?"

He looked up at the sound of Deena's voice.

Busy losing my mind, he thought. He set the weekly aside. "Not really. Made any headway in our little investigation yet?"

She closed the door behind her. "Keep your voice down, Branden. The halls of Dubois & Mellan are seldom empty."

"As the company's new owner, I should be investigating how to trim the fat. That shouldn't come as a surprise to anyone, and if it does, well . . ." He spoke loudly, as if he was addressing anyone wandering outside his office door.

Deena rolled her eyes and perched herself on the arm of the couch that was farthest away from him. She pulled down the slim skirt of her coral suit almost primly.

"You look great," he said in a softer voice. "I'm surprised my new brother-in-law lets you come out to play."

"This isn't play. It's constructive work."

"More like sabotage."

She hummed a little tune. "I prefer to call it encouraging delusional behavior. We don't have to do anyone in. Most people seem able to achieve that on their own, don't you agree?"

"I suppose so." He and Deena had certainly had success exposing their fair share of well-heeled, well-dressed financiers trading in dark pools under shady circumstances, something that the SEC believed had been happening at D&M. It was why they, along with Mike Gaunt and a few other trusted members of their team such as Alex and Frank, were here. And why he really should be focusing on other things besides the delectable Cara Michal.

If anyone could get his mind off Cara, it was his highly intelligent, intensely driven, out-for-blood stepsister. Of his five half and stepsiblings, Deena was the one sister who bounced back time after time from the shit their various fathers put them all through. His mother had been married six times and Branden had done what he could for the sisters he'd acquired over the years to help them through the tough times, but some wounds would never heal.

Deena ran a hand over the back of the couch, as if the taut leather needed additional smoothing. "How long do you think we can get away with our little act this time?"

"Until someone smart gets one step ahead of us."

"That may have already happened. Any news on the Gawker post?"

Branden shrugged irritably. "It's anonymous. They claim to be a news blog and they'll protect their sources. At this time, there's no reason to think it's anything but tabloid fodder. Still, I wish I knew who took that photo of Cara."

"Do you." The needling remark wasn't a question. Deena rose and paced the austerely furnished room. "It would be so nice to not be noticed at all."

Branden's distant gaze didn't seem to see the graceful form of the woman who passed in front of him several times. "But I was. And you may be next."

She turned and faced him squarely. "I don't think so. Not by anyone other than Cara, at least. She's not dumb. She's caught on to my iciness and 'back off' attitude where you're concerned. Something I wouldn't have to do if you'd kept your hands to yourself."

"Yes, dear."

"Cara seems to have captivated the enemy. One that seems to have various connections. Have you seen the second post?"

"No." There was a second post? Cara wouldn't like it. And neither did he. He'd tried to play it cool in order to reassure her, but he'd been pissed by the online publication of that photo. What they'd shared had been intimate. Private. It didn't matter that he was often depicted in the media with beautiful women; that had never bothered him before. This was different.

He hated the idea of anyone witnessing his time with Cara, if that was what had happened, even though only a suggestive outside shot of her alone had been published.

"Actually, it's a link. On a different site. From the time stamp and various comments made, it's been online for hours. Click on it and you go somewhere else that might surprise you. Maybe not. After all, you were there."

Something in the meaningful lift of her eyebrow got him up and in front of his computer again. He pulled up the website and clicked on the link. "Jesus. Oh no. That never happened."

"But there it is," Deena replied softly. "In living color. You and Cara."

A muffled ringing made Cara frown. It was just past eight o'clock and she was home for once, knitting to reduce stress, rather than slaving away at the office, generating even more stress. But where was her phone? Her armchair liked an occasional smartphone snack. She slid her hand between the upholstered back and the seat cushion. The trick was to extract it before it stopped ringing. She answered with a distracted hello, not looking at the number.

"Yo. It's me."

"Hello, Iris."

"Whatcha doing?"

"Contemplating my uncertain future."

"That calls for a stiff drink. I assume someone at work saw that photo."

"Not that I know of. No one stopped by my office."

She left out the conversation with Branden for now, not up for Iris's analysis of how weird that had been. "No one called to chat."

"Keep your head down."

"I'm trying to."

"So I guess you don't want to go out."

"No thanks. I'd rather knit." Cara lifted a tangled pile of yarn from her lap and made clicking noises with the needles.

"Nice sound effect," Iris said. "Are you working on that scarf you started a year ago?"

"Yeah, I just wish it looked more like a scarf and less like a dish scrubber."

"Take a hint from the universe. Use it to scrub dishes," Iris suggested.

"Won't work. It's four feet long. Besides, it's really soft."

"I know someone you could donate it to."

"No one would want this, Iris."

"The laundry room cat doesn't like the sock box anymore."

Cara, who dropped off all her clothes at the dry cleaner's, had spent many peaceful afternoons with Iris in her Brooklyn building's laundry room, watching the suds slosh and the dryers spin while they talked and plugged coins into the machines. Each lone sock was deposited in a cardboard box in the hopes of being reunited with its mate, which never seemed to happen. The calico cat, a stray, had wandered into the building since Cara had last been there and found kitty heaven on earth in the warm, windowless room below street level and the overflowing box.

"Why not?"

"She seems to be pregnant. I think she's looking for a new nest."

"Sure, Socks can have this creation. I'm glad to have a reason to finish this thing."

There was a pause. "When you do, could you make another one?" Iris asked.

"Why? Oh. You're going to take a kitten."

"Two, actually, so they can keep each other company."

For a moment, Cara imagined having a cat waiting for her when she came home. It would be nice to cuddle with something warm-blooded for a change, but her building didn't allow pets. "I wish I could take one," she said.

"Yeah. We figure there will be between four and six."

"We?"

"Me and the new guy upstairs."

"I can hear you blushing, Iris. Louder than thunder." And that was quite unusual for her friend. Iris got around, but a guy who could rattle her with kittens involved was a rare breed.

"Drop dead. I mean that in a good way."

"Is he a new love interest?"

"Sheesh. He moved in last week, Cara." Another pause. "But he is cute."

Cara smiled, liking the idea of a cute guy bringing some happiness to her friend's life. "Keep me posted."

"I will, I promise. So what's going on with you and your new boss?"

Cara said nothing, just kept knitting.

Iris inhaled with dramatic suddenness. "Wait. Did *he* see the photo?"

"I showed it to him." Cara found herself unable to lie. She waited for a reply. "Iris? You still there?"

"Just picking myself up off the floor. Oh my God. What did he say?"

"He didn't think it was anything to worry about. He didn't seem to care at all."

Iris pondered that. "Well, then you're in the clear."

"I'm not 100 percent sure about that. Anyway, he thinks Gawker will drop it and he advised me to ignore it. Just for my own peace of mind, I'm keeping an eye on that website. They took the post down. And that one photo."

"That *one*? You mean there are others?"

"Oh, God, I hope not."

Iris cleared her throat. "Just between you and me, did anything else happen at that party?"

"No. I got kissed by a master kisser. After that, I got my ass home. End of story."

"I want to believe that. I really do. Mind if I check Gawker again?"

"Go ahead. I'm coming up on a purl."

Faintly, she heard a keyboard being tapped, the rhythm almost identical to her knitting needles. Friends forever, clickety-click.

"They dropped the item. Completely. Nowhere to be found."

"Good."

"Maybe not. I wonder why."

Iris tended to be a worrywart, for all her freewheeling ways. But then again, she knew how sites like Gawker operated and Cara didn't.

"Keep purling. I'm looking elsewhere."

A minute or more passed.

"Cara. Oh my God. Are you sitting down?"

"Yes. Why?" Her heart sank. Just her luck. There had to be a second post that was somehow more incriminating than the first.

"I think you're going to need that drink. I'm coming over."

Chapter Eight

"So I found this on HotnSaucey. Besides all the heavy breathing clips they post, it's a fucking minefield of escort ads," Iris said, setting aside her untouched gin and tonic and taking a bite of the bulging tuna sandwich Cara had made for her.

"You could have sent me the link." Cara was glad, though, that Iris had insisted on coming over. Whatever the latest revelation was, she didn't want to face it alone.

"No way. HotnSaucey is loaded with viruses and malware." Iris tapped at the keyboard of an ancient laptop, frowning at the flickering screen. "C'mon, start already. There's a reason I call it the *craptop*."

"Is it broken?" Cara almost hoped so. She raised her glass and gulped down a large mouthful, then sputtered. Apparently she'd gone too light on the tonic, too heavy on the gin.

"Let's just say it sort of works. But basically it's a piece of junk. My former roommate left it behind on purpose when she moved out." The screen suddenly glowed blue and stopped flickering. "Hey, we're in business. This thing does come in handy. I wouldn't risk my new laptop on a site like HotnSaucey. You ready?"

Cara swallowed another mouthful of icy gin and wiped her mouth, dreading what was about to appear on the screen. "Yeah." She shivered as she set the cold drink down and forced herself to look.

"There you go. That's definitely Branden, though he looks younger."

He certainly did. He was also half naked. He and the woman with him were both stripped to the waist. They weren't in a room, exactly. More like a space with blank walls. He faced the lens—when he wasn't looking at the other participant. All Cara could see of her was her back. Yellow hair that had been styled to scary straightness swung over her shoulders.

"That could be you."

"It's not," Cara said quickly.

"I mean," Iris replied as if she were choosing her words very carefully, "that could be you if people wanted to think so. Like, if you were walking away from them."

"Good to know. I don't have a thing to worry about, right?"

Iris didn't answer.

"Right?"

"I know that's not you and—well, if anyone else thinks it is, just laugh it off. Besides, you would never do a sex tape."

Iris was loyal as the day was long and that was true enough. But nothing she said changed the fact that it *was* Branden they were looking at. Cara drank in the sight of golden muscle broadening his chest and tapering to taut abs. The beginnings of the sexy lines that defined his groin on both sides of his torso were visible as he slid his hands down over smooth skin into what Cara assumed were the good parts.

The video had stopped. "Is that all?"

"The clip was a free download. I didn't buy the complete tape because that would have involved sending my credit card information to some weird little country where they laugh at the law and the joke's on you."

The video began again, at the beginning. This time Cara studied his face. Was he enjoying himself? He only glanced at the woman, who stayed in the same spot, not approaching or touching him. But that hot gleam in his dark eyes was familiar, and so was the teasing, sensual half smile.

The memory of having seen both close up at high intensity nagged at her. Forget it, she told herself. Don't flatter yourself. You just happened to be lolling around on his long black couch and he found you, not on purpose. Good thing you got out when you did.

Men as hot and as rich as Branden Duke didn't sleep alone unless they wanted to—or had tired themselves out with a harem for hire. He had probably paid for exactly what he wanted in this goddamn video. Thanks to her own unwillingness to give her credit card information, Cara would be spared seeing how far Branden could go. Although she secretly wanted to find out.

"Okay. Here's what I think," Iris began. "And I do have some media experience."

Branden's strong hands were sliding toward his groin again. Cara noticed this time that he was looking at the woman's face, as if he wanted to watch her watching him. As if he wanted *her* to watch him.

"Uh-huh."

In another few seconds, her rational mind gave in to the sensations her real body was experiencing. Heat. Lust. Sexual instinct that won out over intellect. She wanted that man more than anything. Desperately wanted to be that woman. And damn whoever was playing both of them for being so incredibly, wickedly good at the game.

Iris cleared her throat. She used the touchpad to pause the video.

Cara trembled, on the verge of giving in to a nameless fear that rose within her. She stared at the frozen image, stunned and silent, unable to fight the feeling that someone had looked right through her, ransacked her mind, and hijacked her private fantasies about Branden Duke. She could have been made of glass. About to shatter, when it got right down to it.

Iris picked up a pencil to point at the screen. "That's professional lighting. No harsh shadows, no glare reflections."

"So?"

"Branden didn't film this."

"Duh. He's got his hands full."

Iris snorted. "That's one way of putting it. But this is definitely not a set-the-timer-and-hump amateur production."

"If you say so." Cara couldn't take her eyes off her big, strong, bare-chested boss.

Iris gestured with the pencil. "And note how she stays at the edge of the shot."

"She's teasing him."

"Exactly. It's like she's there to liven him up, get a reaction, make him less nervous—take your pick."

Cara mostly noted how turned on he seemed. In a healthy way. Like he wasn't acting. Just naturally aroused. Maybe the teasing woman was the pro and he was— She didn't think for a second that he, not to be judgmental, used to be . . . an escort or something.

He had to be acting.

"Okay. No need for another go," Cara said. "Eat."

"Mmm. Good tuna," Iris mumbled through another bite. "I just wanted to make sure you saw it before you got slammed with rude questions at work."

"Nobody mentioned the Gawker thing and it's gone

now." But this video was a lot more titillating, and it had been up on the Web for hours. Despite her hopes to the contrary, it was very possible someone could have seen it.

Iris chewed thoughtfully. "I bet Branden had something to do with that."

"Maybe. Could be I just didn't hear the comments. The best thing about having your own office is shutting the door." But with this new video? If people were making comments, she'd probably be able to hear the sneers and snickers no matter where she tried to hide.

"I never had an office, so I wouldn't know," Iris said. "But maybe I will in my next incarnation. Yours is nice."

She raised her chin and straightened her shoulders. Even as dread and fear chased through her, she knew she had to pull herself together. Someone was messing with her. With her career. And she wasn't going down without a fight. "And I plan to be there for the next year at least."

"I know. So we have to stay on this. Because the more I look at her, the more I think that she"—Iris pointed at the screen—"could be mistaken for you, if people were so inclined."

As crazy as it was, part of her wished the woman on the video *was* her. Whoever the unknown woman was, Cara envied her, which was totally irrational but sort of understandable. Silent for several moments, Cara studied Branden's gloriously masculine nudity while the tape stayed on pause.

Iris used the pink eraser to point to the woman with him. "Now that I've seen it several times—"

"Just because you want to help me, right?"

"Of course." Iris seemed almost offended. "Pay attention. Important observation coming up. Notice how her back is always to the camera?"

"Give her time. It's a clip. Not even a minute long."

"Granted. Still, potential buyers of porny product want the woman going *ooh, ahh, give it to me, big boy,* and all the rest of that phony moaning. But Branden is like, um, the star of this."

"Your point? And would you please put down the pencil? I feel like I'm in a seminar."

Iris set the pencil on the coffee table and picked up her drink, taking a big swallow and coughing a little. "Is this all gin?"

"Except for the ice and a too stingy dash of tonic water, yes. Would you like a lime wedge?"

"No. My point, Cara, is that this probably isn't a sex tape per se."

Cara looked at Branden's silken skin and rippling muscles and back at Iris. "Then what is it?"

"Could be a screen test."

"For porn? Are you telling me that the great and powerful Branden Duke, our new CEO, was once so broke that he— Oh no. That's not possible."

"Anything is possible." Iris hemmed and hawed a little. "But it's not necessarily *porn* porn. I mean, it could be soft core, which isn't so bad."

"I refuse to believe it."

"You don't have to. And I'm just guessing. It could also be a commercial."

"For what? Condoms?" Cara found it possible to believe that much. She stared at the golden stud on the screen as the image dwindled to a dot and then went black. Fucking screen saver had to kick in just when she was memorizing every visible inch of his glorious body.

Iris gave her a pitying look that irked the hell out of Cara. "Hey, I know guys who've done way worse things for money than X-rated movies. New York is an expensive city."

"And Branden Duke practically owns it. He's a financial titan."

"Self-made," Iris reminded her. "He didn't inherit his fortune."

"Apparently not."

"Besides that, you found out practically nothing about his past before his meteoric rise to the top, correct?"

"Meteoric rise? I don't remember using that phrase."

"Well, whatever. No one seemed to be holding a gun to his head in that tape. He probably did it for a hundred bucks, paid the electricity bill, and that was that."

"Play it again," Cara suggested. "I missed the part where it looks like he's thinking about his electricity bill."

"Okay. In a sec. Sandwich, come to Mama." Iris took another bite.

"He could be on HotnSaucey right now watching it himself," Cara mused. "Probably wondering who found it and why they sold it. And whether they're gunning for him or me."

"He might never know. Most likely someone on the shoot kept the footage. Now that he's news, what with buying your company and, um, swaggering around like Wall Street moguls do, someone dug it up and digitized it and got it out there."

"The same someone?"

"How should I know, Cara?"

"Realistically, how much money can someone make off an old sex tape or screen test?"

Iris seemed surprised by the question. "Are you kidding me? A lot. But it depends on how hot the tape is, of course. And how famous the former nobody is now."

Cara tried to focus on reality again, wishing she was shameless enough to tap a key and make the laptop come back to life. The screen stayed black. If she wanted to feast her eyes on him again when Iris was gone, she would have to download the clip herself, viruses be damned, maybe even purchase the whole tape for private viewing. If only he had been filmed solo.

"How come you know so much about sex tapes?"

"Because they're click bait for gossip blogs if celebs are involved. Branden Duke isn't A-list in terms of name recognition, but he could be if there are more undiscovered tapes out there with famous females sampling his, um, charms."

"Never mind them." Cara flung herself against the back of the sofa and covered her face with her hands, letting out a muffled groan. "If word gets around and anyone thinks that anonymous female is me, my financial career is toast. I'll fight the good fight, of course I will, but I don't want to. And even if I do, what if it doesn't make a difference. What if I lose everything, Iris?"

Iris put a comforting hand on her arm. "HotnSaucey is mostly for freaks. You work with normal people, right?"

Cara let her hands drop into her lap. "I don't know where you got that idea."

"Well, who knows what will happen. At least you won't be blindsided."

"None of my distinguished colleagues are going to analyze it like you just did." Cara thought of Greg Johnson, who might still be nursing his injured pride. "They'll just scorch the servers forwarding it over and over."

"They have to find it first. Right now it's just a sidebar on a sleazy site. Of course, if HotnSaucey gets lots of hits on it, they'll bump it up to a feature."

After sharing that information, Iris polished off the rest of the sandwich.

"Would you mind if I looked at the clip again?" Cara asked.

"Be my guest."

Cara tapped. The HotnSaucey website loaded slowly

in fits and starts. She saw no sign of the clip. "Hey. It's gone."

Iris sat up straight, wiping her fingers on the napkin. "Scroll down."

"I did."

Iris peered at the screen. "Huh. Maybe the site was paid—or threatened—to take it down in a hurry."

Cara gave her a puzzled look. "Isn't that, like, blackmail?"

"Kind of." Iris sighed. "I guess Branden can afford whatever they were asking. Who else would want it gone?"

"I don't know."

"The blonde, maybe."

"No. Him. You're right."

Now that the mind-numbing sensation of seeing him mostly naked was beginning to wear off, she could think a little more clearly—for one thing, about the bio she'd struggled to piece together for him online. No wonder she'd found gaps. He had unlimited money to edit his private life if necessary and the inclination to cover his tracks fast. That explained his self-contained attitude, too. You sure can pick 'em, Cara told herself. The thought was infinitely depressing.

"Well, show's over. At least you got to see it. Otherwise you'd tell me I was crazy."

"Never. You're my bestest friend in the whole wide world."

"I'm your only friend. You need to open up more. Call me tomorrow," Iris said, shutting down the laptop. "And don't take any questions from the office busybodies."

"Like I would," Cara muttered.

Iris got up and put the laptop on the small table near the apartment door. Then she returned to take her plate to the kitchen sink, calling to Cara from there. "Before I forget to ask, how's the knitted thing for Socks coming along?"

It was astute of Iris to guess that Cara was nervous and tactful of her to offer a distraction.

"What thing?" Then Cara remembered. Right. Socks, the pregnant laundry-room cat, needed nesting materials. "Oh, that. Um, I need to finish off the row I'm on. I'll bring it by on the weekend."

"I'll tell Socks to hold off on the kittens."

"Is it done?" Branden was talking to one of his PR guys, an expert when it came to information online. He could make things appear and disappear. He'd worked his magic with the photograph of Cara outside the mansion, and now he'd damn well do the same thing to that video.

After being assured that the video was as good as gone, Branden hung up the phone then slammed his laptop shut. Going outside and throwing it off the penthouse terrace was not an option, but it was a thought. He'd watched the clip several times, then downloaded it just in case his lawyers would want to have a look. Let them decide what to do. There'd be follow-up snark, but he wasn't anticipating much of that.

It was him and it had happened, despite his protests to the contrary to Deena. He hadn't instantly remembered doing it, but then he'd never seen the tape of the jeans-ad audition back in college. Nothing came of it. A check and a handshake, then thanks for your time, we'll call you, *next*. Over and done with and forgotten long ago.

No telling who owned the rights to the footage by this time. He dimly remembered signing a release after it was all over. Someone had stumbled across the tape somehow and, by his guess, was looking to cash in, but how much could they make? He wasn't that well known outside of New York, and as far as blackmail, forget it. There was no actual sex.

The sight of himself at that age, in that situation, took him back. He'd been young and hungry, that was for damn sure. He hadn't modeled for long, never took it seriously, just did it on occasion for the money. Before the jeans ad, he'd landed a few squeaky-clean catalog shoots. He'd stood under hot lights in a striped polo and khakis, holding a brand-new football and smiling until his face hurt.

The jeans ad had been a bigger deal, part of a national campaign. They'd auditioned a slew of guys and eventually chosen a Swedish exchange student who'd been splashed all over Times Square billboards looking like he had a giant herring behind his denim fly.

HotnSaucey.com had nerve offering a full-length version of the brief audition. Didn't exist. The featured clip was all there was, just over a minute, probably. But when Branden had purchased the entire video for sale, he'd discovered an erotic sex scene with two figures in a darkened room, their features blurry. The fact that the man bore a faint resemblance to him and the blonde bore a faint resemblance to Cara wouldn't stand up to detailed scrutiny, but it could be enough to prolong any speculation that it was the two of them having sex.

Whether the dredged-up post was linked in any way to the Gawker headline was impossible to say. Neither seemed worth an all-out investigative effort . . . but for Cara. He got the feeling she was a deeply private person who had been through some tough times. There was nothing in her personnel file, which was all he had to go on for the moment, to give him a clue as to her past.

Branden got up and moved around the coffee table to the high windows that comprised an entire wall, taking in the panoramic view of lower Manhattan, enjoying the display, which changed by the hour. Night had fallen, brightened by patterns of man-made light on the newer skyscrapers and a few of the older buildings. Some were not illuminated at all, black shapes in the overall darkness outside. He went outside, resting his hands on the railing of the wraparound terrace.

Cara's place was only two buildings down, but even from this lofty height, he couldn't see more than a sliver of it. Just knowing she was nearby made him want her all over again. Here, with him. High above the city and the never-ending hustle of the Street, lost in each other's arms and the enfolding night. He wanted her in his bed most of all.

He normally didn't worry or care about the press. They were hungry little vultures that would be picking bones long after he was gone. But he'd seen how upset Cara was over the photo, and now there was a video to contend with. It was one they both knew never happened, but he had a feeling if she'd seen it, she would be beside herself.

Branden looked at the time—it was almost 9 p.m. He was worried about Cara, and he wondered if he should risk going by her place and checking on her. Since he didn't know who was lurking around taking photos and splicing together videos, it was probably a bad idea.

He really didn't want to alert her to the video if she didn't know about it. But if she did know, he didn't want her to spend a sleepless night worrying about it, either.

He decided to call, and if she didn't seem to know about the video, he would ask her something about one of the reports she'd given him. He looked at the copy of the video he had saved one more time. He felt a stirring in his pants just at the thought of having Cara in any one of the positions the mysterious blonde had assumed in the lurid scene.

He went to his bookshelf, took out an album one of

his stepsisters—probably Rachel, she was always playing Suzy Homemaker—had put together for him years ago, and sat down on the couch, placing the album next to his laptop on the little table in front of him. He linked to the network that took him directly into the computer systems of all of the companies he owned and then into HR at Dubois & Mellan. Pulling up Cara's mobile number, he entered it into his phone and hit send . . .

Three rings and then a tentative, "Hello?"

"Cara, it's Branden."

"So you've seen it?"

That answered the question. "I was hoping you hadn't."

"I have. Part of it anyway. I'm not sure what's going on, but you and I both know that isn't us."

"Yes, well it's not you anyway. I'm going to send you a snapshot. Tell me what you notice about it." He snapped a picture of a photo from the portfolio and texted her.

After several seconds she said, "Those are the same jeans . . . the same pose even. What is this from?"

"I did some modeling in college for extra cash. They took stills as well as a filmed audition for a jeans commercial. That's all it was. Not a sex tape. Just a stupid ad. I was supposed to act sexy. You know, pump the pecs, tighten the abs, thumbs in the belt loops, push the jeans down—"

"I get the idea. So who was the girl?"

"I don't remember her name and I never saw her again. I think she was a production assistant. She agreed to, you know, liven things up."

"I see."

"And they didn't show any of us what they'd taped. Obviously, someone got hold of it, used it, then used different models in bad light to act out a steamy sex scene."

"A steamy sex scene?"

He winced. "You didn't get that far?"

"How—how explicit was it?"

His silence was his answer.

"Oh, God. Why? Who?"

"I wish I knew. I have someone working on it. It should be gone soon if it isn't already."

"I think it is. But that doesn't tell us who's already seen it, who copied it and already posted it to another site, or why anyone would want to do this . . ."

"You're right. I'll do my best to find out for your peace of mind," he told her.

"What about your own peace of mind? You're not bothered by this at all?"

Two things about it bothered him. The seeming connection the photo and video had to his takeover of Dubois & Mellan, and the fact it bothered Cara so badly. He had to wonder if someone knew his true reason for purchasing the company, and if they did, how they'd found out. There was also something about Cara that brought out every protective fiber in his body, and her feeling bad had suddenly become equivalent to him having bad feelings of his own. That was a little disconcerting to him, since his sisters were the only women he'd ever really felt that protective pull toward.

"I don't really care what people think of me, Cara," he told her at last.

"You can afford not to. I can't. I don't have millions to fall back on. My reputation is all I have."

"This won't affect your job, I promise," he said.

"Maybe I won't lose it because of this, but if it gets out that first photo was me and everyone assumes that the video is me . . . it will definitely affect my credibility. Women already walk a tightrope on the Street, you know that. I didn't intend to remain a financial analyst at D&M forever. This could definitely get in the way of my moving up in my career."

"I'm going to protect you on this, Cara. Trust me, okay?"

She didn't say okay, she just thanked him weakly and ended the call.

He hung up with an overwhelming desire to go to her, put his arms around her, and chase all her fears away. He was smart enough to know that would probably only make things worse, so he stayed put, racking his brains over who would want to damage his reputation and harm Cara's at the same time.

Chapter Nine

Cara sat down and tried to deal with her ridiculous-looking, poorly knitted scarf. Of course, all she could do was replay the phone call with Branden.

He'd seemed so confident that the video wouldn't be a big deal, but she still had her doubts. He owned five major trading companies. His reputation already spoke for itself in the business world, and the way society worked, a sex tape or two might only increase his popularity.

Cara, on the other hand, was still trying to make her mark, albeit quietly. People loved to talk, they loved scandal, and rather than viewing that video as an act of passion between two adult single people, Cara would be viewed as a whore, sleeping with the boss to climb the ladder. She could probably kiss her bonus good-bye even if she did end up staying to complete the fourth year of her program. Sure, Branden said he'd protect her now, but things could change in a flash. And really, what did she know about him?

Why did she have any reason to trust him?

She didn't.

Her head was pounding, and she was getting nowhere

going over and over it tonight. She tucked her awful knitting away, took several aspirin, and went to bed, where she tossed and turned for hours before finally falling asleep just about an hour before the alarm screamed to life and expected her to do the same.

Cara was reluctant to get out of bed, and for the first time in her three years of working at D&M she was tempted to call in sick and take a mental health day. She could work remotely—log in to the D&M system and do her job from her home office; they did allow that. She even had the words all planned out in her head as she reached for the phone. She held it in her hand and rehearsed the words before putting the phone back down and telling herself that she couldn't do it.

What would she do all day if she did? She knew herself well; if she didn't go to work she would just sit in the small apartment and let the events of the past several days run rampant through her thoughts. She needed the structure of being in her office. At least at D&M, she could distract herself with beautiful stable numbers. Numbers never let you down. One plus one never said, "I think I'll equal five today."

At the sound of the banging racket of construction equipment, Cara groaned and forced herself out of bed. She showered fast but didn't wash her hair, swaddling herself in a towel before she picked out her most conservative suit, adding a gray blouse with an attached bow that tied at the neck.

Dressing in haste, she tugged and zipped and buttoned up, then looked in the mirror with a frown. What an awful combination. She should have added the blouse to a Salvation Army donation bag long ago, but maybe it was a good thing she hadn't. It definitely lent her a prim and proper air. She dragged her hair back into an approximation of a chignon and stuck hairpins in it to hold it there. It took a little more cover-up than usual to hide the dark circles under her eyes, but otherwise she was presentable.

She was ready. Physically, anyway. Emotionally, not.

Cara steeled herself to leave her apartment. She did know the drill.

She'd had to run a gauntlet in school, when the whispered campaign against her family began and escalated to nasty comments scratched on her locker. She hadn't told her guidance counselor about the harassment, or anyone else, for that matter. There would have been no point in painting over the anonymous words, which were barely visible—by her guess they'd been etched with a metal nail file. Girls could be much more malicious than boys. She'd held her head high and clutched her books to her chest like a shield. *Walk away if you can't walk tall* had been her motto. She could do it again. It was funny what life trained you for.

Wearing a coat and scarf and dark glasses on the street, she still felt strangely exposed. Like everyone who passed had seen her naked and either disapproved of what she'd supposedly done or were turned on by it. Ugh. She flipped up her coat collar and used it to cover her mouth. Avoiding eye contact was the norm in New York, anyway. And maybe it would help to practice before she got to work. An attractive older man gave her a curious look. Maybe it was concern. She ignored him and stepped into the street to avoid brushing by him. It wasn't difficult to dodge the slow-moving traffic, but the blaring horns made her jump.

Her exhaustion was getting to her. That, and paranoia. The predominantly male crowd jostled her once she was back on the sidewalk. It certainly wasn't true that anyone she saw could be a possible suspect, but she couldn't help thinking so. Cara jammed her hands into her pockets, grateful for the concealing lenses that hid her eyes from the occasional masculine glance.

As she walked into the elegant Manhattan office building, it looked the same as it always did, guys in stylish suits glued to their phones or their tablets, rushing here and there, talking loudly, giving no thought whatsoever to the world outside the glass-and-brass doors. No one seemed to notice her. No one pointed or whispered. Malcolm and Gene, two men with offices on her floor, barely said hello as they got in line behind her to go through security, instead remaining deeply immersed in their conversation about the New York Mets, through the security unit, and during the elevator ride. She took comfort in the fact that no one had brought up the photo or video.

Exiting the elevator and stepping into the corridor, Cara looked right and left. The coast was clear. She strode quickly down the hall, still bundled up and feeling uncomfortably hot. She tensed all over when she saw the back of Mike Gaunt's bristled head and the thick shoulders under his wrinkled white shirt. He did look like an FBI agent. On steroids. It occurred to her that Branden had never really answered her question on that score.

Gaunt was in the bullpen, leaning over Jackson Riley, a junior stockbroker, and jabbing a meaty finger at the computer screen as Jackson nodded seriously. Next to them stood Frank, one of the employees Branden had brought in. Cara felt herself go pale. She squinted, trying to see what was on the display, then figured it couldn't be her if those two looked so businesslike. She scuttled past the spot where the office manager would see her if he turned, finally reaching the relative safety of her office.

Coat off, purse stashed, she did a home-run dash to her swivel chair and touched a key, dreading what would pop up in her email. Thankfully, there were no further booby traps waiting for her.

She got busy. Really busy. Excel spreadsheets had never looked so good. Routine was what she needed to stop the roller coaster of emotions that she had been riding since the night she'd locked lips with Wall Street's Most Desired.

The morning passed quickly and without incident. Around noon she suddenly realized that she was so hungry it felt like her stomach was beginning to turn on itself. She dug through her desk, hoping that she had a granola bar or a bag of trail mix, but having no luck. Knowing that she couldn't hide forever, she took her wallet and headed down to the employee dining room. She would just grab a sandwich and bring it back up. She had plenty of bottled water in the office.

Feeling like a criminal, she checked the hallway before stepping out. No Branden, no Mike Gaunt, and no Deena. So far so good. She pressed the down button on the elevator. When it slid open, she was face to face with Greg.

He smiled broadly and said, "Hey there," in a sickeningly familiar tone.

"Hi," she answered grudgingly.

He held the door open but didn't step off. Greg raked his gaze over her. "What's up with the weird blouse and the giant pussycat bow? You look like a high school teacher who doesn't want to get the boys turned on. Unless you're covering up a hickey."

Cara cleared her throat. "Aren't you getting off here?" she asked before she stepped on.

"No, I just remembered that I forgot something downstairs. Which floor do you need?" he asked her.

"Ground," she said.

What is he up to?

He smiled again, and this time it almost seemed menacing. A week ago she couldn't have imagined Greg frightening her, but there was something different about him now. Maybe he was using a little too many of those "pick me up" pills.

"I'm glad I ran into you, actually. You know, Cara," he said after the elevator once again jerked to life, "I really had no intention of leaving you out on the island the other night. I just couldn't find you. I thought for sure you had left me."

"So is that supposed to be an apology? It sounds more like you're laying blame."

"I guess it's an apology if that's what you want to call it," he said.

"I don't want to call it anything," she said, in no mood for silly word games. "I just thought since you'd never actually apologized for abandoning me that night maybe that's what you were trying to do now." She knew in the back of her mind that it wasn't really his fault, but his attitude irked her.

"I didn't do it on purpose. If you had been around like a date was supposed to be, I would have been able to find you. But you weren't, so I don't feel the need to apologize. Besides, judging from the pic in the Gawker, you were doing okay after I left, getting to know the new boss."

Cara felt her stomach drop just as the elevator lurched to a stop and the doors slid open. Greg put his hand out to hold the doors open after he stepped off and grinned at her shocked face like they'd been having a pleasant conversation. Then he said, "Have a great day. I'm sure you'll have a great night. I know I will. I've got a hot video to watch."

He let the doors go and she stood there, mouth probably hanging open for too long, even after the doors closed in her face. It took her another several seconds of standing there looking at the closed doors to remember that she needed to push something to make it open again or go.

Instead of reopening the doors she pushed the up button. Was it possible Branden had been right about Greg after all?

"Where are you going?"

Branden sat quietly behind his desk as Cara described her conversation with Greg in the elevator. Then, without a word, he stood and headed toward the office door.

"I'm going to talk to Greg," he said. "If nothing else, to tell him to keep his nasty insinuations to himself."

Cara immediately stepped between him and the door. "I don't know if that's such a good idea."

The closeness of their bodies registered and goose bumps prickled down Cara's arms and spine. She forced down the urge to go up on her toes and once again feel the softness and power of his sexy lips on hers.

He looked down at her with those smoldering dark eyes. "Why not?"

"If he wanted attention, you'd be giving him exactly that. If he's not the one who posted the picture and video, and he just came across them the way we did, then bringing them up gives credence and unnecessary influence."

He was still looking down at her face. Her mouth had gone completely dry and she felt like she needed to swallow but couldn't. His eyes were shifting back and forth between her eyes and her lips.

He was thinking of kissing her.

A second after she thought it, he pushed her up against his closed office door and his lips were suddenly on hers.

She could have pulled away. She could have at least tried.

She didn't.

Instead, wanting only to forget her worries over that video and the humiliation she'd felt at Greg's jeering voice and expression, she molded herself into his body and deepened the kiss, shuddering as she felt his hot tongue slip between her lips.

Her mind told her to stop. After all, this is what had gotten them into trouble in the first place. But his lips on hers felt too good, too right to stop.

As they kissed, he ran his hands along her curves and she couldn't help but moan against his mouth. His touch was electric, and the fact that they were leaning up against the door of his office with his assistant sitting only feet away outside made it more dangerous somehow and therefore more exciting.

He pulled his lips from hers only to slide them down her face and to her neck. When he reached the bow, his hand lifted, tugging it open and exposing a tender patch of flesh to kiss and nibble. The part of her brain telling her to stop began to scream.

She tried to ignore it. Tried to listen to her body, which was commanding just the opposite.

She was rooting for her body. She wanted it to win.

But before she realized it, her brain took control and she said, "No, wait. Stop . . ."

To his credit, he did. Immediately. Her body was thrown into instant grief and regret.

"Cara," he breathed.

The sound of her name on his lips was like a drug. She had to force herself to be strong.

"We can't do this."

"Why not?" he said in his deep, sexy voice. "I tried to fight this. Tried to do what was appropriate. But Greg saw the video, and it's certain others will have, too, either because Greg told them about it or they found it on their own. All they had to do was Google my name, or D&M, and given I just took over the company, that isn't farfetched. People will already think we're sleeping together. I'm sorry for that. Sorry for the trouble it will cause you. But you already know your job is safe. There's nothing standing in our way from dating. Besides helping you through any backlash with the video, I'd like to get to know you better, Cara. Dinner. Drinks. Conversation."

Her gaze locked on to his. That was no "I'd like to talk politics over dinner" look he was giving her. That was one of those smoldering "Let's shove the meal off the table and have at each other" kind of looks. Everything inside her began to shiver and quake. "Please . . ." she said, not positive what she was asking for.

"Please what, Cara?"

"Please stop looking at me like that." It wasn't what she really wanted to say. What she really wanted to say was, please throw me down on the desk and fuck me senseless.

He slowly pulled away. Shivering, as if the loss of his touch had chilled her all the way to her bones, she fixed the bow of her blouse with trembling fingers. Then she turned to open the door.

"Wait," he said.

She froze. Looked over her shoulder.

He strode to his desk and bent over it.

She imagined that she was lying on top of it, legs spread . . .

Branden wrote something down. When he came back he had a business card in his hand. "I meant what I said when I told you I wanted to get to know you. To have dinner with you. I'm dining at home tonight. At seven. Give this to my doorman. Tell him your name and he'll send you up," he said.

She looked at the card. He'd written *P* on it and signed it. At the bottom it said Manhattan Sky Towers.

"I didn't agree to dinner," she said.

He closed her hand around the card with his own. His touch caused her to convulse once more. She wasn't sure if she liked or hated that he had such a strong effect on her.

"In case you change your mind," he said, "I'll be there by seven. If dinner's too much, just join me for a cocktail or two. In the meantime, I won't talk to Greg, but I am going to keep an eye on him. If he bothers you again, let me know."

She nodded, unable to formulate any words.

He reached out and smoothed down a piece of her hair. That simple act was so sweet and intimate that Cara actually felt the sting of tears in the corners of her eyes. She didn't understand why he had such an incredibly strong effect on her emotions and it made her a nervous wreck. After he pulled away, he smiled and opened the office door.

"Thank you for letting me know about that, Cara. I hadn't realized that venture was losing money. I'll have to keep a closer eye on those stocks."

"Oh, um . . . sure, Mr. Duke. You're welcome." She made eye contact with Jean and smiled.

Jean smiled back.

Cara was probably just being paranoid, but there seemed to be something new in the other woman's eyes, something knowing.

Cara made it back to her office, completely forgetting that she'd left in the first place because she was hungry. Her insides were quaking from that kiss. At least she thought it was the kiss. Maybe it was what Greg had said, or the look Jean had given her. Either way, she needed to shake it all off before her work started to suffer. Her job was the one stable thing she had in her life and she needed it.

Her mother and Glenn were counting on her.

She looked down at the business card in her hand and then shoved it into her pocket.

They were in enough trouble as it was.

She wasn't going to his place for dinner. Because she knew from how he looked at her what would follow dessert.

But there was no denying the fact she wanted to be what was laid out on his table for his pleasure.

After Cara left, Branden returned to his desk and picked up the phone.

"Alex, I need to see you," was all he said.

Less than five minutes later, there was a knock on his door.

"Come in!"

Alex Samuels, Branden's friend and personal investigator, stepped inside. Branden had asked him to be part of the D&M purchase, mostly to keep his ear to the ground and report to Branden anything he heard that could be construed as negative.

"Hey, boss," Alex said, taking a seat across from Branden.

Branden and Alex had met in college over a wild game of Beer Pong and forged a friendship that had survived everything in between—including more Beer Pong and the occasional hostile takeover of a trading company. Now Alex and his brother Lee were Branden's go-to guys for anything or anyone he needed checked out. They worked for him, not for the SEC, not for Deena, and not for Mike Gaunt. After seeing the photo on Gawker, Branden had told Lee to investigate Cara's background on the chance someone from her past was gunning for her. Now, because of Greg's comments to Cara in the elevator, Branden had an assignment for Alex.

"Hey," Branden said, looking his friend over. "Off to play polo with Ralph Lauren?"

Alex, usually a jeans, T-shirt, and boots kind of guy,

currently had on a collared shirt, a long-sleeved peachy-pink button-down, and khaki pants.

"Did you call me up here just to make fun of me?"

Branden grinned. "Nope. I have an assignment for you. But I am wondering what prompted your sudden change of style."

"Are you kidding? My first day here in your fancy trading firm I had not one but two different people mistake me for the plumber. Apparently there was an issue with the toilets on the second floor that day."

"So you went shopping so you wouldn't be mistaken for the custodial staff?"

"Yeah, Leslie took me to Barneys. Not exactly my style, but at least nobody's asking me if they can pee on floor two today."

Branden wondered if Alex had called Leslie, or the other way around. Leslie was one of Branden's five sisters—younger than him by eight years—and had followed him and his friends around like a lost little puppy. Branden had gotten into a fistfight with Leslie's father, stepfather number three, when the douchebag had taken a belt to Leslie's behind after she'd snuck out of the house at night. Alex and Leslie had been friends since they'd met a few years back. Branden couldn't remember if Leslie was dating anyone at the moment.

But the hair on the back of his neck rose at the thought of his baby sister dating *anyone*—even if it was one of his best friends. Although she couldn't do better than Alex. The Samuels brothers were the salt of the earth. Trustworthy. Hard workers. And they'd make great husbands. Unlike him.

Branden sighed and told himself to focus on the matter at hand. "I need you on this quickly. It has nothing to do with the SEC investigation—at least, not that I know of. But who knows . . ."

"Cool, so this is personal. Is she hot?"

"It's a guy."

"Why don't you ever need some hot, lonely cougar type followed? Or better yet, assign me instead of my brother to look into the hot blonde. I was a little hurt over that, by the way."

Something warm stirred in his belly at the mention of Cara. Damn. She seemed to invade his every pore. "You weren't here the day I called for the background on Cara. Lee got that one by default."

"Fine. No hot blondes. What do you need?"

"There's a guy named Greg Johnson. A junior stockbroker, rather obnoxious. I want to know everything about him, including how old he was when he stopped wearing Pull-Ups to bed at night."

"So info you can't get off his employee file. That's it?"

"For now," Branden said. "As soon as Deena gets all the hard drives downloaded and we go through them, I know there will be more. Do you and Lee have the staff and resources you need?"

"We have way too many people at the moment, actually. Got them sitting around watching security tapes and picking their noses all day. It looks like a family dinner at my parents' house."

"That will change soon enough. Get on Greg Johnson ASAP for now. Let me know if you find anything unusual in the guy's background."

Alex stood up. "You got it, boss. Just remember me if any of those cougar investigations come up, okay?"

"Why don't you just go out to the club and find one yourself?"

"You know I'm shy," Alex said with a grin on his way out.

Yeah, right. Or maybe he was too busy going shopping with the woman he really wanted. Branden shook his head and was still smiling when Deena walked in the door.

"You look happy," his stepsister said, taking her perch on the edge of the black sofa.

"Should I not?" he asked, withholding his guess that Alex might be dating their little sister. Sometimes Deena was even more protective of her siblings than Branden was, and he figured Leslie and Alex deserved the benefit of the doubt . . . for now.

"I'm not sure yet. I got the hard copy from an employee's hard drive today. It has some interesting searches on it for information about Serenity and Lindtz Pharmaceuticals."

Serenity was a new medication put out by a little-known pharmaceutical company, Lindtz. As soon as the medication had been approved by the FDA and hit the market, the stocks for the little company had skyrocketed. Anyone who had gotten in on the ground floor of that deal had made a small fortune.

"Who's the employee?" he asked.

"A guy named John Turner. He's been here for ten years."

"Did we look into his financials?"

"He's made several cash deposits recently. All just under ten grand, I'm assuming to keep the IRS at bay. He doesn't own any of the stock for Lindtz, but it seems that he has two brothers, an uncle, and a cousin that acquired quite a bit of it just prior to Serenity being released onto the market."

"Then John Turner is someone we need to be looking at more closely. Mike can handle it."

"Not Alex? I just saw him leaving here. Anything I should know?"

She already knew about the Gawker picture and the shady video, and he thought about telling her about Cara's run-in with Greg, but for some reason that seemed wrong. Like he'd be betraying Cara somehow by sharing. "Nope."

"What's Alex pursuing?"

"Something personal."

"Is this about little Cara Michal?"

"It's about me and my personal privacy," he said.

Deena smiled, but it didn't quite reach her eyes.

Cara worked nonstop all afternoon. When she finally stopped she had a kink in her neck and the sun had already begun to dip low in the sky behind the massive glass-and-steel skyscrapers that lined the street. Her stomach growled and she looked at the time on her computer. It was already close to seven. The time Branden had said he wanted her at his place for a dinner date. No way.

She still hadn't eaten anything and the two bottles of water she drank weren't keeping her full any longer. Her head was even beginning to feel a little light.

After kissing Branden, she'd avoided leaving her office all day, but she was going to have to go find something to eat before she passed out. She'd made up her mind for sure somewhere around three o'clock that she absolutely would not be making an appearance at his apartment at seven, even for a quick drink and conversation. It was borrowing trouble and she had enough already. She picked up her bag and switched off her computer and her office light and headed out for the night. She'd stop at the food cart in front and pick up a bagel or something to tide her over until she got home.

The halls were quiet, but there was plenty of evidence that not everyone had packed up and left. She heard muffled voices and the whirring sounds of copy and fax machines behind closed doors. She smelled the strong coffee still brewing for those who were planning a long night.

She slipped into an open elevator, grateful she was

alone. That only lasted a couple of floors. On the third floor, a man she barely recognized stepped in. Then on the second floor, two men entered. Cara recognized one of them but didn't know his name. She thought he might have been at the party at Branden's place, but wasn't quite sure.

They looked at her, then each other as if they were trying to keep from laughing. She ignored them and stared at the buttons until the G finally lit up and the doors slid open. As she exited, one of the men said, "Gotta thank our mutual friend for sending me that video link. I don't know what the equivalent of an Emmy in porn is, but I'd vote for you."

Cara stopped dead in her tracks, shock freezing her bones. She willed herself to keep walking, but she just couldn't do it. Instead, she turned to face her accusers and studied them closely. They had bags under their forty-something-year-old eyes, broken blood vessels on the sides of their noses that indicated a lot of drinking or a lot of snorting, and bellies that protruded over the top of their pants.

Nothing she could say would make their lives any more pathetic, she told herself. She finally just turned and left.

Once she was out on the street she blinked back tears. She'd worked so hard to get where she was, but a whiff of scandal had eradicated her reputation in less than twenty-four hours. Just like her father, she was being unfairly charged and convicted of a crime she hadn't committed.

But unlike her father, she wasn't going to succumb to the pressure and become a victim.

She couldn't change what had happened. But what now?

Tell Branden about the innuendoes? Part of her wanted

him to beat the crap out of those little shits, but was that what she really wanted?

Her father had allowed the gossips to overrun his life. He'd hidden behind lawyers to protect him and had refused to fight to clear his name. She didn't want that to be her.

No, she wanted to take charge.

She wanted to live her life the way *she* wanted—*truly wanted*—for a change.

And that meant Branden Duke.

But how she wanted him, she wasn't quite sure. Yes, he'd triggered all her sexual instincts and desires—and *then* some—but her attraction to him went a little deeper. The way he almost toyed with her, reeling her in as if she were a fish hooked on a line but then letting her go . . . as if he himself were suddenly the fish and she in charge of the line . . . that sense of give and take, of *trust*, that's what had her focused on him. Not just his drop-dead sexy body.

And yet what about all the women who'd been photographed draped over him? What about Deena Raj? Jealousy had her stomach turning, and she wondered why.

Why would she be jealous?

Why would she care if the man she desired was desired by other women? Wouldn't that simply confirm that she had excellent taste in men?

But she knew the truth, even as it rapped her on the head.

Branden Duke meant more to her than a man whose physique she desired.

She liked him.

It was as simple as that.

There was something compelling about him . . . something that drew her to him, made her want to learn more, propelled her to seek him out even as the steady part of her mind—the old part of who she was—said to steer clear.

She liked him.

She took a deep breath of the crisp night air, feeling reckless and thankful to Tweedledum and Tweedledee back there. They'd convinced her Branden was right— everyone already thought she'd slept with him. That meant she had nothing to lose by going after what she wanted.

But she had a whole lot to gain.

Dinner was just the beginning.

Chapter Ten

Branden looked at the Seth Thomas clock on the wall over the fireplace in his living room. It was seven forty. He'd already eaten the gourmet meal his personal chef had prepared and had put the remainder away in the Sub-Zero fridge. Time to accept Cara wasn't coming. Funny how the realization made his chest burn with disappointment.

Probably for the best.

Yeah, he wanted to get to know her better—*and* wanted her in his bed, but she *was* his employee. Plus, regardless of how strong his attraction to Cara was, he didn't want a traditional relationship, and she seemed the kind who would. His mother had proven to him the hard way that marriage was a farce. To stand at the top of a church aisle, in front of God and family and community, and promise a lifetime of adoration and monogamy and all that bullshit not once, not twice, not three times, but six fucking times? Sure, some might think him a cynic, but with the divorce rate in the U.S. as high as 40 to 50 percent, he figured he was more a realist.

His middle sister, Rachel, constantly told him he'd

simply never been in love, had never felt that intense draw to another person. During one heated argument, Rachel called him a cynic. He'd disagreed and demanded she get back to her studies. With a smile and a hug, of course. She did, but still would occasionally whisper, "cynic" when she knew he could hear.

He took his beer and started to head out on the balcony, only to stop when the intercom buzzed. He activated it. "Yes?"

Nolan, his doorman, said, "Sir, Miss Michal is on her way up."

Branden's heart beat double time and the burn of disappointment that had sat heavy in his chest turned into an inferno of anticipation. "Thanks, Nolan," he said. He tried to remember when he had been so excited at the prospect of spending time with a woman before. He couldn't come up with one. Something about Cara had wormed its way under his skin and taken root. Maybe Rachel was right—maybe he was a cynic. Or maybe Cara just triggered the inner horny teenage boy that lived in all men.

He opened his front door just as the elevator down the hall slid open, slowly revealing Cara to him.

She was looking at him with those wide blue eyes of hers and he wasn't sure if it was fear or anger or determination he saw there. Cara had made it clear she didn't want to sleep with someone she worked for. The fact she was here, even with the worries the Gawker photo and that video had caused her, meant she was as obsessed with him as he was with her. He was glad. He'd never felt the things he felt for her with another woman. Like she was somehow essential to his well-being. Like it wouldn't matter how rich he was. How close to his siblings. How successful. If he didn't have her by his side, in his life, he'd be an empty shell.

Given his musings about commitment just moments

before, that was a problem. But it wasn't one he was going to dwell on now.

"I'm glad you decided to come."

She stepped off the elevator and walked toward him. Her movements and the look in her eyes were that of a skittish animal, and he willed the elevator doors to close quicker behind her. He was afraid she was about to run out on him. So he waited. Held still. And hoped she didn't turn and punch the down button.

She stepped past him and inside.

He shut the door, then helped her remove her coat, placing it on a hanger in the hall closet before turning around and saying, "I'm sorry. You missed dinner. I thought you weren't coming, so I ate without you. But I could rustle up something if you'd like. And I can certainly offer you a drink."

For a few moments she glanced around the room, looking everywhere but at him, then finally settled down, meeting his gaze. "I wasn't going to come, you know."

And it hit him, hard and warm in the chest. She wasn't talking about a dinner date. "What changed your mind?"

Dropping her gaze, she cleared her throat. "I'm not sure you want to know."

He reached out and placed a finger under her chin, pulling her head up until she again met his gaze. "Tell me."

A deep sigh sent her chest rising, then tension seemed to ebb from her. She nodded. "Fine. But I don't want you to do anything about it. Promise?"

Yeah, right. How many times had he heard that line from one of his stepsiblings? They'd always ended up loving it when he beat the crap out of whomever was bullying them. He slid his hand down the column to her neck and the flirty bow on her blouse. He toyed with it for a few seconds, then slid his hand across her shoulder and down her arm, finally stopping to hook his pinky with hers. "I promise not to do anything unless it's absolutely necessary."

A smile ghosted across her lips as she stared at their joined fingers. "A few men got in the elevator at D&M with me."

"And?" he prodded, but he could see where this was going.

"And they made references to the video. Referred to a 'mutual friend' who told them about it, and I can only assume they meant Greg. They tried to do the male-dominance thing and make me feel like I was the size of an ant. And worth as much as a breadcrumb."

Anger tore at him, churning in his gut. Cara didn't deserve any of this. As a self-made business mogul, he'd grown used to the rumors and innuendoes and paid a great deal of money to keep the nasty shit people made up about him out of the hands of the media, but Cara didn't have his resources. Or the experience in dealing with this kind of crap.

But as she raised her chin again and stared at him, a gleam of feistiness in her eyes and strength in her jaw, he realized what she did have was backbone.

"I take it you don't want me to go out and defend your honor? Beat the shit out of the assholes?" he guessed, a half smile tweaking the side of his mouth. Because, God, he sure as hell wanted to.

She grinned back then, her eyes glinting. "You're sweet. And yes, I did have fantasies of you pounding their asses, but I don't want you to take them on. Because . . ."

He waited.

"Because their comments made me realize something."

"And that is?"

"People already think I'm sleeping with you."

"I'd made that point earlier today."

"I know."

"What's changed?"

Surprising him, she rose up on her toes and pressed her lips to his. The shock made him freeze for a second, and she pulled back a little, as his heart rate sped up and his breath came out in a harsh rush.

"What's changed is that I realized I've been following a pattern most of my life. I've avoided conflict. Done everything I can to eliminate gossip in my life. Been a good girl. And look where that's gotten me? A bad reputation, whether I earned it or not. And more important . . ."

She slid her body closer to his and he reacted—going hard instantly. But he knew what he didn't want her to say. Knew he didn't want her to tell him she wanted to sleep with him because her reputation was already compromised. But he waited . . . wondered . . . held his breath hoping that somehow the desire he had for Cara that went beyond the physical was reciprocated.

"But what I realized was more important," she continued, her breath a warm hush against the side of his neck, "was that I'd allowed my interpretation of others' opinions to guide my decisions. I stopped going for what I wanted. I held myself back. And I don't want to do that anymore."

"What are you trying to tell me here, Cara?" he asked, tightening his jaw to stay in control.

"I'm trying to say that earlier today, I wanted to accept your dinner invitation without reservation. I wanted to get to know you, too, the way you say you want to get to know me."

Her hands were now on his shoulders, and her breasts were pressed up to his chest. Her hips were undulating in a slow, sensual rhythm. This didn't feel like a woman who wanted to eat. He needed clarification.

"Are you saying you'd like me to fix you a sandwich and discuss politics and religion with you over a glass of wine?" he asked, barely breathing.

"No," she said, then gently bit the side of his neck. "What I'm saying is that I want you to take me," she said, her words breathy. "Take me hard."

That was all the encouragement Branden needed. He swept her into his arms and kissed her. As their tongues tangled, he moved a few steps forward until her back was against the wall and he let her slide back down to her feet. Pressing up against her, he kissed her harder and pulled her tighter against him. They kissed like they couldn't get enough of each other, like the desire between them was finally standing proud, refusing to be ignored.

As they kissed, he cupped one of her breasts and caressed it through her blouse. Then he let his hand slide down her side to the back of her thigh, lifting her leg off the floor and wrapping it around his hip. He slid his hand to her ass and pulled her in even tighter. She rocked her hips against him.

His hard cock pressed against her, aching to get out. He slid his hand under her blouse, touching her stomach and causing her body to quiver. His fingers moved over the band of her bra before brushing across her protruding nipples. Then he slipped his hand underneath the band so he could play with her bare breasts. She moaned and bit down on his bottom lip.

God, he felt like a man who had been in the desert for weeks without water and he'd finally found his oasis. Each kiss and each brush of his hand against her amazingly soft, supple body made him more desperate. He wanted to touch more, kiss more. He wanted more of her, period.

Their clothes were obstacles he wanted to be rid of. He needed to feel their naked bodies together. He needed to feel those luscious breasts and hard nipples pressing against his chest.

He let out a growl, a sound he couldn't recall making before. He undid the two buttons on her jacket and pushed it off. There were too many buttons on her shirt and they were tiny, causing him to fumble. Shaking with need, he grabbed hold of the top of her shirt, right where the bow was, and ripped. Her buttons flew across the floor, causing a *tap-tap* sound as they did. She didn't seem to notice. Reaching behind her, he unhooked her bra and tore that off, as well.

He picked her up again, but this time didn't nudge her gently against the wall.

She'd demanded he take her.

So he would.

Need riding him hard, he slammed her against it and held her there as she tightly wrapped her legs around the backs of his legs, kicking her shoes off as she did. He could feel her wiggling against him, trying to feel his erection against her pelvis as his mouth covered one of her breasts. She put her hands on the sides of his face and pulled him into her. He took as much of her breast in his mouth as he could while using his tongue to flick and lick and tease her nipple. He was sucking roughly, and he had her pinned tightly against the wall so she couldn't move. It seemed to excite her because she moaned low and long.

He vowed he was going to make her scream his name.

Cara blinked when Branden abruptly set her on her feet. Heat filled her veins, weakening her knees, and she reached for him before realizing he'd backed away only to pull off his shirt. As the fabric slid over his pecs, he was even more gorgeous and ripped than he'd been in that video. She reached out to touch his chest, but before she could, he lowered his head and began to hungrily devour her breasts even as he unzipped her skirt and pushed it down, leaving her in her lacy thong. She shivered, and he manipulated her nipple with his mouth, switching attention from one to the other, working them between his lips before pulling back to flick them with his tongue. Sucking then licking. Sucking then licking. Again and again he repeated the pattern, going back and forth between each of her breasts as if to treat them fairly.

The harder he sucked and the more he used his teeth, the wetter she got between her legs. She was on fire there, craving the same kind of attention her breasts and nipples were getting. She ran her hands slowly up his arms and down to his chest but he stopped her by grabbing her arms and holding them down as he continued his sweet torment of her nipples.

She pulled in a ragged breath. God, how was it she'd come this undone with a man? How was it she'd all but ordered him to take her, instead of accepting the drink and snack he'd offered? This wasn't her. At all.

But it was, her conscience countered, refusing to let her be dishonest with herself. She'd wanted to be with a bad boy, to be bad, all her life. That's what her crush on Tony Spokane had been about. And now this gorgeous, sexy, amazing man wanted *her*.

She'd held her world so steady all these years. Worked hard to make life better for her, her mother, and her brother after her father's financial, emotional, and physical collapse. She'd managed to quash the wild side of her, but it had only led to an unwavering feeling of dissatisfaction with her life. And it had taken this man to make her acknowledge that dissatisfaction and do something about it.

What she felt for Branden was more than a desire for sexual release. Her vibrator could do that for her. No, this need, this want, was about the man who held her in his arms. Who was teasing her nipples into taut, tight buds.

A man who intrigued her. Who made her feel safe even as he exuded an air of danger. The lure of letting him be strong for her had her shaking with want. With need.

Sensing her distraction, Branden raised his head and stared down at her with a fierce expression. "Having second thoughts?"

She had been. She wasn't anymore.

"No," she said breathlessly. "I want this. I need it," she admitted.

"It? Is this about scratching an itch? Anyone would do?"

It would be safer if that were true. It's what she should make him believe. But as she looked into his eyes and saw more than desire—saw a genuine respect and affection for her—she knew she couldn't bear to have him think that.

"No one on Earth can make me feel what you do, Branden. And I need more. Please."

He grinned. "Hang on, baby. Because you think it feels good now? Just you wait and see."

He returned to sucking her nipples, making her hiss and moan, at both his touch and the echo of his words. She was at odds with her own emotions, uncertain about how dominant he was being and completely excited about it. He certainly wasn't inflicting any pain on her, and she felt foolish for her resistance when he seemed to want nothing but to heap pleasure on her body. She forced herself to block out her reservations and closed her eyes, reveling in the exciting sensations her body was experiencing.

"Yes . . ." she whispered, and his hands wrapped around her wrists, holding them down at her sides. Tethering her to him.

Commanding her.

Eventually he picked her up and carried her into his bedroom and placed her on his tall, wide bed. Once she was lying there on her back, he grabbed her panties and pulled them down. She was lying completely nude as his chocolate brown eyes raked across her body, pausing on her vee long enough to make her tremble.

He caressed her face, then held her long hair in his hand, holding on to it firmly, but not tugging or pulling. It didn't hurt, but held her in a steady position as he bent forward to kiss her neck.

She gasped as waves of pleasure coursed through her.

He released her hair and knelt between her legs, then used his knees to press her legs apart just before she heard the rattle of a condom package. Then his hands were on her hips and his throbbing cock was pressing against her opening.

She was soaking wet, but tight enough that he had to guide his cock in with his hand. Once the head of his cock was inside of her he moved his hand and entered her slowly. He penetrated her fully, waited several seconds, then pulled completely out before doing it again.

She thought he was just getting her used to him, but even when it was obvious her body had adjusted and she was grinding back against him in desperation, he continued to undulate into her slowly. Sensually. Holding back his passion, letting hers build.

The feeling of him hard inside of her along with the heat of his breath on her face drove her crazy. She moved her hips, trying to get him to move faster, harder, but the more she writhed, the slower he went. Finally, just about the time she thought she would lose her mind, he began to speed up his movements. His hips slammed against hers roughly with each thrust. She was right there on the verge of an orgasm when he suddenly pulled back.

"No. What are you—"

"I have more to give you. Places I want you to go."

He pulled out of her then, and didn't say anything even as she whimpered. He just pushed her legs open wider and positioned himself in between them. He spread her pussy lips open with his fingers and his tongue was suddenly on her clit. He flicked it then ran it across the edges of her lips. She tried to shift her position, trying to get him to put his tongue inside of her, but he was relentless with his assault of her clit, and the more she moved the tighter his grip became on her legs. She was moaning loudly now, ready to come just as he plunged a finger into her. He continued to lick and suck on her clit as he slid first one and then two and then three fingers in and out of her. She almost came . . . she was so close . . . and then he stopped. She wanted to scream.

Her body was shaking all over as he straightened, leaned in close to her ear, and said, "Do you want to come, Cara?"

"Yes."

"Do you want *me* to come?"

"Yes."

"Where do you want me to come?"

"Inside of me . . ."

"Ask me."

"Oh, God, Branden, come inside of me."

"Beg me."

"Please, Branden, oh, God, please . . . I can't stand it any longer. I need to come, please make me come. Please come inside of me!"

Reaching underneath her, he lifted her hips, raising her core to him, then slipped his cock inside her. She gasped with delight as he began moving his hips. She moved hers, too, and they soon got into a rhythm. This time, the more she thrust against him, the harder he thrust into her. She was crying out and ready to come, harder than she ever had in her life, when she finally felt his body tense and his cock pulse inside of her. They both came then, with an intensity almost too great to bear given the way their bodies shook and the sounds that spilled out of them.

She drifted on a haze of fulfillment.

Feeling like every worry in her life had ceased to exist.

Longing to spend the rest of eternity just luxuriating in his arms.

Chapter Eleven

Cara hadn't meant to fall asleep. She hadn't meant to spend the night. Hot, sweaty sex with the boss was one thing; spending the night in his swanky Manhattan apartment was entirely something else. To make matters worse, she woke up less than two hours before she had to be at work, tangled up so tightly in his arms and legs that she couldn't even sneak out.

"Branden . . ."

"Hmm?"

"I need to get up."

"Huh-uh," he mumbled sleepily.

She shifted and came up to rest on her elbows. Next to her, on his side, slightly curled around her form, lay Branden. With his body fully relaxed and his eyes shut, lashes soft on his cheeks, he looked almost . . . vulnerable.

How incongruent from the strong, dominating man who'd taken her so roughly and thoroughly just a few hours before.

A lightness filled her, as if her heart were floating inside her chest.

"Um . . . yeah, I have to go."

He stirred, but just slightly, and his eyes stayed shut. Softly, he said, "I don't want you to get up. I like you underneath me."

She laughed. "Yeah, you made that pretty obvious. But I have to get ready for work."

"Is your boss a really big jerk?"

"He's not that big," she joked.

He moved his legs. As he did, she felt the brush of his semihard erection against her thigh. He opened his beautiful brown eyes, looked into hers, and smiled. "Good morning," he said.

"Good morning," she said back, and then she sat all the way up. He wrapped his arm around her waist and pulled her back toward him, sliding his hand up across her breast as he did.

"Stop that. I have to go!" she scolded.

"Five minutes," he said like a child who didn't want to get out of bed and go to school.

"Considering last night, I doubt you could stick to that time limit."

"That was a fluke," he said with a grin. "Usually I'm only good for three or four minutes."

"You're lying to get me back in bed," she said. With a moan she added, "And the way you're rubbing that nipple is not helping, either."

"I admit to lying," he said. "But rubbing the nipple is helping. It's helping me . . ."

She turned toward him and planted a soft kiss on his lips. He loosened his grip on her and she squirmed away and jumped out of the bed.

He groaned and tried to reach out and grab her again just as his intercom buzzed. "Shit, it's too early." He put the pillow over his head while Cara left the bedroom, presumably to get her clothes. He groaned in disappointment when she walked back in, clothed and pulling on her jacket, buttoning it up since her shirt buttons were still scattered on the floor.

"It's kind of hard to see how you do so well on Wall Street. You know . . . the early bird and all that."

He took the pillow down far enough to glower at her, then the buzzer rang once more. He rolled over and pushed a button next to his bed and snapped out, "What?"

"I'm sorry, sir. Mr. Alex Samuels is here. He says it's important."

Branden groaned and swiped a hand over his face. "Send him up, Nolan. And I'm sorry I was so short with you."

"Not a problem, sir. I'm not a morning person myself."

Cara caught Branden's eye as he turned back to her. "Um . . . Alex, as in one of the people you brought with you when you bought D&M? As in, a guy from the office?" Last night she'd defied the potential rumormongers and had gone for what she wanted. Branden. But advertising she was indeed sleeping with the boss wasn't such a great idea.

"Yeah, he's part of my internal team, but it's okay. Alex is a friend. He would never say anything about seeing you here," he told her as he swung his long legs over the side of the bed.

Cara couldn't help herself; she had to let her eyes wander over him one last time.

He noticed her look and said, "I'll send him away in a heartbeat if you come back to bed."

She rolled her eyes and laughed. "That's blackmail."

He shrugged and said, "Whatever it takes."

She came over to where he sat and leaned down so that her lips met his. "I'm going to use your bathroom and then sneak out while you keep your guest busy."

"I'll only need a few minutes with Alex. Wait for me and I'll take you."

"I live down the street, so I hardly need an escort. Plus, I still need to shower and get ready for work."

"I'll forgive you if you're late."

"But Mike won't. Your new office manager has us all scared. And despite what I said yesterday, I don't want people—well, any more people than necessary—talking about me. I'd prefer we be discreet about what happened."

He caught her wrist in a tight grip and held her in place. "What's going to *continue* to happen, you mean."

When she said nothing, he drew out her name warningly. "Cara?"

"I'm just thinking," she said swiftly. "Last night was amazing. Of course it was. But . . ."

He stood, and with no concern for his nudity or the fact that he had a friend on his way up, placed his hands gently on her shoulders.

"But nothing. I want to see you again. Dinner. Drinks. Trips to the opera. But mostly naked. In my arms. Taking me deep inside you. Shaking and shuddering as I make you come."

God, that sounded great. More than great. A part of her hungered to be wanted so intensely, but a part of her pulled away. She could see why she was so attracted to this man, but why was he attracted to her? "Why?"

He frowned. "Pardon?"

"Why me? Even with everything that's going on? The gossip and the video . . ."

"You're amazing. Strong. Beautiful."

"I'm not as beautiful as Deena." Oh, God. She wanted to clap a hand over her insecure mouth. This hesitation on her end wasn't about her being jealous, was it?

He dropped his hands and bit out a laugh. Stepped back. Reached for the robe that hung on the back of the bedroom door and put it on. "That's ridiculous. You have nothing to worry about with Deena."

"Yet you just pulled away and dressed when I mentioned her." Like he was feeling guilty and wanted to hide it.

Her instincts had to be right—he was hiding something, of that she was certain. But what?

His mouth twisted, humor appearing there. Humor about Deena, or was he laughing at her obvious jealousy? "I repeat—you have nothing to worry about. You want me. I want you. That's all that matters."

She groped for yet another excuse. "But for how long?"

His eyebrow rose. "It's a little early for vows of forever, isn't it?"

Her cheeks flushed hot. She hadn't wanted to sound like one of those clingy, demanding women, but somehow jealousy and insecurity had laced her words ever since he'd implied he wanted to continue their adventure from the night before. But it was too much. Too intense. She couldn't go there—not with someone like Branden. Someone passionate, intelligent, amazing in bed, and intense . . . and with a hidden past. She needed someone safe.

But she hated boring.

"That's not what I'm suggesting. I—I—" she stammered, then added, "Forget it." She turned and headed to the door, but she didn't make it before he caught her.

"Calm down. Tell me what you meant."

"You're my boss. What happens when this ends? Or when you get tired of people speculating about us?" She jutted her chin out but wouldn't look him in the eye. "And I'm not talking about a relationship—I'm talking about my professional reputation. Last night I was willing to take a risk, and, God"—she swallowed hard—"that risk was so worth it, but you know what they say about the cold light of day. Things look a little different now."

He turned her in his arms. Gently lifted her chin so she would look at him. "No matter what happens with us personally, I will always do right by you as far as your job is concerned. I promise, Cara."

Someone rang the buzzer on the door and she jerked. Looked down. "Fine."

He growled in frustration. "Not fine. Look into my eyes. Tell me you believe me."

Reluctantly, she stared into his eyes. Saw the truth there. Something inside her melted a bit. "Okay. I believe you," she said.

"Thank you." After kissing her softly and slowly, as if he didn't care that Alex had just buzzed again, he pulled back. "I'll see you later."

She didn't confirm his assumption, just said, "Distract him so I can get out of here."

"I haven't done this since I was a kid and trying to sneak a girl out before my sisters saw her."

"Your sisters? Not your mom?"

His face closed up, then he said, "Not sure my mom would have noticed. She was too busy finding my next stepfather. Currently she's working on ex-husband number six. I have five sisters—two of them half sisters, three stepsisters."

"*Five* sisters?"

He cocked an eye at her. "What, I don't seem like the kind of man who has sisters?"

She tipped her head and scrutinized him. Maybe he did, at that. But wait—what was it he'd said? "A kid, huh?"

His expression smoothed out. "Well, a teenager. Surely you snuck boys in or vice versa in high school?"

"Um . . . no, I was a little too busy for such things."

"Busy with what?" he asked. Thankfully, before she

could figure out how to evade answering questions about her painful teenage years, the doorbell rang yet again. "Damn it, Alex, I'm coming!" He sighed as he cupped her face. Gently, he stroked a strand of hair off her cheek and tucked it behind her ear. "We'll talk later, Cara. Promise me."

"We'll talk later," she said. "I promise." She just wasn't sure they'd ever have a repeat of the night before.

No matter how much her body craved it. How much her mind yearned to get to know him. How much her heart raced when mere thoughts of him crossed her mind.

Dropping his hand, he went out to answer the door. She heard another man's voice say, "Did I wake you?"

"Yeah, come into the kitchen. I need coffee."

"What are you doing sleeping so late? Even in college you got up at dawn. Are you sick?"

Cara peeked through a crack in the bedroom door as the men headed for the kitchen. She was surprised when she saw Branden's friend. He had on a short-sleeved, blue T-shirt and both of his arms were completely covered in colorful tattoos. He was wearing a NY Mets cap and a pair of faded blue jeans with holes in the knees. He was really nice looking from what she could see, and he had a body a lot of professional athletes would be jealous of. The perfect kind of guy for Iris.

He certainly didn't look like the type of guy Branden would be friends with.

Of course, how much did she know about Branden Duke? Other than he was fabulously rich, incredible in bed, and seemingly a nice guy in spite of those two things.

In other words, he seemed too good to be true.

Which meant he probably was.

* * *

Branden heard the door snick closed behind Cara. Done distracting Alex, he set up the coffee to brew and then dropped down into one of the kitchen chairs. Alex was giving him a strange look.

"What?"

"Did you get drunk last night?"

"No," Branden said.

"Laid?"

"What do you have for me?"

Alex had a manila envelope in his hand. "You got laid. You make me sick."

"Shut up," he said mildly. "You're on the clock. What's in the envelope?"

Alex gave him a dirty look but then suddenly turned all business. "I haven't been able to find much on Greg Johnson. He seems to be one of those guys that are so plain and average you forget they're even in the room. He's thirty-three, no kids, never married—"

"What about his finances?"

"So far they look squeaky clean. He makes a hell of a lot as a stockbroker."

"So we don't suspect he got mixed up with a loan shark or something like that?"

"Not that I could find," Alex said.

"Then it probably didn't happen." Branden had absolute faith in Alex's abilities. "Keep looking, though. Look more recently."

"Sure, man, I'll look into it all."

"What's in the envelope?" Branden finally asked.

Alex held it out to him. "Lee sent it. It's the investigation he was doing for you."

Branden took the envelope. "Thanks. I think the coffee's ready. You want a cup?"

"Nah, I'm good," Alex said. "I need to get home and change before I go into the office."

"Ralph Lauren?" Branden asked.

"Patrick James," Alex said with a grin. "Your sister's been a big help. Steered me clear of Tommy Bahama. Said it was too casual for the top floor."

"Got something there you want to tell me?"

"Don't wear a palm tree print to the office. Gotta go." With that, Alex slapped his hand on the table, stood, and took off, dashing a wave over his shoulder as he exited the kitchen.

Damn the man. Branden thought the world of Alex, but hey—this was one of his sisters they were talking about. The desire to protect Deena, Leslie, Rachel, Bethany, and Jeannette ran deep. Had for years.

Not like their mother ever did shit to protect the girls.

He flicked off a quick text to Leslie: *Wassup with you and Alex? Clothes shopping? Srsly?*

Two seconds later, she'd responded. *He can't help that he's style-challenged. I'm just giving him some guidance.*

He chuckled and typed in a response. *Not what I'm talking about. I demand you tell me what's up.*

Nunya. As in, none of your business. Let the man be. And stop telling me what to do. You're a pain.

His response was quick. *Pain in the ass if you don't stop dating my friends.*

The reply from Leslie was a grumpy cat face.

He grinned as he poured himself a cup of coffee, then sat down at the kitchen table with the envelope his friend had left. It was the report on Cara, like the others on all the employees he'd had compiled, standard for when he purchased a company. At a glance, it looked like it spanned her twenty-six years and then some. He read through the first few pages, basic stuff like family, demographics, etc. He skipped over high school and jumped right to where a name was highlighted.

Hank Finch.

What the hell?

Cara's father's name was Hank Finch. His was a name

Branden thought he would never hear again. Branden read on, searching for confirmation that his suspicions were correct.

Yep, there on page two was what he'd thought the moment he read the name. Cara's father was the same man his own stepfather had destroyed years ago.

Davies had been just one in a long string of men Branden's mother had hooked up with and foolishly married.

How small was the world that Cara had been a victim of Carl Davies? Did she change her name to Michal because of what had happened or had her mother remarried?

And did Cara know Branden was connected to the man who had ruined her father's life?

He leaned back, contemplating the question. He doubted it. She'd never once given him any reason to think she knew his past, and he paid well to have the Internet scrubbed clean of anything he didn't want out there. And he certainly didn't want the world to know his once tenuous connection to Davies.

But he and Cara had been trying to figure out who would want to hurt them. Maybe they both had been coming at it from the wrong angle. He'd assumed any threat was coming from paparazzi. Someone looking to make some cash.

What if this had something to do with Carl Davies?

Now that he knew there was a connection between him and Cara, he would need to take a look from that angle. He wouldn't be the least bit surprised to find that his stepfather was still dipping his toes in the shady side of the pond.

But why would Davies come around now, all of a sudden?

And why pick on Cara, too?

Chapter Twelve

Despite the adventures of the night before, Cara made it home in time to shower and change and get into work and behind her desk an hour early. She even had her coffee in hand. She sat down and booted up the computer as she shrugged out of her light morning jacket. Taking a sip of her coffee, she leaned back in her chair and let her mind wander back to last night. She really shouldn't be surprised at how intensely she'd responded to Branden in bed. He'd alternately been sweet and dominating, giving and then taking, and taking hard.

He couldn't have gotten where he was at such a young age if he didn't have a dominant personality.

What she was mostly surprised at was herself. She'd had dreams of being sexually satisfied before, mostly since she'd met Branden, but she'd never really thought she'd be able to let go of her control to actually let her body respond in such a visceral, wild way. Or that once she did she would love it as much as she had.

But even more surprising than how sexually her body had reacted was the way her mind kept returning to thoughts of him—memories of how his eyes would light up or go dark . . . how earthy and spicy his scent was . . .

how he'd shown a vulnerable side when he spoke of his sisters . . .

Iris would say she was crushing on this dude, and big time.

Was she?

She forced herself to pull up the spreadsheet she needed to work on today. She worked through the morning without interruption, and at eleven thirty her cellphone rang. It was Iris, wanting to meet for lunch at the food cart outside Cara's office. After Cara promised not to be late, she hung up and dove back into the spreadsheet for another half hour, then finished up the report. She stood, then as she came around the side of her desk, she knocked her cellphone off. She bent over to grab it, and just to prove that the universe was conspiring against her or that fate just liked to fuck with her, Branden walked in while she was bent over.

"The view in here is much nicer than in my office," he said.

She stood up quickly and smoothed down her skirt, as if he hadn't seen everything she had to offer there last night and then some.

Feeling herself blush, she said, "I dropped my phone. What's up?"

Looking amused, he said, "I came to take you to lunch."

She felt a girlish rush of pleasure flow through her, then tamped it back down. She needed time to think. To process. To back away from the ecstasy that had been the night before and rationalize all that had happened. "I'm sorry, but I made other plans."

He frowned. "Cancel them."

Cara felt a tickle of annoyance in the pit of her stomach. That was a clear order. She'd enjoyed being taken hard last night, but what happens in bed should be different from what happens in the workplace. "I appreciate the offer to take me to lunch," she said slowly, "but I don't want to change my plans."

"Where are you going?" he asked.

"To lunch."

He folded his arms. "You know what I mean."

She folded hers, too, and said, "Yes, I do know what you mean. I'm just confused as to why it would be your business." God, she sounded like a shrew, but keeping an upper hand felt important. Years ago, she'd watched as her father caved in front of public meetings. That would never be her.

"And I'm confused as to why it would be such a big mystery. Do you have a date?"

Wait—was Branden *jealous*? The girlish warmth tickled her tummy again. Not what she needed right now. She struggled to hang on to her frustration, needing Branden to understand she would not be walked all over. "I'm meeting my friend Iris downstairs for a hot dog. See, no mystery. Now your turn."

He shrugged. "Now that we're not worried about people seeing us together, I just thought you'd be safer with me."

She wasn't certain she wanted to be seen out with him. Wasn't anywhere near ready to take that step. But wait, what had Branden said about her safety? "Is someone threatening my safety?"

"No, not physically. But people will be less likely to make snarky comments to you if you're with me."

"You're right. I doubt they'd even dare. But you can't follow me around protecting me twenty-four-seven."

"Why not?" he asked. He asked that a lot. She didn't doubt he'd asked it thousands of times in his life—assuming that many people had actually had the balls to tell him he couldn't do something.

"You just can't. I have a life. I've been standing on my own two feet for quite some time now. I can handle it."

He raised an eyebrow like he didn't believe her, and she wondered if it was the statement that she had a life he doubted or the statement that she could handle things. Either thought riled her. She'd worked hard ever since her father's unjust accusation, his subsequent death, and the collapse of her mother and ultimately her brother. Yes, she'd enjoyed being taken hard, against the wall, last night, but that didn't mean she was a panty-waist. Some weak, fluttery woman batting her eyelashes at any man who offered to hold open a door for her.

She could open her own doors. She didn't need Branden Duke to do it for her. "Iris is waiting for me," she said firmly, and jutted her chin in the air as she stalked out of the room.

He begrudgingly stepped away from the door, but just enough that it would be a tight fit when she passed. Controlling her? Or just wanting to touch her again? She wanted the latter but was afraid of the former. She turned her back to him and she could actually feel his breath on the back of her neck as she squeezed by. Didn't matter—she had to make her own way. She couldn't let a man—even Branden Duke—take control of her life. She'd fought too long for independence. To never allow anyone to have such control over her that she'd fall apart if the control was abused. Twisted.

That's what had happened to her dad, and look where that got him. Six feet under, a grieving widow, a son with schizophrenia, and a daughter who was wound so tight she felt like she could explode.

She stewed about the encounter with Branden all the way down in the elevator, and by the time she met Iris in front of the hot dog cart outside, she was practically livid.

"Hey girl! How is life as a financial wizard treating you today?"

"It sucks," Cara snapped, then regretted her tone. It wasn't Iris's fault her world was in upheaval.

"Uh-oh. What happened?"

"Two words," Cara told her. "Branden Duke."

Iris ordered her hot dog and Cara got a salted pretzel with cheese. They walked down Broad Street to Bowling Green and sat on a bench near the *Charging Bull*. It was surrounded by a group of Chinese tourists posing for pictures. The sound of their Mandarin language was like background music, reassuring. Settling.

Cara realized her tension had abated, and focused her attention on her friend. "What are you doing in Manhattan in the middle of the day? You usually avoid this area like the plague. You've said you're allergic to dollar bills."

Iris grinned around a mouthful of hot dog. "I've got an interview at one of the restaurants on the Street."

"Oh good. You'll make a lot better tips down here than you do in Brooklyn."

"Yeah, I like my cheap regulars, but I can't live off them," Iris said with a grin. "So what's up with you and Branden?" she asked. "Is it work, or personal?"

Cara sighed, dipped her pretzel into her cheese cup, took a bite, and sighed again.

"Oh my God! You had sex with Branden Duke!"

"Shh!" Cara said, looking around. "Why don't you just get up on the bull's backside and announce it to the entire Financial District?"

Lowering her voice, Iris said, "I'm sorry, but you did, didn't you?"

"Maybe, but I'm beginning to think it was a mistake."

Iris laughed. "When did it happen? I want details."

"Iris!"

"Not a blow by blow. Eww! I mean how did it happen? Who initiated it? Was he romantic?"

Cara thought about that. Absolutely. But there were other words to describe Branden Duke.

Passionate. Sexy. Erotic.

Even a little vulnerable

She shivered just thinking about the night before and said, "Yes, he was romantic. He actually invited me up for dinner. But I passed. In fact . . ." She hesitated. Iris would typically share all sorts of details about her dates with Cara, even going into explicit detail about the sexual activities she engaged in, but Cara was typically more circumspect. Although, given her decision the evening before, after those two jerkoffs had made their crude statements, to go for what she wanted, maybe it would be good to tell Iris about her activities. That's what she wanted to do, to tell the truth. Share a little of herself with her friend.

"I actually initiated it. Jumped his bones the minute I showed up at his apartment."

"Go Cara! I knew it was about time your dam broke."

Her insides quivered. Fluttered. Sent electric shocks throughout her body as she recalled the fabulous sex the night before. But then Branden's dominating attitude from earlier swept into her mind, and her body chilled. "Maybe I should have listened to my gut and kept him a fantasy, though." She stared at her half-eaten pretzel.

"Why? Was sex that bad?"

"Last night was . . . fabulous."

"You didn't spend the night, did you?"

She blushed. "Um, yeah, I kind of fell asleep."

"In his bed? With him there? Wait—were you in his arms? Did you have morning sex?"

"No morning sex—we both had to get to work. And yes, I spent the night, in his bed, in his arms."

"And the sex was good, right? Just looking for a little clarification here. You usually don't give me this much detail."

Cara looked off into the distance. "It wasn't just good, it was . . . delicious. He took me places I never even knew existed."

"So what's the problem?"

"It's just that . . . today he was a little controlling. Demanding. Maybe he thinks because I slept with him he all of a sudden has rights." But the memory of him sweeping the hair out of her face as she was dressing charged into her mind and wiped away the thoughts of how he'd demanded to know where she was going for lunch. Could her one thought—that he was jealous—be true? The warm and excited quivers in her tummy came back.

She glanced over and noticed Iris was smiling at her.

"What?"

"You've got it bad for this guy."

"What? I just finished telling you how arrogant he is being—"

"Yeah, but it was that light in your eyes when you said it. And you were smiling to yourself. I'll bet you anything you were remembering having sex with him . . . and liking the memory. Admit it, Cara. It's just me here. You have feelings for him. This isn't just about sex."

Oh, God, could her friend be right? But Iris lived on the edge of passion. Logic and planning weren't even on her radar. How could she be unbiased here? "I'm not sure what it's about, honestly. He affects me like no other man ever has, that's for sure. But my life has also gotten a lot more complicated since I fell asleep on his couch. The sex was amazing. He's incredibly sexy. He can even be sweet and funny. But things can't continue."

"Why not?"

She struggled to come up with an answer. "Because he's my boss."

"He was your boss when you slept with him."

"Maybe an error in judgment."

"Was it?"

She sighed. "He makes me feel like a schoolgirl. All boy crazy and crush focused. These feelings are only because he made my body reach nirvana. But honestly? It isn't that Branden is my boss, it's that I can't risk getting into a situation where I end up leaning on someone. And with Branden, I could. It would be easy to let him take control in all ways. Too easy. And I'd get screwed in doing so."

Iris shook her head. "You're crazy, you know. That's what falling in love is all about—being vulnerable. Leaning on someone else. You don't lose yourself in the process—you grow."

"That's just not me, Iris, and you know it." Trying to change the subject, Cara said, "How's the cute neighbor?"

"He's . . . cute," Iris said. She didn't sound enthusiastic, though. It made Cara think about the man she'd seen at Branden's this morning. Alex something or other.

"I saw a man this morning and the first thing I thought was *Iris*."

"Thanks. Do I need laser hair removal or what?"

Cara laughed. "No, I mean he looked perfect for you. Like someone you could have fun with. He was all tatted up and buff and from what I could see, really attractive. He just had this kind of manly aura around him."

"Well, it's probably a good thing I wasn't there. I'm trying to avoid those types. They're the ones that get me in trouble."

"True," Cara said. She finished the last bite of her pretzel and took a long swig of her water before saying, "But then again, sometimes a little bit of trouble can be fun."

And of course, she was thinking of Branden again.

*　*　*

"You're not listening to a word I'm saying."

Branden pulled his gaze away from where he was staring out his corner office window and looked up at Deena.

"I was thinking of something else. What did you say?"

She leaned back in the guest chair in his office, crossing her legs and arms simultaneously, and cocking a brow. "Where in the world is your head today?"

With Cara. How he'd missed her at lunch. How he wanted her again, her naked body posed under him, quivering and waiting for him to plunge into her. Her face, turning to him, eyes luminescent, lips soft and curled, skin glowing . . .

"I'm listening now."

"Jeannette turned in her applications to Harvard, Stanford, and UCLA yesterday. Bethany got the lead in an Off-Broadway play that shows in three months and you're to buy the whole front row of seating. Rachel may or may not be a lesbian."

He frowned. "Lesbian?"

"*That's* what you focused on?"

Looking back out the window, he said, "I wondered when Rachel brought that girl Lili home for Christmas. They seemed rather close. All snuggled up on the couch and stroking each other's hair. I hope she knows she can tell me and I'll be supportive."

"You always are," Deena said quietly. "When I married Gerald, you weren't sure if he deserved me, but you were on my side the whole way. Walked me down the aisle, even."

He turned and smiled at her. "No man deserves one of my sisters, but Gerald is a great husband to you. I was proud to walk you down the aisle. But I'm assuming you have more to tell me than an update on our family."

She crossed a leg and frowned. "Larry Gills. He's a stockbroker. He worked at D&M almost twenty-two years before your acquisition. He used to be one of Max's biggest producers. He brought in new clients before most people were out of bed in the morning and he put the stocks to bed each night."

"And then?" Branden asked.

"And then he talked his clients into investing in the wrong stock. It seemed like a solid investment in his defense, but you know how fickle this business can be. Overnight, his personal clients with the firm lost millions. Most of them pulled out and Max took a big hit financially. He blamed Gills pretty publicly for it all. Max is a good guy, but he has a big mouth. He kept him on, but Gills never really found his stride again. He's a bit of a pariah around here. His commissions became few and far between and he ended up losing his house and the wife went with it."

"So you think Gills may have had a bone to pick with Max and he decided to do that by means of insider trading? I find that a little far-fetched."

"That's good, because that's not what I was saying, which you would have known had you let me finish."

Deena was nothing if not blunt. That bluntness had often gotten her into trouble with stepfather number one, who had no problem resorting to force to make his kids step in line. There were many times Deena had needed her older brother to have her back, and Branden had done just that. Thankfully, his other sisters' fathers weren't physically abusive, but their various addictions—ranging from drugs to gambling to sex—had still made his sisters' lives hell.

Branden had done what he could—making sure the girls were well fed, dressed, safe, and warm, even if he had to sacrifice himself.

Branden gave Deena a nod to go on.

"Larry took one of the young brokers under his wing about a year ago. His name is Rafe Sampson, and from what I hear, the kid attached himself to the old man, telling him he wanted to learn the business from someone who had been around awhile and really knew how things worked. I suppose that was what made him seem suspect to me in the first place. The kid. Why would an up-and-coming young broker attach himself to the oldest broker with the most tarnished reputation in the firm?"

"He needed a fall guy?"

"That was my thought. I'm going through the hard drives of both computers now, but I'm guessing that anything we find will be on Gills's and not Sampson's."

Again, images of Cara drifted through his mind. Not good—he needed to focus. He was supposed to be helping the SEC with its investigation of D&M. He didn't need to be distracted by a beautiful woman, no matter how amazing she was in bed. And out of it . . . "And I'm assuming you've found something already or you wouldn't be here."

"There are two dummy corporations set up offshore that Gills has been selling a lot of stock for lately. As a matter of fact, his sales have almost doubled over the past six months."

"But you're convinced Sampson is the bad guy here and not Gills? How does Gills not know these are dummies?"

"I'm convinced that Larry thinks he's just doing his job, maybe getting his stride back. Sampson is one of those charming, manipulative sociopathic types. Flatters Gills right and left, and blows smoke up his rear. You would have to meet and talk to them both and then you'll understand what I'm saying."

Something tickled the back of his mind. "Wait—what floor does Sampson work on?"

"Third." Deena gave him an odd look, as if his sudden question had held more emotion than warranted.

He placed his elbows on the desk and steepled his fingers. Deena didn't need to know about the sexual harassment Cara had experienced. Some things he could keep between him and Cara. "I don't want it to look like they're suspect. I'll go out this afternoon and make my rounds. Try to talk with them." And figure out if Sampson was one of the little shits who'd made Cara so uncomfortable. He'd promised Cara he wouldn't take action, and he planned to respect her need to control the situation, but if the man was engaging in shady deals and was the fucker who'd insulted Cara, he'd enjoy firing the man's ass.

"Good," Deena said, standing. "In the meantime, I'm going to get a list of the dates and times that these Internet sales were made in Gills's name. I'd hate to see the man doing federal time for something he didn't have anything to do with."

Branden nodded again and said, "And what about the other guy you were looking into? Turner? Did anything come of that?"

"Not yet, but we're still looking."

After Deena left, Branden let his thoughts drift back to the ones that she had interrupted. Cara had been on his mind all day. He hadn't meant to come off the way he had when he'd asked her about lunch. He knew she thought he was being a possessive, controlling jerk. He was genuinely concerned for her, if not her physical safety, then her professional reputation. If his former stepfather Davies was involved in the online harassment, there was no telling how far the man would take things. He thought about the file that Alex had given him this morning. He was still dealing with Cara being Hank Finch's daughter.

He picked up the phone and called Lee. He wasn't as close to Lee as he was to Alex, but Alex's brother had been there for him time and again, and was an excellent sleuth.

"Hey, I need you to find out where my beloved stepfather is, and what he's been up to lately."

"Sure," Lee said. "But which one?"

"Number four. The only one who didn't give me a sister." And the one, unfortunately, who was partly responsible for Branden's current financial success.

Davies had once been an integral part of his life, showing him the ropes of investment at an early age. Ropes that involved some kinky knots—not all Davies did was aboveboard—and once Branden had discovered that, he'd wanted nothing more to do with his stepfather. That had been well before Davies's actions had ruined Cara's father.

"Thinking of a family reunion?"

Tension whirled around his chest at the thought of seeing Davies again. Yeah, right. Some reunion that would be. "Depends on what you find. Either way, once you find him, I'd like you to pay him a little visit. Then we'll decide."

Chapter Thirteen

Cara was wearing her red and blue Penn sweatpants, a white camisole with a red sports bra underneath, and a purple bandana over her blond hair while she dusted her bookshelves. She loved to clean; it was cathartic. It helped her clear the rest of the world out of her head, and sometimes after a stressful day at work she would clean into the wee hours of the morning. Iris thought she might need to see a therapist because of it . . .

Earlier, she'd finished the scarf for Socks. The cat and her soon-to-be-born kittens would never have to know how much swearing had gone into its completion. They wouldn't mind the dropped stitches—besides, it was nice and soft. She shoved it into her tote bag, intending to give it to Iris the next time she saw her.

She had her music cranked up so loud that she almost didn't hear the knocking on the door. She was a little hesitant to open it since the doorman hadn't called up. Maybe she'd missed the call because of the music.

She turned it down and approached the door. "Who is it?"

"I have a package for Ms. Cara Michal."

She looked through the peephole. A guy stood there

wearing a Yankees hat and a black jacket and jeans, holding a medium-sized manila envelope.

"Why didn't you leave it with the doorman?" she asked.

"There wasn't a doorman down there, lady. You can call down and check if you like, I'll wait. But not too long, this is my last delivery. I wanna go home sometime tonight."

Cara looked at the time and realized that it was already after nine. That was why Joe, her doorman, hadn't been there. He got off at nine and the building was locked up. But the management was strict about no one buzzing people in blindly.

"Just leave it," she said.

"I had strict instructions not to do that. I was supposed to hand it to you."

"Then you won't make your delivery at all," she told him. "Leave it and go away, or just go away. Your choice." She wasn't about to open the door to a stranger at nine fifteen at night when she was alone. She continued to watch him. He looked annoyed and kept glancing at his watch.

Finally, he said, "I'm setting it here at the door. If I get my ass chewed about not handing it over, it's on you, lady."

"I doubt I'll be able to sleep tonight worrying about it," she shot back.

He threw the envelope down—telling her there probably wasn't a bomb in it since nothing went *boom*! She watched him go over to the stairs and disappear. She went to the front window of the apartment and looked down at the sidewalk. After a few seconds she saw a man coming out of the building. He looked like the guy who was just at her door, but it was hard to tell. The street was well lit, but she was pretty far up.

She went over to the door and looked out the peephole again. The hallway was still empty. She considered calling Branden before she opened the door and picked up the package, and then chastised herself. Hadn't she just been telling herself she couldn't rely on him? She had to take care of herself, just like always.

She took a deep breath, unlocked the door, reached out quickly, and grabbed it. Then she slammed the door and relocked it. She felt silly about the way her heart was pounding in her chest. Branden's talk earlier about her needing "protection" was playing tricks on her mind.

She carried the package over to the sofa and sat down with it. It had her name on the front, but no other writing, no postmark, no packing slip . . . nothing. She started to open it before deciding being safe was better than being sorry. Feeling extremely paranoid now, she went to the bathroom and got a pair of rubber cleaning gloves. She went back over to the sofa and opened the envelope, sliding the contents out onto the table in front of her. It was a stack of paperwork that had her name on it.

Cara reached down and picked up the paperwork. It was some kind of dossier. The first page was a list of her demographics: address, phone number, workplace, work address, work number. Iris was listed as a "known associate" and at the bottom of the page were her parents' names: Janine and Hank Finch.

She turned the page. There were copies of her driver's license, her passport, Social Security card . . .

What the hell is this?

She turned another page, and there was evidence of her graduation from the University of Pennsylvania, pictures of her at different social gatherings with an old boyfriend from college, pictures of her with her mother, pictures of her with Iris and . . .

A picture of her father.

For a few seconds she smiled as she looked at it. Then she realized the photo had been taken from the local paper in her town when her father had been disgraced and accused of things he hadn't done. Her smile disappeared, her face flushed, and her hands shook.

She tossed it down on the coffee table and that was when she saw the last page with pictures of her and Branden.

Oh, God.

The photos were of her going into his apartment the night before. His body was framed in the doorway as he let her in, and then there was one of her sneaking out the next morning. He lived in one of the most secure buildings in the city. How could this be?

She was both confused and frightened. Why would someone have all of this information on her and her family, and why would they leave it on her doorstep, specifically wanting her to have it? Why had they taken photos of her and Branden? And again, how?

She picked up the phone and called Branden.

"Is everything okay?" he answered.

She tried to keep her voice level as she spoke. She didn't want him to think she was a whiner who couldn't handle her own business. "Someone delivered a manila envelope, and it's full of information about me. It goes all the way back to when I was a kid. There are also pictures of us in it from last night, pictures that had to be taken in the hallway of your secure building."

"Damn it," he spat out.

"Who would spend all that time gathering all of that information and then just have it delivered to my door . . . and why?"

"I don't know, Cara. But I'm not comfortable with you staying there alone. Not until we figure this all out. Come to me."

As soon as he said the words, she wanted to. Wanted

to rush into his strong arms and let him help her. She wanted it too much. "This is my home. Besides, the pictures of us are being taken at your apartment, not mine."

"I'll send the car to get you. You *will* stay here."

No. She couldn't. The night before had been an aberration. She'd thought she'd made a change in who she was and wanted to stop running and hiding the way her father did—that she'd go for what she wanted and whom she wanted. But that decision had been made without enough thought. Her actions had been impulsive. The morning had brought clarity and resolve. She wouldn't sleep with him again, wouldn't open herself up to that emotional vulnerability. She had to stay in control . . . especially now. Now that someone was out to get her. And maybe someone who was linked to what had happened to her father.

Besides, she didn't think she could focus if she were that close to Branden. To his body. His scent. The dazzle of his smile. The way he touched her face with his hand, and her heart with the way he looked at her, as if she were the only person in his universe. She'd succumb to temptation and end up back in his bed, enveloped by his heat and his essence.

Her insides quivered with want and need and desire to accept the offer to stay with him, but instead she forced herself to say, "No, thank you. No one has threatened me, and if you know something that I don't, I wish you would share it with me."

"That package is threat enough."

"Maybe," she conceded. "But it's only been when I've been with you—at one of your homes—when I've been photographed. How are they taking those photos with all that supposed security?"

"I intend to find that out tonight. But listen to me, okay? I have something I need to tell you."

A long pause followed his statement and she waited, dread filling her chest.

Finally, he spoke. "I know who your father was."

Her heart pounded. She opened her mouth, then shut it as his words permeated her mind, swirled around, then settled into clarity. There was silence on her end. What was she supposed to say to that? If he knew who her father was, did that mean . . .

"Carl Davies," she whispered.

"He was my stepfather. And as far as I'm concerned, he was—and if he's alive, still *is*—the scum of the earth."

Oh, God. Oh, God. What was happening? She'd slept with Carl Davies's stepson? "Why wouldn't he be alive?" she asked. Not that he deserved to be.

"I just haven't heard anything about him in a long time. A guy like Davies can make enemies as quickly as others make friends. He probably takes his life in his hands each time he steps out his door."

"You think he's the one taking photos of us and sending things to me, or that he's having someone else do it?"

"I don't know that, either. But as soon as I realized the connection between Davies and your father, I started looking into it."

"How did you find out, about me and my father? I changed my name because of the scandal. Tried to give myself a fresh start."

"I had you investigated," he said, as if it were a normal, everyday occurrence.

"Excuse me? What makes you think that my past is any of your business at all?" Her words weren't overly heated, though. She'd done her own brand of investigation on him. She just hadn't hired someone else to do the legwork.

"Cara, I investigate all my staff. And you're my employee . . ."

She sucked in a breath. "Suddenly that's all I am? Last night it didn't seem that way."

"You can't have it both ways," he said calmly. "You say that I have no rights where you are concerned, yet you take offense at the implication that you're only my employee and not something more."

She hated it when he was right. This man exasperated her like no other. "Well, whatever we are, that just feels like such a violation. But if you had me investigated, you know my father was Hank Finch. He was a good man."

"I'm confident he was. Davies is not. Please stay at my place until we get this all ironed out, Cara. I'll stay out at the mansion if you prefer."

"You can't think I'm in any kind of danger from your former stepfather," she said dryly. "I mean, the guy ruined my father, but what he did to my dad was financial, not physical. My father's life was never in any danger. So don't you think you're overreacting a bit?"

"Cara, I don't know what's happening. But someone is harassing you, and I won't stand for it. Harassment is personal—and when things get personal, they can quickly escalate to violence. I get that you've been independent and in control of your life for years now, but let me help, even if just a little. Let me at least know that you're safe."

She snorted. "In a building where someone took photos of me."

"I already messaged security and my friend Alex as we've been talking. There will be added security guards stationed throughout the building and a bodyguard right outside my door, as well as another who will escort you wherever you go. Covertly, of course. You won't even be able to spot him."

"Branden . . ."

"Cara. I've seen some bad shit go down in the financial world. I don't want you to be a casualty. That's not something I can take. Stay at my place. Do it for me. Please."

It was the simple *please* that undid her. That made her melt inside, just a little. The word had come out of his mouth so soft, almost pleading, in complete contrast to his demands and domineering method of communication. As if he'd placed his entire heart on the line with the one word.

"Fine," she said. "I'll stay at your place, but only until this is ironed out." Whatever *this* was.

Chapter Fourteen

Branden's driver was there within half an hour, just as Branden had promised. He escorted her to the front desk, where a security guard greeted her. "Mr. Duke asked that I accompany you upstairs," he explained. They rode the private elevator to Branden's floor, and when they stepped off the elevator, a tall, broad-shouldered man wearing a dark suit and a grim expression was standing sentry just outside Branden's front door. He must be the bodyguard that Branden had talked about. He looked like he could eat nails.

The security guard knocked on the door, which was promptly opened by Branden. It didn't look like he had any plans to leave for his Long Island mansion as he'd said. He was wearing faded jeans, a fine silk shirt untucked with the sleeves rolled up. His feet were bare.

"I thought you were going to stay at the mansion," Cara blurted out.

His furrowed brow relaxed and a hint of a smile formed at the corner of his mouth. "Thank you," he said to the security guard after he set down Cara's bags. When the door closed behind him, Branden turned to

Cara. "I said I would if that would make you more comfortable. Is that what you'd like me to do?"

Her mouth opened and shut. She knew she should say yes. But she was here now. And he looked so wonderful. She felt safe. "I don't care," she finally said.

She did, though. She cared that she wanted him around. Cared that she liked the feeling of him taking care of her. And cared that it felt like she'd suddenly lost control of her life. Frustrated, she plopped her weight into one of the sumptuous leather chairs in his living room and curled up into the buttery-soft depths.

"Are you okay?" he asked, sitting in a matching chair beside her.

"I will be. I just don't like other people messing with my life, and really don't like other people being in charge of it."

"No one else is in charge of your life, Cara. This is all about helping you and keeping you safe."

"Safe from what, though? I don't understand why you think that I'm not safe. Still, receiving that package . . . it scares me."

"Do you remember the comptroller who was killed in an accident after the scandal that happened with your father?"

She pulled a face. "Yes. To be perfectly honest, I remember being happy when I read that in the paper. I know that sounds terrible, but my father's death was still fresh and my wounds were still wide open. I needed someone to blame."

"Don't feel bad, he was a terrible man. But his death was suspicious. His brake line supposedly broke. And yet he was driving a brand-new car. I checked and there were no reports of other such incidents with that vehicle since."

Swallowing, she used the moment to think. Oh, God. "You think Davies killed him?"

"I think Davies might have had a hand in it, yes. After all, the man was killed before Davies was brought to trial."

"So you're worried about Davies coming after me? Why would he, after all these years?"

"I don't know if he would or not, and if this is him, I doubt he's after you. I think I'm the one he has the problem with." His face closed off and his expression became inscrutable.

Was he hiding something behind that mask that had so easily slipped into place? But if so, what?

Branden leaned forward and clasped his hands between his knees, boring into her with an intense gaze. "Davies taught me a lot. He married my mother when I was in my late teens, and took me under his wing. Taught me about money—not how to earn it, but how to grow it. How to take capital and make more. He saw what he called 'genius' in me, and started to groom me to join him in his misadventures. Turned out I had an ethical streak he couldn't break, though, and when he dumped my mom, I dumped him. I had no interest in getting involved with the shady side of the law where he seemed to operate."

She scoffed. "What he did to my father was hardly on the shady side—it was full-on evil."

He nodded. "Your father never should have been blamed for losing your town's investments, Cara. That was all on Davies. I can't even begin to tell you how sorry I am for your family and what my stepfather put you all through."

"My father died because of the scandal," she said simply.

"I know," came his quiet response.

She sucked in a shuddering breath. "And now you think Davies might be after you because . . ."

"No clue. It doesn't seem like him, but I have no real

answers for you right now, except that this feels personal. Unfortunately, you just happened into my life at the wrong time."

Cara thought about that. "Am I in your life, Branden? I mean, other than at work . . ."

He reached out and touched her face. His fingers grazing her skin were like being touched by a live wire. She both loved and hated it at the same time.

"I'd like to think so," he said.

He bent down toward her and she knew she should turn away. If she let this go on . . .

His lips touched hers just as his doorbell buzzed.

Branden closed his eyes. "The man has the worst timing."

"Who is it?" she asked.

"It's Alex. He's working for me as an investigator. I asked him to come take a look at the pictures of us. You brought the envelope, right?"

She took it out of her bag and handed it to him.

The buzzer rang again. He stood and strode to the intercom, then pressed the button. "Yeah, Nolan, is it Alex?"

"Yes, sir."

"Go ahead and send him up. Thanks, Nolan."

A few minutes later, Alex, the guy with all the tattoos Cara had seen that morning, strode through the front door.

"Alex, thanks for coming," Branden told him. "This is Cara Michal. Cara, Alex Samuels."

"A pleasure," Alex said, shaking her hand.

"Nice to meet you," Cara responded. "Though I wish it was under different circumstances."

"Me, too. I should have introduced myself this morning before you snuck out."

Her face flamed. So she had been noticed.

"Knock it off." Branden held the manila envelope, but

there was a strip of clear plastic between it and his skin. "This was delivered to Cara's door."

Alex slipped on a pair of latex gloves that he retrieved from his pocket and dumped the envelope's contents onto the table in front of them. He used an unsharpened pencil to shuffle through them. When he got to the last two photos of Branden and Cara he said, "This is last night and this morning?"

"Yes."

Alex scrutinized them, then walked back over to the doorway and looked out into the hall. "Can you both come over here and stand exactly where you're standing in the photo?"

Cara wasn't sure what he was after, but stepped out into the hall as Branden positioned himself in the doorway. Alex had the photo in his hand as he stepped across the hall and backed up against the wall. He slid along the wall in one direction, and then back in the other until he seemed satisfied he was in the right spot. He looked up and down, and then to Cara's surprise, he began tapping on the wall. He tapped up and then down slowly, finally pausing in one particular spot. He kept his hand on the wall and said, "What's on the other side of this wall?"

"As far as I know, nothing," Branden said.

"Can you get the super or someone up here for me?" Alex asked.

"Of course."

Alex and Cara went back inside, where Cara made tea and Alex wandered through the entire penthouse with some strange device, sweeping for bugs, he explained when Branden got on the phone with Nolan. Once Alex finished his sweep—he assured her there were no additional surveillance devices—he looked over the other documents in the package, and when he came to the photo of her and her college boyfriend, he asked, "Who is this?"

"His name is Trevor Halstead. I dated him in college."

Alex nodded and pulled out the second photo.

"Where were you in these pictures?"

"One of them was a winter formal–type thing and the other an awards banquet."

"What was the award for?"

Thinking that was a strange question, Cara said, "I was given an award for completing a year's worth of financial data in a matter of weeks. It's a special award that's specific to Penn."

Giving no indication of why he'd thought it was important to ask, Alex nodded.

Branden came back in and said, "The night manager is on his way up."

"Good. I did a sweep, and there are no bugs or cameras in your penthouse."

Branden gave a quick nod, then he and Alex made small talk while they waited and Cara fixed herself another cup of tea. The night manager, a middle-aged, balding little man with a big, bright smile arrived within a few minutes and introduced himself as Bob Cartwright. Cara could tell that underneath his cool, calm facade he was nervous about being called to the penthouse at 10 p.m. He had a fine layer of sweat sitting on his upper lip.

After the introductions were made, all four stepped into the hall under Alex's direction.

"What's behind this wall here?" Alex asked Cartwright.

"Um . . . as far as I know, nothing. I mean, it's just a wall."

"Nah, I don't think so," Alex said. "Come here, I'll show you what I mean." He tapped on the spot he had earlier. "Did you hear that?"

"I didn't hear anything," the man said.

Odd that he'd answered that way, Cara thought. The spot that concerned Alex sounded kind of hollow, while the other two spots sounded full.

"Okay, listen." Alex knocked above the spot and then below it. "Now . . ." He knocked on the spot that concerned him. "Can you hear the difference?"

Cara certainly could. Why was Cartwright still claiming he couldn't? She cast a quick glance at Branden, who firmed his lips and tipped his head slightly, as if informing her to keep silent.

Alex looked at Branden and said, "I'm gonna go get my saw. I'll be back."

"Wait! You can't saw open one of our walls!" Cartwright said, sweat beading on his brow.

"Then I suggest you start talking," Alex said.

Cara looked at Branden. He was still just watching as if he was an impartial witness to a drama unfolding in front of him.

"I don't know what you want me to say."

"I want you to tell me what is behind that wall. If you don't, then I will get my saw and I'll bring an officer of the law with me to witness it, because you and I both know that there is a camera located behind this wall and trained on Mr. Duke's door. So, I may get in a little trouble for sawing the wall, but you're going to get into a whole lot more. Besides," Alex said, jerking his head in Branden's direction, "I have friends in high places."

"Okay, okay. There is a camera back there," Cartwright admitted. "But you don't have to cut open the wall to get at it. There's a crawl space that you can enter from the roof."

Branden suddenly stepped forward, right into Cartwright's personal space. In a low, terrifyingly blunt voice he said, "Who put it there? Who controls it?"

"I don't know," Cartwright said. The sweat was rolling down the sides of his face now.

Branden stepped even closer. Cartwright's bald head was almost touching the underside of Branden's chin.

"Who?" he demanded again.

"I really don't know. The day manager is the one who told me it was there. He paid me to not tell anyone. I'm sorry. I was going through a divorce and I needed the money."

"Call him and tell him you need him down here, tonight."

"He won't answer the phone. I'll call him, I'm not refusing, but he won't answer. He comes in at five, though."

"And that gives you six hours to warn him."

"No, I won't, I wouldn't . . . I don't even like the guy. I told him all of this wasn't right." The sweat stains under his arms were spreading.

"Hmm, what do you think, Alex?" Branden asked his friend.

"I think he's full o' shit," Alex said in a suddenly thick Brooklyn accent.

"Yeah, I think you're right. Take care of him, will you? I'll talk to the other one in the morning when he comes in for his shift, unless you come up with something before then that means I won't even have to talk to the bastard. Come on, Cara."

Branden turned and walked back into the apartment.

Cara was watching Alex and Cartwright, her stomach churning, and wondering what "Take care of him" had meant. Branden had been domineering and controlling before—all alpha male, all the time—but this? This was different. There was something feral about him now. Something not quite civilized.

Something that both scared and comforted her.

"Cara, let's go."

Another one of his commands. Cara resisted momentarily, but knew he and Alex were trying to scare Cartwright, and she needed to play her part. She turned as if obedient and followed Branden into the apartment, leaving Alex and a quivering Cartwright alone in the hall.

Once inside, and with the door closed behind them, she turned to Branden and asked, "What's Alex going to do?"

"Kill him," Branden said deadpan.

Cara didn't believe him . . . too much. "No. Really?"

"Don't worry, no one will ever find the body."

Cara wanted to believe he was kidding, but Branden didn't kid . . . did he? After all, she really didn't know him well. His face was totally serious, and even his posture hadn't changed.

"Branden, please tell me you aren't serious . . ."

He suddenly burst out laughing, shocking Cara. "You should see your face. It's classic."

Cara punched him in the arm and said, "It's not funny, you big jerk!"

"It was kind of funny," he said. "But my sisters would have my hide if they saw me teasing a woman I'm dating the way I tease them."

Cara had never seen him drop the serious, professional demeanor. Even during sex he was all intense. Focused on the task at hand. His laughter softened all of his features, and as handsome as Cara thought he normally was, she found him absolutely beautiful at that very moment.

"What is Alex really going to do?"

"Alex and his brother will just talk to him, I swear. Cartwright will crack, though. They've got that Brooklyn born-and-bred tough-guy thing going on." Branden shook his head. "I really wish you could have seen your face. What do you think I am? The Godfather?"

"I honestly didn't think you were the type to joke around."

Branden stepped up close to her. Too close. She could feel his breath on her face. Her insides were shaking but she didn't step back. She stood her ground as he said, "I'm human, Cara."

Oh, she knew that very well. She could smell his humanness. His manliness. Damn him! He was seducing her with his presence alone. His imposing and strong body. His dark, sexy eyes. His bulging biceps. The soft and loving way he spoke of his sisters. He was walking sex appeal, and how was she supposed to resist that?

She rose up on tiptoe. She wanted him to kiss her and he didn't disappoint. First he just brushed his mouth against hers. Then he kissed her face, up one side and down the other. Finally, his lips crushed down on hers.

She parted her lips so that he could slide his tongue into her warm, wet, willing mouth. She'd come over here with no intention of having sex. Well, Iris would challenge her on that one, and she'd be right. One look from this man was all it took to break down her resolve. She wondered how strong it could have been in the first place.

Chapter Fifteen

Oh, God, she wanted this. Wanted him. Needed him.

She kissed him back, with intensity, moaning as his hands slid up her sides, and whimpering when he pulled his mouth and hands away.

In her ear, he breathed, "Cara," then he gently spun her around so she was facing away from him. Taking her hands, he placed them high against the wall and said, "Stay."

She stayed.

He walked over to a remote-control panel and pressed a few buttons, and suddenly every drape in the condo moved into place, remotely ordered to do so by Branden. He was protecting her. Protecting them.

He came back to her, and his strong hands were warm as they slid down inside her tank and underneath her sports bra. The palms of his hands rubbed firmly against her hard nipples as she leaned her body back into his big, hard chest. He rubbed his face against her hair and slid his lips down to lick and suck on her ear, and then down to her neck. He nibbled and licked along her most sensitive areas. She had goose bumps all over her body and her spine felt electric. He had such an incredible effect on her.

When she rubbed her butt against his erection she heard him moan, and she realized she had the same effect on him. And she loved it.

While he kissed her neck and pulled and twisted on her nipple, she felt his hand between them, unzipping and unbuttoning his pants. She shivered when she realized he was stroking himself against her. She moaned and ground herself against him. He was the sexiest fucking man in the history of the world.

He broke their kiss and turned her again to face him. His erection was pressing against her pelvis now and she reached back and grabbed his butt, pulling his hips into hers, rubbing herself against him. She felt like she could orgasm right then and there. Branden groaned and put his hands on her shoulders. He only applied the slightest pressure, but she knew what he wanted and she wanted it, too.

He'd been so giving to her the night before. Had made sure she was satisfied, and in such an erotic and talented way. She wanted—no, *needed*—to reciprocate. To make him feel as enthralled as he'd made her feel.

She dropped to her knees in front of him and he guided his erection to her mouth. She tried to take it deep, but he wanted to tease her first. He held it in his hand and traced her lips with it, running it back and forth across the tongue she was reaching out with. When he was finally ready, he slipped the head of his penis between her lips and she sucked it out of his hand and all the way into the back of her throat. She shivered with excitement and desire as she felt him wrap both of his hands in her hair and tug gently on it, guiding her head up and down, watching his shaft slide in and out. She ran her tongue along the underside of it, scraping very gently with her teeth, not enough to hurt, just enough to entice.

The sound of his deep, sexy voice spurred her on as he said, "Ahh, yes, Cara . . . that's it. Oh, baby, that feels so good."

He moved his hips, thrusting them forward, pulling in and out of her mouth in a steady rhythm. Each time he pulled himself out, he would quiver and shake, then he would plunge back in, deeper each time. As she sucked and licked with abandonment, arousal spiked inside her.

They were close. *She* was so close . . .

She groaned loudly as he pulled himself from her mouth.

"You want that, Cara?"

She loved the sound of her name on his lips. "Yes."

He smiled down at her and then slid his hard penis back into her mouth, this time moving his hips quicker, more frantically. His breaths got shorter and his fingers gripped her hair tighter. She shook . . . trembled . . . quaked at the intensity. At his strong and sensual scent. At the sensation of velvet and steel in her mouth.

She was still shaking when he released her hair and pulled himself out from between her lips. He was panting, and she knew he had been right on the verge of his own powerful climax when he stopped. His self-control was impressive.

He stood over her as she remained kneeling on the floor, looking up at him. He reached down and ran his fingers gently along the sides of her face and down to her neck and then her shoulders. It was a soft, loving touch—a true caress. She closed her eyes as he touched her, savoring the tender moment and then suddenly, she felt herself being lifted off the floor. Gasping, she draped her arms around his neck as he carried her to the bedroom. He kissed her as they walked, letting his tongue plunge in and out of her mouth in a deep, passionate kiss.

When they got into the bedroom, the sight of the plush white comforter brought back memories of their previous time together, making her shudder. As he laid her down on the big, soft bed, he broke their kiss and she slid her arms down off his neck. He began to undress her then, tossing each piece of clothing aside as he slipped it off of her. Then he stood at the side of the bed and stripped off all that he was wearing, as well.

He took a long look at her then, running his eyes like a fiery touch across the contours of her body. She smiled at him and he licked his lips and reached down and grasped one of her wrists, raising her arm up over her head, like he was posing her. She wondered what he was doing before she suddenly felt silky material being wound around her wrist. Once. Twice.

She gasped, and caught his gaze with hers. He stared at her, steady, frozen in motion, waiting for . . . for what?

For her to decide, she realized. He'd heard her the other night, when she'd said she was done hiding and running and was going for what she wanted. He'd heard her, too, when she'd argued against being controlled. He'd known, somehow, that her arguments had been a subtle message that she'd in fact wanted to. To be taken care of. To have someone else take control and let her simply be.

I should protest. Shouldn't I?

But she didn't. Somehow, Branden knew her. Really *knew* her, and with that knowledge came trust. So what she did was actually put her other arm up over her head, too. As she did, she could feel her core throb. Yes . . . she wanted this. She wanted to be possessed. Taken. And to ultimately be in control.

Because Branden had made it clear, even in his silence, that she was in control here, even as he took her over.

He wrapped that wrist, too, then wrapped the ties around the posts of the bed. When he was done, he placed the loose ends of the wrap into her open palms, closing her hands around them so that she knew getting loose was her choice, if and when she was ready.

He moved his mouth down to her breasts and wrapped his lips around one of her taut nipples. He sucked it in hard and fast, flicking it with his tongue. She moaned and writhed on the bed, and he placed his hand on her other breast, twisting and manipulating that nipple while his mouth continued to devour the other. He slipped his free hand down between her legs to massage her there. She ground her hips down, so wet, so hot, and so ready. He released her nipple from his mouth and she thought about grabbing his head and forcing him back down before she remembered the silk ties. She wasn't ready to give that up yet, and in a few seconds she was glad she'd waited. He was only switching sides, and as his mouth sucked in her other nipple, he caught her by surprise and plunged two fingers into her wet, waiting depths.

As he moved his fingers in and out of her, he used the edges of his teeth to scrape gently at her turgid nipple. He reached up to her face and used his other hand to caress her lips. When she felt his fingers there she sucked them into her mouth, making love to them the same way she'd made love to his penis just a little while ago. He slipped a third finger inside her and she began to buck her hips wildly and thrash about on the bed. She cried out his name.

"What, baby? You like that?"

"It feels so good."

"Is there something else you want? Something else I can do for you?"

"I want you inside me."

"My fingers are inside you."

"No! I want your penis inside me."

He smiled and slipped his fingers out of her. She let out a frustrated little cry until she felt his mouth replacing them. He ran his tongue along her slit, grazing her swollen clit as he did. Every nerve in her body felt exposed as he plunged his tongue deep inside of her, using his fingers to open her up so he could push in deeper, making her squirm and cry out, making her want to scream.

She strained hard against the silk binds but she still didn't slip loose. Swiftly, a powerful orgasm washed across her body. Branden kept up the gentle pressure on her sensitive clit with his tongue, riding her through the orgasm, which seemed to go on and on.

Her body slowly lost its rigidity as she came down from her climax, and a fine sheen of sweat coated her body. She lay there, completely relaxed. She could have gone to sleep right then and there and slept like a baby all night if not for the fact that he hadn't had his release yet, and she wasn't willing to leave him in that state.

He climbed over her and between her legs, then held there, waiting. Teasing. Making her want and need and moan. She lifted her hips and draped one leg across his back, trying to draw him in, seeking to fill her heat with his. Instead, he just held himself against her and let her slide up and down, rolling her hips and pressing against him. Finally, when she thought she might go mad at the teasing, he grabbed her hips and pulled her to him as he thrust into her. She cried out and he let out a long, deep moan, both of them lost in the feeling. As he moved in and out of her, Cara closed her eyes and let the feelings wash over her.

Wrapping his arms around her torso and pulling her

against him so tightly that she could barely breathe, he began pounding her relentlessly. She didn't just *want* to scream any longer, she did scream. She screamed as she climaxed, and she felt Branden grow and swell inside of her just before he cried out and climaxed as well. They lay there panting and gasping for breath, both of them able to feel the heavy beat of each other's hearts in their chests.

"That was . . ." She breathed out, unable to form a coherent thought. "Sorry. I can't seem to find the right word."

He chuckled and nuzzled her neck. "How about fabulous? Incredible? Fantastic? Wonderful? Marvelous?"

She still shook and her breathing wasn't quite back to normal, but she giggled anyway. "Any more adjectives in that mental thesaurus of yours you'd like to add?"

He kissed the tip of her nose. "I can come up with more. Mostly to describe your amazing body. And how brilliant you make me feel. I'm on fire when you're around, Cara. On fire, and at peace." He rolled onto his back and ran a hand through his hair, but kept an arm around her, holding her close. "I've never felt that way before. You're beyond compare, Cara."

She hitched a breath. Yes, men had told her sweet nothings before. But mostly as a perfunctory act. Like it was their job to tell her she was pretty or she made them feel good. None of them had ever made her believe it before.

None of them had been Branden.

She realized his breathing had settled into a regular, deep rhythm and his arm under her had relaxed. He'd fallen asleep, with her in his arms. A wry grin crossed her face. He'd left her tied up. She opened her hands, gathered the silk in each one, and tugged.

Her binds were released in an instant.

She lay there, relishing the steady rise and fall of Branden's chest and wondering what it was about him, what kind of power he had, that made her so willing to do anything . . . as long as it pleased him.

The more it pleased him, the more it turned her on.

She hitched around and came up onto her elbow to stare at him. The drapes in the bedroom hadn't closed completely, the corner of one caught on a modern glass bookshelf, and the faded light of New York's nighttime illuminated the room with a yellow-gray glow. Under the muted light, sound asleep, Branden looked younger. The vulnerability she'd seen in his eyes when he spoke of his sisters now was prevalent in every line of his face. The soft way his lips were gently closed. The ease around his eyes. The lack of frown lines furrowing his brow.

In sleep, the powerful mogul Branden Duke looked sweet. Soft. So very real.

He looked like someone she could fall in love with.

And that thought scared her more than the knowledge someone had spied on her and taken pictures. Scared her more than any exam she'd ever taken at school. Scared her almost more than the day she'd come home from school to see her mother in the cold and dark living room, shaking with sobs, unable to talk—to form words to say her father had died.

She closed her eyes and snuggled into him. She would analyze it all tomorrow. Tonight she just wanted to sleep and feel the strength of his arms around her.

Once again, Branden and Cara were awakened by the doorman's buzzer. Branden noticed that he was alone on his own side of the bed and Cara was curled up on hers.

Then realized he was thinking of that half of his bed as Cara's.

When had that happened? And why so suddenly?

He'd never identified any part of his life as belonging to a woman he'd dated before.

"Oh dear God, does that thing ever stop buzzing?" Cara asked.

"Not when Alex is involved," Branden said in a sleepy voice. He reached over and hit the button and said, "Good morning, Nolan. Is it Alex again?"

Nolan let out a little laugh and said, "Yes, sir."

"Send him up."

"Sir, he has several police officers and two detectives with him, as well. Is it okay to let them all come up?"

"Yes, Nolan. Thanks."

Branden groaned and rolled out of bed. He turned to look at Cara, who was still lying with her face in the pillow. Her blond hair was splayed out and she was only covered to the waist with the sheet. Her slim, smooth back was so tempting he wanted to touch her.

He knew if he did he wouldn't be able to stop, so he forced himself to walk to the door.

She groaned loudly again and flopped on her side. Now her creamy breasts were exposed, and without his consent, his erection moved to full staff.

"Why did you move way over there?" he asked.

She peeled her eyes open and looked to see where she was.

"Oh, on this side of the bed? I have no idea," she said. Then with a sleepy grin she said, "Don't take it personally, big guy, I was asleep. What time is it?"

"Four," he said.

Her eyes widened. "Are you kidding?"

"Nope. It is officially O-dark-hundred." He gave in to his urge, walked back to the bed, leaned down and gave her a kiss on the side of her face. He reached out and tucked a silky piece of hair behind her ear and then he kissed her mouth.

"Too early," she moaned.

"For my kisses?" he asked.

"For anything."

Branden laughed again and went out to let Alex in. When he opened the door the men, including the police officers, were yakking away, not giving any thought to the fact that it was only 4 a.m.

It was a good thing Branden owned the entire floor.

"We're going to have to stop meeting like this," he said wryly to Alex.

Alex looked toward the bedroom and said, "Or maybe you need to stop getting laid on the weekdays."

"Maybe if you had your own sex life, you wouldn't have to be so concerned with mine." Branden looked at the men, who were fiddling with several items. "What are they doing?"

"You see that wire and the little black box on the end of it that my buddy Detective O'Reilly there is holding?"

"What is it?"

"It's a pretty high-tech little system and it was living in the wall right outside your door. It automatically takes a photograph anytime your front door opens. It saves the photo here on its little hard drive, but it also transmits it out to another system. It turns out that your little day manager, Nate, was getting paid to look the other way as the . . . renovations . . . to your hallway were being made."

"Paid by whom?"

"That's where it gets tricky," Alex said. "He says he never got a name, just a suitcase full of cash."

"Who gave him the suitcase?"

"When Detective O'Dell and I first started talking to him, he wouldn't say. By the way that was well after midnight. Do I get overtime pay?"

Branden gave him a look. Grinning, Alex went on.

"Anyway, we spoke from around 1 a.m., when he said that 'some guy' gave him the bag, until approximately 3 a.m., when he suddenly was able to give us a first name of Chuck and a description of a man. The detective is going to introduce him to a sketch artist later on today."

Branden stifled a groan and said, "What about Cartwright?"

"Uh, well . . . I have to make a phone call . . ."

Branden laughed and said, "Where did you leave him?"

"I plead the Fifth. Let me just call my brother and ask him to release . . . um, I mean . . . excuse him."

"So how long has the camera been there?"

"According to the day manager, Nate, who by the way is just a lovely man, it was installed just about a month ago."

Huh. About the time he'd started formally working with the SEC to investigate Dubois & Mellan.

So was this related to Davies, or to his and Deena's investigation? Had someone tipped off the crooks buried in D&M that the SEC was investigating? Could this be business and *not* personal, as he'd first assumed?

For a moment, Branden frowned as realization hit. For all he knew, the SEC could have planted the camera. If so, why? To make sure he wasn't playing both sides?

"Do you think there's something similar set up at the mansion? That was where the first photo came from."

"I sweep the place on a regular basis, and nothing's turned up. But I'll run out there when I leave here," Alex said.

"Okay, good. We're going to have to check the office. And Alex, I want this done discreetly." Which was Branden's way of saying he didn't even want Deena to know about it. He trusted his stepsister implicitly, but he had to rule out an insider at the SEC.

He could tell immediately by his expression that Alex understood him. "I'm all over it," Alex said. "Then I'd like to put Lee and my other men in place while I take a little plane ride."

Energy shot through him, revved him up. But the energy was dark. Heavy. "Davies? Lee found him? He's alive?"

"Alive and well and currently in Punta Cana. It's a tiny sovereign nation in the Caribbean. They have no extradition treaty with the U.S. Offshore banking is very big. Nice beaches."

Branden cursed. Davies should not be toasting his scaly, aging flesh on a tropical beach. He should be rotting in hell. Just thinking about him made Branden's blood boil.

"If he's involved in all this, he's pulling strings."

"And I'll find out who the puppet is."

Branden thanked him and walked him out. Cara was in the kitchen when Branden got back into the apartment. He told her what Alex and the officers had found in the wall.

"Wow, so this is a lot more than catching the interest of the paparazzi," she said. "Whoever put that camera there wanted a photo of every single person that comes into or leaves your home. It's almost like you're being stalked."

"Yes," Branden agreed. "This is serious, and I need to be prepared."

"So does finding this out give you any new ideas about who it may be, or who they may be working for? Could it still be Davies?"

"I'm keeping an open mind. Given our backgrounds, I'm still betting on Davies, but the big question is motive. I'm just not sure . . ." He paused, then turned to her and caught her face in his hands before kissing her, soft and sweet, cherishing her lips. Her scent. The way she trembled under his hands. When he pulled back, he frowned. "And, Cara, no matter what, I'll keep you safe. I *will* protect you."

Chapter Sixteen

Everyone had their own way of dealing with stress. Some people golfed, some ran, some sat in dark, seedy bars and drank gallons of alcohol. Cara ran numbers. She took comfort in the fact everything added up and made sense.

It had been three days since they'd discovered the camera inside the wall at Branden's apartment. They had a sketch of the man who had put it there, but so far the police told Branden they hadn't found a match in any of their databases.

Alex had also found a camera hidden deep inside one of the rocks in the gate that marked the entrance to the mansion. It was a high-powered camera that picked up images five hundred yards away with stunning clarity. The lens was no more than a dot, the same color as the rock it was hidden in. If Alex hadn't known to look for it because of the one they'd found at the penthouse, it would likely have never been found.

Cara was still staying at Branden's penthouse, and she was often present for Alex's daily updates. They were no closer to making sense of Branden's stalker or Cara's role in things, but she and Branden had ample time to become more obsessed with each other.

And oh, God, was she ever obsessed.

Agreeing to stay at his penthouse while the threat was still out there had been both a blessing and an undoing. Because except when they were at work or dining out, they were having sex. Lots and lots and lots of sex. In every position known to man, and some she'd never even imagined in her wildest fantasies.

But what shook her world most was how, after they collapsed, physically and sexually spent, they fell asleep in each other's arms, fingers entwined, legs scissoring, her head on his chest, rising and falling with each breath, his heartbeat strong in her ear. His breath gently moving her hair.

She knew now how he fell asleep—how right before he'd completely drift off his entire body would stiffen then jerk, as if jolted by an electrical current, then he'd sigh, pull her close, kiss the top of her head, and drift off.

She knew how he'd wake in the dead of night and reach for her if she'd drifted away from him in sleep. How he'd curl around her and cup her breast in his palm. Kiss the back of her neck. Make small, warm sounds in the back of his throat.

And she knew how he'd sometimes whisper her name when he thought she was asleep.

What she didn't know, however, was what was happening to her.

For once, Iris wasn't returning her calls or texts. She'd sent one brief text, saying *Spr bsy—job hunting—will txt in a few days.* Cara hadn't known what to do without having her friend available to discuss the chaos that was currently Cara's heart and mind.

Because chaos was the only word she could use to describe the churning of emotions and thoughts that wouldn't leave her alone during those empty moments. The moments when she wasn't crunching numbers or when she wasn't having sex with Branden or when she wasn't laughing with him over some stupid thing he used to do to his little sisters. She'd come to not only respect him over the last few days, but like him a lot. And need him more than a little.

And that scared the shit out of her. After her father died, her mother had fallen apart, leaving Cara to bear the burden of responsibility for herself, her mother, and her brother. Her mother had been dependent on her father for everything—her dad had always been in control of the major decisions in the family, including the finances, and her mother had been lost upon his death. No way did Cara want that to ever happen to her.

She made her own way in the world.

And she could never come to need Branden. That would set her up for a huge fall.

But God, resisting his help, his care, his concern, was getting to be difficult.

Crunching numbers not only kept her aware of her job, but kept her mind off Branden.

Mostly.

A knock sounded at her office door and she jerked. Before she could say, "Come in" or "Go away," Mike Gaunt stuck his head into her office.

"Hello, Ms. Michal. I know it's Friday and you're probably going to want to get out of here early, but do you have a few minutes?"

"Yes, of course," she said. That wasn't the answer she really had on the tip of her tongue, but what else could she say?

Mike stepped in, looking as nervous and uptight as always and carrying a folder in his hand. He sat down across from her and put the folder down on her desk. "Can you help me understand this?"

Cara glanced at the folder but didn't pick it up. "What is it?"

"Look at it, please. I came across it purely by accident. Before I take it to Mr. Duke I wanted to give you an opportunity to explain."

Cara didn't like the sound of that. She picked up the folder and looked inside. It was one of her reports related to the sale of stock in a company located in Switzerland. She had run the report, then given it to Max. It listed out the terms and what the share cost would be in a "lit market," a traditional exchange. Presumably, Max and his brokers had run with the information, offering the stocks to high-frequency traders who used incredibly fast technology to view the offers and to buy or sell within milliseconds. The price wasn't listed out to the public until after the sale was complete. That was how most business at D&M was done. They were one of the biggest dark pool traders on Wall Street.

Cara was staring at the report and as she did, she could feel Mike Gaunt's eyes on her. After a few minutes, she looked up.

"I'm sorry, Mr. Gaunt, I'm not seeing any issues with this."

Mike made a face that made it evident he didn't believe her. He put his hand out. "May I?"

Cara handed the report back to him.

"Who is S. M. Mahoney?" he asked.

"I have no idea."

He held the paperwork out for her again, saying, "Look at the sender and recipient of this email."

Cara did. It appeared the report had been forwarded— *by her*—to someone named S. M. Mahoney. That didn't make sense, though. She always sent a copy to Max, or now Branden, and cc'd it to Jean . . . but that was it. The original email, sent to Max and Jean, was attached to this one that had been forwarded to a man she'd never heard of. And she'd certainly never pass on confidential information.

Tension ate at her gut. "I don't know who that is, or why he or she was sent a copy of this report."

"It's a he. His name is Samuel Mason Mahoney and he is the CEO of Whitaker Enterprises."

"The company that ended up purchasing this stock?"

"The very same."

"But I don't understand. I didn't send this report to him." By now bile filled the back of her throat and she swallowed hard against the acrid taste.

"It came from your email address."

"That's what this indicates, but I didn't send it. I sent it to two people, the same way I do every report, and if it goes anywhere from there it's up to them. I did not forward this. It had to be someone else who accessed my account somehow."

Gaunt sighed and said, "I was really hoping that you would have an explanation for this. One that made sense."

"Well, I don't," she said, her tone both angry and defensive. She wasn't going to let her fear show. "Because I didn't send that and I don't know who did. Therefore, there is no way that I could possibly explain it. Would you like me to make something up?"

"No. I'd like the truth, however. I'll have to take this to Mr. Duke."

"That's fine," Cara said. "I'd like it on the record that I'm not happy about you saying that like it's a threat. I have every confidence that Branden—Mr. Duke—will believe me when I say I didn't send it."

Gaunt raised an eyebrow, which indicated loud and clear that he'd heard the rumors about Cara and Branden. In his defense, they were no longer just rumors, but it still pissed her off that he was sitting there thinking she would get special treatment.

She didn't need special treatment. She did her job to the very best of her abilities, and she hadn't sent that report to someone other than the people she was supposed to.

"That will bode well for you, then," Gaunt said. "And as for what's on the record, I'm not threatening you. Mr. Duke hired me to do a certain job and that's what I'm doing."

"Good for you," Cara said. It probably wasn't wise to be so snippy. Gaunt seemed like the type who would hold a grudge, but he had very effectively ruined her entire day with his false accusations.

He stood and started to go, but at the door he turned around and said, "For what it's worth, Ms. Michal, I do believe you. Unfortunately, my opinion doesn't really count for much around here."

Somehow she found that hard to believe. She figured anyone who worked for Branden was the best for the job, and therefore his opinions would hold a huge amount of weight. Still, Cara now felt bad for having cursed Gaunt under her breath. "Thank you," she said as he went out and closed the door.

She picked up the phone to call Branden, then hesitated.

It was exactly what Gaunt and others would expect her to do. Exactly what she'd told herself she *wouldn't* do.

Run to her boss. Her lover.

She put the phone back in its cradle. She would let Mike Gaunt do whatever he needed, and when Branden asked her about it, she would state her case. She couldn't mix business and the pleasure Branden gave her after hours.

Cara returned to what she'd been doing before Mike interrupted her, but the numbers swam in front of her face. Something bad was going on at D&M, and somehow she'd gotten involved.

Less than a half hour later, there was another knock on her door. She debated not answering, even hiding under her desk, but eventually called, "Come in."

The door opened and Gail stepped inside. "Sushi? Or Thai? We're going out to lunch today and wanted to see if you'd take time away from your precious numbers to join us."

Tammie appeared behind Gail, all smiles. "I vote Chinese, actually. And there's a new mani-pedi place that has a lunchtime special. We can bring in boxes of lo mein and eat at the same time."

Cara pursed her lips. She didn't get out much, and with Iris busy job hunting, she'd missed female companionship. Maybe lunch today would be a good idea—Tammie tended to talk nonstop, which could be a nice distraction.

Suddenly, Deena Raj appeared in the doorway. She was dressed in a white Chanel suit with a perfectly tailored A-line skirt and a red silk camisole just peeking out from underneath her jacket. Both the white and the red looked stunning with her olive skin and raven hair. She smelled like Chanel No. 5.

Cara stood up. "Hi, Deena," she said, forcing a smile.

"Hello, Cara," the woman said, and smiled pleasantly at Gail and Tammie.

"Um, lunch another time?" Gail asked, obviously nervous to have the other woman suddenly appear.

With a smile, Cara tipped her head, then gave a quick farewell wave as her two coworkers exited her office. She turned her attention back to Deena Raj.

"Please sit," the woman said.

Cara did so, and Deena sat in the same seat Mike had occupied less than an hour ago. Actually, she didn't sit so much as melted into it. Everything she did seemed to be done with such grace. Against Cara's will, jealousy spiked through her spine.

"Cara?"

She suddenly realized that Deena had been talking and she hadn't heard a word.

"I'm sorry, can you repeat that?"

Deena raised one perfectly designed eyebrow and said, "I asked who else has the password to your D&M email account."

"No one. This is about the report Mike showed me awhile ago?"

"Yes. Since Branden's busy, Mike brought it to me. I'm not your boss, Cara, but I am helping Branden clean house around here. This report is exactly the sort of thing we're concerned with."

"I can see why. I can only tell you what I told Mike. Not only do I not know S. M. Mahoney, but I never send my reports to anyone other than Max and Jean . . . and now Branden. If it was forwarded from my computer, it wasn't me who did it."

"I understand. Unfortunately, who struck the key on the computer will be a difficult thing to prove. Mahoney bought that stock at a very low price. He sold it the following week at market value. He made over ten million dollars off the sale. This looks very much like an insider tip . . ."

Deena's gaze was so direct Cara felt like it was penetrating her brain. She actually wished that it was, so that Deena could see Cara was telling the truth.

"I don't know what to say, Deena. I promise you I had nothing to do with this, other than preparing the report and sending it to whomever I was supposed to. I can't prove that, but if you check my other reports you'll see that I never sent them to anyone other than Max, Jean, and then Branden after he took over."

"We will check those. Again, it's unfortunate that history alone won't be enough to prove anything," she said as she stood up.

Cara stood, too. "Am I in some kind of trouble?"

Deena studied her intently, as if seeing Cara for the first time. "I'm not sure. But Cara, if you have done something wrong, don't think warming Branden's bed will protect you. Because it won't. And I'll do anything to see Branden protected."

Branden had been in a meeting when the calls came in from Mike and Deena. Now, standing in the hallway, he checked his messages.

The one from Mike said, "Mr. Duke, I've found something interesting that involves Miss Michal. I'd like to speak to you about it as soon as you have a free moment."

The next one from Deena said, "Call me. Your girl-friend has found herself in the middle of a mess."

Branden looked at the time: eleven thirty. He had another meeting at twelve thirty. He called and rescheduled, then instead of calling Mike or Deena, he held the phone in the palm of his hand, staring at it as if the weight was unfamiliar. Uncomfortable.

He shouldn't call Cara first. She wasn't his girlfriend, as his sister had said. He hadn't had one of those since college. But what he did know was she was *his*.

Ownership came easily to him now. But finding a way to get what he wanted had been a learned skill.

He'd grown up with *nothing*.

His shoes and clothing came from the church give-away basket. Toys were things he found in the garbage or in the edges of the local park, like the deflated soccer ball with the red streak down the center he never could tell was Sharpie or a bloodstain, or the armless GI Joe he'd come across while Dumpster diving with Deena one hot summer afternoon. Those items may have been small, but they were his. With those rejected things he'd ended up with, he'd learned to hoard. To possess. To claim as his.

And when he wanted something he couldn't find in a Dumpster? As a small kid who didn't hit his growth spurt until his senior year in high school, fighting for what he wanted wasn't in the cards for him. But negotiations? That's where he'd made his fortune. If he saw a kid at school with something he wanted, he'd watch for a while, assessing the kid, figuring out what he wanted.

Then he set about getting it for him.

He'd traded a beat-down of the class bully in order to get one kid's collection of Pokémon cards in the first grade.

Exchanged a month's worth of homework for another kid's lunchtime Twinkies in the sixth grade.

The more he'd grown into his looks and the more wealth he attained, the more people had begun to want things from him, women included. He'd been fine giving them what they wanted, be it money, jewelry, clothing, vacations in Fiji, even cars. The reputation of being seen with Branden Duke. He gave plenty—but he refused two things: one was bragging rights—he usually had women sign a confidentiality agreement before sleeping with them. The other was his heart. He'd had a few women tell him they loved him, or ask to be loved, or hint about weddings—the minute he felt someone was inching too close to the whole in-love thing, he bailed. And he usually told women up front that his heart was off-limits.

Although with Cara he hadn't asked her to sign the confidentiality contract, and he hadn't given her the no-love conversation.

Maybe that was because he hadn't yet figured out what she wanted from him.

And what he wanted from her.

Odd that out of all the women he'd been with, he

couldn't figure out what Cara wanted—jewelry? Prestige? A Hawaiian vacation? Keeping her reputation aboveboard was what she'd claimed she wanted, but once the world thought they were sleeping together, she'd accepted his invitation to dinner and had made it clear she wanted to sleep with him. Money? Yeah, she needed more than most, as his background check had shown, since she was basically supporting her mother, but she was doing so well at D&M that he didn't think she was insatiable about money, and she'd never asked him for a dime. Sex? She'd loved every damn thing he'd done to her body, then had turned around and given right back to him what he'd given her.

So what did she want?

And now Cara was supposedly in a "mess" at D&M, but hadn't called him to fix things for her.

No, she probably wouldn't ask for his help even if it was the very thing she needed.

The woman was too independent for her own good.

So wait—was that what she wanted? Independence?

But that didn't make sense. He had everything to offer her—money, position, security . . . but she resisted anything he could give her except orgasms.

Fuck. He needed to get the hell out of his head and just call the woman. Ask her straight-out what it was she'd dug her way down into.

He punched the autodial button assigned to her, and when she answered, bluntly said, "Join me for lunch."

A brief silence met his statement, then Cara quietly asked, "Have you spoken to Mike or Deena yet? Because that might affect whether you really want to have lunch with me."

"I was in a meeting. Got messages from them both. I know they're concerned with something having to do with work. I'd rather hear the news directly from you, but you were the only person I didn't have a call from. Is everything all right?"

"No."

Frustration pitched over him. This was exactly the problem he had with Cara. Her determination not to ask for help. Not to need anything. Not to need *him*. He resisted stating the cliché—"no man is an island"—and instead blew out a slow breath, then said, "Yet you didn't call me."

"I don't want to run to the principal's office with my every little problem," she said. Branden could tell by the sound of her voice that she didn't think whatever was going on was a "little problem."

"Fine. You're being called to his office and he'll force you to talk . . ."

Cara laughed and said, "That actually sounds like fun. Kinky, but fun . . ."

Branden smiled. This woman either had him completely fooled or had absolutely nothing to hide.

And he figured it was the latter.

"How about Inatesso in about an hour?"

"Sounds good. I'll see you then."

"Great. I hate to eat pizza alone."

Chapter Seventeen

"So it seems pizza was a good idea," Branden said.

Cara felt her face go hot. She looked down at the warm slice in her hand. They had been talking about the email Mike found and she hadn't even noticed that she'd just picked up her third piece. She put it down and glanced around Inatesso, wondering if the other people enjoying gourmet pizza had noticed her shoveling food in her face. But none of the other well-dressed men and women seemed to be paying her any attention. "It's stress eating. Pizza's my comfort food. That and Ben & Jerry's."

Branden grinned. "From what I've seen, a few pieces of pizza aren't going to hurt you one bit. Go ahead and eat. I didn't mean to embarrass you."

"I'm not even hungry. I really am just stressed about this email business."

"I understand. But you know you didn't send that email, and I know you didn't, so case closed."

"Not really," she said. "Why are you so sure I'm telling the truth?"

"Because I have a gift for judging people, Cara. You work too hard to color outside the lines."

"Well, someone sent the email and now Deena and Mike both know about it, and I don't think either of them are going to just let it go."

"I'll tell them to stop. No need for them to waste their time investigating you," he said. "They need to move on and find the real culprit."

She frowned. "Branden, it's not that I don't appreciate your faith in me, but why aren't you more concerned? Someone that now works for you sent that email to Mahoney, and that someone and Mahoney both committed a crime. In fact, more than one crime, since it was sent from my email address. And let me emphasize again—that someone almost positively works for you. I mean, I know email can be hacked, but an outsider wouldn't be as likely to know who to hack in this massive company to get that specific information, right?"

When Branden nodded, she went on. "I know you want to protect me, and I do appreciate that, but you can't just sweep it under the rug. I don't want it to look like we are doing anything inappropriate." Her mouth twisted. "Any more inappropriate than what we actually are doing."

"I didn't say I'm going to sweep it under the rug. Believe me, I take this seriously, and the person responsible will be caught. But that's my job, not yours. Promise me that you'll leave it alone for now."

Cara had a sneaking feeling that there was something Branden wasn't telling her. "I don't know if I can do that. This is my reputation. Someone wants to shred it by suggesting I slept with the boss. That's one thing. But framing me for a crime I didn't commit . . ."

"I will find that person, Cara. I promise. You trust me in bed. Trust me in this."

An odd feeling, something like panic, worked its way under her skin. Her father had said nearly the same words to her and her mother after he'd been indicted.

Trust me—I'm not guilty. I'll fix this. Her father's voice echoed in her mind and she shuddered, as if shaking off the ghosts of the past, then quietly said, "I don't know if I can. Not because you aren't trustworthy, but because I've been taking care of myself for a long time. And truth be told, the fact that we have been sleeping together, well . . ."

"What?" Branden frowned.

The waiter interrupted them then, asking Branden if he wanted lunch added to his account. Cara took the time to check her phone for emails or texts—nothing. She knew Iris was busy job hunting, but God, Cara could use her advice right about now.

Because she had to break things off with Branden. She didn't want to, but she couldn't keep hiding behind him. Couldn't allow herself to accept his protection, especially from whatever was coming her way.

But as the thoughts entered her mind, tension entered her body. And a sense of longing, of missing, swept over her.

They exited the restaurant, and instead of heading to the busy street to walk back to D&M, Branden cupped her elbow in his hand and guided her to the alley out back.

"What are we doing?" she asked, her heel catching on the uneven ground.

"Hashing a few things out."

"In an alleyway?"

He slid his hand down her arm and entwined his fingers with hers. "No view from above, and we can see if anyone comes around the corner. Little chance of anyone photographing what I'm about to do to you."

"And that is?"

He halted then, and with swift movements, backed her up against the brick wall and slid a hand up the back of her neck. Gripping her hair in his hand, holding her face motionless, he kissed the hell out of her.

She melted. God, no, this wasn't what she wanted. What she needed. She'd been considering ending things with him and now he was kissing her senseless.

On purpose?

She twisted under his hold and he relaxed his grip on her hair. Pulling her mouth from his, she sucked in a breath before speaking. "I'm not sure this is such a good thing . . ."

"You're not talking about making out in a Manhattan alleyway, are you?"

She bit her lip. "Branden, I just think that until we figure out who is behind the rumors and photographs and who's setting me up, I should—"

He nudged a knee between her thighs and pressed her firmly against the wall with his hips. His erection ground against her belly, and his breath blew wisps of hair off her forehead. "I won't accept you walking out of my life, Cara. Not because of some external threat that has no basis in fact. You want me. I want you. We're together. End of story."

She struggled to think. "You think it's as easy as that, do you? You notify me how things are going to be and I'm just going to go along with it?"

"Yes. Because how I want things to be is how you want them to be, too. You're just freaking out. Rightfully so, given what's happening, but if you'd just listen to me and trust me—"

"You can't control everything, Branden. Can't have everything go your way just because of who you are and how much money you have."

"You're wrong. But even if you aren't, I'm not asking for everything. You're all I want right now, Cara. Unless you can look me in the eye and tell me you don't want me, don't want to explore more of what we've had, you're not walking away."

He spoke the words with finality, as if attempting to argue with him would be the same as trying to argue with the brick wall against her back.

He waited several beats, giving her time to answer. To lie.

To tell him she didn't want him.

When she didn't, he kissed her again.

This time, the kiss was sweet. Soft. His lips brushed hers, hesitated, then covered hers firmly. Warmly. As if he was holding back his passion and arousal and simply communicating with her through his lips . . . communicating that he cared.

When he pulled his mouth away from hers, backed up a few steps, and shoved his hands into his pockets and simply stared at her, she knew then that she would not be walking out of his life. Not now, at least.

After lunch, Cara went back to work and Branden went off to do whatever millionaire moguls do during the day. He told her not to wait on him for dinner because he had several meetings lined up for the afternoon that would likely run into evening. She assured him that after three pieces of pizza, dinner would be the furthest thing from her mind. She wrapped up her day around seven and headed for the penthouse. It was a nice night so she walked and on her way she called Iris.

Finally, after days of not returning texts or calls, her friend answered.

"Hey! I haven't heard from you in a few days. I was wondering if you heard anything back from your interview the other day."

"I did. That's why you haven't heard from me. They actually called me the very next day and I've been training ever since. I was scheduled at my current job the last two evenings, so I'm exhausted."

"Congratulations! I'm happy for you. Am I interrupting your rest?"

"Nope. I just parked it on the couch and I haven't moved. I don't want to, either, so talk to me and give me an excuse to stay here on my butt. I don't even care that it's Friday night and I'm dateless."

Cara laughed. "So do you like the new job?"

"Let's put it this way. I've already made more tips in one night than I make all week in Brooklyn."

"Good. But you know what that means. You get to pay for the next spa day."

"Count on it. So how has your week been? Still having hot, satisfying sex with Mr. Rich and Sexy?"

Thinking about what she'd been doing over the last few nights, she blushed. "You're so bad!"

"I know, but so are you. You're just bad behind closed doors, right?"

"I don't kiss and tell," Cara told her primly. "But just between you and me, I have never been so satisfied."

During Cara's walk to the penthouse, they caught up on the events of the last few days, then hung up with the promise of getting together for lunch one day in the upcoming week.

Nolan greeted Cara and called the elevator down for her. When the doors slid open on the top floor, she looked at the wall that had already been completely repaired and she shuddered a bit. Just the idea of someone watching her . . . It really creeped her out and she had to force herself to shake it off as she went through the dark apartment, switching on lights and checking in corners. Alex swept the corridor and the penthouse daily, but still. When she was confident there was no one about, she took a quick shower, dressed in a comfy nightshirt, and explored Branden's DVD collection.

Eclectic, like the man. Pink Floyd's *The Wall*, romantic comedies from the 1940s like *The Philadelphia Story*, some Federico Fellini and François Truffaut, and *Caddyshack*. She moved from the DVDs to take in his bookshelf. Again, the man's possessions showed diverse taste. Antique first editions were nestled next to recent bestsellers. Everything from Euripides to Dickens, Laura Hillenbrand to a dog-eared copy of the first Harry Potter book, in paperback. She pulled out a copy of a book on *shunga*—Japanese erotic woodcut art images—she'd noticed tucked away in a dark recess of the bookshelf, and went into the kitchen to make herself a cup of tea.

And to fantasize about doing some of the sexual positions with Branden.

Because if she wasn't leaving this situation with him right away, she'd enjoy the hell out of the time they had left to be together. Who knew how long things would last? For now, she was content to be surrounded by him, immersed in him. But she vowed the minute she felt her heart give way . . . the minute she felt that dumb little flutter girls always talked about when they started to fall in love, she'd bolt. Branden Duke's reputation was that he wasn't a forever kind of guy . . . and she'd never be a forever kind of girl.

She just had to keep reminding herself of that.

Branden liked the image of Cara standing in his kitchen wearing only a nightshirt that came down to just below her knees. The light from the buildings outside shone through the blinds just enough to cast her in a luminous glow. She had a cup of tea by her elbow and her nose buried in a book that was perched on the counter. The teakettle was on a back burner, the flame underneath adding a warm, luminescent light.

"Honey, I'm home," he called out.

She gasped and slapped the book shut, then turned and grinned at him. "Cheesy, but cute. How was work?"

"Fine." More than fine, actually. He'd received an update from Alex that he'd found Davies, complete with straw hat and loud, ugly Hawaiian shirt, in Punta Cana. Alex had tailed him to a meeting with two men, whom Alex had dubbed Dreadlocks and Surfer Dude because of their distinct appearances, and then followed the other men after they'd left Davies. To no one's surprise, they'd headed straight to the bank where they'd visited the safe deposit box area. Last he'd heard, Alex was going to attempt to make contact with the men in order to determine the nature of their business with Davies. He'd jokingly told Branden that if he had to light a joint or two to make them talk, he was up for the sacrifice.

Branden set down the briefcase he'd been carrying and walked toward Cara. "What are you reading?"

Even under the pale light, her cheeks turned a little pink. "Um . . . something I found on your bookcase."

With a fingertip, he spun the book around so he could see the cover. Then smiled wide. No wonder she'd blushed. "See anything you want to try out?"

She gasped when he slid a hand up her thigh and shoved the nightshirt up to her hips. "I—I . . ."

"Tell me," he demanded, stroking the side of her very naked hip with his palm, aware how she undulated under him. How she leaned toward him, as if craving his touch. "Tell me, or I'll step back."

"You wouldn't," she said, although the word came out almost strangled.

He cocked a brow and gazed down on her. "I would. Now tell me."

"The one where the man is looking at the woman's . . ."

Oh yeah, he knew exactly which woodcut she'd been aroused by. And he'd make that happen for her. But not just yet. For now, he'd simply tease her a little. Make her want him a lot.

Because he loved that flush on her cheeks. Loved the way she sucked in a delicate breath. Loved how her chest rose up and down in rapid succession.

Loved knowing he could bring her to ecstasy.

Leaning down, he pressed his lips to her neck, then slid them up so he could nibble the outside of her ear as he flicked the inside lightly with his tongue. He could feel the goose bumps rise as they ran down her arms.

He pulled her in closer, settling his hands around her waist. He turned her around and pulled her in for a kiss. She was tense at first, but as his tongue slipped in between her soft lips he felt her relaxing in his arms, and then kissing him back. He ran his hands up and down her back and on the last pass he caught the bottom of her shirt and pulled it up so he could grab her ass with both hands. He slipped his hands down inside her lacy underwear and kneaded and massaged her as they kissed.

His touch on her bare skin seemed to incite her and their kiss grew more passionate. She moaned as he continued to knead and his fingers slipped lower and lower so they could lightly graze where she was already wet. Cupping her there, he steered her up against the counter.

"In the kitchen?" she breathed. "Naughty boy."

"Naughty girl," he said, joining in on her teasing. "No, naughty *woman*, actually. Beautiful and exquisite woman."

He slid his hands up her body, lifting the shirt up as he went. She made a soft sound in the back of her throat.

"God, I love it when I make you moan," he said, then nipped the side of her neck. "It's a delicate sound, but earthy. And your eyes close when you do it—I love seeing your eyelashes on your cheeks. Beautiful. Like you."

He twisted her shirt in his hand, then pulled it off and tossed it to the floor.

He leaned down and kissed first one of her breasts and

then the other. She shivered as his tongue shot out and flicked across one hard nipple. He sucked it in, hard, causing her to gasp and grab his face to hold him in place.

He reached underneath her, still holding one nipple gently between his teeth, and lifted her up onto the counter. He pulled off the panties she was wearing and let them join the nightshirt on the floor. The kettle began to rumble as the water boiled, so he reached over and turned that off before he crouched between her open thighs.

"Beautiful," he whispered.

And she was.

Soft. Pink. Like petals on a flower. "Branden . . ." Cara whispered, and tried to pull her knees together.

He put his hands on her knees and spread her even wider. He knew she wanted this. Wanted him to look at her and adore her the way the woodcut husband had looked at and adored his wife.

"I won't stop. I have to see you."

"But I'm . . . it's not . . . I mean . . ."

He knew what she meant. "You are, though. Beautiful. Alluring. Seductive. And I see you. Completely."

When she sucked in a shuddering breath, he cast his gaze upward, and caught sight of her face—eyes squeezed tightly shut, the corner of her lip held by her white teeth, tension across her forehead.

"Believe me, Cara. Trust me."

With those words, spoken with all the truth he had in him, her face relaxed. Softened. She stopped biting her lip and sighed, allowing her mouth to curve into a smile.

She trusted him. Trusted him to take control. To give her what she wanted. What she needed.

Something unfamiliar entered his bloodstream, poured through his veins, infused his pores. Something warm. Soft. Intense.

He fought against the rising sensation, struggling and battling against—what? Emotion, maybe? Whatever it was, he didn't want it. Not now. Not ever.

He bent forward and licked her wet pussy.

A shudder hit him—God, she tasted good. Clean. Earthy. All woman. And so exquisitely Cara.

Cara groaned and wrapped her fingers in his hair. He used his tongue to slowly part her lips, wanting to immerse himself in her scent, her taste. Finding her swollen clit, he lapped at it hungrily as she squirmed and moaned on the cold tile counter. He licked her for several long moments before he sucked and nibbled on her clit. She cried out and the shudder came back, traversing his spine—he loved hearing her cry. Loved knowing he was giving her pleasure. Making her lose control.

"Oh, Branden," she said, throwing her head back against the cupboard as he entered her with a finger and began to swirl it around inside her. Her moans grew louder and more intense and her body quaked. She was on the verge of having an orgasm.

He slipped a second finger inside and went deep as her body shook and she cried out his name a second time. As he felt her tighten around his fingers he pushed in and out harder and faster. She screamed out his name as the orgasm hit her and he could all at once feel her tightening around his fingers. She continued to move her hips and he left his fingers where they were until she shuddered again and her body went slack.

Finally dropping his hand, he leaned in to kiss her while he pulled his pants and boxers down and let them fall to the floor.

When he broke the kiss she said, "Do you want to move this into the bedroom?"

"Soon, Cara. Soon." When she nodded, silent, he stripped off his shirt and tie, then, after grabbing a condom from his wallet, sheathed himself with it. Then he

put his arms around her and lifted her off the counter
with her legs wrapped around his back. He carried her
over to where the wall was solid, and in one motion he
slammed her back against it and entered her. She was so
wet that he slid all the way in. Cara cried out again and
he felt the scrape of her fingernails down his back. He
gripped her ass tightly with both hands and began
thrusting, pumping in and out of her as she sat sus-
pended above the floor.

God, this was good.

"I love being inside you, Cara," he whispered.

She held on to him tightly and kissed and licked his
bottom lip in response, sucking it in and running her
tongue along it as she held it in her teeth. He moaned,
and folded his arms underneath her ass and slipped her
up so that his cock was barely inside of her and her
breasts were where he could get to them with his mouth.
He sucked on her nipples, thrusting his hips harder, but
given their position he could only fit about half of his
cock inside her. He needed more, so he reluctantly pulled
back from her breasts and let her body slide down so
that he could once more press his full length inside her.
While he kissed her, she moaned and he could feel the
vibrations of it against his cheek.

He had only intended to play with her in the kitchen,
get her worked up a little bit, but he couldn't make himself stop.

"What are you doing to me?" he growled, knowing
there was no answer.

"Branden," she moaned. "You. It's . . . it's you."

With each stroke, a fire in the pit of his stomach grew
hot, and as he drew closer to climax, Cara thrust her
hips into him harder and sucked his tongue into her
mouth. He felt that familiar pulse and surge of blood
that signaled he was ready, and when his body began to
shake it seemed to trigger something in hers. She shook

with him and pulled her mouth from his, crying out as another orgasm tore through her. Seconds later he groaned loudly while he experienced his own. When they both stopped shaking, he lowered her slowly to the floor and kissed her softly on the lips.

And had to ask himself, *what the hell just happened?*

Chapter Eighteen

Cara finally had her tea, not that she was complaining. Tingles from their last encounter still rushed over her, but she forced herself to focus on the here and now. After they'd both climaxed, they'd shakily dressed again, and she'd poured herself a cup of tea and Branden a Scotch and soda. Now she was seated on the couch in his living room, her feet in his lap and a teacup cradled in her hands. She couldn't help thinking how nice the evening had been and how "domestic" it had felt.

How lovely it would be if every night could be like this one.

And that thought alone worried her immensely.

Cara had never really been interested in a man enough to think about living with him. And she wasn't kidding herself now. Whatever was happening with Branden was a temporary thing that would eventually burn itself out, probably as soon as they figured out what was going on and who was messing with them. Because a man like Branden was way out of her league. She needed to keep her emotions in check—because if she didn't, she'd get hurt. And badly. She'd never experienced heartbreak, but she'd held Iris's hands plenty of times as her friend had cried over boyfriends who'd moved on. But even as she gave herself mental warnings, a part of her wondered if maybe it was already too late.

Because these feelings she was having—missing Branden's scent when she hadn't seen him for several hours, experiencing the rush of tingles in her belly when she remembered the sensation of his penis entering her, the way his eyes lit up when he spoke of his sisters . . . all these feelings were real. And deep. And maybe even more than just a crush.

"What are you thinking about?" Branden asked her.

She glanced at him. She couldn't tell him the truth . . . that she was wondering if she was falling in love with him, but lying wasn't an option. Stick with the truth, even though it might just be a partial truth. "I was just thinking that this is nice, sitting here with you."

"It is nice," he said. "So you're not worrying about how that illegal email ended up coming from your email address?"

She made a face. "I'll have to worry about it sooner or later, but I don't want to think about it tonight."

Wiggling his eyebrows he said, "Then maybe we should come up with an activity to keep your mind and body occupied."

He'd already fulfilled plenty of her fantasies in the kitchen. Playing dumb, she said, "Like club dancing?"

"You like to go dancing?"

"It's a good stress reliever. I just dance like nobody's watching."

"Let's go then," he said, sitting up suddenly and spilling her feet from his lap.

"What, now?"

"Why not? It's Friday night, and we live in the city that never sleeps. Plus, I have a cool sports car you haven't even ridden in yet . . ."

Cara grinned. "It does sound like fun."

"Did you bring dancing clothes with you when you packed?"

"I threw a dress or two into my suitcase. Just in case."

"Perfect. How long do you need to get ready?"

Not long, it turned out. She picked out a black cocktail dress with a layer of sky-blue lace that just peeked out around the neckline and then again along the hem that ended just above her knees. She had a pair of four-inch heels that matched the lace and a bag that would work well.

She brushed out her hair, leaving it loose around her shoulders, and applied a light layer of foundation and powder before lining her eyes with a soft blue crayon. Her final touch was a layer of mascara and a shiny pink lip gloss. Satisfied, she went to find Branden. As she passed the large walk-in closet that was bigger than most people's apartments, she heard a long, low wolf whistle. She turned and saw him standing there in the doorway of the closet.

"Damn, you look hot," he said.

"Thank you. You look pretty hot yourself." He had on a soft-looking pair of black trousers and a short-sleeved blue silk button-down. His hair was stylishly mussed and Cara thought he looked so good that she might reconsider and change her mind about going out.

Branden called the valet and when they got downstairs, the blue Maserati with the racing stripes was waiting for them. The valet left it running and held open Cara's door. Cara slid inside.

Immediately, she realized what the phrase "soft as butter" was referring to. She'd never seen or felt anything like it. The dash was filled with all the latest buttons and gadgets. It was like being in the Batmobile. She looked at Branden and thought, *I'll bet he and Batman have never been seen in a room at the same time.* Then she laughed at herself. She suddenly realized that in spite of all the chaos that had invaded her life lately, she was happy.

Branden drove carefully and obeyed all the speed laws, but just the sound of the car and the vibration of its powerful motor sent little tingles of pleasure through her body. Only a few minutes passed before they arrived at their destination. It was a private club on the Street. Cara had heard all about it from executives at D&M, but she'd never been there. It was one of those clubs where you had to pay a monthly fee to even be allowed in for a drink.

When they walked inside, the large airy room had bright red carpeting and a cherrywood bar with an etched gold mirror behind it. Tall stools with soft, puffy seats surrounded the bar, and they all looked to be filled with men in suits. The big, soft-looking booths were red and black and there were several large-screen televisions hanging around the room. One of them was playing a baseball game with no sound, and the other two were showing music videos. The sound was off on those as well and soft music was playing overhead.

Branden led her through that room and into the next, where there was a large stage and people were bustling around like they were getting ready for a show. Several of them smiled and said, "Hi, Mr. Duke," as if he was a celebrity or owned the club.

Maybe he does, Cara thought.

The next room was the nightclub. The volume of the music was much louder due to the live band playing in the corner on an elevated black stage. The rest of the room was decorated in red and black like the bar. The wood dance floor was black and shiny and there were already quite a few people on it. The lighting was soft and high-top tables surrounded the dance floor. Branden took her hand and led her to one near the dance floor that was marked with a Reserved sign.

"This is your table?" Cara asked him.

"Yes, but I don't use it often."

She raised an eyebrow, doubting that was true considering the pictures she'd seen with various model-types hanging on his arm. She looked over and saw people coming in through a door on the side of the room that was flanked by bouncers who were checking IDs. She hadn't thought about it, but people had barely glanced at her when she and Branden had come in the other way.

"Did we come in the back way or the front?" Cara asked.

"We came in the private entrance. It's a perk of my membership," he told her with a grin.

The cocktail waitress came over and took their order.

When she was gone, Branden surprised her by saying, "You are so pretty."

"Thank you," she said.

He had his eyes locked on hers again. Sometimes just the way he looked at her made her panties wet. Right now? Mission accomplished.

The band started playing dubstep. She was wiggling her legs and feet to the music when Branden stood and held out his hand to help her down off the high stool. "Shall we?"

He was being such a gentleman tonight. Not that he was ever rude—his manners were impeccable—but something just seemed different about him. She thought back on her little "domestic" fantasies earlier in the night and found herself wondering if he ever had any of those himself. She almost laughed out loud when she remembered who she was thinking about.

He led her out onto the dance floor and they found an empty spot. They both began to dance and she couldn't help but notice how every woman on the floor looked at him with lust and her with envy. He was, of course, a great dancer. He danced like he did everything else. Perfectly. Cara was glad that dancing was something she'd always been good at. She'd taken ten years of dance classes before her father lost his job.

Her mind suddenly turned to her mother, who she needed to call. Needed to visit. She'd been allowing herself to enjoy the fantasy of being with Branden, but that wasn't real life.

Branden pulled her tightly against his hard chest and leaned down so that his lips were almost touching her ear. The feel of his hot breath sent little jolts of electricity down her spine. "None of that tonight."

She turned her head slightly, and when she did his lips were just inches from hers. She'd only had a few sips of her drink but she felt drunk. "None of what?"

"Whatever's going on in that pretty head of yours. Tonight, I want you here with me. Completely."

She still couldn't take her eyes off his lips. She was hoping he had more to say, because being this close as she watched them move was lighting a fire of desire in the pit of her gut. She had her hands on his shoulders and she slid them upward, wrapping them up behind his neck. She rested them there, but allowed her fingers to dance along his hairline.

He had his hands on her waist, but as the beat accelerated and then decelerated, he slid them up, stopping briefly on the sides of her breasts before running them back down to her hips. As they swayed to the music, Branden turned her in a slow circle and pulled her back into him. His hands now ran freely across her abdomen, every so often venturing upward to brush her breasts.

People could see them. He had to know that. He obviously wanted them to see. Wanted her to know they could see.

Cara shivered and arched her back, fitting herself up against him. When the music slowed again, she matched the movement of her hips to it, grinding against his

growing and stiffening cock. She leaned her head back
on his shoulder. He bent his head and ran his lips across
the sensitive flesh between her neck and shoulder. She
had her eyes closed, oblivious to the hundred or more
people around them.

Cara felt her heart pounding in her chest. It was dancing to the beat of the music, as well. Branden slid his
hands back and forth across her abdomen, causing her
to push back harder and grind herself against him. He
leaned down and whispered in her ear, "You keep that
up and I won't be able to walk out of here."

She turned her head slightly and shot him a wicked
look over her shoulder. "Should I stop?"

"Hell, no," he growled out.

"But what about the crowd? What if someone takes
our picture and posts it online?"

His fingertips gripped her hips more tightly and he
pulled her hard against him. "Let them. We're doing
nothing wrong. And anyway, if that happened, then
people would know you're my woman."

His woman.

The phrase hung there, heavy, like the beat, then dis-
sipated and melted into the air when Branden rubbed
his big hands along her hips and upper thighs, letting
her skirt rise and fall with the motion, not exposing anything but leg, but coming so very close to the warm wet
place he knew was there.

While his hips swayed and his long legs moved in time
with the music, he flipped her around once more, this
time to face him. They kissed softly and then followed
each other with their eyes and their bodies. Each time
Branden would pull her in toward him, she ground her
pelvis against the front of his pants. Then he would push
her away again, and for a few minutes she would dance
for him, and he would undress her with his eyes before
he reached out and pulled her back in. His chest and her

breasts would bump as he brought her in and they would dance slow and close. Her nipples were so hard that she knew he had to be able to feel them through both of their layers of clothes.

He pushed her back again, and this time when she danced for him, she ran her own hands slowly down her body and back up again. She raked her eyes over his body as she danced, pausing over the large bulge in his pants and swiping along the outer edges of her lips with her tongue. He grabbed her with two hands then and brought her back in.

Dropping his mouth to hers, he kissed her long and hard, deep and passionate, while squeezing and kneading the cheeks of her ass. When they finally broke for air, it took her a moment to realize the music had stopped playing, that the dance floor was clearing out.

Slightly embarrassed, Cara grabbed Branden's hand and tried to lead him off the dance floor. He refused to go and instead reached out and wrapped one hand through her long hair, pulling her back for another long, possessive kiss.

This time, when they stopped kissing, he let her lead him off the dance floor. He stationed her back at his table, then when the cocktail waitress didn't immediately appear, he headed off to get her water.

Almost as soon as Branden left, Cara's phone rang. She frowned when she saw the call was from her mother. Since it was late, Cara assumed there was some kind of emergency. And usually, emergencies were about Glenn.

"Hi, Mom."

"Oh, Cara. I'm so glad I caught you."

"What's wrong, Mom?" Cara glanced over her shoulder; Branden was still at the bar.

"It's Glenn."

Cara's stomach flipped. "Is he okay?"

"I got a call from the center. They said they couldn't reach you . . ."

Cara pulled the phone away from her ear and glanced at the screen. She did have a missed call. It had probably come through when she'd been dancing with Branden.

"Mom, take a breath and tell me what they said."

Cara glanced at the bar again. Branden was on his way back over.

"Glenn had an episode. I don't think he likes his new meds. The night assistant I talked to said he keeps asking for you. Glenn's convinced himself that you've been killed or kidnapped because it's been so long since he's seen you. I'm sorry, honey, I know you're busy and I would go, but . . ."

She glanced up as Branden reached her. "I'll go, Mom. Just so you know, I was there last week. He was sleeping the whole time, but I was there."

"Oh, honey, I know you take good care of him. You take good care of both of us."

Branden sat down and was giving her a quizzical look.

"I have to go, Mom. I love you."

"I love you, too," her mother said.

Cara hung up and looked at Branden. She accepted a glass of water from him and took a generous swallow. "Thank you," she said. She stared at the glass.

"Is everything okay?" he asked quietly.

"Um . . . my mother needs me."

"Tonight?" He glanced at his watch. "It's awfully late. Are you going to go?"

She nodded. "I—I need to."

"I'll come with you."

Her head jerked up. "No."

"Cara—"

"I'm sorry. I feel bad for cutting short our fun, but you can stay . . ."

He frowned. "You want me to stay and dance without you?"

Of course she didn't. "Or—or you can work. I'm sure you have work to do."

He reached out and covered her hand with his. "Cara. What's going on?"

"What's going on is I have responsibilities. Responsibilities that have nothing to do with you, Branden." *Nothing to do with the fantasy life that you live.*

He frowned. "I want to help you. Take care of you."

"No. I'm used to taking care of these things by myself. I want to keep it that way. I *have* to keep it that way."

"You don't have to. You could try letting someone in every once in a while. You could try letting *me* in."

She stood. "I'm sorry. I have to go. If you'd prefer I go back to my own place afterward—"

"No. I'll send my driver. That's not negotiable, Cara. It's late. Either I take you to your mother's myself or you go with my driver."

"Fine! You might as well take me yourself since your driver will just report back to you anyway."

"Report what? Where are you going?"

"To Suffolk County. Windorne Care Home. And we're not going to see my mother. We're going to see my brother."

Branden walked with Cara down a long hallway. Windorne Care Home was a residential facility—like an apartment complex but with services for those who had special needs. It was very nicely decorated, with big open windows that faced the east and probably picked up the rays of the sun during the day quite nicely. They entered an airy day room with a large-screen plasma television and big, plush couches. The tile floor was new and shiny. There were lush green plants in pots that sat around the room and pictures of colorful flowers and birds on the walls. It looked like a comfortable and safe haven.

Cara turned to him. "Can you wait here? I—I'm not sure what kind of state he's in, and if he sees you . . ."

Branden nodded. "I'll stay out of sight."

She walked to another hallway and past two big linen carts. It looked like staff had been busy distributing the laundry before they got called away. She stopped about halfway down the hall, then glanced at him before entering a room.

It was quiet for the most part; he could hear the occasional snore or the sounds of soft crying here and there. It reminded him that even as nice a facility as this one was, it was still a facility for those who couldn't care for themselves, and that would always carry a hint of sadness.

Ever since she'd received the call from her mother, Cara had tried to hide it, but Branden had sensed the sadness in her. She was tired. She was here for her brother, but she needed help, and he felt like an idiot sitting here. He was curious about her brother even as he wanted to respect her wishes to not be seen.

He walked past the laundry carts and by the open door of her brother's bedroom. Staying out of sight, he peeked inside. She was sitting next to a young man who was reclining in bed. Seeing that the room next door was empty, Branden slipped into it and then into the adjoining bathroom; the door into the next room was slightly ajar. From there, he was just able to hear Cara's conversation with her brother.

"I understand that you must have a good reason for refusing your meds, Glenn, but I would understand all of this better if you would tell me what it is."

"I took the melting tablet, the one that acts fast, when you called to say you were coming. But I didn't take the other meds. Besides, you'll just say I'm imagining it," the young man said.

Branden knew from his investigation that Cara had a brother named Glenn. He was five years older than her and as far as Branden had known, he lived with her mother. There'd been no medical reports to indicate mental illness, but his treatment could have been done privately, keeping it off the insurance information.

"I promise to keep an open mind," she said.

"You won't believe me. No one here believes me. You never believe me."

"That's not true. I've believed you lots of times."

"Name one," he said.

"When you told me my high school boyfriend, Denny, was a cyborg, do you remember that? I believed you and I dumped him right away."

Branden heard Cara's brother laugh.

"I may have been wrong about that one."

"Are you kidding me? I could be married to Denny and have four kids by now!"

"Cyborg kids," he said with another laugh. "When I don't take my meds, my ideas can get a little . . . far-fetched. But really, I'm not making this one up."

"Okay then, tell me what's going on, big brother."

"I see Dad," her brother blurted out.

"You see Dad? Where?" she asked.

"He sits with me at night when I feel lonely. He doesn't say anything, he just sits there. I don't like to be alone. Dad always knew I didn't like to be alone. Remember when I was little he would sit on the end of my bed until I fell asleep, and then if I woke up, he would come back?"

Branden peeked through the crack in the bathroom door. He could see just a sliver of Cara's beautiful face as she smiled.

"I remember," she said. "He chased a few monsters out of my closet at night, too. He was a great dad."

"Yeah, he was the best," her brother said.

"It's nice that Dad is here with you when you're scared or alone, Glenn. I don't have a hard time believing that. What does it have to do with your medications, though?"

"When I take them, I get too sleepy and I sleep all night. I don't get to see him, Cara. I miss him so much."

Branden could tell by the crack of his voice that her brother was crying. He saw Cara lean in and put her hand on the side of his face gently.

"Listen to me, Glenn, okay? Daddy is always with us." She took her other hand and put it on his chest. "He's right there." Then she pointed at his head and said, "And he's right there, in your memories. Anytime you want to see him, day or night, all you have to do is close your eyes and call him up. That's what I do."

Glenn looked at his sister with surprise. "You see him, too?"

"Yes, but I don't see him with my eyes, I see him with my heart. Your imagination has always been better than mine though, big brother. Your mind and heart are probably just projecting an image of him at the end of your bed so you feel safe and protected. You have to remember that the meds are for other things, a lot of things that you do want gone, Glenn, right? Like thinking that I'm dead and your nurse killed me. I can't imagine how awful that must have been for you. But look, I'm here, and I'm real."

"Ow," her brother said.

Cara giggled and said, "I was only pinching you so that you knew I was real."

"Yeah, right," he said with a smile. "But I get what you're saying. I can lose the ugly thoughts and keep the good ones, right?"

"Right, big brother. You're pretty smart; you must get that from me."

He laughed and said, "I think I got it from Dad, but if that makes you feel better . . ."

"Will you go back on your meds now?"

"I will," he said. "I promise. But for a few minutes will you just sit with me?"

"Sure," she said.

"Cara?"

"Yes, Glenn?"

"Will you say the poem for me?"

"Sure," she said again. "Close your eyes and rest your head, okay?"

Glenn laid his head back into the pillow on the recliner and closed his eyes.

It was obvious how much her brother meant to her, and something sharp and hard tugged at Branden's chest. Because in realizing how much Cara's brother meant to her, he realized how much Cara meant to him.

She started speaking in a low melodic voice about darkness wrapping him in a tight embrace, the moon shining rays on his sleepy face, and him sleeping peacefully as the stars kept their nightly vigil.

Branden felt himself relaxing. His own eyes drooping.

God, how wonderful would it be to be held in this woman's arms every night as he drifted to sleep, knowing she would be there when he woke every morning?

Branden heard movement in the hall. Reluctantly, he slipped out of the bathroom and back into the empty room. Seeing Cara with her brother was a firsthand example of how much loyalty and love Cara had to offer someone.

Before he could stop himself, the question formed in his mind: could Cara ever love *him*?

He shut down the thought—the *yearning*—immediately.

Love was a word he'd permanently rejected from his vocabulary, except when thinking of his little sisters. Love wasn't part of who he was. Never had been, never would be.

Love made you stupid. Made you blind. Made you see others in a way that wasn't true—wasn't real. Romance movies weren't real—the shit in the papers and magazines about true love wasn't real, either. Love wasn't real. Yeah, his sister Rachel called him a cynic, but he figured *realist* was the right word.

Because his mother had proven how idiotic "love" was, time and time again, falling in love with men who treated her like shit. Treated her son and daughters like less than shit. Half his stepfathers had beaten the hell out of him, the other half had beaten the hell out of his mom. One had even beaten the girls. And still his mother would cling to their ankles as they tried to walk out the door, suitcase in hand, kicking off the sobbing woman who kept proclaiming her love over and over and over again. Love was about being weak and needy and desperate.

But Cara, gently whispering poetry to her brother, soothing his agitation and sending him off to sleep, had expressed love through each word. Through the lilt and tone in her voice. She hadn't needed anything from her brother. Had simply loved him.

But love couldn't be that simple . . . could it?

Chapter Nineteen

Outside Windorne, Cara shuddered and hunched against the brush of cool wind as Branden opened his car door for her. "You take on too much," he told her.

Cara folded her arms against her chest, refusing to enter the car. "You don't get to say that to me. You're my boss and my . . . lover." But maybe he was more than that. Maybe he was becoming her friend. Because he'd certainly acted like it, given he'd accompanied her here. Whatever she labeled him, she'd been grateful for his company. In a way, he'd made her feel less alone. He'd made her feel like if she needed him, he'd be there for her.

"You hesitated before you said the word *lover*. Why?"

Of course he wouldn't let that slide. She sighed. "I guess . . . I don't really know what we are, and that makes the rules blurred."

Branden put his arm around her, but she noticed he didn't say anything about what they "were." Finally, he just said, "Wanna go get a cup of coffee?"

"It's midnight."

"Are you going to turn into a pumpkin?"

She smiled and shook her head. "I guess you have a point. Let's go get some coffee."

After they both climbed into the car, Branden drove them a few blocks down the street and around the corner to an all-night diner. After the waitress filled their cups and walked away, Branden said, "What's wrong with your brother?"

She put her cup down, hesitated, then said, "When I was in high school, our family went through some . . . serious upheaval. Then my dad died, my mom had a nervous breakdown, and Glenn and I were doing our best to hold it all together. We'd both gotten jobs and everything was . . . well, none of it was good, but it was fine, you know? Then one day Glenn goes to work at the burger stand in our town and we get a call from his boss. He was arrested because he was standing nude in the drive-through window right at lunch hour."

"Nude? That must have been a surprise to hear."

Cara gave a hollow laugh. "I was only fifteen. When we went to the police station to pick him up, the policeman told us that he had been committed on a 5150 for a psychiatric hold and evaluation because he told them that 'the voices' told him to do it. He spent about a week in a psychiatric hospital and they sent him home on meds. That was his first psychotic break."

"Schizophrenia?" he guessed.

She nodded. "Yeah, only it's really strong. They call it 'treatment-resistant.' He does marginally well when he's on meds, but *marginally* is the operative word—he can't function completely on his own, although he's tried several times. My mom couldn't take care of him, so we found the assisted-living facility for him. For the most part, he does well and he's happy there, but the illness sometimes breaks through the meds and he occasionally has another episode. I try to see him every weekend, but it doesn't always happen."

"Wow, so you take care of him and it sounds like your mother, as well. That's a lot on your plate."

She shrugged and said, "Everyone does what they have to, I guess. They're family; you can't turn your back on them."

"I understand that," he said.

"You mentioned all your sisters and seem happy when you talk about them, but you don't mention your mom, just that she's been married a lot. Do you have a good relationship with her?"

"I have as much of one as I can," he said. "When a mother spends most of her time looking for a new husband or trying to get rid of the loser she has, the kids get a little lost in the shuffle. But I love my sisters. I stay in touch with them and help them as much as I can. The poor girls actually have it worse than me; they all had criminals or abusers or alcoholics or druggies for fathers. Mine was just absent."

"And Davies?" she said, surprising him.

"He and my mom didn't have any kids, thank God."

"I saw a post about you on Gawker that had a yearbook photo of you. Underneath that photo it said Branden Davies. You changed your name?"

"With every new father before I was eighteen. My mother insisted. I knew they weren't going to be around long enough for the ink to dry on the court papers . . . but she believed differently. I changed my name back to the one I was born with, not because I was trying to hide anything but because it seemed most honest. And, of course, the less association I could have with Davies, the better." He hesitated, then took her hand. "I'm sorry about what he did to your family."

She shook her head. "Don't be. It's not your fault. I just hope justice is served one day. Sometimes I even wish I could be the one to dish it out."

"I don't blame you for wanting revenge, but Davies

isn't someone you want to mess with, Cara." He looked at his watch. It was almost 2 a.m. "You ready to head home?" he asked.

Home. He said it like his penthouse apartment really was her home. Sometimes he acted like he wanted it to be. Part of her wanted it, too. Not because his home was swanky, but because he was there. And when they were together, Cara felt more at peace.

Was it possible that despite her difficulty accepting it, Branden wanted more from her than just a temporary sexual relationship?

"Sure," she said. "Only . . . We've talked a lot about our pasts. Not really our present or future. What is this between us, Branden? What are we doing?"

Branden took in a deep breath and let it out before saying, "I'm not sure, Cara. I know that I've never felt so strongly about a woman before. I know that every day I discover something else about you that makes me want to be around you. You're beautiful, that was the first thing, but now I know you're brilliant and kind and hardworking. Responsible and loyal and, seriously, better in bed than any other woman could possibly dream of being."

She liked that he seemed as confused by their relationship as she was, but that he was still willing to admit he felt something for her, even if he couldn't quite say what that was. Cara laughed and said, "Maybe we should start a mutual admiration society."

"Do you admire me?"

"How can I not?"

"I want more time with you. Outside of work. How'd you like to stay at the big house this weekend?"

"A few of my best fantasies have involved that place," she admitted.

"And was I in any of those fantasies?"

"Baby, you were the star."

*   *   *

Branden drove them out to his mansion on Long Island. When they got there, he told her he was going upstairs to draw her a bubble bath and she could sit in it as long as she wanted to and let the stress wash away. "There's wine in the kitchen. Make yourself at home," he said before he went upstairs.

Cara poured herself a glass of wine and wandered around the massive house. She'd been there the night of the party, of course, but she took her time drawing it all in again, including the thirty-foot-high ceilings and crystal chandeliers, as well as the artwork that she knew were originals and should probably be hanging in a museum somewhere. The vases in the house were all filled with fresh flowers and one whole side of the house opened up to huge windows that faced out over the ocean.

She was staring at the stunning view when Branden walked up behind her and kissed her neck. "Hmm," she said.

"Enjoying the wine?"

"And the view. It's breathtaking. If I lived here, I don't think I could bear to leave."

"If you lived here, I'd feel the same way."

She sucked in a breath and turned to face him. He kissed her and she marveled that the touch of his mouth on hers was even more breathtaking than the ocean view.

"Your bath is waiting," he said when he pulled away. Taking her hand, he led her up the stairs and into the bathroom.

Cara gasped aloud when she walked into the room. Branden had dimmed the lights and lit several beautifully scented candles. He had soft jazz music playing from speakers that were built into the walls around the room, and the deep, oversized black marble tub was filled with water and bubbles. Next to that was a shower the size of most ordinary bathrooms and it was entirely made of glass. One wall was completely mirrored and the other wall held a marble vanity and dressing stool. The black marble commode was hidden in a separate room off to the side.

"This is amazing, Branden," she said.

"I'm glad you like it. I left a towel and a robe here for you."

"You're not going to join me?" she said with a pout.

"I didn't say that. Why don't you slip in and I'll stay here in case you need any help."

Cara smiled and started stripping off her clothes. She looked directly into Branden's eyes as she took each piece of clothing off and tossed it to the floor. When she was completely nude, she said, "Maybe a little help into the tub?"

The tub was huge and sunken. There were two marble steps that led up on the outside. Branden took her hand as she stepped up to the top and held on to it as she entered the water. Sinking down into the warm, soft bubbles she moaned in pleasure.

"Is the temperature okay?" he asked.

She leaned her head back against the vinyl pillow that was built into the side of the tub and closed her eyes, "Mm," she said with another smile. "It's perfect."

Branden sat on the side of the tub and picked up the soap. "May I?"

She opened her eyes and sat up. "Please."

Branden picked up a big fluffy sponge and saturated it with the body wash. It smelled like lemon and sage, and the aroma of it alone relaxed her.

Branden lifted one of her arms and caressed the soapy sponge from her shoulder to her hand, massaging as he went along. He did the other arm next, and then started on her shoulders and neck, moving the slick sponge in slow circles. He ran it down her spine and she shivered with delight, and then he ran it back up to her shoulders and repeated the process until he'd washed her entire back.

Gently, he nudged her back and she leaned against the pillow again. She closed her eyes as he began to work on her chest. He washed and massaged near her neck, and then made his way down to her breasts. He circled them with the sponge, making her squirm as he cupped each one in his hand and lifted to wash underneath. He pinched her nipples, sending shivers down her spine.

He moved down to her abdomen then, and it was hard for her not to arch her back and beg for him to touch her between her legs. He washed down her sides and then across the top of her pubic mound, causing her to squirm and groan. He moved the sponge to her inner thigh and worked his way very slowly down her leg, across and behind her knee, over her calf and to her foot, which he lifted up out of the water and caressed as he washed it. Then he sat that leg down gently and began washing the other.

When he made it to the top of that thigh, he grazed her pussy with his fingers and she convulsed.

He leaned in and set down the sponge behind her, pressing his lips to hers as he did. He took her hand in his and stood up, urging her along with him. He turned on the massaging, handheld showerhead, made sure the water was warm, then began rinsing the fragrant bubbles from her body. He rinsed her neck and shoulders and then each arm and leg. Then he changed the setting on the showerhead and she suddenly felt jets of warm water pelting her breasts and nipples. The sensation was electric and Branden had to put his hand on the small of her back to keep her from falling into the wall.

When he finished tantalizing her breasts he moved down to her abdomen, and finally to the aching spot between her legs. He adjusted the spray once more so that it was a single, concentrated jet. Then he doubled her delight by using his fingers to hold open her lips and allowing the jet of water to land directly against her hard, swollen clit. She moved her hips and moaned and shivered.

He turned her around to face the wall and brought her arms up so that she was leaning forward against it. He began rinsing the top of her back, over her shoulders, the small of her back, and across the soft cheeks of her firm ass. He used one hand again to open her up, this time from behind. He let the water hit her pussy from that angle and then he concentrated between her ass cheeks.

He worked her there for a while, until she felt like she would come from the spray of the water alone. She'd never felt anything like it, and she almost laughed at herself as she thought, *I gotta get me one of these.*

He moved the spray to the backs of her legs, then washed down to her feet. He turned off the water and twisted to grab a towel behind him. He dried her off from head to toe, pausing only to kiss her lips, and then brush his tongue across each one of her hardened nipples. When she was completely dry he helped her into the fluffy robe and pulled her in for another deep kiss.

Then he said, "I'm going to take a quick shower."

Shaking, she took a seat in front of the glass shower on the vanity stool. She watched him strip and took note of his beautiful erection as he did. He stepped in, and with his back facing her he put his head and shoulders underneath the spray. She watched as it cascaded down over his shoulders and back, rolling off of his hard ass and dripping down into the floor. He took the bar of soap off the shelf and turned around to face her, then grinned as he realized she was watching him. He finished soaping the rest of his body and rinsed.

He toweled off and put on his own robe. Then taking her hand he said, "I want to show you something." He led her through a gigantic master bedroom to a set of glass doors. He opened them and they stepped out into the cool night air. The view from the balcony was magnificent. The ocean rolled across big, jagged rocks that jutted out from the hills surrounding the mansion, and Cara could actually taste the salty air on her tongue. Positioned so that no one could see them from above or below, it was a private alcove perfect for making love.

He reached down and undid her robe, opening the front of it and doing the same to his own.

"Are you sure we won't be seen?" she whispered.

"I trust Alex with my life. There are no cameras or bugs on my place. Plus, we're totally hidden from view from anywhere here."

He pulled her up against his chest and covered her mouth with his. She pulled herself up on her toes and deepened the kiss, pushing the robe off him completely and running her hands across his strong back and shoulders. He steered her to a lounge chair by the door and then brushed her robe away, as well. Sitting in the chair, he pulled her into his lap, facing him. Her legs straddled him and his hard cock pressed up between her legs. She pressed her clit against his shaft, moving up and then back, using him for her own pleasure.

The cool night air caused new sensations as her body heated. She rubbed herself against him, coating him with her natural lubricant. She turned her face down toward his for another kiss, sliding her tongue in and out of his mouth seductively. They were both breathing heavily and he put his hands on her ass, pulling her in tight against him and then pushing her back. He broke their kiss to bend his head down and take one of her firm nipples in his mouth. He sucked it in hard and fast, causing her to gasp and then moan.

Branden suddenly stopped and stood them both up in one fluid motion. Then he stepped back and looked at her.

"You are so fucking beautiful," he said. He reached into his robe pocket and pulled out a condom, which he swiftly put on. Then, reaching around her head, he wrapped his fingers up in her flowing mane of golden hair. He used that hand and her hair to pull her in for a kiss, and then pushed her back again, spun her around, and bent her over the side of the chair. With his hand still entwined in her hair, he pulled her head back and buried his entire length inside her.

Cara cried out in ecstasy as he began plunging in and out of her with such force that the chair wasn't holding up.

"Hold on, baby," he said as he stopped and pulled himself out of her. He picked up one of the robes from the ground and draped it over the side of the balcony railing before leaning her face-first against the rail and plunging inside her again. She let out a cry. He didn't keep her pressed up against the railing long. After several long, hard thrusts, he spun her to face him. "You make me *want*, Cara. So damn much."

With a trembling smile, she knelt in front of him, on the robe that was now at his feet. She touched the condom that glistened from being inside her. "Do you have another one of these?"

When he nodded, she slowly rolled off the condom, set it to the side, and opened her mouth. Groaning, he slipped his cock into her mouth. Reaching down, he squeezed her nipples as he thrust in and out of her mouth

with almost the same force he'd used when he filled her
pussy. Cara sucked in the entire length of him each time,
loving the feel of the head of his cock at the back of her
throat. She dug her nails into his hard ass with each
thrust. Branden began to grunt in rhythm to his thrusts
and very quickly was ready to explode. Cara braced herself, but he stopped and pulled her up to his mouth,
locking her into another passionate kiss.

He reached down and pinched a nipple, then trailed
his mouth down to bite and suck on the other. She
moaned with pleasure as he switched and moved his
mouth over to the other side. Then he reached down
and ran a finger across her clit, making her shiver violently. He kissed and licked his way down across her
abdomen, then plunged his tongue inside. Her legs were
shaking so hard she could barely stand. He nudged her
back down into the chair, and she sat forward with her
legs spread wide to allow him full access. Cara wrapped
her fingers in his hair now and used her hands to guide
his mouth and tongue to the places that gave her the
most pleasure. Branden licked and sucked and nibbled
on her clit until she was once again on the verge of an
orgasm. Then he stopped.

"More," she mewled.

He chuckled, then picked her up in his arms. "Oh,
Cara, I promise you, sweet one . . . you'll get more."

He carried her inside to the huge bed. He lay her down
on her back, produced the second condom, put it on,
and climbed on top of her.

He leaned in and kissed her mouth as his cock slipped
easily inside her. They moved together until at last settling into a steady rhythm, both of them lost in the sensations that coursed through their bodies, the sounds
that each of them were making and the smells of their
lovemaking. Soon, Branden's body tensed and he cupped

her butt, pulling her up and into him as he exploded with the orgasm he'd been holding back since she was in the tub.

Cara found her own release and then lay shaking and quivering in his arms until they both fell asleep.

Chapter Twenty

Sunday morning, after a quiet Saturday spent reading, watching movies, and making love to Cara, Branden left a sleeping Cara in bed to work in his office. He received another update from Alex, who was still in Punta Cana and was partying with Dreadlocks and Surfer to the point the other two had passed out, giving Alex the opportunity to search their house. He'd found bonds and texted Branden a picture. There were a lot of them. Branden immediately guessed that the bonds were stolen and that Davies had paid the men to move the bonds in order to cover the trail. According to Alex, the men were headed to Indonesia next, then to California to "catch some swells."

Branden had read something about drugs being brought into the country inside of hollowed surfboards. Figuring it was worth checking into, he talked to a contact he had at Interpol. Ernest was an agent who'd helped with SEC investigations when money was being illegally traded into different countries. He told him what he thought Davies was up to, and then he texted him the picture of the bonds. Ernest told him that he'd start working on things from his end, trying to find out if a hefty number of bonds had been reported missing or stolen recently.

After Branden finished his call with Ernest, Deena called. "Hey, sorry to bother you on the Lord's day, although I'm sure you're only worshipping at the temple of Cara."

"Did you call just to be sarcastic?"

"No, but that part is a bonus. I called to tell you that I'm brilliant, in case you didn't know."

"Of course I knew," he said. "What are your bragging rights today?"

"The email that Cara supposedly forwarded to Mahoney was routed through her computer, but it originated from an entirely different ISP address. It was crazy hard to figure that out, and someone with lesser abilities might have missed it altogether," she told him. "That address is the private domain of Larry Gills."

"Private domain? That would mean it came from his home PC. That derails your theory about Rafe Sampson setting Larry up, doesn't it?"

"Not necessarily. I still get the feeling Larry's being duped. Sampson's smart enough to make it look like that email originated from Larry's computer. He'd also be smart enough to know Cara would deny sending the email in the first place and that we'd investigate it."

"So he's setting Larry up for the fall. What's our next move?"

"We need Larry's home computer. Because it's not at the workplace, we need a warrant. I'll call you when my department is ready to move. I'd like to be there."

"Me, too," Branden told her. "Is it going to happen today, you think?"

"We'll probably go in next week. I'm going to have them include the office. Even though you can give the okay for us to search the office, he might have personal items like a cellphone, notebook, etc., that I want a look at, too."

"And what about Sampson?"

"Lee's been trailing him just like you asked. He got into the office today before 6 a.m. Not too uncommon for an ambitious up and comer but still . . ."

"Can we name him in the warrant, as well?"

"We have nothing on him. If we could charge him with being a workaholic, they could use that to hang us all."

"Okay, just keep me posted," Branden told her.

He hung up and called Lee. "You still on Sampson?"

"Yep. He just stepped into the Bull's Den."

"The Bull's Den on the Green?"

"That's the one," Lee said.

"Okay, good. I'll be there soon. Keep an eye on him, okay?"

"Will do, boss."

"What about the Bull's Den?"

Branden turned and found Cara standing in the doorway.

"I was just asking a friend about it. I was thinking of taking you out to lunch, if you're interested."

"Mm, yes I am interested," she said. "And excited! My friend Iris just started working there this week. I think she's working today."

"Perfect then," Branden told her. "Are you ready?"

The Bull's Den really had nothing to do with bulls. It was a metaphor for the "aggressive force on the move" that is Wall Street. When Cara and Branden walked in, Cara saw Iris at the bar, picking up a drink order.

"I'm going to go say hello," she said.

"Okay, I see someone I need to talk to, as well," Branden told her. He watched her as she approached Iris, waited until she had a moment, then greeted her friend. Strangely, she reached into her bag and handed Iris what looked like a scarf. Iris laughed, took the scarf, and gave Cara a hug.

With a smile, Branden scanned the restaurant. He saw Rafe Sampson and another man sitting in a booth near the back. He headed over, passing Lee on the way.

Lee was a bigger, slightly more serious version of Alex. Short dark hair. Olive skin. Broad across the chest and shoulders, a little bigger than Alex. No visible tats, though he had several on his back.

Sampson looked up and saw Branden just before he made it to the table. He looked nervous for just a fraction of a second before he caught himself. Putting on a big smile, he stood up and said, "Mr. Duke, I thought that was you. I've never seen you in jeans before."

"Rafe Sampson, right?" Branden asked, acting like he had to think about it.

"Yes," Sampson said, putting out his hand. "I'm honored that you even know who I am. We only met briefly in a meeting."

"I remember you," Branden told him. He actually felt like there was somewhere else he should be remembering him from. He'd seen the guy in the office, but hadn't paid much attention to him. All of a sudden he got a strong feeling that they'd met before . . .

Branden wanted to hear him talk again. There was something familiar about the way he moved his mouth. "You and Larry Gills have been teaming up on a lot of projects lately, right?"

"Larry's been good to me, showing me the ropes." Sampson glanced at the man sitting with him. "I'm sorry, Mr. Duke. This is Robert Stacks. He's a good friend and also a mentor to me."

Branden shook the other man's hand. "You're a broker?" Branden asked the other man.

"Retired," he said. "I teach classes now over at NYU. Rafe here was one of my best and brightest students."

"Well, I'm glad D&M hired him, then."

"Can you join us for a drink, Mr. Duke?" Sampson asked.

"Maybe another time," he told him. "I just wanted to say hello."

Branden told the other man it was nice meeting him and shook Sampson's hand again. He went over and found Cara, still talking to Iris. She introduced them and after pleasantries were exchanged, they took their seats.

Cara glanced over at Sampson and his lunch companion. "Friends of yours?"

"Not at all."

"Good. Because I have to say . . . Something about him reminds me a lot of Davies."

Branden jerked with surprise. "I'll be damned," he said. Now that she'd said it, it made sense. Now he had to determine if it was in fact true. He leaned over and kissed Cara on top of her blond head before standing up. "You're brilliant," he said with a smile.

"Thanks," she said, confused. "Where are you going?"

"I need to ask your friend a favor. I'll be right back."

He went over to the table that Iris was cleaning off and said, "Hey, Iris."

"Oh, hey, Branden," she said.

"I have a really odd favor to ask you."

She laughed and said, "Odd is my specialty. What's up?"

"Do you bus all your own tables?"

"Not usually, but the busboy called in sick and they haven't found a replacement for him yet, so today, yes. Why?"

"Okay, don't look because I don't want this guy to

know I'm talking about him, but there's a younger guy in a fancy suit sitting over there in the far back corner with another man. When you pick up his glass, can you hold it by the stem and bring it to me?"

She looked at him curiously and then said, "It sounds so cloak-and-dagger. Sure, I can do that."

He grinned and said, "There'll be a nice tip in it for you."

"That's even better," she said.

Branden thanked her and went back to Cara. When he sat down, Cara smiled and asked, "What was that about? Are you hitting on my best friend?"

"Are you kidding? She's cute, but she's got nothing on you. No one can compare."

Cara's smile widened but she dropped her gaze, as if . . . embarrassed? Pleased? When she peeked at him from behind her lashes, he figured his second guess was right. She'd not just felt flattered by his honest compliment, she'd taken it to heart.

And that was sweet. Really, really sweet. Her reaction stirred something inside of him, but before he could figure out what it was, Iris came over and they gave her their order. A few minutes after she went to put their order in, Branden saw Sampson and his friend get up. He looked over at Iris who saw them, too; she gave Branden a little nod.

When Sampson and his friend headed to the door, Lee followed them. Iris was right; this was all very cloak-and-dagger.

Branden and Cara finished their lunch and Iris cleared their plates. Then Iris came up to them carrying a small white bag. She handed it to him. "Here's your leftovers. Enjoy!"

She's good, Branden thought. He'd have a lab run a DNA test on the glass. If and when the authorities found Davies and brought him into custody for those stolen bonds—which Branden suspected would happen eventually—he'd make sure they got DNA from Davies to compare to Sampson's. Failing that, Branden would raid his mother's house. She was a pack rat bordering on a hoarder, one who was prone to keeping items that belonged to all her exes, be it old clothes, empty beer bottles, or a piece of old wedding cake. If he could find something with Davies's DNA, he could have it tested against Sampson's to confirm whether the two men were indeed related.

"Shall we go?"

"Maybe," she said. "But first, I'm curious about something. A place like the Bull's Den isn't really the spot where you get a doggie bag, and you're hardly the kind of man who'd accept one without even asking. Are you going to explain all of this to me?"

"It's probably best if I don't. It has to do with business, and when it comes to mixing business and pleasure . . ."

Her eyes grew hooded and she glanced away. "Right. Things are complicated enough as it is. Besides, it's not like you really know me."

As she turned from him, he took her arm, unable to bear that clouded expression that she now wore. What was it with this woman that made him want her to know him deeply? That made him want her to trust him?

"I know enough about you, Cara. This isn't about trust. It's about protecting you, the way I promised I would. You hear me?"

She bit her lip, then nodded. "Yes. Before we go, I want to say good-bye to Iris and use the ladies' room."

"I'll take care of the bill and meet you by the door."

After he settled the bill, Branden saw Cara come out of the ladies' room, and he was just thinking about how beautiful she was and how he couldn't wait to get her home when the man sitting at the end of the bar said something to her. He didn't hear what the man said, but he did see the uncomfortable look on Cara's face. She continued past him and the man actually stood up and grabbed her arm.

Branden saw nothing but red as he crossed the bar. When he got there, the man was still holding on to her wrist, despite the fact that Cara was trying to walk away.

"Take your hands off of her," Branden said. The man dropped his arm, but that wasn't good enough. Branden shoved him several steps back. "Who the fuck are you?"

"He works at another trading firm," Cara said, her lips tight, her skin white. "Apparently he's a friend of Greg's."

The man held his hands up, palms out and said, "Hey, sorry. I didn't mean anything by it."

"By what?" Branden said in a dangerous tone.

The man swallowed hard, but he didn't say anything.

Branden looked at Cara and said, "What did he say to you before he put his hands on you?"

"Branden, it's fine. Let's just go."

"What did he say, Cara?"

"He called me the boss's slut," Cara told him with a look of distaste.

Branden immediately grabbed the man by his collar and almost jerked him off his feet.

"Branden, he's not worth it," Cara said.

"Oh, I disagree." Branden pulled his fist back and punched him in the face.

When Branden let him go, he did so with a little shove so that the man landed facedown on the wood floor of the bar. Cara let out a little scream, as if she couldn't believe what Branden had done.

Branden couldn't really believe he'd done it, either. It had been years since he'd been in a physical fight. He was so angry that he was actually tempted to pick the bastard up and punch him again.

"No one, and I repeat, *no* one, messes with my woman," he ground out, then grabbed Cara's hand and dragged her out of the restaurant, as the phrase "my woman" ran through his head over and over and over again.

Chapter Twenty-one

Monday morning, Cara was still feeling slightly shell-shocked at having a man come to defend her honor in such a way. After the fight in the bar, she and Branden had driven back to his penthouse apartment. Then he'd left, taking the bag Iris had given him with him, without even discussing the fight. Or the fact that he'd called her his woman. Was she his? But she couldn't be. Branden Duke was a lone wolf. Untamed. Never to be confined by what a real relationship would bring.

They were just playing, right? Having fun while they could?

After he took off, she'd showered, crawled into bed, and done something she hadn't done in a very long time.

Cried herself to sleep.

When she'd woken, Branden was beside her, but on the other side of the bed, his back to her. Given he hadn't woken her when he'd returned, she suspected he was maybe regretting how far he'd taken things with her already.

Calling her his woman, for a man like Branden Duke, was a lot. He probably hadn't meant it and was now regretting the statement. They hadn't talked before going to sleep last night, and though they'd talked in the morning, it had all been friendly. Oh so polite. No morning sex, not even any cuddling. Just the one soft kiss on the mouth he'd given her before she'd left, though granted it had been a lingering one. And by the way his hands had cupped her face, it had seemed like he'd been reluctant to let her go. Yet he had. Let her go. And the only explanation she had for his taciturn change in behavior was that he'd had second thoughts. That he'd begun to think she wasn't worth the trouble of punching that man in the face. That he regretted it and everything they'd done together. And that made her heart ache almost unbearably.

Now, at work, she felt like putting her head down on her desk and crying all over again.

She didn't understand what was happening to her. She'd never been one to be ruled by her body or her heart, yet despite everything that had already happened to jeopardize her professional reputation, she'd let Branden get inside her—and not just with his body.

Trying her best to put Branden out of her mind, she turned on her computer, almost groaning at the number of emails that had poured in over the weekend.

Minutes later, trembling and feeling as if all the color had leached from her face, Cara leaned forward and put her head in her hands. She was so tired of all of this, and suddenly all she wanted was her comfortable, boring life back. She was determined to get it back, but in truth she didn't even know if it was possible given what she'd just seen. If there was any hope for it, she had to stop seeing Branden and move back into her apartment, pronto.

But first she had some sleuthing to do.

Then she had to show Branden what she'd just read. And seen.

* * *

A half hour later, Branden entered her office and closed the door behind him. He didn't reach for a chair or even ask to sit down, just stood there, studying her with an expression of wary concern.

"What's going on?"

"Emails." Cara rose and turned her desktop monitor toward Branden so he could read for himself. "They were waiting for me when I logged in."

He came closer, standing so near that she could sense the warmth of him. She didn't edge away. She refused to act like a nervous schoolgirl. She needed to maintain her control for once and prove that she could handle this. That she could handle him.

Admit it, Cara. You were the mystery babe outside the mogul's mansion. You looked hot. Hotter than hot.

Branden cursed softly.

Cara tapped the scroll key so he could read the second email.

Silently, she reread the second one with him, feeling sick all over again. Branden's thick brows drew together in a scowl. "Holy shit."

Got your attention? Good. I want you to know something else. I went upstairs after you did and Branden followed. You two didn't hear me. Guess what? There's more photos of your private party.

"So where are they? That could be a bluff," Branden muttered. "Nothing attached, I see."

"No. Here's the next one," Cara said.

His dark gaze rapidly scanned the opened email.

But you both kept your clothes on. HotnSaucey delivered the goods. Branden Duke loves blondes. Always has. The one in the sex tape got him all excited. But I couldn't see her face. Was that you, Cara?

"I want these traced." Branden's voice was rough with anger. "If I find this fucker, he'll be happy to go to jail."

"What do you mean?"

"He'd prefer jail to what I'd do to him."

"How do you know it's a him? Could be a man or a woman. The emails aren't signed." As she spoke the words, she realized how dumb they sounded. Creep etiquette didn't require real names.

Branden gave a slight shake of his head, unconvinced. "Sounds like a guy to me."

"You're probably right." She took a deep breath. "There's one more email. And this one did have an attachment."

"Show me."

She clicked on the email and video link. Then, biting her lip, she saw herself on the screen. With Branden. She was undulating against him, her blond hair tangled, her skin slick with sweat. He slid a hand into her hair and pulled her head back, making her cry out with a wild lust until he released her. She arched against him, her back to his chest, offering herself to the strong hands that cupped her breasts. His circling fingers tugged at her nipples until they were red and hard.

She twisted and turned, rubbed against him, moving to a throbbing beat that came faintly from the speakers.

It was a spliced and CGI-enhanced video that had been manufactured from the night they'd gone dancing. The movements were theirs, and it was her face, but somehow Cara's clothes had disappeared so that she was completely naked.

Start to finish, it was only a few minutes long, but it seemed as if it would never end. She had to tell herself over and over that she was looking at computer-generated imagery, created with obvious expertise.

Branden was actually himself, heart-stoppingly handsome with a lot of character. Her body double was an invention.

Her erotic response to her lover was all too real.

His strong hands roamed avidly over "her" body, stroking "her" skin. Just watching was almost unbearable. Her mind refused to acknowledge her intense physical delight in seeing Branden pleasuring a naked woman who was and was not her, his lovemaking skill very much in evidence.

His hands moved lower. Her body double arched against him. The rest was a mystery—like the modeling tape, it stopped short of the ultimate satisfaction. There was no sex, per se. Just a scorching prelude to it meant to stimulate and excite.

It worked on both counts.

It was a true feat of technological genius.

It wasn't real, but yet it was.

It wasn't as if Branden was blameless, but he could live this down—he was too powerful and too wealthy for a minor indiscretion in his past to mean much. Hell, he'd probably be touted as "the Man" and receive back slaps for weeks.

For her, though? Sexy dancing in public was one thing. She'd been a little concerned about cameras the night at the club, but had agreed with Branden—photos of them together that night wouldn't have done much to harm either of their reputations. People already knew they were dating. No shame in a little sexy dancing.

But a sex tape? One where she was without a doubt an active participant?

That was a big deal. *That* could break her.

He remained silent, and she could feel the vibrations of emotion coming from him. She hadn't looked at him once since the video started, and now a horrifying thought made her body jerk.

What if he'd already seen it? The video could have been sent to every computer in the office, awaiting the first employee to arrive that very day. And sent to online media, who would post it immediately, complete with an adult content warning or strategically placed black bars. She shuddered when she thought of the headlines. Someone was bound to identify her by name sooner or later.

Greg Johnson might, if he was still pissed off at her. She wondered fleetingly if he had made the video. The answer was on a spectrum from unlikely to impossible. His sense of humor was juvenile, going no further than the occasional frat-boy-style prank directed at a male coworker. The whoopee cushion and fake dog poop he'd used on his office mates were testimony to that. Besides, he was a numbers nerd, not a computer geek. He wasn't capable of creating a sophisticated CGI fake like this, was he?

The game that someone—who had to know them both—was playing was malicious and manipulative. The rules, if there were any, had just changed radically and the stakes had been raised.

Her screen saver appeared, a stock photo of a mid-night ocean. Moonlight shimmered on the tranquil dark water.

She wished she could sink beneath it and disappear herself. Soon she'd have to walk out of this office. What if there were whispers? Open stares. Worse than that, the not-looks, the tactful silence, from colleagues who were kinder or less judgmental. She knew their underlying pity would be harder for her to take than open contempt or salacious interest.

What could she do? What could she say?

It wasn't me in the tape, you jerk. Not at all. Okay,

the face was mine. But not the body. What do you mean, prove those weren't my tits? I can, though. Look. She imagined the sound of popping buttons and horndog yelps, or maybe she hallucinated both. *See the difference? See?*

What if—oh no. Iris would be sure to find out about the second tape. And eventually, her mom, who had yet to hear about the first one. Although that would take awhile, because her mother's bulky old computer didn't work well and the cable bill went unpaid every other month, and she didn't subscribe to any newspapers and rarely left the house.

It didn't matter.

Cara bit her lip to keep from crying.

"Cara," he whispered, reaching for her, but she pulled away.

"Had you seen it already?"

"Of course not."

"I checked what I could." Cara pointed to the screen. "That URL is for the desktop computer that some of the interns use. It's in the traders' bullpen."

The rows of connected desks were unoccupied, the several monitors on each showing blank blue screens. Wall-mounted TVs tuned to money news that were never turned off had been switched to silent mode. The few desks that held only phones, for discussions with secretive clients who preferred deal making without emails or paperwork, were also empty. A row of large clocks bearing the names of foreign cities in different time zones, financial centers on a par with New York, ticked away the hours.

Fortunately, she'd known which computer to look for. tempstation@dubois.mellan.

"The time stamps on the emails are 3:01, 3:02, 3:03, and 3:04. As far as I know, no one can even get into the building at that hour. Any ideas?"

His answer was blunt and immediate. "We got hacked. Those emails didn't come from that computer, they came through it."

"That doesn't mean an outsider is responsible."

"Hard to say."

"What? Are you still thinking this is Davies?"

"I doubt it, considering Alex found him in the Caribbean and he's been busy with his own shady shit as usual, but who knows. He can have someone working for him. In any case, Deena needs to know about this right away."

"No!"

He ran his fingers through his hair, his facial features tight and dark. "Come here, Cara," he said quietly.

"No. And stay right where you are," she said quickly when he moved to come toward her.

"Damn it, Cara."

"We're over, Branden."

"The hell we are," he growled.

"We should never have started. This is my fault."

"No, this is the fault of some bastard coward with too much time on his hands."

"Time he *or she* is clearly using to try and take us down. I won't give that person the satisfaction of going to her for help."

His brows went up. "Are you saying you think Deena is responsible for this?"

"I'm not ruling it out."

He shook his head. "That's ridiculous."

"Is it?" The antagonism she'd felt on first meeting the glamorous tech expert hadn't gone away. Neither had the memory of the lovely hand on Branden's shoulder, staking a hidden claim. "Even if she isn't responsible for this, she feels something for you, Branden. Don't deny it. If she thinks you're hers, showing her these will only lead to more trouble."

He laughed out loud. "Deena doesn't think I'm hers. Not the way you're implying."

It irked Cara that Branden defended Deena automatically. Then again, he'd brought her in as part of his new team. The nature of his relationship with Deena otherwise was none of Cara's business. Especially now that anything personal between her and Branden was over. Still, for him to say he meant nothing to Deena . . .

"Bullshit," she said.

His expression grew serious. "Careful, Cara. I'm already pissed off about all this. Don't piss me off any more."

"Or what? You're going to fire me? Maybe that's what you were thinking about this morning. Regretting not only that we ever got together, but that I even work for you. Maybe this video just gives you the perfect excuse to do it."

"What the hell are you talking about?"

At the incredulous look on his face, she closed her eyes. She knew she wasn't making sense. But the memory of his distant behavior this morning, coupled with the shock of this new video—it was too much for her to handle. Her *feelings*—feelings that clearly went beyond sexual—for Branden were too much to handle.

"You want to know what I was thinking this morning, Cara? Why I probably seemed distant?"

"No."

"Well, I'm going to tell you. I was dealing with the fact that what I told that bastard after I hit him was the complete and utter truth. I was dealing with the fact that my days as a single man are over. That you *are* my woman, Cara, whether you're ready to admit it or not. I was thinking of how to do it—how to feel what I feel for you, yet give you the time to come to terms with it and sort your own feelings out, too."

What he was saying caused joy and terror to soar

through her. She was too wary of the transient nature of joy to hang on to it, so she grabbed on to the fear instead. The fear was what would keep her safe. "This was all a mistake. Whatever you feel for me, Branden, whatever I feel for you, it's too complicated. I can't continue seeing you. I can't continue *working* for you."

"Of course you can. You're not a coward, Cara."

"No. But what I have been—careless and reckless and stupid—ends today. You know what happened with my father, Branden. You know how he died. It's horrible, but I think some part of me always blamed him for giving up. For having a heart that wasn't strong enough to get past all the stress and shame that Davies caused him. But the truth is, I'm just as weak. You make me forget what's important and risk things I can't."

"No, I'm not making you do that. You've finally allowed yourself to go for what you want. You said so yourself. I believed you when you first came to my penthouse and told me that, and I believe it now. Cara, life is about taking risks. About feeling. Enjoying. Allowing yourself to have the things—and people—you want. Things you haven't let yourself have for a damn long time. And I'm telling you right now, you're not quitting."

"Not right away," she conceded. "I have three weeks vacation time. I'm going to take that first while we try to track down the person responsible for this. But I can't—I can't be here, I can't stand all the looks I'm going to get from people—"

Her voice broke and before she knew it, Branden pulled her into his arms. For a second, she leaned her head against his chest, wanting the comfort he so readily offered, but that just made her feel weak. "Please let me go," she said, her voice brittle with tension.

Slowly, he did. "Maybe you're right," he said. "Maybe

it is best if you take some time off while I look into this. It's probably safer for you."

She pulled back. "Safer? Really, you still think this is about personal safety? Because I think this must be about revenge. Someone is gunning for you and using me in the process."

"You're right. And I'm sorry about that, Cara. I really am."

She stared at him, then sighed. Rubbed her temple. "I know you are, Branden. I'm not blaming you. I got myself into this situation with my careless actions. It's just finally time for me to act like a mature adult for a change."

He crossed his arms over his chest. "Which means denying yourself any kind of life, you mean? Any form of entertainment or pleasure as you take the world's troubles on your shoulders?"

She shrugged those shoulders. "We can't all be millionaires. Some of us have to live in the real world."

"And your real world doesn't include me, is that right?"

"No," she said after taking a deep breath. "It doesn't."

"Cara." Branden put a finger under her chin and tipped her face to his. Her lips parted as she drew in a breath.

"Don't," she whispered.

His dark eyes searched hers. Then he took a step back. "As I said, I agree that taking some time off is for the best. But things aren't over between us, Cara. Not by a long shot."

She swallowed hard, walked around him, and reached for the doorknob.

"You've been in here much too long. Doesn't look good. So . . ."

She opened it.

"Hello, Cara." Apparently, Deena Raj had been about

to walk through the door. She smiled at her. And then at Branden. "There you are. I was looking for you. Do you have time to talk?"

"Yes," he bit out. He turned to Cara. "I'm looking forward to the complete report on those collateralized debt obligations, Cara." He walked past her but glanced back and stopped. "Your preliminary calculations look rock solid. I know how many hours went into them. It's definitely time for you to take some vacation time. Enjoy yourself and I'll see you soon."

Deena's finely arched eyebrows went up but she didn't ask any questions. Just slid her arm through Branden's and walked away with him down the hall.

Cara did the best she could to concentrate on work the rest of the day. She got a call from HR around 3 p.m. telling her Branden had approved her vacation request even though she hadn't even put in for it yet. That was fine; she needed to get out of there, and the sooner the better. She left immediately, heading to Branden's penthouse to get her things. When she got there, the doorman gave her an envelope. After slipping into the elevator, she read Branden's message.

I asked the housekeeper to gather and pack your things for you. I'll be staying at the mansion tonight if you need anything. You are welcome to stay at the penthouse tonight and I'll have my driver take you and your things to your place in the morning.

—Branden

Cara had to wonder if she really was losing her mind. Reading that note made her feel like someone had kicked her in the stomach. It looked like his promise to see her later had been quickly forgotten.

She felt the tears rolling down her cheeks and couldn't figure out why she was so upset. This was what she'd wanted. She'd needed to end things between them and get her life back to normal, whatever that meant, given she'd soon be unemployed. But to her amazement, it wasn't her impending joblessness that had her so upset as much as the fact that she would no longer be seeing Branden.

She chastised herself as she got off the elevator. She was not staying at the penthouse one more night. She was going home.

She had a vacation to plan.

Chapter Twenty-two

"Dad, can I come home yet?"

Branden had Alex on speakerphone and Lee was in the room, as well.

"Dread's still not talking?" Branden asked, ignoring Alex's joke. Branden's friend Ernest in Interpol had discovered the bonds in the picture had indeed been stolen. Dread and Surfer were in custody. Davies was still at large.

"No, and I doubt that Davies is stupid enough to still be hanging around."

"He's been untouchable for as long as I've known him, but his luck can't possibly hold out forever. He'll slip up enough to get caught eventually."

"So that's a yes, I can come home? I'll be good, I promise. I miss my mother . . ."

Lee laughed and said, "Mom told me she was relieved that you were finally gone. She's getting tired of taking care of a twenty-six-year-old infant."

"That sounds more like she was talking about you," Alex snapped back.

"Okay, I hate to break up this love fest between broth-ers," Branden said, keeping his laughter to himself, "but

I have a lot to get done today. Come home, Alex. Lee will have a list of things for you to do when you get back."

"Thanks, boss. Hey, Lee, guess which finger I'm holding up."

Branden disconnected the call with a shake of his head. He looked back at Lee and said, "Tell me what you found out about the latest emails and that video Cara received."

After Cara had shown him the emails and videos, then told him she was going on vacation before handing in her resignation, it had taken everything Branden had to walk out of her office instead of doing what he really wanted to do—throw her over his shoulder and lock her in his apartment. Chain her to his bed. Chain her to him.

The only thing that had stopped him was how thoroughly freaked out she'd been. And how furious he was at whoever was playing games with them.

How furious he was at himself.

He'd fucking promised to protect Cara, and instead he'd allowed someone to get close while they'd been dancing and endanger her yet again. As she'd pointed out before, she seemed to be the most vulnerable when she was with him, and as such, maybe if she went away for a while, she'd be off the madman's radar long enough for Branden to figure out what the hell was going on. That was the only reason he'd arranged for her things to be packed and left her that note. He'd also arranged for Dexter Howe—a member of his security team and a former cop who was a tough-looking son of a bitch with deadly hand-to-hand skills, as well as sniper training—to watch over her, just in case. So far, Howe had spotted no threats to Cara.

"I checked interior security video," Lee said. "You were right. Someone went through the company computers to send those emails. Either that, or we're dealing with a freaking ghost or the Invisible Man, because the cameras picked up nothing."

"What else?"

"Cara's the only one who's received the video so far."

"How can you be so sure?"

"Deena created a portal so we can view everything that comes in to Dubois servers when she's not around. I can do that here or remotely. And that video hasn't shown up."

"Not anywhere?"

"No. She also set up auto-monitoring for Web mentions of your name, photos, things like that. The Gawker thing is permanently gone and the HotnSaucey clip is, too. There's absolutely nothing new out there."

"At least there's that." It was also a double-edged sword. Because it confirmed that whoever had made that video was focusing all his insanity on Cara.

Suddenly, keeping away from her didn't seem the wisest course at all.

The thought of losing her . . .

God, when was he going to catch a break here?

"What about the DNA test? Any word yet from the lab Gaunt recommended?"

"Not yet. He told me he was going to rush it, but it would probably be the end of the week at best."

"What about the background on Rafe Sampson?"

"That's a little more interesting," Lee told him. "He was raised in Scarsdale and both of his parents were in the home until he was four. At that time he got into an accident and he lost a lot of blood. As it turned out, his father, or at least the man who was on the birth certificate, didn't have the right blood type. There was no way that his mother and stand-in-father's combined blood types could have created his. Daddy left the nest not long after. When little Rafe was a teenager, he tracked his dad down. Apparently, Mom hadn't told him that she was the one who broke up the marriage. She'd let him believe it was Dad. Dad was more than happy to tell him that he wasn't his father. You were right about Sampson reminding you about Davies. His father was a man named Carl, who his mother worked for when she first got married."

"So Davies *is* his father. I guess the DNA test will just confirm that. Do you know if he ever contacted him?"

"Rafe finished out high school, and then moved on to NYU on a full-ride scholarship. The summer of his senior year was when the scandal happened with Davies and Cara's father. It's possible that the press from that alerted him to where Davies was and who he was with at the time."

"My mother," Branden said.

"Do you want me to go get him and bring him in for a talk?"

"Not yet. All I can really do is accuse him of photographing me. We need more than that. I want to bring the bastard and his bastard of a father down. But right now, I need you to do something even more important for me, Lee. It involves Cara Michal."

When Cara got to her own apartment, she called Iris.

"Hey, are you working tonight?" she asked.

"Just got off. How's your big, strong, protective man doing? God, the way he laid that guy flat was so darn sexy."

"Violence isn't supposed to be sexy," she said.

"Oh come on, Cara. You can be so uptight sometimes. It's not about the violence. That blowhard needed to be popped in the mouth and Branden took care of it. That means something. Men don't do that for women unless they care a lot about them."

"Well, things are over between us."

"Wait . . . *what*?"

"You heard me. And I'm taking a few weeks off work."

"You're taking time off? What the hell is going on?"

"I just . . . I need some time away." She thought about telling Iris about the emails and the newest video, but somehow she just couldn't muster the energy.

"You're running," Iris said flatly.

"What?"

"I saw how you looked at Branden yesterday, Cara. And I saw how he looked at you. There's something crazy strong between you and that's freaked you out. You're running scared."

"Maybe I am," she cried. "What I feel for Branden isn't healthy, Iris. He makes me forget common sense, for God's sake."

"That's what passion and love is supposed to do."

"I'm not in love with him," she said flatly.

Iris's silence said loud and clear that she didn't believe her.

"I'm not, Iris. But . . ." She hesitated, then said, "But I could see myself falling in love with him. And that's crazy. He doesn't represent the real world."

"Fuck the real world," Iris snapped. "What has the real world gotten you besides losing your father and having to take on responsibility for your mother and brother? You deserve more than that, Cara, and if Branden's willing to give that to you—"

"He's not," she said. "He had his housekeeper pack up my things and he approved my vacation, Iris."

"That makes no sense."

But it did, Cara thought. Sure, he said he wanted her gone to keep her safe and that things weren't over between them, but Cara wasn't a fool. After he'd left her office with Deena, he'd obviously come to the conclusion that her leaving was for the best. Why else would he have written that note? He sure as hell hadn't come after her.

"It makes perfect sense, Iris," she said quietly. "Now, can we stop talking about Mr. Branden Duke and focus on the first vacation I'm going to be taking in years? I'm sitting here with the laptop open, staring at deals for vacations. I don't want to go out of state, in case something happens with Mom or Glenn, so I was thinking about Niagara Falls. I've lived in New York my entire life and I've never been up there."

Iris didn't speak for a while, and Cara knew she was struggling with dropping the subject of Branden. Cara gave that to her, thankful when Iris finally said, "That sounds like fun. I'm jealous."

"I'd love to take you with me. Think of all the fun we'd have."

"Yes, but I just started a new job. I'd have a blast and come home unemployed. You'll have to just have fun for me. Send me lots of pictures and I'll live vicariously."

"I will," she said. "I'm going to book my flight and try to leave by Wednesday if I can. I'll go see Mom and Glenn tomorrow and make sure all is well there."

"Have them call me if they need anything. I would be happy to check in on them, too," Iris told her. "Have your vacation, Cara. You take care of everyone else; go take care of yourself for a change."

Her friend's support bolstered Cara in a way nothing else could. "Thanks, Iris. I love you."

"I love you more," Iris said before hanging up.

Cara booked the flight, got herself a hotel room, and then went to bed. She would get up early tomorrow and go visit Glenn and her mom, then spend Tuesday night at her apartment before catching her flight first thing Wednesday morning.

*   *   *

In his Long Island mansion, Branden prowled the room in which he'd first set eyes on Cara. His skin was itching with the need to call her. With the need to command her to come to him and forget going on vacation by herself.

He could only imagine how she'd react to that.

Despite his frustration, he smiled.

She had to be the most exasperating woman he'd ever met. She was also the strongest, softest, sexiest, smartest . . . He could go on and on, and he could even use different letters of the alphabet. The problem was, he didn't know what to do about it.

She seemed scared by the fact that she was so uncharacteristically reckless around him, but the truth was he felt the same way about her. He'd never let his desires rule him to the point where he'd gotten involved with one of his employees. And he'd never, ever called a woman he was seeing "his." Nor had he ever seen himself staying with one woman, but whenever he closed his eyes and thought about his future, he saw Cara by his side. The idea of spending the rest of his life with Cara filled him with joy.

What the hell was up with that?

A text from Jeannette caught him off guard. *Big sis Deena says your balls are gone. Some woman has them. Do tell!*

Before he could respond, another text came through. This time from his middle sister, Rachel. *Cynic no more? Is love smacking you upside the head like a cold fish? Welcome to the real world, Big Bro!*

Branden rolled his eyes. Deena shouldn't have talked out of school, but the sisters had always been close. She never would have divulged information about work, but apparently had no problem informing their sisters he was seeing someone.

Two more texts flashed through, one from Bethany and the other from Leslie. The one from Bethany asked him to please invite his new girlfriend to the opening of her play, and the one from Leslie asked if she could be a bridesmaid.

Holy hell, what had Deena said in her texts to their sisters?

He'd always been deliriously happy in his bachelorhood. He'd never wanted a woman underfoot, telling him what he could and couldn't do. He liked being completely in charge of his own life. He wasn't looking for a partner. He needed women, sure, for sex and companionship, but anything beyond that reminded him too much of his mother's fruitless search for love.

He and Cara were only meant to be temporary, but the thought of her quitting and permanently walking away from him made him want to punch someone again.

Suddenly his thoughts became clear. He'd focus on figuring out who was gunning for them and protecting her from any further harm. He'd figure out his confusing feelings for Cara. But he wanted Cara close by while he did so.

He picked up his phone and dialed a number. "Hey, Lee, what do you have for me?"

"Cara Michal used her credit card to book a flight to Buffalo that leaves on Wednesday morning at 9 a.m." Lee gave him the flight information and Branden wrote it down. "Then she used it to book a room at the Falls Resort, also in Buffalo. You want me to keep Howe on her?"

"Keep him on her until she gets on the plane. I'll take over from there."

"Figured that might be the case."

"Thanks, Lee. I'll talk to you in the morning."

"No problem, boss."

Branden hung up and then he made another call. This one was to a travel agent that he used for all of his travel needs. She always took his calls no matter what time of day or night it was. He paid her handsomely for it.

"Hi, Branden."

"Hi, Greta, I need a favor. I want to go to Buffalo and I want to leave on Wednesday from JFK and I want to be on Transamerica flight number 714."

Greta laughed. "That's very specific," she said.

"Can you do it?"

"Of course I can," she said.

"One other thing, can you upgrade seat S11 to first class?"

"Absolutely. Where are you staying?"

He gave her the name of the hotel and thanked her again. He hung up knowing how pissed Cara was going to be when she saw him on that flight.

He'd just have to make sure she got over it.

Chapter Twenty-three

Tuesday morning, Cara dressed and ate yogurt while standing by her living room window, looking absently at the ongoing construction across the street. The entire building was shrouded in black netting by now, the scaffold barely visible between it and the building's walls.

They could be adding a new facade. It was the quickest way to revamp an older building and turn it around for sale or rental. But the constant din told her otherwise—maybe it was being gutted and turned into lofts. Cara wasn't actually sure if it was originally office or residential space. The building had just been there, solid as a mountain, rather nondescript with not much in the way of architectural ornamentation.

Her phone, which was on the kitchen table next to her laptop, buzzed with an incoming text. After finalizing her vacation plans, Cara had stayed offline. She was too afraid the video of her and Branden would pop up everywhere, or that she'd discover another version, one that its creator had done more with, gotten really down and dirty, turned her into a flaming whore for his own delectation.

She didn't actually need the laptop that much. She had

her smartphone to read and send email. When it buzzed again, she put her yogurt cup down and picked it up. It was vibrating with a text from Iris marked Urgent. Cara tapped the little screen.

Sox had six!

The kittens. She was glad she'd delivered the scarf thing ahead of time. She responded. *Great. Bet she's glad it's over. How cute are they?*

Another vibration. *Unbelievably cute. All different colors. Mama doing well.* Iris attached a snapshot of the plump little fur balls lined up at the milk bar.

Awwww.

Iris texted back. *I spell it awwwesome. K, gotta go. Cute neighbor Fred's here.*

Ah. Cute neighbor guy had a name now—Fred.

Cara would have liked to see the kittens but didn't want to be a third wheel. Besides, she had a lot to do already what with visiting Glenn and her mom.

She set the phone down. She'd already arranged to rent a car, and when she walked to pick it up, the beautiful spring day should have cheered her. Unfortunately, it didn't.

She stopped to see Glenn first. He was happy to see her, and they played Scrabble for a couple of hours. She didn't tell him she was going away, just that she'd see him soon. If he needed her, she'd be able to get to him and she didn't want him to worry or get upset.

After visiting Glenn, she drove to her mom's.

"It's good to see you, honey. Come on in. The place is a mess. Sorry."

It always was. A sign of depression, probably, but Cara had long ago given up on trying to get her mother into counseling, or on an antidepressant. Cara cleared off a seat next to the one her mother always used at the cluttered dining room table.

"Maybe you can help me. I got this budget book." It

had been left open on the table. Her mother sat when she did and smoothed the mostly blank pages before she picked up a pen from a desk organizer engraved with her married name, Janine Finch.

"Nice." Cara saw no reason to point out that similar books could be found under the heaps of stuff with no more than a page or two filled in before they were abandoned.

Her mom took the rubber band off a wad of unopened household bills. "First I have to sort these out so I can begin to track expenses."

That was a step in the right direction, a new one for her mother. Cara sucked it up and took on the task without criticizing. "Okay. Done."

Janine gave her a wan smile. "Not yet. There's more where those came from." She nudged a plastic crate out from under the tablecloth, crammed with more papers, more unopened bills, outdated flyers, and junk mail.

Cara allowed herself an inward sigh. She was here, she would help. But the atmosphere of defeat and depression she always felt in her mother's house seemed heavier and more oppressive today. The autumn wind rattled the closed windows. She wanted to fling them open and let the chilly wind blow away the dust that had long since settled over the clutter everywhere. But she stayed put and kept working.

The crate was emptied of its contents in another hour and the filled-up columns in the budget book ran to several pages. The final tally was discouraging. Cara couldn't put a positive spin on those numbers.

"What am I going to do?" Her mother's voice was weary, as if the reality of her situation was more than she could bear. She glanced once more at the book, then closed it.

"I'll think of something."

Her mother sighed, reaching across the table to retrieve a faded velvet box. "I have jewelry that I don't wear anymore. The place down the street buys gold for cash."

"Please don't sell anything Daddy wore."

"I wouldn't do that, Cara." Her mother raised the lid on the box, looking at the jumbled contents. "There's his signet ring. You can have it now if you want. And the old pocket watch that belonged to your grandfather. Take both." She lifted them from the box and held them up.

Cara accepted the offering in silence. Her mother must have searched hard for the velvet box, which Cara vaguely remembered had once held a set of silver spoons. It had been a very long time since Cara had seen the ring or the watch. Her mother had put Hank Finch's effects away long ago. God only knew what had made her find them again.

"There's that hideous bracelet from my cousin," her mother said, breaking the spell. "She never liked the damn thing, so she gave it to me. I can't say I'm sentimental about it." She lifted it out and let it dangle from a finger. "Fourteen karat. And it's heavy. That takes care of the next heating bill, wouldn't you say?"

"I suppose so. Just don't sell anything Daddy gave you, either."

Her mother rubbed the wedding band she'd never removed. "I never have and I never will."

"Thanks for these." Cara tucked the signet ring and watch into her purse. "I don't really have anything that was specifically his."

"Now you do."

"Were they in the attic with his things?"

"No. I'd put them away for safekeeping. Then couldn't find them, of course. So I turned the house upside down. Can't you tell?"

"Not really," Cara answered honestly. "It looks about the same as it always does."

"Ungrateful child you are." But there was a gleam of laughter in her mother's eye. "So ... Everything's planned for your trip?"

"Yes. All set."

"What if something happens to Glenn while you're gone?" Her mother's voice quavered a bit.

"Then they'll call, Mom. Iris is going to be checking in with you and Glenn while I'm gone. I need this time away."

"I know, honey. You work so hard. I'm sorry, I just worry . . ."

Cara leaned over and gave her mother a hug. "I know, but don't, okay? I will come back refreshed and renewed and everything will be fine. Glenn is in good hands, and Iris will take care of anything you need while I'm gone."

"Okay, honey," her mother said. "Do you mind if I take a nap before we eat?"

"Of course not. Get some rest and then we'll go someplace fun."

While her mother napped, Cara tried to read and just relax, but her mind kept wandering to work and Branden.

Eventually she put the book down. Having her father's ring and grandfather's watch made her want to see some more of her dad's old things.

She climbed the pull-down stairs into the attic and found the boxes of things she and her mother had packed up and brought from the other house after her father had died. When she was younger, she'd come up here and sit next to the boxes and think about him, but she hadn't had the strength to go through them.

Now she felt compelled to. She figured going through her father's things would give her strength and ground her in her decision to leave Branden and D&M behind.

After all, she and her mother had started anew after her
father's scandal. Her father hadn't had that chance, but
if he'd lived, Cara liked to think that he'd have done
whatever he could to move on.

She sat down on the floor and began going through
the boxes. She found his things from college, and his
commendations from work. There were photos of him
graduating high school. He looked so young and hope-
ful . . . it broke Cara's heart that his life had been cut so
short.

She pulled out a stack of paperwork; in it was his high
school diploma, his college diploma, a copy of his degree from his business school, and some paperwork
from his job with the city that must have been put into
one of the wrong boxes.

One of the papers was a spreadsheet printed out on
the city's letterhead. It was a graph that had been charted
with red, blue, and green lines. The right side was a list
of employee benefit funds and the top was a list of years.
Across the bottom were monetary figures. The chart
spanned the five years before her father was arrested. It
had a date on the bottom indicating when it was printed
off of Excel. That day had been a week before her father
had been arrested.

Cara felt a tickle of excitement in the pit of her belly.
Her father had been accused of embezzling from the
city's pension fund. Could this document have had
something to do with that? Had he been looking into it?
But if he had, why wouldn't he have said so? Perhaps he
had been looking into it but hadn't come up with anything definitive. There was certainly nothing on the
graph, as far as Cara could see, to exonerate him or in-
criminate Davies any further.

Cara tucked the graph safely into one of the file fold-
ers and took it downstairs with her. When she got back
from vacation, she'd go through the rest of these boxes.

* * *

As Cara drove home, heavy clouds obscured the highest buildings in the Manhattan skyline as she headed west over the bridge. The signet ring was too big for her but she wore it anyway, on her thumb. She had a gold chain somewhere she could slide it onto. The pocket watch needed repair—did anyone still repair watches? Whatever the cost, it would be worth it to her. Her father had treasured the old timepiece, opening the engraved gold lid for her when she was very small so she could hear it tick.

New tech just didn't have that kind of old-timey magic. She dropped off the car at the rental place below street level in a parking garage and walked the few blocks home, still full after eating most of her entrée at the diner.

Her apartment was sunk in shadow that the hall light slashed into—she had forgotten to turn on a lamp before her departure. Cara moved swiftly across the living room and switched on a light. The warm illumination made the ordinary furniture look welcoming and chased away the gloom outside. She'd forgotten to lower the blinds, too.

It seemed like too much trouble to do it now. Besides, the construction workers were long gone. The black-shrouded building across the street was virtually invisible.

She took off the signet ring and set it next to the pocket watch on the table that held her closed laptop. That seemed ordinary again, a neutral object with no power to hurt her.

She still wasn't tempted to open it and watch a movie or anything that was streamed. She could do that on her smartphone if she squinted and turned the volume way up. An hour or so of a rom-com would kill the time between now and crawling under the covers.

Cara wandered into her bedroom and put on the pajamas she'd left on the floor, then settled in on the couch.

She had a text from Iris. *Check out our kittycam. Live from the laundry room.*

Cara grinned when she saw the link and clicked on it. The blurry image resolved into a tangle of six small fur balls. The returning mother cat stepped back into the box and bumped the kittycam. A black blur filled the screen. Cara waited. Apparently Socks was actually sitting on the lens.

"Okay. I get the message. You want to be alone."

Cara gave up and sent Iris a text to that effect, not expecting a reply. None came. She puttered around her apartment, leafing through a few magazines she'd read before, bored after a while. Then her eye caught her laptop.

Fuck it. What were the chances of another sex tape arriving at the exact second she went online?

Cara ignored the odds and booted up. She browsed the news, shopping sites, tomorrow's weather—there was nothing of interest. Sometimes the Internet was only good for making you sleepy. She yawned, about to shut down the laptop again, waiting for the hard drive to cooperate when a voice stopped her cold.

Just a voice. Not a tape. It was robotic, without an accent of any kind, without inflection. Obviously male, on the deep side. She guessed it had been digitally altered from the first words she heard.

"Hello, Cara."

She looked around, instinctively making sure that there was no one in the apartment. The voice seemed too resonant for her laptop's small speakers.

"No need to look for me. I'm not far away."

The chilling statement was not reassuring. It was terrifying.

"Who are you?" she whispered. Maybe it was better not to respond, not to engage at all, but she couldn't help herself.

"No one you know." The monotone voice gave equal emphasis to each word. "But I know you. What you want. Who you want. You can't have him, Cara. Not for real."

"Are—are *you* real?"

She suddenly wanted to keep the robot talking. There was a hint of something familiar in the altered voice. She couldn't place it. Cara strained to hear.

"I used to be a real man. Strong. Respected. Not anymore."

Whatever he might mean by that didn't matter. She picked up on the sullen self-pity underlying the carefully chosen words.

Skip the psychoanalysis, she told herself. Keep him talking. She stretched out a hand toward her smartphone. Maybe she could record this weird conversation. The little light above the camera lens in her laptop shell wasn't on. The robot wasn't watching her.

"Who do you think I want? Branden?"

"You can't have him," the voice insisted. "Not for real. All you'll ever be to him is a good fuck. That's why I make the tapes for you, Cara. So you can see what you are to him. So the world can see what you are. Branden Duke's lay. His big hands all over you. Feeling you. Bare-assed slut. You two like to play a little rough. He gets you hot, doesn't he. *Doesn't he.*"

The voice-altering software apparently didn't allow for question marks.

"Yes." She grabbed her phone, looking away from the laptop, desperately trying to find the record function. Was that it? The microphone icon? Cara tapped it without knowing for sure whether she'd guessed right. "Is there more? Do you have another tape for me?"

"Yeah." The single word burst from the speakers, edged with ominous roughness. The beast was straining at his chain.

The laptop screen exploded with obscene images, each erasing the other at strobe speed, a shifting kaleidoscope view of dark acts and hidden desires. Cara could not be sure that the woman she saw tied to a chair was herself or that the hooded man in leather leggings and strapped boots was Branden.

The ugly show went on for several more seconds. It was all about anger. Humiliation. Punishment. The strong against the weak. There was no pleasure in it. Just a soul-consuming, self-degrading lust that overwhelmed all else. She couldn't watch. Cara raised her hand to slam the laptop shut when the voice spoke again.

"You can make it stop forever, Cara." There was a fractional change in the tone. The voice was less robotic. Faintly coaxing. "Branden has to meet with me. You have to make him do it. By himself. You can't watch what happens. Just get him there."

She heard herself whisper. "How?"

"We will talk again. But first I want to show you that I'm real. Look out the window."

And be shot at? No way. She went sideways off her chair to the floor and crawled under the window.

"You look sexy on all fours. I want you like that, Cara."

Oh, God—was he watching her?

"Yes, Cara. I can see you. The camera light doesn't have to be on for me to see you. You don't know much about hacking, do you."

The robot was back, droning again. But she caught a tinge of pride in his icy voice. She was in shock. He could see her. She'd read about such a thing before. The ability to hack into someone's computer and observe them without so much as a video light to give you away. She just figured that was something the FBI did, not your everyday stalker. But she should have known that given the CGI-enhanced videos he'd produced, this guy wasn't an average anything.

"You don't have to answer. And I can see you're too smart to stand up. But I want to show you something. Peek at the black building. Sideways. From where you are. Right across from your window. Do you see."

In less than a second, a thin red line traced a shape on the shroud of netting. It was a heart. Imperfect but a heart. The laser outline burned inside her eyes before it vanished. Cara closed them.

"From me to you, Cara. I told you I wasn't far away."

Chapter Twenty-four

Cara fell back, collapsing onto the floor. She stayed down for a few agonizing seconds, her mind a blank, in shock, her senses numbed by fear. Her eyes stayed closed until she dragged in a raw breath and summoned up the nerve to crawl below window level toward her phone.

What if he saw her? What if he had a rifle? She would know the answers when she reached up to the table. Cara propped herself up on one forearm and fumbled near the laptop. She could see it but not the phone.

There was nothing but the smooth surface of the table. Then she had it. Cara flattened herself to the carpet, clutching the phone, expecting the zing of a bullet overhead.

There was only silence.

She breathed out a prayer of thanks, knowing good and goddamn well she wasn't out of danger. She started to dial 911, then hesitated as she envisioned how that conversation would go.

Please state the nature of your emergency. A heart? You saw a heart out your window? And someone sent you nasty pictures? That's all?

The cops wouldn't rush over.

But Branden would.

All she had to do was call him.

She wanted to. Just thinking about calling him made her feel better. Safer. She knew he'd do everything in his power to protect her. But there was a madman after him. A madman that was trying to use her to get to him.

Branden has to meet with me. You have to make him do it. By himself. You can't watch what happens. Just get him there.

No. She couldn't tell Branden. She knew him. She knew he would meet the man. To stop this. To protect her.

And in doing so, he'd put himself in danger.

Cara knew what her stalker wanted, and it wasn't to chat with Branden or even to extort money from him. For some reason, he wanted Branden dead.

Cara wasn't going to let that happen.

Shaking, she put her phone down next to her on the floor and curled into a ball. She thought of Branden. How happy he'd made her, in bed and out. How kind and honorable he was despite the ridiculous amounts of money and power he had. She wasn't a match for someone like him.

She'd always believed her father to be a coward. A good man, but a coward nonetheless.

It turned out that Cara was the biggest coward of them all.

The shrill sound of her phone ringing caused Cara to jerk awake. For a moment, she was disoriented, uncertain why she was curled up on her living room floor, her bones aching from having obviously fallen asleep there.

Then the memories came flooding back.

It was morning. She was supposed to be leaving on

vacation, but that creepy voice and heart had kept her locked in her apartment all night.

She cringed as her phone kept ringing, unsettled by the default ringtone. Not anyone she would know. She used pop songs for friends and her mother. Then she stiffened with fear.

Oh, God—was *he* calling her?

She stared at the phone until the ringing stopped.

Then it started again. Cara lifted her fingers and saw Branden's number on the screen.

"Hello?" she whispered. "Branden?"

"You sound freaked. You saw it, didn't you? Another fucking freak show starring you and me."

"Where are you?"

"The link came up on my work computer. Where are you?"

Curled up on my floor like the pathetic coward I am.

Instead of saying that, she said, "I'm freaked, Branden. But not just because of the video. He—he *talked* to me. He could *see* me from my laptop. He hacked into my video feed."

"What did he say?" His voice held barely controlled fury.

"Crazy crap. Threats. Then, bam, the video." She swallowed hard, trying to calm down. "Branden—he's outside somewhere."

"You mean in your building?"

"No. But close to it. Maybe across the street."

"I'm coming over."

"No! No, you can't. Promise me you'll stay away, Branden."

The line practically quivered with tense silence. "You said he made threats. He threatened me, didn't he?"

"He's crazy and he wants to meet with you, Branden. He wants me to set it up."

"Then that's what you'll do."

"No," she said, forcing strength and authority into her voice. "I won't let him hurt you. I won't be the one he uses to try, either. Now promise me you'll stay away."

"I'll be right there, Cara. Don't open your door to anyone."

"Branden—"

But he'd already disconnected.

He was on his way to see her.

And despite everything, despite her genuine desire to keep him safe and away from harm, she was so glad he was.

Cara crawled into a corner to wait for him. She called the doorman at the lobby desk and let him know she was expecting a visitor. She described Branden and provided his name, emphasizing that he was the only person to be allowed up.

"Yes, Miss Michal. Someone was just here, though, asking for you. A man."

A sudden sense of dread held her motionless. "What did he look like?" Branden couldn't possibly have gotten here that fast.

She had no idea what her stalker looked like. But any description would help.

"Ah, I can't say exactly. Not young, not old. He was bundled up. It's cold out."

"Yes, I know. What was his name?"

"I didn't get a chance to ask that. Sorry, Miss Michal. Another resident was picking up a delivery and when I looked up he was gone. Do you think he was your visitor? Hold on, please. May I help you?"

A huge wave of relief washed over her when she heard Branden give his full name.

"That's him. Send him up."

"He has a friend with him."

Had to be Alex. "That's fine."

The fear that had her half paralyzed made it hard for

her to stand. She hugged the wall, keeping her gaze on the windows, ready to drop to the floor again.

Reflexively, she looked at the building across the street. The black netting let the sunlight through the window openings in the facade. She could see some of the steel beams that had been left in place to hold up the walls. But there were no floors.

A gust of wind lifted an unsecured part of the black netting from the gutted structure, revealing the steel-and-glass walls of the skyscraper Branden lived in. With nothing in between, it was possible to draw a direct line from his building to hers, something she hadn't noticed before.

But that wasn't what troubled her most. There were no floors in the gutted building. There'd been nothing for her stalker to stand on to point a laser beam. How would he have positioned that heart for her to see?

Maybe he hadn't pointed the laser from the building across the street.

Maybe he'd pointed it from her own.

Pausing in front of Cara's door, Branden turned to Dexter Howe, the man who'd been watching over Cara the past few days. "Don't let anyone in here unless I approve it."

"I won't, Branden. They'll have to get through me first."

With a nod, Branden knocked.

He'd barely been keeping it together as it was, but the instant Cara opened the door, pale and obviously scared out of her mind, he wanted to kill someone. "I brought backup."

Her tight expression seemed to relax somewhat when she saw Howe. "Not Alex?"

He shook his head. "Not for this kind of work."

When he closed and locked the door, she retreated several steps, her arms crossed against her chest. She was trying to hold it together, just like him, but he could see she was shaking.

"Cara, baby—"

"He's crazy and he wants to hurt you, Branden. He won't leave us alone until he does. Oh, God!"

Her knees buckled, but Branden grabbed her arm before she fell, holding her close to him. He pulled her into his body, wrapping her clumsily in his open coat, rubbing her back.

"Take it easy. I got you," he whispered.

"He was in the lobby. Just before you got here. What if—"

God, the bastard's games had done their job. She was terrified, and truth be told, so was he. He couldn't believe the man had talked to her. Had gotten so close to her. He blamed himself. He should never have allowed her to leave the protection of his building. Of his arms.

It was a mistake he wasn't going to make again.

"You're safe now." He pressed a kiss against her tangled hair. "I'm not going to let him hurt you."

She pulled back and grabbed his coat by the lapels, shaking him. "You're not listening to me. He's fucking with me, yes, but you're the one he's after. He wants to hurt you!"

He covered her hands with his. "And you don't want him to. Why?"

She tried to pull away but he wouldn't let her. "What do you mean? I wouldn't want anyone to be hurt. You're my boss and—"

"Don't you fucking say I'm your lover, Cara, because that's not all I am. And it's high time the two of us admit that to one another. You care about me. Admit it."

"Fine! I care about you. I don't really want to go on a vacation, not without you. And I don't want to quit my job. I want to spend more time with you. I want to get to know you. I want you to get to know me. Is that what you wanted to hear?"

"Fuck yes," he growled before pulling her up on her toes and kissing her.

Her taste exploded on his tongue and the tight knot that had been inside his chest ever since she'd told him she was leaving finally loosened. He was still tense, still worried and furious that someone was threatening her, but having Cara in his arms calmed him in a way nothing else could.

He ripped his mouth away from hers. "I care about you, too, Cara. More than I've ever cared for any woman. I don't know where things will wind up for us, but I promise you this. We're going to find out, and that means I'm not going to let some sick bastard play his games with us any longer."

"You can't stop him! You've been trying to find out his identity but have come up empty. He's smart. He—"

"He wants to meet me. So I'm going to meet him. This is going to end."

"No."

"Cara—"

She cupped his face. "No, Branden. We just admitted we have feelings for each other and you think I'm going to let you walk into some death trap a madman has set up for you? Absolutely not. We'll think of another way."

There is no other way, he thought. He remained silent. Because she was touching him, he could feel her still trembling. He could hear the way her voice rose as she talked, as if she was becoming hysterical.

"Shh," he said, rubbing his palms soothingly over her back. "I'm here. We'll figure something out, but right now I'm here."

"That's right. You are." She buried her face in his chest and muttered, "And you're staying here."

Chapter Twenty-five

An hour later, Branden was lying in Cara's bed, holding her as she slept. She'd told him everything before she'd nodded off. It wasn't a peaceful sleep but one plagued by restlessness and nightmares. For the past fifteen minutes, however, she'd been sleeping soundly.

In the meantime, Branden had been making plans.

"What are you thinking?" she asked suddenly.

He glanced down at her, mouth tightening at the sight of the dark circles under her eyes and the fear she still couldn't quite mask.

"That you should be sleeping, not worrying what I'm thinking. You need your rest, Cara. That's another thing someone has to pay for. I didn't want you leaving but you deserved vacation time. Forget Niagara Falls. When this is all over, I'm going to take you away someplace warm and exotic. How does that sound?"

"Like a pipe dream. But wait a second. How did you know I was going to Buffalo? Did you have my travel plans investigated?"

"More than that. I was all set to be on that plane with you today. I wanted you safe, but I couldn't shake the feeling that you'd be safest with me. Maybe I was wrong—"

She shook her head and laid a hand on his chest. "You're not wrong. Whatever is happening, we have to stick close to one another."

He cupped a hand around her neck and drew her in to kiss her, his tongue sliding hotly against hers for several moments before pulling away. "You were cutting it close by going into work this morning, though. You might have missed our flight," she teased him.

"I couldn't help it. I needed to see that video."

Slowly, she pulled away and sat up, and Branden did the same. "Wait. What? You knew the video was coming? How?"

Branden reached into his shirt pocket. He pulled out a small plastic bag holding a folded torn-open standard envelope clipped to a sheet of white paper. "This came in the mail. The return address is bogus. I checked."

Cara read the single sentence, which wasn't handwritten but printed. The envelope had a printer-made label and a freebie return-address label from some charity solicitation. The sender had used a Forever stamp. With a heart.

Tune in tomorrow morning for more hot stuff. Not Workplace Appropriate, but that's where to find it.

"So I went in, waiting for it. Unfortunately, my fingerprints are all over this envelope and the note, but there may be others. The envelope and the stamp are self-stick, but I'm going to ask Lee to have the whole thing checked for DNA traces anyway. Hell, maybe I'll ask Mike Gaunt. You never know."

"Gaunt?"

Branden set down the envelope and shifted until he leaned back against the headboard. Then he pulled Cara into his side. "I have to level with you. He *is* an FBI agent—undercover. It's funny that you picked up on it. He's good at covering his tracks."

He felt the shock vibrating through her. "That's not an explanation."

"Wait for it. Dubois & Mellan has been under suspicion for stock fraud. It's a real can of worms. And no, Max Dubois never had anything to do with the scams. But they did happen while he headed up the firm and that's why he decided to step down and sell. The SEC is investigating . . . with my help."

"Holy cow. So you're a—what?"

"The CEO. I don't have a secret identity. I'm a financier. Name it, I've done it. I came up the hard way. Started as a stockbroker, moved into venture capital, hedge funds—"

"You can skip the résumé. I Googled you when you took over."

He grinned. "Due diligence, huh? Anyway, I really did buy Dubois & Mellan and I really do own it. When the SEC heard of my initial interest in the company, they asked if I'd help with their investigation and I agreed. I've helped them with investigations in the past. Mike's an expert on cyberfraud, which, given Deena's expertise, was a bonus but not a necessity. Not exactly a fun guy, but we needed a pit bull and we got one."

Those cold eyes and thick neck—the description fit, but it wasn't flattering to pit bulls. Cara hadn't ever warmed up to Mike.

"I generally use Alex and Lee when I need information," he continued. "Frankly, I enjoy their company more, and Deena usually works with Mike."

"So Deena . . . What's her role in all this?"

There was a note of dread in her voice, one he was glad to finally address.

"She's an SEC investigator. Has been for years. She's

also my stepsister, Cara. And she recently married the love of her life."

"Holy shit," she said. "I hated her guts. I was so jealous of her, imagining . . ."

She bit her lip, and Branden reached out and rubbed it until she stopped. "She's protective of me. We're protective of each other. But you have no reason to be jealous of her or any woman."

She blushed, and for the first time since he'd seen her again, her eyes sparkled. "Good. But what does all that have to do with our stalker?"

"Someone must have realized what we're doing and is trying to get to me. Through you. He—and by the way, I doubt he's acting alone, though he may want me to think so—is probably not as crazy as he acts. That's all I can say for sure right now."

"So you no longer think Davies is involved?"

He shook his head and explained what had gone down with Alex. "Davies is being hunted as we speak. I have no doubt he'll be taken into custody soon, but unless our stalker is someone who's taking orders from him, I think someone else is at work here."

Cara's mind was reeling.

She'd known Branden Duke was a financial genius, incredible lover, and overall good man, but he was more than that. He was a freaking hero. She felt like she'd walked into a movie.

But that didn't mean she was safe and there would be a happy ending, she reminded herself. It also didn't mean that just because Branden was a hero he needed to handle what was happening here alone.

She'd been doing a lot of thinking over the past hour as she'd rested in Branden's arms. And what she'd been thinking was she wanted this. To relax with him, open up to each other, and explore what could develop between them when their lives weren't consumed by safety and professional concerns.

But that meant they had to deal with their stalker once and for all.

And she'd come up with a plan to do so.

The only question was whether Branden would go along with it.

Slowly, she pulled out of Branden's arms and stood up. He raised a questioning brow. She pointed at her phone and laptop, which they'd brought into the bedroom with them and placed on her dresser.

"I want to do something," she said. "But first, I need you to call Lee."

As Branden listened to Cara's plan, he had to admit it was a good one; it was a long shot, yet posed no real physical risk to either of them. But if it backfired, there would be no going back—she would have handed the enemy the means to destroy her professional reputation and personal peace of mind. The fact that she was even willing to consider it made him realize just how much he did mean to her. She'd sacrifice everything she'd worked for in life rather than risk him being harmed.

When she was done with her explanations, he shook his head. "No. I can't let you do it, Cara. I know how much your privacy and reputation mean to you. We'll think of something else."

"There is no other way. Please, call Lee. Trust me the way you've always asked me to trust you. Let me prove to you and myself that I'm strong, and that I'm not going to let my fears control me any longer. That I'm not going to let someone terrorize me and stop me from finally having what I want."

"And what is it you want, Cara Michal?"

She smiled wide. "I want you, Branden Duke."

He hesitated. Read the certainty and clarity in her gaze. Then he picked up his phone. "And I want you. I always will." He dialed Lee's number.

"Lee. Are you at D&M? Good. Because I need you to do something important for me. You listening?"

After he hung up with Lee, Branden watched as Cara walked to her dresser and opened up the laptop. She pointed it so the screen faced the bed. Then she bent down and stared into the screen.

"You want to play games?" she taunted. "Let's play. Because you're not in control here. You said I couldn't have Branden? Well, you're wrong, and I'm going to show you how wrong. You've been creating fake videos of us. Now you can watch us firsthand. Record us. Do what you want with the video. You're nothing. You'll always be nothing. And most of all, you're no threat to us."

When Cara turned away from the camera, Branden stood beside her. His mouth crashed down on hers and he kissed her, deeply and passionately. His tongue found hers as he stripped off her pants, leaving her standing with her back to the laptop, her bottom covered only by silver panties.

Decent, but barely.

Cara tried not to focus on the fact that a creep might be staring at her almost-bare ass. The fact that Branden's kiss was getting deeper and his hands were running possessively across her lower back made it easier to forget.

He grabbed her then, and suddenly tore open the buttons on her shirt, sending them flying across the room. Then he used the shirt to pull her forward against his chest and kiss her again. He pulled back and stared at her, his expression one of pure, unadulterated, animal lust. His chest heaved as he quickly unbuttoned his own shirt and shoved down his pants, keeping his boxers on. While he undressed, she shrugged her shirt the rest of the way off, leaving her bra on.

Less decent, but still covered.

He spun her around so they were in the same position they'd been in in that first CGI-enhanced video, with her back against his bare chest and his hands cupping her breasts. Unlike the CGI-enhanced video, however, she was clothed enough—if the creep did end up publicizing this video, she'd be able to rely on that, at least.

Branden growled against her neck. They may be faking it for the video, but Branden's response to her body was real—of that she was confident. She felt his throbbing erection pressing against her lower back. She arched her back and stretched her neck, giving access to his searching lips, teeth, and tongue.

Each lick and nibble sent a fresh jolt of electricity shooting down her spine, all the way to her toes. He kissed a trail of hot breath and cool tongue down her neck to her collarbone. Flipping her back to him, he began to work his way down her chest.

He raised his head, looked into her eyes, and said, "You're mine, Cara."

He stroked her face, then leaned in close to her ear. "He's had enough visual for now, don't you think?" He tore his shirt off, then threw it, as if casually tossing it aside, but instead making sure it landed on the laptop.

Now the creep could hear them, but not see them.

Even as they were setting up the man, Branden was protecting her.

And she loved it.

"I want you, Cara," he said harshly.

"I need you, Branden," she said in response. A simple

statement, but one that carried weight. That held meaning.

He turned until he faced her laptop.

"Nothing," he said, repeating her earlier words. "And no one. No one will take this from us, Cara. I'll fucking kill anyone who tries."

Then he strode to the laptop and slammed the lid down. He immediately returned to Cara, sat on the bed, and kissed her temple. Pushing back her hair, he held her gaze. "I wasn't just playing for an audience, Cara. I meant every word I said."

She felt a wave of pleasure, bordering on orgasmic, at the sound of his words. Unable to stop herself, she kissed her way down his chest, stopping to lick both of his nipples before allowing her mouth to travel lower to its intended destination. He was still wearing his boxers, and she nuzzled her face against the soft cotton, causing his cock to twitch and jump violently.

As she kissed the head of his cock through the cotton material, she ran her hand up his thigh and into the bottom of his boxers. Her hand carefully found his testicles and she began to tug and roll them slightly between her fingers. Branden moaned as she wrapped her other hand tightly around the shaft of his cock while her mouth continued to nuzzle him.

Finally, she grabbed the waistband of his underwear and jerked it down. She immediately found his cock with her anxious mouth and sucked it in, taking it all the way to the back of her throat. She still had a hand wrapped around it, jerking as she licked the underside then swirled around the head of it with her tongue before sucking it all the way back in. She slid her mouth down to his balls and took one into her mouth. She used her mouth and tongue to gently massage it and then she moved to the other one.

"Oh, my sweet girl!"

While she pleasured him with her mouth, she dragged her fingernails across his chest and stomach and down to his thighs. She kept eye contact with him the entire time. She loved watching the pure, raw emotion on his face when he was in the throes of passion. He was usually so controlled, but not when she had her lips on his cock.

Cara could feel him twitching and swelling in her mouth. The muscles in his legs were tense, and she knew he was getting close even before he pulled her up by her shoulders and kissed her. He swept her into his arms and carried her to the bed, where he stripped her completely.

He laid her on her back with her legs hanging off the side. Kneeling between them, he lapped at her swollen, aching clit, then nibbled on it gently. She felt her orgasm starting in her toes and she gasped for breath as it worked its way up. She squeezed Branden's head between her thighs as she let out a little scream. Wave after wave of glorious orgasm rushed through her, but Branden didn't stop. He rode out the orgasm, continuing to lick and suck until he'd wrung every last drop of response from her.

When she'd calmed, he cupped her bottom and shifted her higher on the bed. She saw him slip on the condom. Once he had the length of his throbbing erection covered, he draped her knees over his strong biceps and, still standing, plunged his cock into her. He moaned loudly, beginning to thrust quickly at first and then slowing down to keep them both on the very edge. As he moved in and out of her, he stared into her eyes. They rocked like that for a long time, both of them enjoying the simple pleasure of being connected.

Nothing else mattered. The rest of the world disappeared.

Cara licked her suddenly dry lips and said, "I'm yours,

Branden. And you're mine. Nothing can change that. Nothing."

Branden froze, then he began thrusting harder. Faster. His head was thrown back and his breaths were so ragged they could hardly be doing him any good. Cara had to grab hold of the comforter and hold on tight as he bent down and gave her all he had.

"Come again for me, angel," he moaned. "Now. Come with me."

Her body exploded at his command, and then he stiffened and shook, groaning with his own release.

Moments later, he covered her mouth with his and cupped her face so he could stare into her eyes. There was an intense desire reflected in their depths. A feral gleam of possession. Even so, when he kissed her, he did it softly.

Cherishing what he held in his arms. Acting with the implicit intention to protect what was his.

Chapter Twenty-six

Branden pulled the sheet over Cara so she was covered. He smiled, placed a soft kiss on her lips, then said, "We should get dressed. I want to be prepared for anything when Lee calls me back."

Cara nodded and slid out of bed. Swiftly, they dressed.

According to their plan, several of Lee's men were supposed to watch from the D&M building's security room and notify Lee, who would be waiting outside with more men, if anyone in the office, in particular Rafe Sampson or Larry Gills, suddenly became agitated or upset. In any event, if such person left and headed to Cara's building, he or she was to be detained.

When they were dressed, Branden checked in with the bodyguard outside.

"No sign of trouble," he said when he returned. "But Howe's on red alert, as is the security guard downstairs."

She felt a sudden chill and rubbed her arms. "My God. I feel so helpless here. Trapped."

Branden pulled her in for a hug. "You're not trapped. You're safe. And until we figure out what the hell is going on, that's how you're going to stay."

After holding her close for several minutes, Branden pulled away to look out her living room window. He examined the street below, then drew the shades. The tension in the air was palpable, the dim lighting symbolic of the pall that had overtaken them. They alternately sat or paced until Cara burst out laughing.

Branden looked at her, his expression wary.

"We don't even know if anyone saw our little show. We can't just sit here watching the clock wondering when Lee will call." She stood, turned on the lights in the kitchen, and took out her frying pan. "Did I ever tell you I make a mean batch of pancakes?"

He smiled. "I didn't know that about you."

"There's probably a whole lot you don't know about me. Why don't we use this time together to fix that? Ask me anything you want."

He cocked a brow. "Anything, huh?"

"Yep." She pulled a box of pancake mix from a cabinet, and eggs and milk from the fridge. She started prepping and mixing, and Branden moved to the counter and sat on one of the bar stools, facing her.

"Okay. When did you—"

His phone rang and when he looked at it, he tensed. "It's Lee."

She swallowed hard and turned off the burner on the stove.

"Talk to me," Branden said.

As Lee spoke, Branden's expression morphed from concentration to understanding to disbelief. "Right. Is Deena there?" He nodded. "Okay, I'll be there right away."

He disconnected the call and locked eyes with Cara. "Larry Gills. Do you know him?"

"I've met him. He's a trader. Older . . . Oh, God. Is it him?"

Branden's jaw ticked. "Deanna suspected that Rafe

Sampson was using him to orchestrate some shady deals. Setting him up to take the fall. We've been waiting, trying to find what we needed to take down Sampson and possibly clear Gills. Lee said about ten minutes ago Gills lost it. Started shouting and throwing things around in his office. He's barricaded himself inside and he keeps screaming, 'It's not supposed to be this way,' over and over again."

"What about Sampson?"

"He never showed up to work today. Mike is trying to track him down even as we speak, and he's got the help of NYC's finest at his disposal."

"So Gills . . . you think our plan worked? That he was watching us? That he's the one that's been doing all this? Why?"

"He probably suspected he was being investigated. Thought to use you as a bargaining tool, which is why he's asking for me now. To bargain. The police are there, but Gills says he has a gun."

"A gun? What about the others in the office—are they safe?" Gail's and Tammie's faces charged into her mind. What if something had happened to them? She'd resisted getting too close to the women for so long, thinking only to protect her own emotional vulnerability. How wrong she'd been.

"Everyone's safe—no one's been hurt. And Gills swears all he wants is to talk to me."

"And you're just going to go? No. It doesn't even make sense. He has to know there's nothing you can do to help him. He broke laws!"

"The guy's obviously not thinking straight, but I need to get over there, Cara."

"Branden, he has a gun—"

"And I won't do anything stupid. I'll be careful. Listen to the police. But if I can defuse the situation by talking to him, I have to try."

"I'll go with you."

Branden shook his head. "I don't want you to be part of that ugly scene, and if Gills knows you're there, it might just agitate him further. He might demand to see you. There's no way I'm letting that happen. I want you safe. In my penthouse. Howe will stay with you, but the security in my building is a hundred times better than your place."

"Okay. But, Branden . . ." She grabbed his arms. "I—I—"

He covered her mouth with his. When he pulled back, he ran his knuckles down her cheek. "No worries, Cara. I'm wealthy, but I wasn't truly rich until I found you. No way am I letting anything get in the way of you cooking me those pancakes and telling me more about yourself. Then we're going on that beach vacation. Understood?"

"Understood," she whispered.

After taking Cara to his penthouse apartment and making sure she was secure there, Branden made his way to D&M. All the employees had been sent home and the floors had been evacuated. The only people on site were the police, Lee and four of his men, Deena, and now Branden.

"Any news on Sampson?" Branden asked Deena.

"Not yet. Something must have tipped him off. Mike's tracking him down now. I'm wondering if he called Gills. Warned him and that's what set him off."

Branden didn't say anything about the trap he and Cara had laid for their stalker. Hopefully, there was no physical evidence of it and no one would ever have to find out.

He jerked his head at Gills's office door. "It's quiet."

"He hasn't responded for the past ten minutes. The police have been strategizing about forced entry. I convinced them to wait for you in case you can talk him out. We'll tell him you're here but that you're going to call him to communicate from an internal line. Sound good?"

"Sounds like it's the best choice. 'Good' would be this over and me back with Cara."

"Is she okay?"

"She will be. I'll make sure of it."

Deena smiled. "I'll enjoy getting to know her when she doesn't think I'm a coldhearted bitch screwing around on my husband with you." She fake shuddered. "As if."

"You can get to know her eventually," Branden said. "But after this, I'm taking her away and spoiling her rotten, Duke style."

Deena smiled, then her expression sobered. "All right, big brother, let's get this done."

They'd braced for a showdown of majestic proportions, but the reality of Gills's surrender was relatively tame.

A half hour later, the man was in custody. All it had taken was for Branden to get on the phone with him and Gills had immediately said he wanted a lawyer there to represent him before he came out. One of the best, he'd told Branden, as if he really trusted Branden to pick out good legal representation for him. Unsure what new game Gills was playing but willing to go along so that he could get Gills contained and back to Cara as quickly as possible, Branden didn't hesitate to contact a well-known defense attorney with a long list of various financiers—many convicted but some acquitted—as clients. Branden stayed, then watched as Gills was unarmed and carted away by NYPD in the company of his new lawyer.

Branden wanted to interrogate Gills himself. Wanted to search his office and home in order to make sure anything that could embarrass or hurt Cara was destroyed. But he knew doing that would merely jeopardize the prosecution's case against Gills and Sampson, giving them the means to cry entrapment or tainted evidence. So Branden did the next best thing. He contacted his own lawyer to work closely with the police and move for any protective orders necessary to ensure that anything found having to do with him and Cara was kept under seal.

"Branden!"

He turned at the sound of Deena's voice. "Mike's on his way back. Sampson is in custody," she said. "Mike said Sampson cried like a baby when they stopped him at JFK and said enough to implicate both him *and* Gills. There's more work to do at D&M, but at least those two have been stopped."

It was over. It was all over.

And Cara was safe.

Thank God.

"Thanks for telling me. Can you handle things from here? Because I want to get back to Cara, and we're both going to take a few days off."

"Go," was all she said in return.

Fifteen minutes later, Branden strolled through the vast lobby of his apartment building, detoured around the indoor grove of ficus trees, headed for the penthouse elevators, and jabbed at the elevator button.

"Branden."

Branden turned to see Mike Gaunt standing beside him, a nylon duffel bag over his arm.

"Mike. What are you doing here?"

"I just missed you at the office. I wanted to talk to you about some concerns I have about Sampson." He patted the bag. "I have new information on the investigation. I was thinking we could have a cup of coffee. I understand if you'd rather do that at the office, but Deena mentioned something about you taking vacation time."

The elevator finally arrived. He held a hand against the side of one of the opened doors, ignoring the beeping. He'd rather have a quick meeting with Mike now than go into the office tomorrow. He hadn't been lying to Cara—he wanted to spend some alone time with her over pancakes and then he wanted to take her out of the city someplace special.

He thought of the residents' lounge on the fourth floor. Two coffees, a fast look at whatever it was that Mike thought was so important, a request for a printed report instead of a lecture, and he'd be home free.

"Uh, I can give you fifteen minutes. But I have to contact someone, say I'll be late. Can you hold that door?"

"Sure."

Branden took out his phone and turned away from Mike to send a fast text to Cara.

Be there in twenty. Unavoidable bullshit delay. Sorry.

He stared at his screen, unable to deny it.

He'd been about to add an automatic *love you*. Even during the intense emotions they'd experienced making love, they'd studiously avoided the slightest mention of that dangerous emotion so far.

Branden hit send, then waited until he got her reply.

I'll think of all the ways you can make it up to me.

With a smile, he slipped the phone back into his pocket. Hell, what was the point in fighting it any longer? He was in love with Cara Michal.

But he sure as hell wasn't going to tell her that for the first time in a text.

"You first."

He waved Mike into the elevator and pressed the number four. Above five, the elevator went express all the way to his penthouse.

"Thanks so much," Mike said in a flat voice.

Was it because he was annoyed with the other man, or did Mike Gaunt's voice sound more monotonous than ever?

Branden told himself to suck it up. Mike Gaunt had put in a lot of overtime on the investigation—he didn't seem to have a personal life, or at least he never mentioned one—and his tenacious attention to the smallest details was invaluable.

The elevator rose and the numbers lit up. Two. Three.

He felt a sudden explosion of pain at the back of his head.

Felt the bone-jarring impact as he fell to the floor.

Felt a heart-stopping moment of fear for Cara.

Then felt nothing as he blacked out.

Cara had just poured two glasses of wine when she heard the penthouse door open and close. Footsteps came down the hallway. She smiled and called, "You're early. I'm not ready yet." Of course, he probably wouldn't mind that she was barefoot and bare legged, her body concealed only by one of his big T-shirts. But she'd been planning on being completely naked and splayed out on his bed when he arrived. With a wineglass in each hand, she turned and walked into the living room, frowning when she saw Mike Gaunt.

Confusion flooded through her. "Mike? What are you doing here?"

Gaunt smiled. "I ran into Branden in the lobby. He's on his way up. Howe let me in."

"But why would he—wait a minute." Cara stepped back. The confusion made way for something different. Something more instinctive. Concern. Worry. "You shouldn't be here."

"But I am."

Fear. The cold sensation of dread ran up her spine,

making the hairs on the back of her neck rise. Her eyes never left him even as she slowly edged toward a phone on a low table. "Get out."

"I just got here. I'd like to look around." The tension between them seemed to vibrate in the air. He covered the distance between them before she could lift the receiver. He grabbed the phone from her hand and unclipped the cord. One swift pull and the other end of it came out of the wall jack.

"What did you do to Howe?"

Gaunt shrugged. "He, unlike you, believed me when I said Branden had sent me up. Big mistake." He wrapped the cord around his hand and advanced toward her, backing her into a corner.

Terror caused her body to tremble.

"I like it when you look at me like that," he muttered. "You never have. In the office you always look right through me. And when I've followed you, watched you, you never saw me at all, did you, Cara?"

She swallowed hard. "You mean—the videos. You made those?"

"Yes. All three of them. I saw you fucking awhile ago, just like you wanted me to see, but I didn't record that. I couldn't. So I'm going to have to record something else."

She seized a bronze figure on the bookcase in back of her, clutching it like a weapon.

Mike advanced toward her, unafraid. She swung at him with it and lucked out, catching him on the temple.

Cara tried to dash past him but he stretched out his arms and caught her in a viselike embrace.

"No. Stay with me."

She kicked and scratched at him, then bit him.

"Ahhh, yes," he hissed.

Oh, God. Her fighting was turning him on! She opened her mouth to scream and he clamped his hand over her mouth. He forced his leg between hers, crushing her bare foot under his heavy shoe to keep her off-balance and under his control.

She kept fighting.

"The fourth video will be the best of all," he said. "I have everything I need in my bag."

Branden dragged himself up from all fours, using all his strength to hold on to the elevator railing. His battered brain still worked, enough so that he didn't bother with analysis or reasons why.

Mike Gaunt had been behind everything that had happened. He was the only one who knew everything about everyone in the office, a classic loner steeped in hate who hid it well. Paranoid. Utterly twisted. And without a doubt, a killer. Branden had only been in his way. Gaunt's target was Cara.

Branden stared dully at the dangling wires coming from the elevator control panel. Something was clipped to them. A flash drive. He reached for it just as the elevator descended, picking up speed until he fell down again.

The thumb-size drive dangled, flashing red.

What had it been programmed to do?

He made another grab at it, then nearly passed out when the elevator jerked hard and whooshed upward again.

Branden gasped for breath as he dragged himself up. His head throbbed with fierce pain. He put a hand to his face, staring at his bloody palm. He could barely think. There was something—he could survive—if—why couldn't he think?

He banged his head against the paneling.

It came back to him.

The manual override. Secretly installed after he'd bought the penthouse. His idea. Hidden behind the official notice of inspection in the small metal frame above the control panel that no one ever noticed.

He braced his arms and legs, fighting the rocket ride, waiting for the jolt.

When it came, he was ready. The frame opened at the pressure point when he jabbed it. He waited again for the ride up, staring at the override lever. Would it work? He had never used it.

The car rose, gaining speed but not fast enough for him. Less momentum going up. The slowness was excruciating. He felt a sickening drop that lasted too long and squeezed his swollen eyes shut. Then came a full stop.

He wasn't aware that the doors had opened until he blinked. The car had gone all the way up to the top of the building. He staggered forward before the doors could close again, his sleeve button catching on the extracted wires, yanking off the flash drive. He didn't know why it was there, didn't hear it tumble through the thin gap between the car and the shaft. The doors slammed against him, pinning him hard, slamming and slamming. Branden fought free. The doors shut behind him. The free-falling car screamed down the cables.

Branden didn't wait to hear the crash of the elevator hitting the ground. He ran toward the penthouse door, cursing when he saw Howe, face bloody and lying prone on the ground. A quick check confirmed he was unconscious but still alive.

Oh, God. Oh fuck.

Cara.

As soon as he entered the penthouse he heard them. He ran into the living room. The thick form of Mike Gaunt was bent over Cara's arched body as he tried to catch her hand. She was fighting him furiously, punching him with one hand, not screaming, saving her breath, trying to save her life.

Branden reached them in a split second. Powered by uncontrollable rage, he ripped Mike away from her and threw him against the wall. He grabbed him by the shirt and smashed his face into the coffee table, shattering the glass. Blood gushed from the other man's bristled scalp as he crawled free.

Cara's soft cry made him turn. She held up her other hand and Branden saw the cruel cord that bound one wrist and the blue skin and hugely swollen fingers. He kicked the crawling man in the belly and flattened him before he turned to her.

He picked the hard knot loose and rubbed her wrist.

Gaunt dragged himself up and got to his feet somehow, then made it to the open door. And out.

"Stay here," Branden commanded Cara, then ran after him.

The man looked back just as the elevator doors opened.

"Gaunt!" Branden yelled.

But it was too late. Gaunt stepped forward. He screamed as his arms windmilled and he tried to regain his balance but failed.

His body fell out of view.

A feral howl of despair echoed. Grew fainter. Then, from far below . . . a thud.

Branden slowly walked toward the elevator shaft and peered down, jumping when he felt a touch on his shoulder.

It was Cara, her face drained of color. "Back up. Please back up."

He did, dragging her with him and pulling her into his arms. She buried her face in his neck.

"Thank God," he breathed. "Thank God you're okay."

She nodded. Looked up at him almost dazed. "You

saved me, Branden." She looked over his shoulder. "Please. Can we go inside?"

Branden remembered Howe. "We need to call an ambulance. Get help for Howe."

Cara clutched his hand. "He hurt you. I want you to go to the hospital, too."

He lifted her hand and kissed it. "Fine. But I'm not letting you out of my sight."

Hours later, he was still watching her. He'd gotten medical attention, and then they'd made their reports to the police. CSI had already come in and photographed the crime scene. Finally, because it was apparent Cara was swaying on her feet and suffering from an adrenaline crash, he'd drawn Cara a long bubble bath and then put her to bed, where she'd conked out immediately. Branden had made himself a stiff drink of subzero-temperature vodka splashed with whatever was in the smaller green bottle. That way he could think of it as a martini and not just a belt of booze.

He'd taken the drink into the bedroom, wondering if he was already a little buzzed just from the vapors emanating upward from the iced glass. Maybe so.

There she was, sleeping right in the middle of the huge bed, the superking coverlet tugged around her in a puffy white whirl. He could discern her shapely form all the same. She lay half turned so that her bare breasts, which he couldn't see, were up and her hips to the side, one leg bent at the knee and the other stretched out. One bare foot was visible. Her round ass almost begged to be patted, even though it was completely covered.

Earlier, he'd tried to kiss her when he tucked her in, but she'd turned her face away and his kiss had landed somewhere on the side of her mouth. He'd reached for her, but she'd pulled her arms in tight, as if unable to touch him. To be touched.

He understood.

Nearly being killed did odd things to a person, and he'd give her whatever time she needed to bring herself back up from the depths of wherever her mind had taken her to survive.

Exercising manly self-control, he pulled on the coverlet and covered up her foot, too. After changing his clothes, he settled himself into the armchair nearest the bed to begin his midnight vigil.

Eventually he'd crawl in beside her. He was so tired he might not have to finish his drink, so tired he thought he might drop off sitting up.

Branden tossed the vodka down, shivering from the cold feeling in his gut. He warmed right up when he looked at her again.

Cara was stirring. She dragged the coverlet higher, revealing not only the foot he'd so tenderly covered but her entire bare leg. The way the other leg was bent gave him a fantastic view. Fortunately for his sanity, she stretched that leg out over the one beneath it and settled into a more modest position.

Which didn't keep his stupid cock from springing upward. Branden put a decorative pillow over it and rested his drink on top, holding it in both hands. His cell phone buzzed—he pulled it out from his back pocket where he'd stuck it earlier and noted a text from his youngest sister.

Big Sis said you all had guns to your heads today. Dude, you still alive? Can I have your condo if you're not?

He gave a crooked smile. Apparently, Deena had informed their sisters of what had happened. It was clear Jeannette knew he was alive—just messing with him.

She'd group messaged, and his other sisters started chiming in.

If Jeannette gets the condo, I get the Maserati—that car totally goes with my actress glamour, was the text from Bethany.

Don't be dead, dude—I need my older brother to chase Alex away. Actually, scratch that. Croak all you want, Branden, I wanna jump Alex, came a text from Leslie.

Hah! She did want to date his friend, even though she'd claimed otherwise.

You little idiots. Big Bro is alive and well, like I told you all earlier. Now go to bed. That one was from Deena.

How's your girlfriend holding up? Trust Rachel to remember Cara.

He typed out a quick response: *No one gets the condo or the Maserati—earn your own goodies. And do what your older sister says and go to bed. Cara's safe and with me now, right where she belongs.*

He dropped the phone onto the nightstand and glanced back at Cara. His wanton angel slept on.

Then Cara sighed.

Not in a sad way. The sound was breathy and sexual. What was she dreaming of?

If only he knew. He couldn't help thinking of the hot, raw, turbocharged sexual connection between them. Couldn't help hoping that it could soon be given free rein. But right now he wanted only to share his strength with her, body to body, bring her back to him in every sense of the word. And go further still. Tell her how much he loved her. That he was serious about making her his forever.

Chapter Twenty-seven

"They found something interesting in Mike Gaunt's office," Deena said to Branden a week after Gaunt's death. "Come and look. It's all set out on his desk."

Branden glanced at the clock. It was past seven o'clock. He'd already texted Cara that she should have dinner without him. If she kept to the schedule she'd been on the past week, she'd be getting ready for bed soon.

She hadn't been herself since Gaunt's attack. He knew that would pass, but this feeling of helplessness? This feeling that there was an invisible wall between them, one that grew taller and stronger with every day that passed?

It drove him crazy to think about. Which is why he'd finally returned to work a few days ago. She seemed to need the time to herself or with Iris, who'd popped in several times, plus at least work managed to be an intermittent distraction.

He sighed and nodded at Deena. "His desk, huh? He kept that little room neat as a pin. I heard he emptied out his own wastebasket."

Branden had conceded to Gaunt's request at the onset

of the investigation that he would be given the smallest
space available at Dubois & Mellan, with no windows
and no art on the walls. The man had his few possessions strictly organized in a black bag he brought in
every day—and took home with him, now that Branden
thought of it—and kept straight things like pencils
aligned with the edges of the immaculate desktop. Branden had noticed the quirk but considered it nothing
more than a hallmark of an old-school Fed like Mike
Gaunt. Extra points for extreme neatness.

"Really?"

"I didn't follow up on it. So what was there to find?"

"You'll see."

Branden had no trouble keeping up with Deena's
long-legged strides. But she didn't usually move this fast.
His curiosity was piqued. There were a lot of unex-
plained things about Mike Gaunt, in life and in death.

"A place for everything and everything in its place.
Didn't he used to say that sometimes?"

"Yes," Deena said. "As if he'd just invented the motto,
too. I never knew whether I was supposed to agree with
it or not."

They stopped at the open door to the tiny office.

Branden held out a hand, silently asking Deena to give
him a minute. He could barely swallow past the sudden
lump that had formed in his throat. Unlike Cara, he
hadn't been plagued by nightmares of Gaunt's attack,
but now, faced with the prospect of seeing God-knows-
what evidence of Gaunt's insanity . . . Faced with the
very real possibility that it would involve Cara . . .

Branden closed his eyes and sucked in a deep breath.
Cara.

Every night since the fatal confrontation, he'd curled
around her, bodily protecting her from danger that no
longer existed. Cara lay still, offering no resistance when

he gently pulled her against him, her back to his chest, her bottom nestled against his thighs.

Sometimes they woke up that way. Or rather, he did first. She had taken to sleeping much longer than he ever could.

But that was because of the pills. Before she'd begun taking them, she'd barely slept at all.

"These are stronger than what we usually prescribe," the doctor had said. "She can't get addicted but she may experience some side effects."

It seemed to Branden that she did. After what had happened, her distant manner and reluctance to say much broke his heart. All he could offer was purely physical warmth and comfort, an instinctive, animal response that she seemed to welcome when she was asleep, as if taking shelter inside his arms.

She refused to see her mother—would just walk out of the room when he mentioned a trip to Brooklyn.

Denied that her brother needed her. Calls from Glenn's assisted-living facility were ignored. Brushed off, as if they meant nothing, but Branden knew better. Just that Cara couldn't deal with Glenn's needs right now.

Iris even brought over a kitten, which mewled and gazed up at Cara with soft eyes, but Cara simply stared at the peach and gray ball of fuzz and didn't reach out to pet it. This had worried Iris immensely, and she'd confided to him that Cara had always wanted a pet, but that her building didn't allow them. Branden had immediately arranged to acquire one of the kittens from Iris, who said she'd hold on to it until Cara was feeling more like herself.

Thankfully, that looked like it was going to happen sooner than he'd expected. Last night, something seemed to have shifted inside her, and she'd accepted a drive out to Windorne Home to see Glenn, then to Brooklyn to see her mom.

And go through her father's things in the attic.

But she'd still come home that night and had curled up in bed, not reaching for him, not spreading her legs and welcoming him in.

In sleep, she stretched and relaxed in his embrace, giving sleepy little moans that took him back to their hottest encounters instantly. *Tough*, he'd told himself. *Tough fucking luck. You, Branden Duke, will live through this night and the next night and the next. However long it takes. Until she's ready for that again. Ready for you.*

And she would be. Together, they'd work through the shadow Mike Gaunt had cast. And in order to do that, to help her do that, he needed to know everything there was to know.

Opening his eyes, he turned to Deena and nodded.

He opened the door to Mike Gaunt's office.

A slender woman in her forties with brown bobbed hair was paging through two books set side by side, turning the pages of each at exactly the same moment, like an automaton. Her bifocals had slipped down her ski-jump nose but she didn't stop to push them back up.

Deena knocked softly to get her attention.

She looked up and smiled in a very real way. "Come in," she said. "I'm Louise Callahan, a forensic psychiatrist and investigator. You must be Branden Duke. Deena said she would bring you by."

"Well, here I am. What's going on?"

Louise got to the point. "We found Mike Gaunt's journals in his black bag, which had a false bottom. These were concealed beneath it." She nodded toward the bag, which now sat on a chair. It seemed to be completely empty. Branden was more interested in the thick journals, which weren't printed but handwritten. Each held what seemed to be hundreds of pages between hard black covers, spiral bound.

"As you can see, these are actually artists' sketch-books, with high-quality paper suitable for watercolor paints and ink, no bleed-through."

Each page was covered in tiny cursive script, on both sides. He could make out a few dates—the microscopic numerals were easier to read than the dense handwriting.

"He started these in the late 1990s. Yes, they go back that far," she said in response to Branden's surprised expression. "Each entry is quite short. He created a meticulous record of his descent into insanity, perhaps as an attempt to control it. Mike Gaunt was a deeply troubled man."

Branden and Deena exchanged a look.

"What I find most fascinating is the parallel structures of the text," she said. "One book mostly about men. One book for women. Notes for each gender appear in each on the same day. His observations are much less organized and it's not perfectly consistent, of course. Whatever came into his mind was written down. If you like, I can read you some of the material. But the books themselves will be kept as evidence."

She paused and gave a little cough.

"It's almost ironic that no one can physically touch these books without gloves now because they're evidence in a criminal investigation. Mike had been obsessed with germs, but he'd also craved contact. More than the interaction he had with people during the day, apparently. So he invented his own world, in a way, and peopled it with actual human beings from his daily life. On paper, he could control them. When digital editing software was developed, he could make them do anything on film he took secretly."

"What did he write?" Branden hated thinking about what he might learn. He had seen what Gaunt did with videos. The books couldn't be as devastating. Ink and paper didn't have the power of moving images. "Don't go back too far. I want to know what he wrote about Cara."

Louise nodded and flipped pages of both books backward with the same simultaneous motion. "His hatred for you started years ago, when you started working with him and Deena in prior SEC investigations. Once you came to D&M, however, he never wrote about her without writing about you. It was as if you two were inextricably linked in his mind. But even on paper, he prevented you from touching."

Deena stayed where she was but Branden moved closer, standing where he could read over Louise Callahan's shoulder. She pointed to a relevant entry in the men's book with a gloved fingertip.

Branden Duke acts like a fucking king. I hate him. Wall Street is full of liars and thieves like him. The game is rigged. Honest men can't win. Good men, grown men who take their responsibilities and training seriously get shoved aside by these fucking punks. His youth—he takes it for granted. His success—he doesn't deserve any of it. All that money. Women are always touching him, like they can feel something good under his clothes. But Cara stays away.

Louise pointed to the women's book. "He picks up the thought here. Note the same date. It's like a dialogue in his head."

Cara is pure. Conservative clothes. Not too much makeup. I could be wrong about her, though. The way she walks is sexy. I keep thinking about what she looks like naked. But she keeps to herself. No flirting. I think she hates Branden, too. It doesn't matter. To her I'm nobody. Just a middle-aged man in a clean white shirt who follows the rules. But I have a lot to offer. She just doesn't know it. I want to teach her that rules are good. She needs to learn to obey. I will have to touch her to teach her. She might fight me. But I'll win.

"I have to warn you both that many entries are obscene. Some are violent."

Branden fought back a rising fury. These books would be filed away in an evidence locker somewhere in DC. Mike Gaunt's words no longer had the power to hurt others or to heal his psychosis, to use Callahan's lingo. His fantasies, his brooding rants were effectively as dead as he was.

He let Louise turn more pages.

I followed Cara and Branden into that dirty club. I had to tape her. It was a way to keep her close to me without touching her. But she danced like a whore. She rubbed herself all over him on the dance floor. I was disappointed in her. I was angry. She needed to know someone was watching her. So I sent her the tape.

"Flip back a couple of pages," Branden asked quietly. "I want to know where he got the original tape of me that he digitized."

Louise obliged.

I tagged him online. I have a record of every mention of his name. The HotnSaucey tape of him was available for complete ownership and transfer of copyright. I paid what they asked. It would never be shown online again. It was mine. Safe in my hard drive, ha ha ha. With all the girl porn I used to make my own Cara. And now I had Branden Duke in the flesh. I cut off everything he had below the waist. Him with his hands on those tight jeans. Touching himself. I had to keep him from touching Cara like that. I had to figure out a way to punish them both. I wanted them to be scared.

"Sick fuck." Branden looked at Louise. "Sorry. Had to say it."

"There's no need to apologize. The psychiatric term is really too long."

"A dead sick fuck." Branden avoided Deena's reproving glance.

"Yes." It didn't seem possible to ruffle Louise Callahan. "Do you want to read more?"

Branden frowned. "Go forward. To the day before he attacked Cara. I want to know what he was thinking."

"The handwriting got bigger and more agitated in the final pages," the psychiatrist said. "I would guess that he was rapidly losing control. There are numerous signs of progressive mental disintegration, fueled by obsessive hatred. He begins to mix up the male and female entries, for one thing. And he seems to be standing outside himself now and then, observing and admiring his own actions."

She called him and he brought his own bodyguard with him—Howe. He knows me. They don't know that I took over an empty apartment in Duke's building. A real badge and the right bullshit gets you past any doorman. No one asked me questions when I roamed around the skyscraper, either. Because now I look like the *man*. In charge. An authority figure. Experienced and disciplined. A man who can make bodies disappear without a trace. A man who can kill. No. A man who *wants* to kill. I have a plan. In my head. I don't need to write things down anymore. I need to act. Kill her. Kill him.

Louise Callahan flipped to the last page. The meticulous handwriting had changed completely into a messy scrawl that was too big not to crowd the margins. Gaunt's focused rage had exploded.

He has everything. I have nothing. He has her. But I can take her away. Today. Today.

Thank God he hadn't succeeded in his plan to take Cara away from him, Branden thought. And what a complicated, well-thought-out plan it had been.

He'd rented an apartment in Branden's building. Gained access to the new skyscraper's computerized heart, including the key code to Branden's door and to his private elevators. He'd even planted malware that only he could activate to run them in different ways. All he'd needed was the opportunity to get Branden on those elevators and to Cara.

So far, there was no evidence that he'd recorded the trap Cara and Branden had set for him. He hoped it was because he hadn't.

Even after spending the last week with her, with all known threats to them eliminated, Branden was still paranoid. He'd assigned several men to guard her while she was in the penthouse and when she was out of it. While some part of him wanted to keep her protectively locked indoors, he refused to give Gaunt that type of power over them. Cara wasn't meant to be caged. She was a beautiful woman who loved life, and he was going to spend the rest of his spoiling her and showing her all the wonders and luxuries that were hers for the taking. That included making sure her mother and brother were well taken care of as always, with the major difference that Cara no longer felt she carried that responsibility alone.

Tomorrow they were leaving for the beach vacation he promised her. He hoped the time away from New York would finally enable them to move beyond the nightmare they'd experienced and become intimate— physically *and* emotionally—again.

During the visit with her mother last night, Cara had shown him her father's paperwork that she'd found in the attic. She held hope that the paperwork would hold the key to exonerating her father once and for all. Branden wanted to give that to her, but from what he'd seen so far, he wasn't sure he could—Davies normally covered his tracks pretty darn well. However, he was currently in custody for trying to move those stolen bonds, so who knew? Maybe Branden was giving him too much credit. He'd make sure to look over every piece of paper himself once he and Cara returned.

As for Gills and Sampson, Deena would handle the investigation while Branden was gone. It wouldn't be difficult given how cooperative Gills was being now that he'd heard Sampson was talking and spinning things in his favor. Gills told Deena that his life had been wasted "chasing numbers" and that he'd gotten talked into "doing illegal things" by Sampson, who might or might not be Davies's son—Sampson was denying the connection, and the glass Iris had pilfered hadn't provided usable traces of DNA.

According to Gills, conspiring with Sampson had initially given him a thrill, an adrenaline rush. But then he had heard about the death of one of his longtime acquaintances, a man who'd been arrested for insider trading. The man had dropped dead of a heart attack while in jail awaiting his trial. Larry told Deena that he tried to stop after that, but Sampson had too much on him and blackmailed him into continuing. He was old and tired and had decided he couldn't go on the way he had any longer.

Based on what Deena had uncovered so far, Sampson could be charged with violating at least four sections of the Securities Exchange Act of 1934, and as far as sentencing, if found guilty, he would be forced to repay his ill-gotten gains, plus prejudgment interest, preventing him from serving as an officer or director of a public company, and permanently enjoining him from future violations of those provisions of the federal securities laws. Gills probably wouldn't fare too much better.

But that wasn't Branden's concern. And it certainly wouldn't be Cara's. He didn't plan on sharing what he'd learned today, especially the snippets from Gaunt's journals. Maybe someday he'd tell her, but right now he wanted her completely at ease, the memory of Gaunt's attack wiped away as much as possible.

To that end, he left D&M and headed home.

To Cara.

Chapter Twenty-eight

After arriving at the Andros Island Airport, Branden and Cara caught a private ferry to Kamalame Cay, a Caribbean barefoot-chic retreat with nineteen luxurious seaside suites set in charming bougainvillea-draped cottages, peak-roofed Balinese beach houses, and classic Plantation-style villas. Each cottage had access to a mile of its own private beach.

They were greeted at the Great House, which was furnished with a grand collection of South Asian and Bahamian decor, art books, antiques, and collectibles. The concierge led them through a garden terrace along a white sand path, passing an outdoor tiki bar with an open grill and a heated freshwater pool edged in breathtaking, towering silver palms.

The Great House was mind-boggling enough, but when Cara saw their villa . . .

"It's gorgeous," she said, then laughed at how she'd been gushing.

"You like?"

"I love! It's like nothing I've ever seen before, straight out of a magazine . . . or a dream."

"I aim to make your fantasies a reality, Cara."

In the past few weeks, she'd been so distant with Branden, ever since Mike Gaunt had tried to . . . what . . . kill her? Sure felt that way. But Gaunt had taken her somewhere she'd never been before—that no one ever should be. Bouncing back from a crazed man's attack wasn't the same as bouncing back from a fractured wrist or a tumble on the sidewalk.

But she was almost there. Almost back to who she was before the attack. She had to hope Branden would keep waiting . . . and had to hope she'd heal, and soon.

And that when she did, Branden would still be there.

Because she still hadn't said those words that meant so much to her. She still hadn't told Branden Duke she loved him.

And she did. Not because he'd saved her. Not because he'd examined the paperwork from her mother's attic and found a couple of discrepancies that had proven her father was indeed innocent of what he'd been accused of—something he, Cara, her mother, and Glenn had celebrated with tears and hugs of joy and toasts to her father—but because of all he was. Kind. Sexy. Strong. Honorable.

She scanned the villa. It had a peaked roof and a wood frame. The open windows in the front room left it bright and airy and splashed with sun. The ceilings stretched upward as tall as the sweeping palms they'd passed on their way in. Outside, there was a covered spacious veranda that looked out onto their mile-long private stretch of white sandy beach that led to a clear, aquamarine ocean.

The bathroom had a sunken marble tub with built-in jets and a walk-in shower with two heads. The bedroom was huge, with an oversized king bed and privacy curtains draped around the hand-carved four posters that held it up. The glass doors opened directly onto the beach.

Finally, a small kitchenette was already stocked with a variety of fine wines, premium spirits, snacks, and teas. They were all her favorites, right down to the brand. Branden must have tailored the selection to their liking when he made the reservations, and his attention to the smallest detail, all designed to spoil her rotten, made her heart clench and then expand. Branden slipped the young man a tip, a very large one judging from the look on the other man's face, and asked that they not be disturbed again. The young man explained their "walkie-talkie" system, saying that guests wouldn't be bothered unless the guest initiated contact with the staff.

When the young man was gone, Cara turned to Branden. "This is incredible."

"It is beautiful, isn't it?"

"Yes, although I'm not even sure beautiful covers it. Just look out there," she said as she stared out the big glass windows. "Can we go for a walk?" she asked excitedly.

He hugged her from behind, resting his chin on the top of her head. "Walking wasn't exactly what I had in mind, but there's plenty of time. This is your vacation, Cara. I want you to do whatever you want."

She sighed and turned her head to receive his kiss. He pulled open the glass doors and gave her a little nudge. She stepped onto the veranda and bent down to slip off her shoes. When she straightened she caught Branden staring at her behind.

"Like what you see?" she teased.

Branden made a growling sound deep in his throat.

Cara smiled and held out her hand. "Come on, let's walk."

After sliding off his own shoes, Branden took her hand. As they walked, the sand slipped between their toes and the warm, clear water lapped at their feet. A small breeze played lightly through Cara's hair.

She suddenly felt a raindrop on her face and wiped it away. A few clouds had moved in while they walked.

"Do you want to go back inside?" Branden asked.

She shook her head and tilted her head back so her face pointed toward the clouds. The drizzle of rain was light, the air warm. Both caused Cara's thin cotton dress to stick to her curves. The wind shifted in intensity, spattering her with raindrops—warm, wet, heavy raindrops that plopped on her skin like a happy song, sending joyful sensations shooting across her skin.

It hit her—she was *alive*.

Alive, and full of energy.

Alive, and with Branden Duke by her side.

Gaunt hadn't won. *She* had. She'd faced her enemy with a show of force, unlike her father. Sure, she'd been wounded along the way, but she'd ultimately won. No more hiding behind her conservative clothes and quiet demeanor, no more playing the part of the "nice girl." No more withdrawing from emotional connections just because someone might hurt her.

No, she was done avoiding life.

Years ago, because her father hadn't fought back, Carl Davies had succeeded in ruining the happiness of her entire family.

But when Mike Gaunt had tried to ruin her life, she'd finally fought back.

And there was no stopping her now.

She turned and faced Branden, who stared at her with a perplexed look, as if surprised by the joy she knew was suddenly written across her face. She knew he'd been worried about her the past few weeks. Worried that Gaunt's attack had irreparably damaged her. Worried that the rift Gaunt had built between them with uncertainty and fear would tear them apart when they'd only just found each other.

He didn't have cause to worry.

The patience and gentleness he'd shown her had only strengthened her resolve—Branden Duke was hers and they were going to spend their time together with gusto. She wasn't going to let anything—be it her fear of the intensity of her feelings for him or her own unease at how ridiculously wealthy he was—stand in the way of her exploring the possibilities that were Branden.

Mike Gaunt, in his odd way, had taught her to let go of fear. To let in love.

With an impish glance at Branden, she untied the strings that attached behind her neck and let her dress fall to the ground, leaving her standing on the beach in a very thin white lace bra and matching thong.

A flicker of surprise flashed across Branden's face and she laughed. She placed her hands on her hips. "What? This beach is private, right?"

"It certainly is." He stepped toward her, narrowing his eyes when she playfully backed away.

"The water looks so amazing," she said. "Can we go for a swim?"

"Whatever you want, angel. Remember?"

She waded slowly into the water and looked back over her shoulder to see Branden slipping off his shirt. "It's like bathwater, Branden. Come in!"

After stripping down to his black boxers, he waded into the water with her. "Damn, that's nice," he said with a grin, but he was staring at the outline of her nipples showing through her white bra.

She splashed water at him. "Such a lech."

"Just stating the truth, baby." He reached out to grab her.

She took a step back and he lunged at her. Squealing, she tried to run away. His hands closed around her waist and pulled her back into him. He held her tightly, his erection throbbing against the curve of her ass, the gentle motion of the waves creating a soft humping motion.

She laid her head backward on his shoulder and closed her eyes. His hand glided across the soft, wet skin of her stomach and settled just below her breast. Cara reached for his other hand and brought it up to her lips. She kissed the tip of each of his fingers before sucking the middle one into her mouth and stroking it with her tongue.

His cock jumped as if anticipating when it would be its turn. She gave his finger one last flick of her tongue before Branden moved both hands to cup her breasts. Cara reached back between them and unhooked her bra, letting it drop into the water. Branden ground his palms against her hard nipples. When he kissed and nibbled on her shoulder, she pressed back into him even harder, moaning out, "Oh, God, Branden. That feels so good!"

Her breathing grew more ragged with every twist and pull and stroke of his hand. She cried out loudly when he took one of her nipples, twisting it vigorously between his fingers, pulling on it, stretching it. His hips rocked gently into her.

When he flipped her around, she wrapped her arms around his neck and rose on her toes to kiss him. Cara shuddered as Branden sucked her bottom lip into his mouth then ran his tongue across it with teasing licks as he held it between his teeth.

Cara reached down and ran her hand along the shaft of his cock and he moaned loudly. His kiss became more voracious, his tongue plunging in as deeply as it could. Reaching down, he grabbed her ass with one hand; with the other he ripped the thin material of her thong off and let it join the bra in the depths of the sea.

Branden lifted her, and Cara wrapped her legs around his waist even as he gripped the back of her neck, controlling the angle of their kiss. She pulled back for a second, gulping for air, and then she began to kiss his neck and shoulders, scraping her teeth gently across them as she did.

He pushed her higher until her breasts were level with his face. He kissed each breast and then drew one nipple into his mouth even as he slid a hand between her legs and a finger along her lips, teasing her swollen clit. Cara threw her head back, making little sounds of pleasure as she slipped into another dimension. She cried out loudly as he finally took her clit in between two fingers and began to rub it.

"Oh, Branden. Yes!"

"You like that, angel?"

"Yes!"

"How about this?" he asked, suddenly applying more pressure to her swollen clit and then biting down on her nipple.

She became a wild woman in his arms, writhing and arching, her fingernails digging deep into his broad shoulders. She hardly noticed as he carried her out of the water and back up to the shore. "You're the sexiest woman in the world, Cara. And you're mine."

"Yes, Branden, I am yours. Always."

Holding her hand, he led her over to their private veranda, stripping off his boxers before sitting down on one of the overstuffed chaise longues. Lying back, he stretched out his long legs before reaching for her again. She straddled his lap, dangling her legs off each side of the chair. Hands on her hips, Branden lifted her up before settling her down on his hard length. Cara used her legs to push up and down, and they both cried out in ecstasy as they merged.

The rest of the world ceased to exist.

Her entire being was focused on Branden, sensations surging through her body, each nerve standing on end, exposed, feeling everything.

Gradually, their pace increased even as their rhythm

grew more erratic. He groaned and she felt his body tense.

"Oh baby, I'm going to come. Come with me . . ."

Cara bounced harder. Branden groaned louder. Within seconds they both exploded, hotly and loudly, reveling in the fact that this was only the beginning of their vacation.

Only the beginning of their lives together.

Branden pulled her gently up his body and cupped her face, staring into her eyes. "I love you, Cara."

Cara had never felt as happy as she did in that moment. Never felt as safe. Never felt as loved.

"I love you, too, Branden. So much."

She laid her head on his chest, sighing as he ran his fingers through her hair.

Her life had radically changed the moment she met Branden Duke. While she couldn't say it would be smooth sailing for them from here on out, she was looking forward to every single moment of the journey.

Find out more about the Belladonna Agency in
Virna DePaul's first book in the series

TURNED

Chapter One

Seattle, Washington
A few weeks later . . .

Back in the Bronx, Eliana Maria Garcia's weapons of choice had been a smart mouth, the occasional threat of a knife, and her fists. Now, standing with her back pressed against the brick wall behind Monk's Café, Ana Martin had something even better—a gun. One she was hoping she wouldn't have to use.

Confronting the man who'd been following her, however, was unavoidable. She'd noticed him at the bank yesterday, then the market. But last night she'd seen him outside her house. And moments before? Across the street.

That was one coincidence too many. She'd left Primos Sangre over seven years ago, but if there was one thing the gang had taught her, it was that survival meant confronting danger head-on rather than running from it. Since she didn't trust the cops—didn't trust anyone—her only choice was to handle this herself. Her way.

If only she wasn't so scared. But she'd put her old life behind her, and even though she wasn't happy—could never be happy without her sister—she was often content. Sometimes when she looked in the mirror she even managed to like the person she saw looking back at her. The thought of losing that scared her more than any threat of physical harm ever could. And it scared her enough that she was willing to fight to make sure it didn't happen.

The sun had set long ago. Now and then a stab of light from a passing car pierced the shadows of the alley where Ana was hiding, forcing her to dodge back. Invisible, shrouded in darkness, she waited. When she heard footsteps, she knew it was him.

Forcing her near-numb fingers to tighten their grip on the gun, she watched as he walked past her, then made her move, coming at him from behind, pressing the barrel of her gun against the back of his head.

He didn't even jerk.

From the back, he looked big. Broad. Muscles rippling. Dangerous.

But from the front? Even from a distance, he'd looked more than dangerous. He'd looked deadly. Beyond handsome. Midnight hair and eyes just as dark. Savage and sophisticated at the same time. She'd never seen his equal. Certainly never met anyone that came close.

Part of her knew she'd gotten the drop on him a bit too easily. That perhaps she was doing exactly what he'd been expecting. Hoping.

But it was too late to go back now.

"Hands where I can see them," she managed to get out.

Slowly, he raised his hands in surrender. Only she still wasn't buying it. Her nerves screamed at her to run, but logic kept her feet planted firmly on the ground. Somehow, she knew if she ran, he'd only come after her.

"Why are you following me?"

No answer. No surprise.

With her free hand, she patted him down, the way she'd learned to do in the gang. By the time she'd frisked him from the back, she was the one who was sweating. And not from exertion.

Nothing about him was small. He was tall and buff, more than big enough to overpower her slight frame. Sangre-style paranoia set in, and it occurred to her that this guy might be undercover. She instantly recalled the run-ins she'd had with cops as a teenager. The way they'd often pulled her long dark ponytail, hard enough to make her back arch and breasts lift. The way they'd sometimes copped a feel or implied they'd leave her in peace if she made it worth their while. She'd never given them that satisfaction.

But no, she decided. This guy's vibe was just too different. Not so much cop as outlaw.

His entire body was contoured with interesting ridges and bulges and planes. This close she could smell him, a subtle spicy scent that managed to convey unabashed maleness and warmth despite what seemed to be a rather low body temperature. The man held himself in control. Unlike her. Gritting her teeth, she ignored the rush of heat to her cheeks and moved faster to disguise the telltale trembling of her hands.

"Turn around," she commanded.

Slowly, he did.

Despite the heat in his gaze, his mouth was tipped into a mocking smile, as if he knew how affected she was by touching him. What he didn't know—*couldn't* know—was how confused she was by her reaction. He made her feel . . . restless. Edgy. Vulnerable.

She hated it.

As such, she hated *him*.

Methodically, she frisked him from the front, delving between his denim-clad legs to make sure he wasn't packing more than nature had provided.

He grunted slightly and said, "Keep that up and you might find more than you want, princess."

His accent was clipped and tidy—upper-crust British. Despite herself, her gaze shot to his.

"Don't call me that," she said automatically, just before she found the gun tucked into a sleek holster concealed inside his waistband.

She pulled it out, and the sight of the Luger didn't surprise her. The well-made weapon suited him. Swiftly, she slipped it out of his holster and into the front of her own waistband.

The only other time she'd seen a Luger was when she'd delivered a package to Pablo, the leader of Devil's Crew, another street gang, and he'd insisted on inspecting the contents before he paid. He'd told her the guns had been stolen from some Richie Rich who liked fancy cars as well as fancy guns. When he'd asked her what kind of car she drove, she'd told him the truth. None. She'd only been fourteen at the time.

Even so, her youth hadn't stopped her from fighting the gang leader when he'd decided to inspect more than the package she'd delivered. All she'd gotten for her trouble was a beating and the ugly scar on her face.

To her, big and male was synonymous with power and violence.

"I'm not going to hurt you," the man in front of her said softly, as if he'd read her mind. "If you'll listen to me, I can help you, Ana."

The fact that he knew her name shocked her . . . and scared her even more. "Fuck you," she snapped without meaning to. Swearing was an old habit, one she'd fought hard to break, but sometimes it came out. When she was angry . . . when she felt threatened . . . the tough girl inside her lost control, cursing and spitting and speaking Spanish in an effort to protect herself despite the fact that it merely revealed how vulnerable she really was.

How weak.

She bit her lip, furious that he'd sensed her fear. Furious that his offer of help made her easily long for things she couldn't possibly have.

She'd gotten soft. Too soft. And once again she was paying the price. The only question was how high the price would be this time.

"Move." She gestured with her gun. "Face the wall." He had her so rattled she was second-guessing herself. She needed to frisk him again. Make sure she hadn't missed anything the first time.

He merely stared silently at her, and she forced herself to snap, "Now."

Unbelievably, he practically rolled his eyes just before he obeyed, cursing when she suddenly shoved him face-first against the brick; Eliana Garcia, gang member, was quickly chipping away at the civilized, respectable woman Ana had been trying to become.

But instead of retaliating, he waited while she frisked him yet again. When she was done, when he failed to make a move on her, she relaxed slightly. "Face me."

As he did, she saw the slight trickle of blood now dripping from a cut on his forehead. She felt a momentary pang of guilt. Along with it came the strange temptation to wipe the blood away and kiss the wound better. To kiss *all* his hurt away. Hurt she somehow sensed was there.

Which was beyond ridiculous. Like one of those tear-jerker movies where the love of a good woman saved some useless son of a bitch.

He didn't need her to wash his freakin' pain away. He needed to know who was boss. Besides, she didn't take care of anyone but herself anymore. It was better that way. Safer.

Instinctively, she gripped her gun tighter while he leaned back against the wall and crossed his arms over his chest, no longer smiling but watching her with an intensity that made her shiver.

"You've been trailing me since yesterday," she said, "and not just because you like my coffee. *¿Porqué?*"

At her lapse into Spanish and the thickening of her accent, Ana clenched her teeth, then deliberately modulated her voice so it was once again white-bread Americana. "Why are you following me?"

He smiled again, as if her speaking Spanish had amused him.

Embarrassment washed over her and she wavered, accidentally lowering the gun. "Answer me, *bastardo*—"

In a blur of movement, he grabbed her wrist, wrenched the gun from her hand, flipped her to the ground, and covered her body with his much larger one.

Reflexively, she struck out, striking him in the face before he pinned her arms and his body simply weighed her down. Damn it, she'd known it had been too easy. He'd set her up. And the way he'd moved . . . Faster than anything she'd ever seen before.

But oddly enough, he had his body braced so his full weight wasn't on her. As if he wanted her pinned but not hurt.

As if he was taking care of her.

Breathing hard, she stared into his mesmerizing face. His scent would be all over her, she thought absently. When he shifted, rubbing his lower body against her, she blinked at the unexpected warmth that flooded her. He was cold, yet he made her feel so good. So hot. Literally. For another crazy second, she wanted to grab either side of his face, pull him closer, and kiss him.

Ah Dios. She was losing it.

He tsked. "It was your f-bomb that finally got to me, you know. Normally, you hold back. You don't have to. Your cursing. Your use of Spanish. I like it. I *more* than like it. I just had to see if you felt as good as you look. As you sound."

Again, that dazzling smile. The British perfection in the way he modulated his words. Those cold eyes. Danger emanated from him like a flashing red light, while charm oozed from him like honey.

He leaned closer and whispered. "Lucky me. You feel even better than I'd anticipated." When she failed to respond, he raised a brow. "What? I've rendered you speechless? Or are you just holding back again? I told you I'm here to help. That starts with offering you a job."

Now *that* she hadn't been expecting. She snorted and shifted underneath him, working to twist her way out from under his weight. The intoxicating feel of her limbs rubbing against his made her want to move slower. To relish the contact.

Instantly, she ceased her attempts to get away from him.

"I'm not stupid or gullible—" she began.

"No. In fact, Téa believes you're extremely smart. One of the smartest she's ever worked with."

Ana went rigid with hurt. Téa—a woman she'd thought was the closest thing she had to a friend—had sent him here with no warning? "Please get off me," she whispered when what she really wanted to do was scream. Cuss. In Spanish *and* English.

He kept his gaze locked on hers for several seconds, then said, "As you wish." Pushing himself to standing, he held out a hand to help her up.

She ignored him and scrambled to her feet, immediately backing several steps away. "How do you know Téa? Why did she—"

"Ana!"

Ana jerked when she heard Paul, one of her employees

at the coffee shop, call her name, but she didn't take her eyes off the man. "I'll be right there," she shouted back.

The man in front of her didn't bat an eye.

She shook her head. "Téa misled you. I don't want anything from you."

"Not even information about your sister?"

Her heart stopped beating and for a moment the world around her blurred. She fought against the wooziness, focusing on the man's face. Excitement tickled the back of her throat and sent a buzzing up her spine.

Ana hadn't seen her sister, Gloria, for seven years, not since Ana had tried to jump them both out of Primos Sangre. Gloria had only joined the gang after returning from living with her grandparents. Ana had barely recognized her. Gloria had been angry. Distant. Wanting her sister's company one minute and hating it the next. After the shooting, she'd written Ana in prison, making it abundantly clear she blamed Ana for her injury and never wanted to see her again.

Had Gloria changed her mind? Had she sent this man to tell her that? A wash of excitement shot through her. Buoyed her. Maybe the stranger that had returned from living with her grandparents had finally turned back into the loving sister Ana remembered. Without even realizing what she was doing, she stepped closer. "You know Gloria?"

"I know about her."

"But did Gloria send you to find me?" she asked, hope reducing her voice to a whisper.

"No."

Disappointment. Suspicion. Dismissal. All cut through the excitement and hope, scattering them to the wind.

Nothing had changed. As such, this man had nothing she needed.

As if he could read her mind he said, "I told you, I'm here to offer you a job."

"I'm not interested in anything you're offering." Slowly, her eyes never leaving him, she retrieved her gun, tucked it into her waistband right next to his, covered them with her sweater, and started walking backward toward the cafe entrance.

"I'm quite fond of my gun, you know," he called out.

"It's mine now."

"It's also a violation of your parole for you to carry a firearm."

That made her freeze, but only for a second. She turned and walked to the coffeehouse door, her steps slow and lethargic. Over her shoulder, she muttered, "So tell my parole officer. Téa always knows where to find me."

Ty sighed as Ana walked back into her coffeehouse. She moved fast and loose, as if tackling a guy in an alley and pointing a gun at him was par for the course. He supposed given her background it was like riding a bike—you never forgot how, not when your very survival was at stake. But that didn't mean she hadn't been shaken up by their encounter.

She seemed to fit in well with the college crowd she served. In fact, in her uniform of short tees and tight jeans, she could have been a student herself. She worked. She went home. She kept to herself.

But she wasn't happy with her life. Far from it. She'd simply convinced herself she couldn't have more. Sometimes, however, her true nature came through despite her best attempts to hide it.

Soon after he'd arrived in Seattle, Ana had ceased to be a fuck fantasy. The hot ex–gang member with the checkered past turned out to be a woman to admire. She kept her distance, but she was hardworking and good to her employees. He'd also been right about her smile. She didn't use it often, but when she did, her hotness ratcheted into heart-stopping beauty.

His surveillance had also alleviated any lingering concerns he'd had about her refusing to do what they wanted. Because as hard as she tried to keep herself apart from others, she clearly longed for the type of connections she didn't allow herself.

He'd seen how she'd stared longingly at the couple playing footsie in the corner of her coffee shop. How she'd stared at two women at the grocery store, arm in arm, obviously loving sisters. And how she'd helped a frail young man with MS across the street; she had watched him walk down the block until he turned the corner and disappeared from view.

Over the past few weeks, his protective instincts had kicked in. So many times, he'd wanted to go to her. Wrap his arms around her. Comfort her. But of course he hadn't. Because she would have fought him, yes, but also because his hunger had grown almost unbearable.

When she'd confronted and challenged him, he'd managed to hang on to his control, but just barely. He'd known she was waiting for him in the alley and he'd been prepared for her to touch him, even if it was simply to disarm him. Although he'd allowed himself to touch her back, he'd done so with ruthless restraint. He'd led Ana to believe he was just a strong human rather than a hungry vampire lusting after her blood and her body. His sheathed fangs ached the way his dick did, longing to penetrate and take everything from her: her sweet blood and her complete surrender.

Once again he reminded himself it wasn't going to happen. No matter how he admired her, and no matter how she made him feel, she was a job and that was all she could ever be.

He took out his cell and punched in Carly's number.

"You found her?" Carly's voice was husky. Feminine.

It was flat-out sexy—deliberately so—and he couldn't help compare it to the gravelly, clipped speech that Ana had used, her occasional melodic slip into Spanish aside. Despite the sentiment behind her words, the flow of them combined with the touch of her body had made him hard, harder than the brick wall he'd been pressed against. The intensity of his desire as well as his decision not to push her too far—yet—had been the only reasons he'd remained against that wall. Despite carrying an illegal gun, Ana had turned her life around. He didn't want to take that away from her. And she had no reason to hurt him unless he gave her one. Besides, it wasn't as if one of her bullets could kill him anyway.

As far as he knew, nothing could.

"She's not going to be as easy as the others," he said in response to Carly's question.

"I wouldn't say the others have been easy."

"She's good. Even managed to get my gun."

"Right," Carly answered, her tone laced with the knowledge that if Ana had gotten Ty's gun, it was because he'd let her do it. Just like he'd let her spot him watching her in the first place. "Did she shoot you?"

"No, she did not shoot me. She cursed me, though. In Spanish. Something that seemed to bother her." It had certainly bothered him, but only because he'd liked it. Too much.

He closed his eyes and replayed her words, enjoying the way it made him think of heat and skin and sweaty, slippery silk sheets. With her golden skin, cinnamon eyes, and dark hair, he could easily picture her spread beneath him, begging him for release as he crooned back to her in her native tongue:

Todavía no. Not yet.

Un poco más largo. A little longer.

Dé a mí. Give to me.

He bit back a groan.

Give to me.

Even now his dick twitched, ready to get busy, ready to immerse itself in Ana's warmth.

He couldn't have her. Not sexually. Not in ways that might involve her heart as well as her body. And that made him angry.

It fucking made him want to kill someone.

Thankfully, Carly seemed oblivious to his internal struggle. "Excellent," she said. "You're right about that, she hates it when she speaks Spanish. She's trying to deny who she is—who she was—but even after all these years she can't. She's still the tough little girl from the Bronx."

"Yes. The little girl packs quite a punch, too." Raising a hand, Ty rubbed at his mouth, grinning when he saw the blood. She might not be able to kill him, but she sure as shit could make him bleed.

"Was that before or after she got your gun? Pity. I know how fond you are of it."

His silence just seemed to amuse her. True to form, she pounced on it.

"Oh my. Are you saying you can't handle this one?" she purred.

God, he hated Carly sometimes. Hated her bitch-on-steroids act. Hated the necessity to partner with her at all. But she hadn't always been like this. Years ago, as a fellow newbie agent with the FBI, she'd been good at her job but she'd had a gentle side, too. That part of her had long been quashed. And now? Sure, she'd helped Ty and Peter when they'd needed her most, but her assistance had been more about using them than saving them. Carly was doing what she needed to adjust to her new life, part of a team but very much alone. Just like him.

Ty glanced in the direction Ana had disappeared. "No," he said, this time letting a trace of humor leak into his voice. "I can handle her. I'll just have to be a little more direct, that's all."

"You don't have authority to reveal what you are, Ty," Carly snapped. "Not yet. We have one month until the leaders of Salvation's Crossing attend the Hispanic Community Alliance fund-raiser, and we need Ana fully invested before we show our hand."

"I have no plans to tell her I'm a vampire right now. But she still has my gun, and I have no intention of letting her think she can take anything from me and just walk away."

GOING HUNGRY

2/10 = 2
4/10 = 2
4/11 = 3

"[*Going Hungry's*] authors defy many of the stereotypes about eating disorders, and who suffers from them."

—*Newsweek*

"[An] eye-opening collection."   —*People*

"Taylor writes with grace and insight of her self-imposed malnourishment."   —*The New York Times Book Review*

"Those struggling with an eating disorder are sure to find among these personal essays at least one that will help them better understand their own condition, and provide company and hope."   —*Publishers Weekly*

"In *Going Hungry*, writers of different ethnicities offer thoughtful personal perspectives on eating disorders. Of particular interest is the theme that anorexia nervosa can be an expression (albeit a harmful one) of a positive drive to accomplish something noteworthy and that such aspirations can be redirected into meaningful, productive endeavors. These messages inspire hope and provide a powerful counterforce to stereotypes that associate eating disorders with superficiality and vanity."

—Dr. David Herzog,
Director of the Harris Center for Eating Disorders,
Massachusetts General Hospital